CARE FOR THIS LOVE

MY NAVY ROMANCE
BOOK 1

HOPE SNYDER

SUNNY
LAUREL
BOOKS

Care For This Love

MY NAVY ROMANCE – BOOK ONE

HOPE SNYDER

For my Grandmommy from Mexico, my Ita from Colombia, and all the generous, sacrificial women who have poured love, advice, and grace into my life.

Most importantly, to my mom.

CONTENTS

AUTHOR'S NOTE

Spoiler alert: No one dies and it all ends happily ever after.

However, here are a few topics touched on in this book that some readers might be sensitive to:

- Toxic, manipulative dating relationships, on page
- Death of a parent (past) and discussion of ensuing grief journey
- Parental abandonment (past), brief mention of addiction

CHAPTER 1

THE SUNNY SANDS and foaming blue waves of San Diego call to me from my phone's lock screen as I check the time—half past noon. My curly-haired cubicle mate Hughie is singing "Hey, Soul Sister" under his breath, as I text Bryce with a smile on my face.

TIA

Almost time for our Wednesday lunch date! Where do you want to meet?

BRYCE

Ah, sorry, I can't. Slammed right now.

TIA

Oh...we missed last week too.

BRYCE

So sorry, babe. Next week for sure.

I do my best to stifle my disappointment. It's not personal, it's just work. Sometimes it's busier and that's okay. We'll get back into our routine soon.

TIA

Aren't we going to meet your parents in the Outer Banks next week?

BRYCE

Oh, right. Well, we'll definitely be getting lunch together then!

It'll be nice to have him all to myself for our road trip from Washington, D.C. to North Carolina. His boss definitely overworks him, but Bryce keeps impressing everyone with his ambition. He's making a name for himself.

TIA

Do you want me to bring you some food?

BRYCE

That'd be nice, but you don't have to.

TIA

Salad or burger?

BRYCE

Burger, but not from the place nearby, from Shake Shack.

That's nearly an hour round trip, walking and taking the metro. But it could be worth it for a strawberry milkshake.

TIA

Okay!

BRYCE

Cool. Thanks, Tia.

I reach under my desk for my tote bag, swap my court heels for flats, and log out of my computer. I turn to Hughie, who should be tracking voting methods by constituency, but instead is researching an up-and-coming congressman everyone's taken to calling X, like he's a secret government lab project. The guy is nothing more than a fast-talking go-getter from Florida, but his persona has been heightened by this "Congressman X" moniker.

"Hughie, I'm going to Shake Shack, want anything?"

"Oh, for real? Yeah!" He rattles off his order and promises to send me money for it. "Hey, do you know if Sutton is going to try to hop on the bandwagon and work for X?" He points back to his computer screen.

"Why would she?"

"She's doing PR for the national committee, right? I'm sure she thinks she's a rising star, and her star will rise further with this guy."

"We may share an apartment, but I have no idea what she's thinking career-wise. She's pretty tight-lipped about her work."

Sutton and I found each other via a Facebook apartment-hunting group for young professionals. We started at a polite level of acquaintance, both of us being clean and respectful, then gradually moved towards the exchanging of facts (the oven takes forever to heat up, the bathroom tile is so crooked and it drives me crazy, you can use my curling iron if you want), then information and gossip about who works where, who was talking to whom, which events we were both invited to. She's not exactly a warm personality, but she's a cool apartment-mate.

About a year and a half ago, she told me about her guy friend from college who had seen me around and was asking about me. The next week, she introduced me to Bryce, and the rest is history.

"You'd tell me, right?" Hughie says with a furrowed brow, bringing me back to the present. "If you get wind she's going to throw her hat in the ring, let me know. I have a few strings I could try to pull."

It grates to hear people say things like "strings I could pull." But this is D.C., people are constantly trying to get ahead by any means possible. Not everyone does it that way, but it seems the increasing competitiveness of Capitol Hill has made my particular circle of friends more jealous and insecure. It makes me sad.

"I'll bring your food up after I drop off Bryce's."

"Oh, shoot, do you think Bryce will try to switch to working for X?"

I shake my head. "He's in a really good spot. You know his boss is on all the magazine covers and Bryce has played a big role in making that happen. Talk about a rising star." I leave with a little smile of pride in my boyfriend.

I tap in a mobile order as I walk down the long, imposing corridor of the Longworth House Office building. Humidity hits me square in the face the second I pop out the south exit and I grimace as I make my way to the Capitol South metro station. I've immediately started sweating, even in a sleeveless blouse and pencil skirt.

One glance at my lock screen makes me sigh again. I would give anything to be back home feeling a California coastal breeze right now, not the damp heat and mild air conditioning of congressional offices. I'm dreading another sticky Washington, D.C. summer, and it's barely even started.

A notification comes through that my order has been accepted —at the wrong Shake Shack location. Dang it, I'll have to go to Dupont Circle instead of F Street. Oh well.

"Is that the 'Queen of the Field'?" A voice booms from behind me as I get on the long escalator down to the metro platforms. I turn to see Tim and Eliza, teammates from my recreational soccer team.

"Hey!" I say with a grin. "How are you? I miss seeing you guys every Saturday."

"Same," says Eliza, coming down a few steps to catch up to me. "Hey, what happened with the championship game last month? We needed you."

My face falls. I glance up at Tim, whose expression mirrors Eliza's question.

"Food poisoning," I reply with a grimace.

"Right," says Tim. "From what?"

"A bad oyster," I lie.

"Bummer," says Eliza in a flat tone. She doesn't believe me for a second. "I mean, of course we had a few subs, but no one plays with your hustle and enthusiasm. There's a reason you're our Queen."

She's really heaping the burning coals on my head.

"Well, here's to next season and having our best mid-fielder back with us," says Tim.

"Yeah, definitely."

The guilt about missing the last game of the season comes and goes, even though it wasn't my fault. The night before the championship, Bryce had texted to say he was going out with a few of his college buddies for a guys' night, so I went to bed early, ready to be well-rested to play my heart out.

Except I got a call at three in the morning that he was drunk and belligerent, bleeding from a fight.

I took an Uber to Georgetown, brought him back to his townhouse, and got him in the shower, clothes and all. He started sobbing about how he wasn't good enough, how he didn't know how to be good enough. He kept saying, "Is anyone good enough for life?"

After a lot of gentle parenting, I got him changed into dry clothes, bandaged the scrapes on his face, and tucked him into bed around five a.m. He made me swear I wouldn't leave him alone.

"You're a good girlfriend, you're so good to me, you won't leave, right?"

How could I, when he asked all sad and vulnerable? He didn't wake up until well after noon, and I missed the championship game.

I don't know why I'm lying to save face for Bryce. Somehow, it feels like the truth is too intimate to share with people who don't know him, who haven't learned to understand his nuance. His walls of bravado and bluster are hard to get over, but I'm sure he has a soft heart behind them.

After a few more bits of small talk, I wave goodbye to Tim and Eliza, and we part ways to head to our respective platforms. The air down here is damp but cool, trapped underground by the arches of concrete overhead. Across the tracks, between an ad for the Smithsonian and another for the Kennedy Center, is a giant banner of the U.S. women's national soccer team.

The goalie stands in the middle of the collage of player photos, holding a soccer ball between her gloved palms and glaring down at me. It feels eerily personal. I can almost hear her saying, "Come on, Tia, protect what you love." I look away.

As the metro takes me northwest, I think about the two constants in my life—soccer and art. Since I was a kid, they have been an essential part of what makes me Tia Lopez. I love soccer, I love my team, and next season will end on a better note. I love art, but I've neglected my painting for a while, partly due to time constraints, partly due to feeling like I've lost the magic a bit. I'll pick it back up after next week's road trip. I know I shouldn't allow my passions to fall by the wayside, but it's...complicated.

I'm a block away from Shake Shack when I spy one of my favorite things and one of D.C.'s redeeming features—random art. At the confluence of two busy streets is a statue in a sliver of a green park. I'm a sucker for a good statue. The crosswalk is open, and I take a quick detour to go see who this memorial is for. I turn the corner, pause to take it in, and find myself smiling.

Set in solid bronze, a man is seated wearing flowing academic robes, his bearded chin resting on one hand, and his other hand holding a book. One finger keeps his place in the pages, a delightful little detail. I wonder if he felt the sculptor was interrupting his precious reading time. The reddish marble base of the statue says "Longfellow."

My phone vibrates with a notification that my order is ready to pick up. I'll have to google "Longfellow" later. I take a quick photo of the statue to study on the metro ride back, zooming in on his face, then go grab the bag of food. On the walk back to the metro, Sutton texts me.

SUTTON

Have you heard of anyone else applying to work for X?

TIA

Are you thinking of quitting your job?

SUTTON

Just wondering if you've heard from Bryce or Hughie if they're thinking of trying to get in with X.

I roll my eyes, flick the notification away, and google "Longfellow." Oh, of course, the poet, Henry Wadsworth Longfellow. I go to pull up a few of his shorter poems to read but get interrupted by Bryce texting.

BRYCE

Are you almost back with the food?

TIA

Yeah, heading back now, be about 30 minutes or so.

BRYCE

Sweet, I'm starving.

I hustle down the escalator, and as the train car takes me back to Capitol South I go back to studying the picture of Longfellow's face. The soft hint of curls in his beard blends upwards towards his ears, then waves of his hair come down and meet them. I wonder if I could paint that. I wonder what it would look like at night, what kind of shadows form when the light catches on those bronze curlicues of hair.

The noon heat is turning oppressive as I pop back out of Capitol South and head back to the Longworth building. Just as I get to the second floor and am about to turn the last corner towards Bryce's office, I hear my least favorite laugh: Bryce's high, condescending chuckle of disbelief.

CHAPTER 2

I TUCK BEHIND THE CORNER, steeling my nerves. When he's like this, he can be...hard to deal with. Bryce says something, then pauses. He must be on the phone. His shoes tap down the hall towards me, and I flatten myself against the wall, but when he speaks again I can hear him perfectly.

"Are you serious? Marry Tia? Nah, I'm not marrying her. She's not awful, but I mean, there's a reason she's never met my family."

I shake my head. Um, what? I almost want to laugh at how ridiculous that sounds.

"Yeah, they don't even know about her. Endgame is some trust fund girl from an old-money family with houses up and down the East Coast."

I couldn't have heard him right. No, that's...this is all a front, he's just swaggering. But then again, it feels all too honest. I struggle for air, like I've been punched in the stomach. I want to run, but I can't remember how to move.

Endgame is some trust fund girl. Not me. I had no idea I was competing against an invisible woman. Or...no, I am the invisible woman.

"Good to hear from you, man. It's been too long since we partied it up at Alpha Sig. Yeah, for sure. Later."

Bryce's footsteps start to retreat, and I wheel around the corner.

"Bryce?"

His tall, lean body whirls around and he at least has the decency to turn pale. Pain radiates through my chest, as if there's a literal knife sticking out of my heart.

"What was that?" I ask.

"Tia, I don't know what you think you heard—" He brushes his strawberry-blond hair to the side and straightens his red-striped tie.

"Why would you say that? It was a lie, right?"

We're good together, we were just cracking up at a Washington Nationals baseball game last week. We're going on a road trip soon. I always wondered if we had kids, if they would have his fair coloring or my olive skin tone.

It would not be out of character for him to make up some story to impress an old frat buddy. It has to be a lie. In every way he described, I am the opposite of his "endgame." I have a small savings account, no living biological parents, and my uncle, who raised me and whom I refer to as "Dad," rents an apartment above a bait shop in Cozumel, Mexico.

A flicker of decision crosses Bryce's face and his eyes go cold.

"Tia, you're not allowed to police my private conversations," he says.

I watch his expression grow more and more distant and I want to reach inside him and drag out small, vulnerable Bryce. But he's gone. The door to his heart is slamming in my face.

"Are we even going to meet your family next week?" I ask in a pained voice.

He has the inconceivable nerve to look me dead in the eye and say, "They had to cancel."

So it was not a lie. Not at all.

It's like scales falling from my eyes, the last click of the combination lock, a sharp tug of the final thread holding a tattered tapestry together. I finally see him for who he really is—a manipulative, selfish man. The facade is gone. I've spent months pretending everything was fine, promising myself he would change over time, but now I see I was hoping to uncover someone he could never be.

I laugh. It starts as a slow chuckle of sheer disbelief, then morphs into a hysterical belly-laugh of relief as I shove the bag of food into his chest and storm past him.

"Tia," he says down the hall.

I run down the stairs and he makes no move to follow me. No, why would he? I'm simply seeing myself out, sparing him the effort of eventually dumping me when the right rich girl comes along.

The emotional whirlpool is spinning me in circles. All the little red flags I've been suppressing in the name of maturity, acceptance, and hope pop up like a hundred jack-in-the-boxes with wicked grins. But right alongside them are hundreds of good memories, laughter and sweet smiles and tender, private moments.

He played me so well.

My breath is coming in weird gasps as I run outside. I can't carry this by myself, it's too much. I dial Sutton's office number. She's the only one who can help me try to make sense of this.

"Hey, are you okay?" she asks impatiently.

"No."

"Do I need to call 911?"

"No, no, it's nothing like that."

"Okay, then say it. I've got minutes to finish this press release."

"I went to talk to Bryce and overheard him on the phone with someone and he..." Oh, no, I can't start crying. Sutton can't stand it when other people cry. She'll hang up on me. I take a sharp inhale. "He said he wants to settle down with a rich girl whose dad has vacation houses all along the East Coast. And he said his family doesn't even know about me. At all."

I thought he was it. He could be so kind, so vulnerable, so sweet when he wanted to be. I was okay with his moodiness, his white lies; no one is perfect. We totally could have made it work.

Sutton is quiet on the other end of the line, and I hear typing in the background.

"Sutton?"

"My dad has a house in the Hamptons, does that count?"

I pull my phone away from my ear and study the screen. Did I call the wrong Sutton?

"Excuse me?"

"You were just dating. Low commitment, you know. Were you even exclusive?"

My eyes go wide, and my eyebrows scrunch together. "What is that supposed to mean? He's my boyfriend, and we've been together for a year and a half!"

It was not low commitment to me. I was ready to settle down and have some stability, even if it meant giving up on the idea of fairytale love and settling for satisfactory. He gave me enough glimpses of a softer side that I believed in that part of him. I thought with time and love, it would grow. He was charismatic, I liked being on his arm when he shook hands with magnates and moguls, he knew exactly how to tease a sardonic laugh out of me.

Sutton cuts through my thoughts. "Just...Tia, I'm sorry you feel betrayed. Can we talk about this later? I'm glad you're fine, go back to work, we'll order pizza and drink wine tonight, okay?"

I hang up.

I am not fine. My breath is squeezing out of my chest in short gasps. I'm twenty-six years old. My life should be full of great beginnings by now. Instead, my world is caving in, a gaping black hole of emptiness.

The humidity is cloying. I close my eyes and inhale, but the air is feeling thicker, stifling. It's getting harder and harder to take a breath.

Why am I here? What am I doing here? I don't even like D.C. I took this job because it fit my degree and I knew it would make my family proud of me. I thought it was patriotic and contributing to the greater good to work for Congress. I don't love spreadsheets and emails and phone calls, I love art and creativity and doing things that challenge me. I want authenticity, genuine friendships, and kindness, not talking behind people's backs, lying, or playing coy political games.

I don't want to be here anymore. All I want right now is a sea breeze. I want a wide-open beach. I want to paint a happy sailboat bobbing in the ocean. I want to kick a soccer ball on a grassy field. I want a Southern California summer. I want to go back to my happy place.

And why can't I? I have savings, I have family, I have a place to go.

My phone vibrates with a text from Hughie.

HUGHIE

Food?

TIA

Be right there.

Forget Bryce. He doesn't get to lie to me, break my heart, and get my lunch. I march back inside and storm into Bryce's office. The five legislative aids crammed into the side room all look up as I stride across the carpet. Bryce has the audacity to be on the phone, talking about a new tax bill with zero shame about what he just did to me. I swipe the Shake Shack bag off his desk, send an uncharacteristic rude hand gesture his way, and head back to my office.

I'm biting back tears as I set the food on Hughie's desk.

"The hero returns triumphant!" he says. "I nearly perished from starvation."

Sorry for the delay while I got my heart stomped on, I'll do better next time.

"Oh, wait, wait, wait, I almost forgot," Hughie says as he

chomps down on a crinkle-cut french fry. "While you were out, Rich came in and talked to Dan, and the word on the street is your position is about to be made redundant. Like, soon."

My stomach bottoms out. My job too? "Wait, what? What exactly did Rich say?"

"Oh, Dan's coming over. Shh, sit down."

"Hey, Tia," says Dan on his way past our cubicle with another cup of black coffee. "Just out of curiosity, if you weren't working here, you got something else you would want to be doing in D.C.? I don't know, lobbying, a nonprofit, something corporate?"

"I'm sure I'd find something," I say with a false tone of reassurance. Dan nods to my white lie with a satisfied smile.

If that's not a hint, I don't know what is. It's time to ditch D.C.

———

I CLOCK out early with shaking hands, running through the pros and cons over and over. I'm not a whimsical woman. I don't get harebrained ideas and spontaneously act on them. But I'm not happy here and I haven't been for longer than I care to admit.

Once I'm home for the night, I lock myself in my room with some leftover pad thai and a quarter of a bottle of white wine. When Sutton arrives, she gently knocks on my door.

"Tia?"

"Maybe later," I say as a sob lodges in my throat. There are plans to be made and a big cry waiting to happen, and I don't need her commentary on either of them.

When I open my laptop and see the picture of Bryce and I as the background, the ensuing tears fall hot and angry. I think of my secret Pinterest board called "B + T" filled with wedding ideas, and I feel equal parts sad and stupid. I had a picture in my head: him and I at the end of the aisle, just married, our loved ones cheering behind us, and Bryce with that sweet, happy smile I love so much. What a joke.

I weep into my pillow long enough that I hear Sutton turn off the TV, flick off the lights, and whisper, "Goodnight, Tia," before closing the door to her room.

However much I'm mourning a lost future, a strange, sweet relief follows on the edges of my tears. I am free of him. I no longer have to put up with his moods, his whims, his half-truths. I don't have to twist myself into his idea of what I should be like. It doesn't outweigh the shock of today, the way he took the full measure of me and found me wanting, but it helps.

In the quiet darkness, I lay on my back on my bed and stare up at the ceiling. There's nothing keeping me here now. I grab my phone, intending to look up ticket prices to San Diego, but my browser opens on a Longfellow poem I had pulled up earlier called "The Light of Stars." I read to the end, my breath shaking in quiet sobs over the last stanzas.

> *The star of the unconquered will,*
> *He rises in my breast,*
> *Serene, and resolute, and still,*
> *And calm, and self-possessed...*
>
> *O fear not in a world like this,*
> *And thou shalt know erelong,*
> *Know how sublime a thing it is*
> *To suffer and be strong.*

CHAPTER 3

I'M GOING to go home. I'm going to redeem this summer. I'm going to change my life.

It's not too late to call California. Great Aunt Marisol—Aunt Mari to me—picks up on the first ring and says I'm always welcome to come stay with her for a visit, it's been too long.

My airline points will cover a one-way flight to San Diego first thing in the morning.

I email the office with my notice that I'll be taking Thursday and Friday as sick days followed by two weeks of vacation. Here's hoping they'll let me go and give me some severance instead of me quitting.

I drag my big suitcase, my duffel, and my little carry-on out of the closet and start throwing my essential belongings into them. Packing never felt so good.

———

I COCOON into my sweatshirt on the early-morning flight, wiping my tears with my sleeve. Last night was utterly sleepless as I turned everything over and over in my mind. I'm making my way past anger and heading towards simply grieving now, sad and worn down. For some reason I almost miss the way Bryce used to say, "Bye, babe," whenever we ended a conversation. I'll never hear it again. In fact, if I do, it means I've made a massive mistake and a terrible judgment call.

"We will not be doing that," I promise myself.

My whole trip to the airport, part of me was waiting for him to call and explain, to make something up that would let me come back. Instead, it's been complete radio silence from him, which is a wake-up call in and of itself.

Anxiety and longing rise in my chest. I wanted him to be the last person I dated. I wanted to finally have something or someone I could count on. Now how do I find that?

My heart aches for a place to call home, for people in my life who will always be there for me. I want to choose something that will give me security and stability and have that thing choose me back. I tried D.C. for a few years, and it chewed me up and spit me out. But what should I have expected from the easy, safe choice?

My future self will be pickier, will set firm boundaries, and will never settle for satisfactory. If I want stability, I'm going to have to make it for myself on my own terms. And this is the first brave step.

———

THE LAST VESTIGES of morning fog are breaking up as I exit the airport. San Diego must be fighting to hold on to its June Gloom reputation. I pull my hood up, hoping it hides my unbrushed hair and my red, puffy face, and check my phone. Aunt Mari texted she'll be curbside soon and to look for her silver electric Mustang. I keep my eye out for the car that is as cool as she is.

I wave as soon as I spy her coming towards the terminal. She waves back and pulls up, hopping out and coming around to me as the trunk opens. She gives a little sound of tenderness and hugs me tight.

"*¡Ay, mi corazón preciosa!*" she exclaims in my ear with affection and excitement.

My heart skips with happiness, hearing her familiar greeting in her Mexican accent. Every summer of my childhood used to start like this, a big hug and a million *besos* from Aunt Mari.

"Come, let's go home now."

AUNT MARI DRIVES us onto the 5, then over the long swoop of bridge connecting mainland San Diego to Crown Island. The curving bay below us is sparkling blue in the now-bright sunlight, the white sailboats bob at their moorings in the harbor, and the radio plays a doo-wop tune from the 50s. I can barely make out the line of the fence distinguishing the divide between North Island, the Navy base with aircraft carriers and airfields, and Crown Island, with its neighborhoods full of white mansions, gorgeous gardens, and a simple, Main Street, USA feel.

I can't wait to be able to walk four blocks from Aunt Mari's house to stick my feet in the sand and smell fresh saltwater. This is the idyllic island homecoming I've been anticipating, and it meets every expectation.

"Are you happy to be here?" asks Aunt Mari.

"Very happy," I reply with a grin.

When we pull into the driveway, I take a deep, satisfied breath to see the house is just as I remember it: a cream-colored, mid-century California ranch house with ivy climbing up the wall next to the ornately carved wooden front doors. A big tree shades the small front lawn and red geraniums are sprinkled around in terracotta pots.

I carry my bags inside and my sense of relief doubles at the familiar layout. The living room is in front, the kitchen to the right, the dining room tucked around the side of the patio, just off the kitchen. Aunt Mari gives me the full house tour all over again, including the highlights of which pieces of furniture were bought for a bargain.

A long hallway to the left leads to the bedrooms. The first one on the left used to be reserved for me and Julio's summertime visits. Our bunkbeds are gone, and it's now a chic, neutral guest bedroom with a blue batik rug (Facebook Marketplace for five dollars, *increíble*) and a queen bed with a polished brass frame (estate sale, two hundred dollars) and a white duvet. Across the hall is a petite office with dark green walls and a few bookshelves (solid wood, furniture store in El Cajon was closing, very cheap). Then, of course, Aunt Mari's yoga room and her bedroom across the hall.

The only thing significantly different is the hallway bathroom. Aunt Mari had it redone with a new white bathtub and white tiling, oak cabinets, and modern black fixtures. Nostalgia kicks in —I miss the old brown tiling and tub and the dark cabinets.

I put my three suitcases in my old room—the new guest room —and settle a few things in the drawers and wardrobe. So far, Aunt Mari hasn't mentioned that I appear to have overpacked for "a short visit." I'll find the right time to bring it up, to ease into what's happened and why I'm here.

I find her bustling around the kitchen with red reading glasses balanced on her nose. She's wearing a colorful apron with "Gibraltar" printed in big blue letters across the front over a white blouse with the sleeves still buttoned around her wrists. I can tell by the rich tomato smell she's making *sopa de fideo*, and she hasn't gotten a drop of the deep red broth on her blouse.

"*¿Qué está cocinando?*" I ask because the sentence popped into my brain fully formed. My Spanish is terrible, nearly non-existent, but every so often a phrase forms itself without too much effort.

"*¿Quieres practicar tu español?*" Aunt Mari asks, turning from the stove and eyeing me over her glasses.

"Not right now," I reply. "Maybe soon."

She waves her wooden spoon towards the barstools on the opposite side of the island.

"Get yourself some water, sit and talk. Women warm a kitchen."

I have to smile as I grab a glass and fill it with ice and water from the fridge. Aunt Mari always throws out these little pieces of wisdom, cute and pithy. Her short, graying bob, chunky silver jewelry, and a high sense of fashion are all part of what makes Aunt Mari my favorite.

I pull out a wooden bar stool and sit as she picks up a cutting board of vegetables and turns to the stove to dump them into her ancient soup pot, probably made before my great-great grandmother was born.

"What are your plans while you're here?" she asks. Marisol Elena Lopez Ortiz—getting right to the point, always bossing everyone around, taking care of us with commands and food.

"Hanging out with you, of course. I've missed being here. Missed too many summers."

Aunt Mari smiles then narrows her eyes at me, filling me with terror. "*Bueno, pero* your three suitcases filled up the trunk of my car. You haven't said how many days you're staying. Do you even have a return ticket to D.C.? What have you done?"

Oh, boy. There goes any hope of easing into the truth. "I quit my job."

Aunt Mari sucks in a sharp breath of surprise, then whips off her glasses. "Why would you do that?"

I settle for a middle-of-the-road truth. "I don't think D.C. is right for me. It's so fast-paced and kind of toxic. Everyone's fighting to get more power, more influence, more money. I put in my two-week notice and quit my job."

When I glance up, she's still staring me down with suspicion.

"*¿Qué pasó?*" She's boring holes into my brain with her all-knowing glare. I should cave now and save myself the unease of keeping a secret from her.

"I wasn't happy there anyways," I mumble.

"Why?"

"Because it's hot and ugly and cold and dark, and yes, it has its moments. But overall, I don't like the East Coast."

"*Ay Dios,* you quit your job because you don't like the weather?" she asks.

"No, it's not just that—"

"Then why?"

"Because it was all wrong! Everything! The weather, the city, my job, my friends, my boyfriend—"

"What happened with the boyfriend? The tall one who looks like milk, *¿no?*"

"Bryce," I bite out.

"What did he do?"

I don't want to repeat it, but I go ahead and tell her word for word what I heard Bryce saying on the phone and how he reacted afterward. Hearing myself say it out loud, it's stark in its severity. What a freakin'...weasel.

The gasp Aunt Mari sucks in through her teeth makes a sharp hiss, then she calls Bryce all sorts of swear words in Spanish. "That is so very wrong, what a terrible man" she says, sounding more angry than I've ever heard her. She turns to the stove and aggressively stirs, muttering a prayer under her breath. "Okay, well, Gustavo always wanted this house to be a safe place for our family. You stay here, as long as you need."

Bless Great Uncle Gustavo and his well-placed investments in telecommunications and his foresight to have bought a house in the most beautiful beach town in California. Rest in peace, Uncle.

"But you must have a plan, *¿no?*"

This is the part where I need to put on my big girl pants and gird my loins for Aunt Mari's commentary on my plan. "I was doing some thinking on the flight over and...I want to try a different life."

"What does that mean, try a different life?"

"Well, something creative." My cheeks redden as I talk. "I was thinking of going back to painting for a bit. Of course, I'll get a job at a coffee shop or do something in retail to make ends meet while I put together a portfolio. Then I'll see if I can sell some pieces."

I brace myself for the eventual wind-up of her aunt-splaining that art is no way to make a living. My entire family believes it's nice to have a hobby or a creative outlet, but art can never be your job. It makes sense—I was raised to be practical, to think about how to pay bills and save some for myself.

My senior year of high school, I told my dad about the art programs I could apply to for college. Dad paused, a beer halfway to his mouth and gave me a long look, full of exhaustion. "Nina, I didn't save up college money for you to go study art." He shook his head. "Learn something useful, something practical in college. You can always do your art on the side."

I couldn't have felt more ashamed if I tried. No, of course not. Dad's savings from working as a well-respected auto mechanic would go towards something concrete, something real. He couldn't have been clearer and I understood what was expected of me. But that was eight years ago. I did what I thought was right and hated it, basically got rejected by it, now it's time to try a new path. Something I choose for myself.

"You want to paint?" Aunt Mari's voice is pointed.

"It may not be what I do forever," I say, walking back on my dream. "But it would be nice to give it a shot for a season."

Suddenly, Aunt Mari's soup is in need of all her attention. I fade into the background as she chops and stirs and seasons, all with her lips pinched tightly together in thought.

After a tense few minutes, she says, "My friend owns the coffee shop here on the main avenue. I think she'd like some extra help now, since tourist traffic will pick back up during the summer months."

It's an olive branch, a sign of acceptance, and I take it. "That would be great."

"Okay, you'll be here for a while, then. It's fine," Aunt Mari says, rinsing the cutting board and other dishes in the sink, then drying her hands on her apron. "But one thing—promise me you won't run off with one of these Navy sailors and marry them. They are everywhere here."

I laugh out loud. "That's random. But no, I won't be going near any men, Aunt Mari."

"Good," she says, tucking a kitchen towel over the oven door handle. "Now, the soup will cook, and it's time for our movie."

It's tradition that the first movie Aunt Mari and I watch is *Pride and Prejudice*. Aunt Mari has an unending love for Jane Austen because her mother, my great-grandmother, learned her sparse English from watching old Regency romance movies. Like Laurence-Olivier-as-Mr. Darcy old.

We start at lunch time and end up watching all six BBC *Pride and Prejudice* VHS tapes in one sitting and eating soup in the living room. And even though it's late, we decide to follow it up with *Sense and Sensibility,* the Emma Thompson and Hugh Grant version.

I get choked up every time there's any sight or mention of Willoughby, and when Marianne stands sobbing in the rain looking down at Combe Magna, I weep with her. Aunt Mari fetches the tissue box from the kitchen and tucks it next to me on the couch.

Once the credits roll, Aunt Mari clicks off the TV, the light over the stovetop keeping us from total darkness. She gets up, folding the blanket that was on her lap and draping it over the arm of the chair. "You should have a good summer, Christiana," she says, patting my cheeks, then straightening up the cushions on the couch.

"I'm going to paint all day and forget about men for a while and I'm going to play a ton of soccer."

Aunt Mari laughs. "Ah, I forgot your obsession with *futbol.*

You were never far from a ball growing up. I would have to yell at you to keep it out of the kitchen."

Julio and I used to kick the ball down the long hallway, from one side of the house to the other. We regularly overshot our kicks, and the ball would go skidding into the kitchen. We'd be grinning ear to ear as Aunt Mari scolded us.

"I'm going to bed, I have sunrise yoga very early. I am happy you came, *niña preciosa. Buenas noches.*"

"*Buenas noches,*" I say.

She hurries off with a little wave over her shoulder, and I know I'll never be able to thank her enough. She is a mighty woman, and I can't imagine my life without her.

The darkness and loneliness settles around me in a way that's peaceful and calming. I grab my phone and google recreational soccer leagues in the area. I'm here to do what I love, and I swear it's going to be my best summer yet.

CHAPTER 4

One week later

I SET my brush down and take a step back from my easel, studying the nighttime seascape I've been painting since I woke up. Aunt Mari allowed me to make a studio in the office, and after a quick trip to the art supply store, I now have a limited collection of brushes, oil paints, and a mini easel. It's an art space of my own, something I never had in D.C., and it's necessary.

Bryce has finally decided to reach out and text and call over and over. I can't bring myself to give him any attention, to hear his spin on his side of things. I have to build my foundation here and listening to him would be an earthquake, shaking things up. Silencing my notifications and focusing on my brush strokes has been freeing. This is my first painting in my new journey, a healing start.

My seascape is almost complete, I just have to fill in the shadows and highlights, the details that give it enough perspective to show a boat in a harbor with a full moon reflecting on the slightly choppy water. I read another Longfellow poem called "The Bridge" and the last lines were what inspired me.

And forever and forever,
as long as the river flows,
as long as the heart has passions,
as long as life has woes;

The moon and its broken reflection
and its shadows shall appear,
as the symbol of love in heaven,
and its wavering image here.

This intersection of art, poetry, and the inspiration of nature is filling me with new life. I'm tempted to keep pressing on until I'm done, but a growing ache in my neck and shoulders tells me I really should take a break from this session. I need to move my body a bit, and the fresh air coming through the open window is calling me outside. I wipe my brush clean, dunk it in some brush dip, and set it down in a safe space.

"Aunt Mari," I call out, unsure where exactly she is in the house. "I'm going to see if the corner liquor store has any soccer balls."

"*Está bien*," she yells back from the back patio. Now I can see her outside the screen door, watering her plants and refilling her bubbling fountain. "If they don't, check the drug store. Sometimes they have them in the summertime."

"Thanks," I say, waving to her.

I grab my phone and some cash from my bedside table, slip on some flip-flops, and appreciate the fact that I walk out the front door into sunshine and beachy breezes. I close my eyes for a few steps just to see the yellow of the sun on the backs of my eyelids, accompanied by the sound of rustling palm trees. It's heavenly.

The store is only a few blocks away, like most things on Crown Island. Julio and I loved to come here when we were growing up, a dream-come-true emporium of sodas, ice cream, sandwiches, beach toys, boogie boards. Walking through the automatic sliding doors feels strange without him, and I'm sad to see things have changed so much. The laminate flooring has been replaced with gray slate tiles, and the layout isn't charmingly crowded anymore. It looks...modern.

They do have a basket of soccer balls, though, and I fall in love with a neon blue one. I drift over to the wall of beer and zone out staring at all the options. It's my first summer being back as a legal adult, I could grab a six pack of the famous orange wheat beer that's brewed on Crown Island.

"Do you mind if I..." asks a male voice.

I startle, looking left, and make eye contact with warm brown eyes. I quickly drop my gaze to an olive-green t-shirt stretched attractively across a broad chest. I have zero right and less than zero necessity to be noticing that.

"Hi," the guy says, friendly but polite.

"Hi," I reply, averting my gaze back to the beer.

"Sorry, didn't mean to scare you. I was going to get a couple cases of Yuengling right there"—he points to the spot in front of me—"but take your time."

"Oh, please, go ahead."

"Cool," he says. I scoot over as he opens the door and deftly hauls out two large cases of beer. With a tight smile and a quick nod, he heads to the front, ringing the bell to request someone to come to the register.

His pale blond hair is buzzed short. Paired with the amount of beer he's taking to the register and the olive-green crewneck, it dawns on me—this guy is in the military. Maybe a Marine? Or Navy, as Aunt Mari warned about.

"Cole. Cole!" A tall, leggy blonde in jean cut-offs and a black tube top calls out from the store entrance. "I'm going to run down the street and grab a coffee."

She must be his girlfriend. Makes sense—she's pretty.

The military guy pivots from the register. "We're kind of

running late, I can grab you a coffee here. Want a DoubleShot or a cold brew?"

"Ew, can you not? I need keto coffee. I'll be a few minutes, just go wait in the car when you're done."

"Ripley," he calls out, but she's already gone, typing away on her phone as her sandals smack the pavement.

He sighs, heavy enough that I hear it across the store. I should not be as invested in this brief dramatic exchange as I am. I'm here for a soccer ball and might as well grab one of my favorite summer drinks.

But she seems...a little demanding.

I move to the soda section of the fridge, and my eyes go right to the neon green glass bottle with the yellow cap. Squirt, my childhood in a bottle, straight from Mexico. I swing the door of the cooler towards me, ready to grab it, holding the soccer ball under my other elbow.

A loud crack of plastic and thick glue pulling apart echoes through the store and the entire door suddenly falls off the hinges. In slow motion, it looms over me, threatening to fall on my head as it teeters on the edge of the fridge casing. I drop the soccer ball and quickly brace the door with two hands and try to figure out how I can get it back in place. It presses down on me, heavier than it appears, and I struggle to keep my hand from slipping on the glass.

A hefty arm flies up to the left of me, and of course it's the military guy coming to my aid. He helps lean the door backwards, and we prop it back in place against the case.

"You okay?"

"Thanks for the help," I say, shaking my arm out as adrenaline courses through me. "Getting a Squirt has never been so dangerous."

A man in a tracksuit ducks his head inside the front door, then stubs out a cigarette under his sneaker before jogging inside.

"I have never seen that happen. Just had someone in here who got a Coke, worked fine." He shrugs and visually inspects the fridge. "I'll go get some tape to close it off."

He starts walking towards the back of the refrigerated section, then turns and points at me. "Something in the case you wanted?"

I'm about to wave him off when the military guy chimes in, "You said Squirt, right?"

I nod. Of course my favorite drink has to have a name like Squirt. Why couldn't I like something normal like Coke or root beer?

"Can you grab her a Squirt?" he calls to the guy, who gives a thumbs-up before disappearing behind the thick plastic flaps of the cooler.

The military guy pulls out his phone and starts texting. "I'm picking up my buddies from North Island, and then we're all heading to the mountains for the weekend," he says as he types. "I'm in charge of post-hike beers and forgot until just now. I'm letting them know I'll be a few minutes late for our rendezvous."

Oh, he talks like a military guy.

"Thanks again for the help," I say.

He puts his phone away and smiles at me. "I'm Cole."

"Tia," I reply. Technically, I'm Christiana Josefina María Lopez, but I'm Christiana to all my aunts and uncles and relatives, Nina to my dad and Julio, and Tia to everyone else.

He sticks out his hand, and I instinctively shake it. His palm is warm and dry, and his grip is strong and sure. He holds the handshake for just the right amount of time before letting my hand go. We smile at each other.

He seems nice. I wish his girlfriend was kinder to him.

There's a sound of plastic slapping against plastic, and the tracksuit man emerges from the cooler with a few bottles of Squirt cradled in one arm and some tape, paper, and a Sharpie in the other hand.

"On the house," he says, unloading the bottles into my arms. "The ball too—glad you weren't hurt."

"Oh, wow, thank you. Thanks again," I say to Cole with a quick smile and head for the door.

He holds up his hand and looks like he's about to say something, but something breaks his concentration, and he ends up pulling his phone out again to take a call. I leave him standing there in the middle of the liquor store.

As soon as I make it outside, I drop the ball to the sidewalk and dribble it home, smiling to myself the whole time over free drinks and a ball. Small town life is the best. I can't wait to spend a whole summer here in a place that feels far more like home than D.C. ever did.

CHAPTER 5

Waking up in San Diego is somehow significantly easier than waking up in D.C. There's no weight pressing on my chest, and my heart doesn't pound as I drink my morning tea. I think the last time I felt this free was pre-Bryce. Guess that checks out. There's a niggling sense that I need to get closure with him, that things aren't as over and done with as they seem.

The random waves of remorse that come when I'm reminded of him are confirmation of that. Yesterday, it was seeing his profile name on our shared Netflix account. That I pay for. He got booted off as fast as I could click to change the password, and I got teary-eyed doing it. I'm afraid the distance we have is making me go soft, making me forget how terrible he is and how our relationship was a total lie.

My phone rings on the counter next to my mug, and I wince. Sutton. She texted me a few days after I left wondering where I was and what was going on. I told her we'd talk whenever she was free, but we haven't had a chance to connect yet. Now, I have no excuse.

"Hey, Sutton."

"Hello, prodigal daughter. What's happening?"

"I am in San Diego," I say cautiously.

"Yeah. Seems like it's going to be a permanent thing?"

"For now, yeah."

"You're just...gone?"

"Hughie found out I was being made redundant, Bryce and I are over, I hate D.C. summers, it just makes sense."

"Okay...but we're still splitting rent 'til the end of the month. I'll try to find another roommate, but honestly, it might be tough."

That's Sutton alright, goes right on to the next detail, no response to what I said. "You know a lot of people. I'm sure it won't be a problem."

"Just Venmo me for this month, please. What about your furniture?"

"You can keep it. It's yours."

"Oh. Cool."

She goes quiet for a moment.

"Is there anything else, Sutton?"

"Are you, like...okay?"

Sutton and I were brought together by the need for a clean and quiet person to split rent with, and over the years of living together we created a certain level of reserved friendship. She is driven, ambitious, smart, a bit conniving at times, but emotionally supportive she is not.

"I'm fine."

"I ran into Bryce and he was telling me his—"

"Nope, no, no thanks. If you need anything, text me."

I hang up, shaking my head at the phone. Not talking about that at all, especially not with her. Anyway, it's time to head to the coffee shop for my interview. I change into Crown Island's version of business casual—a white linen button-up, olive green joggers, and leather sandals—and head to one of my favorite spots on the main avenue, Cafe 22.

Cafe 22 is an old-world European-style coffee shop featuring golden yellow walls, towering ceilings, a loft area stocked with tabletop games, and floor to ceiling windows facing the main avenue. Every morning, local retired men gather at the two tables outside to chat over the newspaper while their little Shih Tzus and maltipoos and toy poodles nip at each other. It's small-town life at its finest.

Aunt Mari is friends with Elise and Elvin, the owners of Cafe 22, and Elise mentioned they were looking for an extra hand as the summer rush felt more crushing than in previous years. I don't know a thing about making a latte, but I can take orders, I'm good at customer service, and I learn anything quickly.

I turn into the coffee shop, and a girl who looks about my age with dark dreadlocks and thick wooden spiral earrings is behind the counter smiling and counting out change for an elderly lady. I wait in line behind two pilots in green flight suits, who are chatting loud enough for me to overhear as we all wait to order.

"Hey, have you checked your LES recently? Are you getting San Diego BAH or is it still JAX BAH?" asks the shorter pilot.

"Uh, pretty sure it's San Diego now."

"Huh, okay. I need to go talk to admin then. I have a feeling my paperwork got screwed up. Mine hasn't switched over yet."

It's like they're speaking a foreign language. The jargon in D.C. could get technical, but this feels cooler, probably because these guys look like they walked right off the set of Top Gun.

When it's my turn to order, the girl behind the counter looks unhurried and happy as she turns to me with a smile.

"Hey there, how we doing today?" she says. "What are we having?"

"Hi, good," I say, not sure how to say I'm here for an interview, not a coffee.

A woman with a high gray ponytail and a fluff of bangs comes out of the back kitchen section and eyes me with a suspicious smile.

"Are you Tia?" she asks. "You look just like your Aunt Marisol."

"Yes, that's me," I reply with a grin.

"I'm Elise," she says with enthusiasm. "Thanks for coming by, Marisol said you might be interested in helping us out?"

"Oh, my gosh, that would be amazing," says the girl behind the counter with a giant sigh. "I'm Jules. Do you know how to sling lattes?"

"No, but I'm a fast learner," I say.

"Sweet, no worries, do you know how to work POS systems?"

"Um..."

"She means point of sale," chimes in Elise. "Jules is great at making drinks, so she'd love to be freed up to do more of that while you take orders, if that's okay."

My shoulders relax with relief. "Yeah, I can work a register easily."

"Let's go chat about the details," says Elise, tilting her head to the right, where I can see a hallway that leads to a back outdoor seating area.

"Can I get you anything to drink?" asks Jules. "On the house."

"Oh, wow, that's really nice of you. Any iced teas you recommend?"

"Yeah, the white coconut one is bomb. I'll bring it out to you."

"Thanks so much," I say, before I follow Elise outside.

We sit down at a cast iron cafe table set, and Elise smiles kindly at me. "You're from Washington, D.C., right? Left quickly, from what your great aunt told me."

Aunt Mari does tell all. Elise isn't probing for more details, but there's a question in her statement.

"It was a...once-in-a-lifetime choice," I reply. "Based on a bad situation."

"Well, isn't it nice it's in the past, then?"

Her words wash over me like gentle rain, making me surprisingly emotional. It doesn't feel as final as the way she put it, but each day is a small step closer to putting it in the past.

Jules breezes in and out with my iced tea while Elise gives me more details about the job. "We pay a living wage, and Elvin handles scheduling on some internet thing I can't wrap my head around, but I'm sure you'll be a whiz at. We don't tend to struggle with customer service, no altercations or anything like that, but it does get busy and demanding. How are you with dealing with difficult people?"

"Oh, I can handle them. I would say I'm fairly patient and I know how to put on a smile and accommodate a customer." Thanks for the practice, Bryce. Good riddance to you.

"Right, wonderful. I think your vibe matches what we're about, so I look forward to working with you, my dear," says Elise. "It's as easy as that. I'll let Elvin know you're ready for paperwork and to schedule some training, if that's good with you? He can email it over."

She pats the table as if she's patting my hand, and it really is as easy as that. I'm stunned.

I start to feel a faint buzz of excitement as I wave goodbye and start down the sidewalk in the sunshine. I have a job again, a kind boss, and a really cool place to work. Should I buy a lottery ticket?

There's a twinge of regret that comes on the heels of my elation. I should have done this so long ago. I should have come to San Diego as soon as I graduated from college. Instead, I forced myself into a mold. The expectation of a career, a noteworthy job, a stereotype of success—all those could have crushed me if I hadn't left when I did.

But I did. And I'm going to make it here. I'm proud of myself.

Securing a job is a win that deserves ice cream. There's an old-fashioned ice cream parlor across the street from the cafe, a once-a-summer treat for Julio and me when we were kids. The warm sugar smell of fresh waffle cones makes me grin as I treat myself to a double scoop of mint chocolate chip in a cone and tuck a napkin in my pocket for later.

I walk the long way home, a roundabout route that takes me through the heart of Crown Island. I savor my ice cream as I make my way down the sidewalk along the main avenue, noticing what's the same and what's changed. There are still cute stationery shops with floral window displays made entirely out of paper, boutique children's clothing stores with racks of seersucker and sailboat dresses, and plenty of surf shops combined with touristy t-shirt stores. Sprinkled in with them is the bookstore with long green awnings over the windows, a bagel shop, and Mexican Take Out, the best burritos in the world, in my opinion.

Wait, that's new.

Floor to ceiling windows let plenty of light into a narrow art gallery with darker, moodier paintings on display. My breath catches. I quickly finish my ice cream—art galleries never allow food inside—and wipe my hands on the napkin.

A bell rings out as I enter, and a lady at the back raises her head, then waves to me, acrylic bangles clacking together on her wrist.

"Hello, welcome," she says in a warm voice. "Have a look around, let me know if you have any questions."

"Thank you." I give her a smile as I turn to the first painting.

A broody old man with a knit cap pulled low over his eyebrows stands at the helm of a sailboat, a headlamp with a red light the only lighting aside from a streak of moonlight on the water. I try to guess what the connecting theme will be. Sailboats, water, or night? All my fortes. I mostly paint dark and moody night images, but I love a good seascape.

The next portrait is a mother nursing her baby in a gray rocking chair in the middle of the night, a nightlight shooting stars onto the ceiling above them. Then a man proposing under a streetlight. Then a car with its headlights on, illuminating a boy pitching a baseball into the dark. They're all different styles, different color choices, but they're all dark palettes with limited light sources.

"See it yet?" asks the woman, from much closer than I remember, making me jump.

"They're all at night?"

"Mmhmm, people at night. Gives it a spot of new perspective, some interest."

I nod. There's an air of determination in these paintings, one that I'm drawn to. The pull of things happening when most of the world is resting

This is the kind of theme I would want to paint. It has echoes of Longfellow's poems, a confluence of multiple points of inspiration. I've never tried painting people, though I've always been drawn to portraits. I may be overconfident, but...how hard can it be?

Could I do something like this? Something that would be good enough to be displayed in a gallery? I'm barely getting back into it, I should probably practice more before I set my sights this high. Is that kind of pressure something I want to put on my art right now? But, then again, why hold back?

With a pounding heart, I casually ask, "Do you know if any new paintings are being accepted for this display?"

"Depends. I'm picky, but I'm open to one or two more."

"Oh, this is your gallery?" I ask, my heart pounding even harder. "It's stunning."

"Thank you, sweetheart," she replies with a grin.

"I'm an amateur artist, but my favorite thing to paint is nightscapes," I offer.

"Oh, how lovely. Well, for this display, I'm looking for paintings with a person or people as the focal point. Have you had people as your subject before?"

"No, the most recent series I did was the D.C. monuments at night." *Recent* being loosely used to mean over a year ago.

"That must have been special."

"I haven't painted for the last few months, so I feel rusty, but I'm so drawn to these colors and moods. There's a sense of perseverance that I admire."

"Yes! That's what I love too. It would be nicer for these folks to enjoy these things in the daytime, but they're doing what they have to. I'm Lorraine, by the way."

We shake hands as I say, "Tia. Nice to meet you."

"I love that you stopped in. I watched you scarf down that ice cream cone so you could come in and thought to myself, 'Oh, good, she's an art lover.'"

I smile, a slight tinge of heat in my cheeks. "I am. I was so struck by this collection. I guess I would have expected more of the sea, lighthouses and sailboats, or the hotel, the beach."

"I'll tell you what, so many people have stopped by to take a look since I set up this collection. I think it's unexpected and welcome for being out of the ordinary."

"Are they all local artists?"

"Yes, from all over San Diego County."

I nod and study the boy throwing the baseball. Is that a subtle pattern of rain coming down in front of the headlights? So many details to take in and admire.

"Are you just visiting, then?" Lorraine asks.

"No, I'm here permanently now. I quit my East Coast life, and I'm living on Crown Island."

"Wonderful. You got here at the perfect time of year. It's shaping up to be an unparalleled summer, not too hot, not too cold. I expect we'll be busy."

I study the portrait of the mother and baby one more time. "I'd really love to do something in this theme, I just don't know if I can do it justice. I'll have to practice sketching people like that before I dive into a painting."

"Ooh, over here." Lorraine waves me towards the back of the gallery, to a painting that's facing the back wall.

This one is much more painterly, with broader brush strokes, more obvious layers—closer to my style. You can tell the subject is a medical professional in scrubs, drinking coffee at a diner counter, again in low lighting.

"Oh, I like this one," I whisper with appreciation.

"See what you can come up with," Lorraine offers. "I have a price cap of a thousand, but most of these are priced well below that."

My jaw falls open, then a laugh bubbles out. "I've never sold a painting, much less for that price."

"Oh, pish," Lorraine waves away my fears with a smile. "Selling one hundred or none has no bearing on talent."

My eyes roam over the gallery as a hopeful, determined sensation rises in me. I definitely want to have a painting in this gallery. "I'll be in touch. I might stop by every now and then to visit. I'm starting a job around the corner, at Cafe 22, so I'll be in the neighborhood."

"Look forward to seeing you, Tia," says Lorraine, sounding so genuine, it makes my heart squeeze with affection for her.

After one last slow spin to take in the beauty and thoughtfulness of the whole space, I wave goodbye. I'm a bundle of nerves, giddy with the thought of trying something new and challenging.

As I walk home, my excitement is tempered by an email notification from the office, asking if I have time to call and speak to Rich and Dan. Oh no. The nervous, giddy feeling from before is turning to nausea now. I might as well get this over with.

I dial Dan's office number right away and jump in as soon as he answers. "Hey, Dan, it's Tia. I got an email to call you?"

"Tia, yes. I just saw you're on vacation, right? Didn't mean to disrupt your time off. You know, we can have a conversation when you get back to the office."

"What's up, Dan?" Someone clears their throat in the background. "Is that Rich? Look, please tell me what's going on. Am I being let go?"

"Well...okay, no beating around the bush. Your position has been made redundant. Now, not to worry, we have a great severance package for you—"

I pull the phone away from my ear and close my eyes with a smile, biting back a laugh of happy relief. Who knew getting let go could make my day?

CHAPTER 6

Iт's a Friday afternoon and I'm lounging on the back patio sofa, sipping a margarita, and reading a fantasy romance novel. A love story could be a turn-off for someone healing from a break-up, but it's so far removed from my present reality, I find myself enjoying it. I take a deep breath as I finish a chapter, relishing the warm fresh air scented with a hint of jasmine. I set my book down, look around incredulously, then laugh out loud. How is this my life right now?

My phone starts vibrating on the end table, and once I check the caller ID, I answer with a shout of, "Dad!"

"*¿Mija?*" says Dad. I can hear his smile of surprise that I answered.

"Hey, how's it going down there?"

"Good! I'm good. Cozumel's good. Fishing's good. Hey, guess who's here?" I hear Dad call for someone and the sound of a cooler thunking shut.

"Hey, Nina."

My eyes go wide with surprise. "Julio! I didn't know you were in Mexico. I thought you were still in Florida."

"Just here for the summer. What's up? Where are you?" asks

Julio. He already sounds suspicious, and I can imagine him and Dad exchanging concerned glances.

"I'm at Aunt Mari's," I say, raising my voice like it's a fun little getaway I've been planning for months.

They don't buy it for a second. They immediately talk over each other. "Nina, why are you there? Are you okay? What about D.C.?"

"Nothing's like really, seriously wrong," I immediately reassure them. "Well, my life kind of...unraveled in D.C."

"What does that mean?" Julio asks.

"Do you remember I was seeing a guy named Bryce?" Ugh, his name makes me nauseous now, but I press on and tell them everything that's happened, with honesty and transparency.

"Do you want me to come to San Diego? Do you need me there?" Dad asks after I've finished sharing.

"No, I'm okay," I reply with gratitude. "I'm doing fine now."

"I'm sorry, Nina," Julio says, closer to the phone now. "That really sucks. You guys were together for a while."

Eighteen months. Feels significant and yet it meant nothing. It was everything to me and a lie to him. My phone starts vibrating with incoming text messages, but I ignore it as my heart squeezes with emotion.

"It's going to be okay," I say. "Really."

"How long will you be at Aunt Mari's?" asks Dad. "If you need us, we'll come as soon as we can, okay?"

"Okay, thanks, Dad," I whisper, suddenly feeling wrung out and tired from the rollercoaster of emotions I've been on the last two weeks. I miss my family, and I wouldn't say no to a hug from them right now. "How are you guys?"

Dad tells me how many charters he has coming up, and Julio talks about how he's thinking of going back to school for his master's degree in business. We catch up every so often like this, telling each other the surface level stuff and, very occasionally, the emotional things we're going through. Ever since Julio and I went to college, at Dad's insistence, we've all kind of split off into our own separate adult lives. Sometimes it makes me sad, and sometimes I'm simply grateful we all love each other and there's no drama. It is what it is. We're not a normal family, and maybe that's one of the ways it shows.

They both tell me they love me and to say hi to Aunt Mari and we end the call.

I close my eyes and take a deep breath. Yes, today is perfect, but there are still loose ends I haven't dealt with in D.C. Is it time to check all those notifications on my phone?

Texts from Bryce used to be thoughtful and kind. He'd ask questions like, "Do you like how today is going for you? What could make it better?" Or say things like, "I hope you feel fulfilled in your job today. If not, there's always tacos and tequila afterwards. #TacoTuesday." Or even a simple, "Thinking of you," would make me feel seen and valued.

Faker.

Right now, I have a dozen notifications from Bryce, and when I open my messages there are multiple texts that turn out to be paragraphs long. He is definitely verbose when he wants to be. Part of me is curious to see what he has to say, and another part of me is ready to ignore it all and send him one strongly worded text and be done with it.

Curiosity wins, and I start to read his texts. They're strangely formal, like they were written by a father chiding his teenage daughter.

BRYCE

Tia, I am so disappointed by the way you...

As I start to scroll, my chest tightens with a familiar twinge.

I lock my phone and drop it on the couch. No, I am not reading those, I'm not listening to him. I can't do this yet. At some point, the time will be right. Just not yet.

———

THE NEXT MORNING is my first day of soccer and the team is immediately diving in with a scrimmage, not even a practice. Some googling found me a co-ed recreational league that had one spot open, and I registered right away. I arrived in San Diego at the perfect time, right as the season begins, and I am so pumped. I can't wait to feel the rush of the start of a game.

I'm almost too nervous to eat, but I know if I can't get something in my stomach, I'm going to be too weak to play. I manage to get a banana and some toast in me before I need to go change.

My soccer kit had priority in my suitcase, and putting it on again has me grinning ear to ear. I throw my hair up in a tight bun, pull on some black shorts, wrestle my way into a black sports bra, and slip into an old white jersey from my college intramural league. By the time I'm putting on my shin guards and socks I'm breathing hard, but I feel like I could run a 5K no problem with the amount of energy zinging through me.

I grab my bag, pre-packed with water, snacks, and cleats, and the key to Aunt Mari's electric Mustang, which she is graciously letting me borrow. I slip into my slides and head out. The sun is shining as I drive north to Pacific Beach, and the day ahead of me feels light and uncomplicated as I jam to Karol G.

I try to wrap myself up in this moment of me being happy, all on my own. This is how it's going to be from now on. I'm going to have the freedom to choose what brings me joy. I won't bend for anyone, I won't be manipulated by anyone.

With new resolve, I pull into the parking lot of an elementary school with a big field, pretending like I know enough Spanish to lip-synch to *Si Antes Te Hubiera Conocido*. It's all about the vibes anyways.

I turn off the car and sit in the silence, noticing people trickling onto the field. My stomach starts flipping in mini cartwheels of nervousness. I don't know anyone. I hope they like me. I hope I don't embarrass myself. What if they're all retired pros or something? What if I can't hang with them?

"Just go, Tia," I whisper. With a deep breath, I grab my bag and try to pep myself up as I make my way on to the field.

I'm about to reach the sideline, when my toe dives down into a ground squirrel hole, and suddenly the world is somersaulting under me. My ankle rolls to one side as I flail my arms with a squeal, throwing my bag in one direction while my body ungracefully lurches the other way. I end up on my back, staring up at the sky with a whimper. Ouch.

"Are you okay?" asks a masculine voice from somewhere behind me. "That gopher hole gets everyone the first time."

"Yeah, totally fine," I say, heat rushing to my face. Of course I trip in front of someone I'm either playing with or against. Great first impression. I sit up and gingerly twist my foot around, checking the extent of my ankle injury.

"If it's really bothering you, I could take a look at it. I'm a corpsman, by the way, not trying to hit on you."

I wince as I flex my foot. "I think I'll be okay. I'll walk it off."

The guy generously goes and gets my bag, dropping it down next to me.

"I promise I'm not that clumsy in real life," I say.

"You sure? Last time I saw you, you were holding up the door to a liquor store cooler."

I look up and lock eyes with the guy from the corner store. Cole. My painter's eye takes him in by color again. Warm brown eyes, short hair so blond it's nearly white, lightly tanned skin, a pale blue jersey stretched across his shoulders.

"Hey, Tia," he says with a smile.

"Oh, hey, Cole." My nerves settle at the fact he remembered my name. It's a friendly, reassuring sign. Hopefully he's on my team.

From the parking lot, someone whoops and aggressively chirps on a whistle, and we both turn towards the sound.

"Looks like the rest of the team's here. Want a hand up?" he asks.

I take his hand, and he easily pulls me to my feet as I test putting weight on my ankle. No permanent damage, just a twinge of soreness.

A tall, lanky guy with honey blond hair and a sunburn comes over. He lets the whistle he was chirping drop to his chest as he reaches out to shake my hand. "You must be the new girl. I'm Aiden, I go by Denny."

"I'm Tia," I say, shaking his hand.

"Tia? No way," he says, his mouth falling open. "Are you the girl Cole met in the liquor store last weekend?"

I glance over at Cole. His neck, then ears turn bright red. Interesting.

"He told us all about that on the drive up the mountain. Not, like, in a weird way, more like a 'Guess what happened?' His girl-friend wasn't happy," says Denny with a sunrise of a smile. He taps Cole on the arm. "Dude, no way."

A serious guy with dark brown hair, olive skin, and a thick, solid body comes over to join us. He rolls his eyes at Denny and shakes my hand. "I'm Luko. Good to have you," he murmurs.

"Hi, Tia. I'm Anisha," says the next girl in the line-up. She's as short as me, about five-three, with rich bronze skin and a long black ponytail. "Hey, let me give you the relationship rundown and spare you the effort of trying to figure things out on your own." She's peppy and fiery when she talks, pointing to each person as she goes through the list. "Frank is our team captain, and Sarah is his girlfriend. I'm married to Mick, the love of my life. Denny is a lovesick puppy, pining for a girl who will never love him back." Luko stifles a laugh while Denny rolls his eyes. "Cole is dating a girl we all hate for him, and Luko—ugh, Luko—honestly may be a bachelor forever. He's holding out for his one true love, but he's picky."

They're not a random hodgepodge of people thrown together

by the whims of a recreational league commissioner—they've clearly known each other for some time. I'm the infiltrator, the new girl. I bite the inside of my bottom lip, trying to quell my desire to run back to the car and drive straight home.

"Are you single?" Denny asks in a stage whisper.

"Um, newly single." I offer.

"Bad breakup?" asks Luko.

"The worst."

He nods in sympathy. Denny chimes in, "Luko is our Russian bear, the strong and silent type. I'm the class clown, and Cole is the cool one."

I awkwardly laugh. "You guys seem like you've played together before."

Anisha nods. "Denny, Cole, and Luko have been playing together since college, with little breaks here and there. Frank's usually goalie, Denny and Sarah stay up front, Cole and I play midfield, and Luko and Leslie were usually on defense. Leslie abandoned us to move up to Washington with her new husband, so we'll throw you back there."

"But we can switch it up," Denny offers. "What do you like to play?"

I have great endurance and accurate passing skills, so I usually play midfield, but there's no way I'm going to be the stranger who comes in and throws this team out of their groove. "Oh, defense is fine," I reply. "That's great."

"Well, we'll wait for Frank and Sarah to show up, and then we'll give them a good teasing about why they're late, as usual."

"Who are we playing?" Luko asks.

"The Nemesis and his team," Anisha growls. Everyone groans.

"The Nemesis is this insane goalie," Cole offers to me. "Do you know who Kelly Slater is? The surfer?" I shake my head. "Oh, well, google Kelly Slater after you meet The Nemesis. They're practically twins. Bright blue eyes, surfer's tan, bald. Anyways, he's a magician in the goal box."

"Noted," I say.

We wait around a few more minutes, getting our cleats on, and when Frank and Sarah finally show up Anisha shouts at them to stop having sleepovers on Friday nights.

Frank, a fit, blond guy with a man-bun and a sleeve of thick black tattoos shakes his head and rolls his eyes as he carries over a bag of soccer balls. Sarah is about my build, with fair and freckled skin, muscular quads, and a thick blonde french braid. She runs across the parking lot and nearly tackles Anisha in a hug.

Anisha brings her over to meet me, and she's so friendly and warm I have no choice but to like her immediately. In fact, I like this whole team, which is a rarity in the world of co-ed leagues. But they're almost too nice and friendly. I feel like something is going to go wrong—my streak of good luck has gone on far too long already.

The other team arrives and starts their warmup, and I'm getting nerves now, the best kind of nerves. Pregame nerves.

"All right," says Frank, drawing everyone into a huddle at midfield. "Tia, good to have you. Welcome to our unnamed team, Anisha will have come up with a name by the end of the scrimmage, as per usual." Everyone chuckles. "Let's have fun, and if anyone gets hurt, call Cole, not 911."

With a fair amount of backslapping, we fan out across the field. Frank works his gloves onto his hands as he heads to the goalie box.

"Tia, where you coming from?" he calls out.

"D.C.," I answer back.

"You here long?" he asks.

"For as long as I can be," I answer. Feels good to say that.

The referee jogs onto the field and tweets his whistle, and I grin at the *thunk* sound of the ball being kicked into play.

CHAPTER 7

WE LOSE THE SCRIMMAGE.

Turns out The Nemesis really is the best goalie I've ever seen. No one was able to score on him, and the other team got two balls past Frank. Still, it was a ton of fun, and our team spirit is high. I'm grinning ear to ear as I break off from the group and walk back towards the car. I drop my bag on the pavement by the trunk as I prep to unlock the car and pull off my cleats.

Someone calls my name, and I turn to see Luko jogging over with his soccer bag slung across his chest.

"Hey, we're heading to the beach down the street to cool off. Might grab some food after. Want to come?"

"Oh, I..." cannot think of a good excuse why I can't. "Who's going?"

"All of us, the whole team. You'll be the odd one out if you don't come," he says.

"Odd one out" is a phrase that will get me every time. Besides, what am I going to do at home? Paint and sketch? I'm not on a deadline. And spending time with this group might mean I can actually make friends with decent people.

"Yeah, okay. I can meet you there."

"Parking may be tough since it's the weekend and all. Want to hop in with us in my car?"

"Let's do it."

Anisha waves to us as she gets in the passenger side of Luko's military-green 4Runner, which looks like it's seen a dirt road recently. I slide in behind her while Luko throws our bags in the trunk.

"I'm excited to have you on the team. You were awesome today," Anisha says, turning in her seat to talk to me. "This season is going to be so fun."

Cole slides in next to me, and Luko rubs a towel over his sweaty hair before getting in the driver's seat.

I grin at her enthusiasm. "You guys play together really well."

"Sometimes my husband Mick subs in and plays with us. He's a helicopter pilot, but he's deployed right now."

"Oh," I say, not quite knowing what to add. I'm sorry? That's too bad? Right on? Cool? What's the proper response to something like that?

"This is him," says Anisha. I gasp as she shows me the lock screen of her phone. It's a beautiful picture of the two of them in red and gold Hindi wedding attire. Mick looks like he descended from the highlands of Scotland, tall and brawny with a curling thatch of red hair cut to military regulations. He's at least a foot taller than Anisha, but he's looking down at her with nothing but desire in his eyes. They're physical opposites and clearly in love.

"That is a gorgeous photo," I say.

"Isn't it?" Anisha says, smiling down at it. "Anyways, so excited to have you this season. You're faster and better than Leslie was, no offense to her, so we're going to kick butt this time around," says Anisha. "And our team name is going to be the Goal Diggers."

"Welcome to the team," says Luko. "She's a little competitive." He points a thumb towards Anisha.

She rolls her eyes. "Look, if we happen to win the championship after multiple seasons of trying, I won't be mad. We have a shot, right?"

Luko nods, checking the rearview mirror as he backs up. "I'd say we have a shot. For all the glory and the fame."

"It's just rec soccer," I say with a laugh.

"Whoa, whoa, whoa," Anisha says, sitting up tall and turning to address the car. "Listen up, you all. Mick has been floating on an aircraft carrier in the middle of the ocean for months on end. All he dreams about is getting to play soccer on a green grass field again, he lives for my soccer updates, and it's my personal mission to win this championship for him. At the very least, we're going to make this an interesting season. I don't care what we have to do. This deployment has been way too long, and this is my last resort for entertainment. We're winning. End of story."

She's like a little Napoleon, rallying her troops for the glory of winning. I'm inspired to want this for her—and for her husband. I can't imagine not getting to play soccer for months on end.

"What do you say, Tia?" Cole asks.

"You bet we're going to win," I say, holding up my fist. He rewards me with a fist bump and a cute little grin.

———

THE WHOLE TEAM hot-steps it across the burning sand, then surprises me by dashing straight into the waves. Everyone dumps their duffel bags and shirts at the edge of the tide, including the girls, so I join in, running into the ocean in my shorts and sports bra.

Only to scream in shock. "It's freezing, you psychos! What are you thinking?"

No one hears me over the waves. I retreat to where the water is only brushing over my feet and cross my arms over my chest. I'll never get over the shocking cold of the Pacific. It always looks so sparkling and inviting on a warm summer day, making me forget the temperature is the same as barely-melted ice.

Luko's tattooed chest and Cole's thick, defined muscles are on full display as they body-slam each other into the water. I look away before my long glance can be classified as staring. Sarah and Anisha are practically mermaids, and Frank and Denny are already swimming out past the waves. Everyone seems so carefree. I'm sure they all have stuff going on in their lives, like Anisha's husband being deployed, but that doesn't stop them from having fun. It's been so long since I played like I was a kid. Life was so uptight in D.C., and there was so much judgment in my circle. Maybe I just had bad friends.

The girls wave to me, motioning for me to come in farther, but I stay where I am, shivering just thinking about diving deeper into the ocean. As I think about grabbing my shirt and taking a seat in the warm sand, watching to see who's the first to come out with goosebumps and chattering teeth, I hear my name being chanted.

"Tia! Tia! Tia!"

Everyone has waded back to about hip deep, their backs to the waves. They're all looking at me, motioning for me to get in with them.

"I'm going to get hypothermia!"

"Cole will take care of you," Luko shouts back.

"C'mon, it's the best," Sarah coaxes.

"Lunch is on me if you come all the way in with us," Denny says.

"This is a team event," says Anisha. "Call it initiation."

New city, new friends, new courage, new me. Why hold back now? I dive in to the cheers of my teammates.

———

YES, the water's cold, but I forgot how much I love hanging out in the waves. I float with the girls, then Sarah and I bodysurf for a bit.

The power of the waves and the woosh of water coming over my head and propelling me to shore brings back fun memories of doing the same with Julio.

Frank and Sarah get out first and dry off to do the food run for us. When we see them pulling a wagon full of lunch, drinks, and towels across the sand, we all make our way out of the waves, shivering and shaking our limbs.

Sarah tosses me a California burrito and a can of Coke as I sit on a borrowed towel, letting my skin slowly defrost in the hot sun and sand. I take one bite and groan with deep satisfaction. Tortilla, French fries, guacamole, carne asada, sour cream, cotija cheese—an amazing San Diego specialty.

"So good," I murmur to no one as my shoulders melt with happiness.

Luko snags an entire tray of carne asada fries and takes a seat on a towel next to me. Before he takes a bite, I quickly ask, "Hey, can you confirm a suspicion for me? Is Cole a Marine? I'm just curious."

"What are you guys talking about?" Cole asks from behind me, making me jump.

"She asked if you were a Marine," Luko volunteers. Thanks, buddy.

"Why, do I look like one?" Cole's face lights up as if it's a compliment. "I'm actually Navy, I work with the Marines as a corpsman."

"I'm not totally military illiterate, but what's a corpsman?" I ask.

"Oh, I'm like a medic for the Marines. I'm there for anything from heat casualties, to blisters, to actual battlefield injuries. Not that I've been in combat or anything. I mostly deal with dumb Marines doing dumb things and getting hurt. Or thinking they have brain cancer because they only drink Red Bull and preworkout and get super dehydrated. Love them to death, but yeah, not always the brightest bunch."

Denny walks over and joins our circle of towels. I take in the sum of them, realizing they all have pretty trim haircuts. Luko's hair is the longest on top, followed by Denny, then Cole's is the shortest by far. He looks like he recently got a haircut too, with how crisp the lines are. Am I staring at his fade? I shift to looking at the sand.

"Are you all military?" I ask.

Luko nods and finishes his bite before he answers. "We're all in the Navy."

"Do you not like guys in the military?" asks Denny. "I know we get a bad rap because of the bad apples."

"Oh, no, I have nothing against people in the military. I was just curious, that's all."

They're nice and attractive guys in their own ways, but the fact they're all in the Navy will make it easy to keep things on a friendly/teammate level. Based on the little I know about it from pop culture and books and a few military influencers I've stumbled across on Instagram, the military life is not for me, what with the constant moving and going on deployments and the service member going into harm's way. Cole's the only one who's really my type anyway, and he has a girlfriend.

"Are you from around here?" asks Cole.

I shake my head. "I have family here. I'm from L.A. originally, but I'm on Crown Island now. What do you two do in the Navy?" I ask, pointing to Luko and Denny. It's not like I'm dying to know, but I don't love being in the conversational spotlight.

"I'm a SWO—a surface warfare officer," says Denny. "I work on a ship out of 32nd Street, the Navy base on this side of the bridge."

"Since U Been Gone" by Kelly Clarkson cuts into the conversation, ringing out from a phone somewhere. I didn't know people still did ringtones and left their phones on full volume. Denny's bright animated expression vanishes. He dashes to his stuff, grabs his phone, then shows the screen to Luko and Cole, and even I can see it reads "Ellis."

"Dude," says Luko, shaking his head in disapproval. "She's not calling to beg to get back together."

"It's probably a pocket dial, but you never know," says Cole. "You do you."

"I'm gonna go take this," Denny mutters as he heads off towards the parking lot.

"I know how this is going to go," Cole says with a sigh. "I'd better secure his food so the seagulls don't get it." He wanders over to Frank and Sarah's wagon and sunshade to see about storing Denny's fries.

"What about you, Luko?" I ask.

"I fly helicopters out of North Island."

"Oh, cool. I always see Navy helicopters flying overhead when I'm walking along the beach."

"Nice," Luko says with a nod. "I fly Sierras, the kind with the diagonal wheel way at the end of the tail."

The vibration of a phone catches my attention, and I reach over to dig mine out of my bag. There's a group text from Frank with all of our numbers and names in it.

FRANK

Here's the team, Goal Diggers. Cheers to the season.

ANISHA

We gonna win the championship! Let's go!!!

SARAH

When's the first team hang?

"You all know we're sitting right here?" says Cole, with a laugh as he comes back with his phone in hand.

FRANK

Can we still text you injury photos for you to
triage? Like next time my toenail is looking
bad?

I grin as I set my phone to the side. I like these people.

"What do you do, Tia?" asks Luko.

Thankfully he asks me mid-bite, so I have a second to figure
out what to say. My stomach sinks as I think about how to best
answer that. I mean, I should answer honestly, but suddenly it
sounds so lame and oddly...irresponsible? Like it's not something a
real adult would say. But I have to own my choices.

"I work at a coffee shop, and I paint on the side. Like art painting, not house painting."

"Oh, for real?" says Cole. "What do you paint?"

Sometimes people surprise me with their interest in art. I
would not have pegged these Navy guys as art enthusiasts. "I really
like nightscapes. The moon reflecting on the bay, or like a row of
boats with one that has interior lights on. Anything like that."

"Nice."

Frank tosses a football straight at Luko's stomach, which kicks
off the guys playing two-on-two football while Sarah and Anisha
and I hang out and talk. I learn that Sarah works as a classroom
aide at an elementary school and Anisha does freelance graphic
design. We bond over a mutual love for Jane Austen and the whole
team ends up staying on the beach for hours, the time passing in
the lazy, comfortable way it does in summertime.

I'm driving home as the sun is setting, and I realize that after
just two weeks here I now feel settled. I'm here, established, now
it's time to level up. I'll start work at Cafe 22 tomorrow, start
learning how to paint portraits, and play my heart out to get the
Goal Diggers on the road to the championship. Here I go.

CHAPTER 8

THE COFFEE SHOP is bustling and the patrons are restless on this unusually hot Sunday morning. I can sense everyone staring daggers at me as I navigate the POS software on the iPad. It's not complicated, it's just nothing is where I expect it to be on the screen, and I'm struggling to find things quickly enough to keep the line moving at the pace customers expect.

Jules is amazing to work with—helpful, easygoing, and kind. But the line is getting longer as the sun heats up through the big windows.

I feel for the woman at the counter right now. She's got a toddler pulling her arm in one direction and an elderly woman clinging to her other arm. I repeat her order back to her. "Okay, that's one vanilla latte, one kid's hot chocolate, one peppermint tea, one cranberry scone, and two slices of bacon quiche?"

"Veggie quiche," says the woman with a quiet sigh.

"So sorry," I reply. Darn it. I make the adjustment, but it takes a few seconds longer than I would have liked. "Here's your number. Jules will call it when drinks are ready at the counter, and we'll bring your food out to your table."

"I asked for everything to go."

Double darn it. "I am so sorry, I missed that. It's no problem, hang on to that number and we'll get everything packaged up for you."

She gives me a tight smile as she pays and declines to tip. Good for her.

The next customers are a tall, retired couple in tennis whites, rackets slung on their backs in leather bags. I brace myself for a complicated order and lots of questions about our menu.

"Two black drip coffees."

"Easy!" I say, peppy with relief. I turn to quickly fill their cups and slide them across the counter as they pay. They select the highest tip amount on the final screen. Bless their rich hearts. I quickly wipe a splash of coffee off the counter with the bar towel tucked in the tie of my apron.

"How can I help you?" I say, looking up to find myself staring into Cole's brown eyes.

"Hey, Tia, you work here?"

"My first official day," I say, breathless with the bustle of the morning.

"That's wild. I had to be over on North Island for something and needed coffee. You doing okay?" he asks.

"It's mayhem," I say with a smile. "Can I take your order?"

His neck starts to redden. "Don't judge me. Can I get a triple-shot latte with almond milk, two pumps of vanilla, two pumps of white chocolate, and one pump of raspberry? Hot, please."

I bite my lip, holding back a grin as I work through the system to add all his requests to the order, then write it down on the side of a to-go cup with a Sharpie.

"Do you want whipped cream?" I ask, pausing my writing and glancing up at him with a smile.

"I know, it's a chick drink, whatever. I got hooked on them in high school. And yes, I want whipped cream," he replies. He pays and tips generously. "Cool to run into you again and see where you work," he says. "See you Saturday."

"Yeah, see you then."

He waves as he heads down to the end of the bar to wait for his drink. He's so nice.

"Who's that?" Jules whispers over my shoulder.

"A guy from my soccer team," I whisper back.

"Oooooh...interested?"

"Not at all. He has a girlfriend, and he's in the Navy."

"Huh," Jules replies, playfully.

"Don't 'huh' me. I'm serious."

She shrugs and goes back to making a flat white.

———

THE REST of the week passes by at a comfortable, easy pace as I adjust to life in a new routine. I find a new running route around the island, and Aunt Mari includes me in some of her weekly events like shopping at the farmer's market on Tuesdays and getting a fresh stack of novels from the library on Thursdays. And then it's Saturday again, with another soccer game on the schedule.

This time the soccer field is a slick mess of flattened grass. Apparently, the sprinkler system flooded everything the night before. We all struggle to keep our feet underneath us as we start the game, and I slide into unintentional splits a few times too many.

"You good?" asks Cole when I'm slow to get up. "Need a minute?"

"No, no, I'm fine," I say, waving for play to continue even though it feels like I shredded my inner thigh.

Luko and I manage to hold the backfield well throughout the game, but we're both limping by the end. Thankfully, we win our first team victory, putting us on the bottom rung of the ladder to the league playoffs. Everyone has prior commitments they have to jet off to, so our celebration is a short-lived round of high-fives.

I slowly wince my way out to the parking lot afterwards, ready for a hot bath and a nap, only to be greeted with the unwelcome sight of a flat tire. Great. Thankfully, it's not a daunting occurrence, thanks to Dad's instruction and loads of practice in high school. I swear, I ran over every screw and nail in Los Angeles County. I can easily put on the spare, but today, when I'm already sore and tired? Really?

I fling my bag in the back seat and open the trunk, pulling out the spare tire and the jack. I get everything in place, raise the corner of the car to take the weight off the tire, and get the wrench on the first lug nut, twisting it with all my might to torque it off.

Nothing. It doesn't so much as budge, like it's cemented on.

I glance around the parking lot, panic setting in as I realize everyone is gone already. Wait, no.

Cole is about to get in the driver's seat of his black Camaro. The car is a gorgeous design of clean, sleek lines and gentle curves —the newest model. I bet there's a lot of horsepower under the hood. No lie, that car is sexy.

"Cole!"

"Yeah?" he shouts back.

"Could I get your help with something?"

He quickly grasps my situation and hustles over, his left leg limping a bit.

"I can't get the lug nuts off," I say, pointing to the offending tire.

"You did this all yourself?" he asks, scanning the empty trunk and the jack lifting the flat up off the ground.

"What, like it's hard?" I ask, flipping my ponytail.

"Yeah, okay." He chuckles as he lowers himself down to kneel on the asphalt. He throws his all into turning the lug wrench, his shoulders straining against his jersey, his face flushing deep red.

"Geez, that's really on there," he says, breathing hard. He tries a few more times, then leans back, sitting down on the pavement and shaking out his arms.

"Hey, scoot over, I'll take a turn," I say.

"Oh, what, like I loosened it for you?"

"You never know."

Cole moves over, and now it's a matter of pride. I'm gonna get this lug nut off or get a hernia trying. I'm a strong, independent woman, and I might need a man to help, but I'll finish the job on my own.

I nearly stab myself with the wrench as the nut gives and the wrench spins free.

"Shut up," Cole says in surprise. "No way, I totally loosened it for you."

"Sure thing," I say to him, laying into the next nut. But then I have to swallow my pride again. "Okay, this one is stuck too."

Cole gives me a smirk, but we swap positions. I can guess by the set of his jaw he's not giving up on this one until he gets it off. His face is turning close to purple as he tries to twist the wrench.

"Hang on," he says, pausing to breathe. I can hear a vibration coming from somewhere, so I dive into my bag to check. It's not my phone.

"Hey, Ripley," Cole says in a less-than-excited tone, setting his phone on speaker and leaving it on the asphalt as he flexes his hands.

"Where the hell are you?" says one angry female voice.

"At soccer," Cole says.

"You said we were getting brunch today."

"No, I said we were getting lunch."

"You think I'm lying to you? You clearly said brunch, I made reservations, and we're late already."

"Ripley, I said lunch, and I have a plan. It's all going to be—"

"No, you're a forgetful idiot, and you're trying to gaslight me, like I'm stupid. I'm not stupid, Cole. You said brunch."

My blood heats as she yells through the phone. I knew she wasn't the nicest, but this is really bad.

And all too familiar. My mind flashes back to an eerily similar conversation Bryce and I had a few months ago, about whether we had agreed on drinks before dinner or dessert after. Such a minor thing, but he made it seem like our relationship hung in the balance, based on whether I agreed with him. Of course I gave in, even though he was wrong. I felt no taller than an ant by the end of the conversation.

Wow, it was really that bad. But the way Ripley talks is overtly mean, while Bryce was subtler. They're both awful.

Cole rubs his forehead and picks up his phone, quickly scrolling.

"Ripley, the shared calendar says 'Lunch with Ripley' at noon."

She goes silent for a moment. "Did you just go in there and change it? You are so manipulative. I can't believe you."

"I didn't. Do you even want to get lunch? I have to go shower and change still."

"Ugh, let me guess, you're going to go all the way back to your barracks instead of coming to my place."

I hate the way she's spinning him in circles. I wonder if she would talk like this if she knew someone else was hearing her. And is that better or worse, that she would change her tune in public?

"I don't understand," says Cole. "Do you want me to come to your place?"

"No, just meet me at Snooze at noon, and then we'll go shopping after, okay? You can make it up to me."

"I have to study after—"

She hangs up on him. He sighs and slides his phone back in his pocket, his face clouding over. I stand awkwardly to the side, my heart racing in anger over how awfully she spoke to him and how familiar it was to me.

Cole puts his all into getting the rest of the lug nuts off. They don't come easily, but I get the sense he has a lot of fury to fuel him. "Okay," he murmurs, setting the wrench down with a clatter. He moves out of the way, and I remove the flat and get the spare on, fumbling my way through the familiar steps.

I should say something to him, but I don't want to butt in. This is probably one of those things he has to figure out on his own. Why would he listen to a random girl on his soccer team give him relationship advice? What if he resents me for it, or worse, it makes things incredibly awkward from here on out? We're not close, we're barely friends, we haven't known each other that long. I shouldn't say anything. It would be weird.

But I wish someone had said something to me about Bryce. I put the lug nuts in place and wrench them on as tight as I can.

"Can you make sure I tightened them enough?" I ask Cole, buying myself some time to decide what to do.

"Yeah," he says. We swap places again. My heart is pounding, and if I held my hand out flat in front of me, it'd be shaking. I shouldn't make this awkward. It's really not my place. I'm just an acquaintance.

"Your girlfriend is kind of mean to you," I blurt out.

Cole's arms freeze mid-turn. Shoot, that's not what I wanted to say. Crap, that was really awkward.

"She shouldn't treat you that way."

No, that's not exactly it either. What am I even trying to say? "You're...don't stay with anyone who bullies you or makes you feel small. That's not how a relationship should be."

He doesn't say anything.

"I'm sorry, I'm making this so awkward, it's probably not my place to say anything."

He sighs and stares straight ahead at the tire. "Luko hates her. Denny isn't a fan."

"I think your friends care for you," I say gently. "I just don't want anyone to make the same mistake I did and hang around, thinking it's all fine. It's not."

Cole nods and finishes checking all the lug nuts. He stands and hands me the wrench with a tight-lipped smile.

"Thanks for the help," I say. "I'm sorry if I overstepped."

"No, it's okay," he says, his eyes focused on the ground. "Have a good weekend."

"You too."

CHAPTER 9

MY EYES ARE BURNING, an unintentional side effect of me trying to forget what happened at work this morning. I was helping Jules with an order and I wheeled around, saw a suit and red tie at the register, and for a millisecond, I hoped it was Bryce. I hoped he was heartbroken, repentant, here to win me back. Of course, it wasn't him. The cold reality is that Bryce would never lower himself to be penitent, much less fly across the country to see me.

After my shift ended, I threw myself into study mode. I'm serious about getting a painting into Lorraine's gallery, so I've been watching YouTube video after YouTube video on how to sketch and paint faces. I'm starting at square one: the student level. Doing a portrait will take so much practice, but it'll also take settling on a specific subject to know which new skills will be the most demanding. If I paint something with backlighting, then the face details won't be so obvious, but if I put the light source in front, shining right on the subject, then I'll need to be really detailed.

Aunt Mari has some leftover chilaquiles in the fridge, and I microwave them, then sprinkle cotija cheese on top, squinting at the time on the oven clock. Have I really been watching videos for...four hours?

I sit down at the island, take a delicious bite of fried corn tortillas baked in rich salsa, and nearly melt into the barstool over how good it is. I should ask Aunt Mari to teach me how to make this.

I brainstorm as I eat, thinking about the themes of courage, bravery, perseverance and the mode of nighttime and limited lighting. What subject would tie all those together? I could fall back on my experience painting the D.C. monuments. Or try to recreate my new favorite statue and poet, Mr. Longfellow. But I think the idea is to have a *person* doing something.

Oooh, I could do Aunt Mari cooking late at night, making one of her dishes that requires a slow simmer overnight. A halo of illumination from the soft light above the stove, her back to the viewer, worn apron strings tied in a limp bow, a pot of something on the stovetop, an ever-so-subtle blue glow from the gas burner. I could add in a picture in a colorful frame sitting on the counter nearby to emphasize she's cooking for others.

I grab my sketchbook from my room and set up the kitchen scene the way I imagine it, a pot on the stove, the light on dim. There's an old family photo in the living room that I relocate to the counter. I take a seat on the barstool and allow a minute to let my eyes roam over everything, drawing out the lines with my eyes, noticing the shadows and highlights and the general color palette.

With a pencil and some basic lines, I start to transfer that mental image to the textured paper of my sketchbook. It takes patience as I add in some curves and smaller shapes, but the vision comes alive. I can't help thinking the still life of the kitchen will look so good next to the other paintings in Lorraine's gallery.

I'm nearly ready to go grab my watercolors and start doing a color study when I hear a key in the lock and the sound of Aunt Mari shuffling in with arms full of shopping bags.

"Christiana, *ayúdame,*" she calls out.

I leave my art supplies on the counter and go to help her.

"Wow," I say, taking in the sheer number of bags she's loaded onto her arms.

"The sales, you would not believe the sales," she says, nearly breathless. "*Ay, mis pies.* I need to sit down."

She goes to the living room and sits down on the couch with a sigh while I line up about ten shopping bags from Banana Republic, Gap, and of course, Chicos.

"What did you do today? Did you eat?" she asks.

"*Sí, comió.*"

"*Comí.* We should really work on your Spanish," she mutters with a laugh.

"I should listen to Spanish shows or something while I paint. I've been working on learning some sketching and painting techniques on YouTube."

"For what?" she asks, blowing her nose with a wrinkled tissue that materialized out of nowhere.

I may as well go ahead and bring up the portrait idea now instead of agonizing over it for weeks. My stomach clenches.

"Well," I brace myself, wringing my hands behind my back. "There's a gallery near Cafe 22 that is accepting paintings in the style similar to the way I paint." I bite the inside of my cheek. "And I was wondering if I could do a painting of you cooking? In the kitchen?"

Aunt Mari waves me off. "No, no, not tonight."

"It doesn't have to be tonight," I say quickly. "It could be anytime, whenever you're next preparing something. You don't have to go out of your way for it."

Aunt Mari looks up at me from behind her glasses. "Christiana, is this your plan for the future? A painting for an art gallery?"

"No. I mean, yes, it's just kind of a stepping stone. I just..." I hate having to defend myself. Why can't she be excited for me? As tears prick at the backs of my eyes, Aunt Mari's expression softens.

"If you see me doing something and you want to draw it, *está bien. Buenas noches.*" She slowly gets to her feet. "I'm going to take a bath. Just remember, art is never going to pay your bills."

I know what she's saying, I know she's looking out for me. She's of a different generation and a different mindset, where money and numbers need to make sense for any risk to be worth taking. She's telling me she's worried, she cares. But it still stings.

——————

FOR THE NEXT FEW DAYS, any time I'm not working, eating, or sleeping, I'm drawing. I'm sketching like a madwoman, my hand cramping around charcoals and pencils, watching hours of YouTube videos, checking out library books, taking up whole sketchbooks with drawings of eyes, noses, mouths, eyebrows, and more.

I practice shapes, shading, structures, spacing. I draw pictures of Julio, Dad, Aunt Mari, and then I start reaching for any face in my mind. The soccer team, customers at the coffee shop, random strangers who pass me going for a walk on the beach.

It's difficult to tell if I'm making any real progress. The process is trial-and-error, try and try again. Faces are hard, requiring precision and fine lines and more exact highlights and shadows than I'm used to. I think I'm getting the hang of it as I flip through my sketchbooks, but I'm not quite brave enough to start testing my newly learned techniques on a painting yet.

I hang around the kitchen whenever Aunt Mari is cooking, taking down notes and working on the proportions of her small body in front of the large cooktop and oven. I put together rough color palettes in the margins to see how I can best adapt them to fit the moodier pieces in Lorraine's gallery.

Sitting on the barstool at the island does gift me with something new—it gives me the chance to talk with Aunt Mari as an adult. We begin to delve into conversations we've never had before.

I was in high school the last time I came here; there are aspects of life I couldn't have understood then. But now, I have a chance to learn about her past.

"Aunt Mari, what did Uncle Gustavo do in Mexico?" I ask as she chops onions for *salsa fresca*.

"It had to do with telecommunications, satellites, television, television antennas, I don't know. But what I do know is when we came from Mexico to America, he invested his money very well, and it's those investments that continue to provide for me."

I don't really remember him. He passed away when I was young. I have a vague impression of him with a bristly mustache and a gray polyester suit, but I'm not sure if that's from a photograph or an actual memory.

"Why did we start coming here in the summer? I can't even remember the first time we came."

"You were two and Julio was four. Miguel was so tired, he needed to take a break from being a father. *Mi sobrino precioso.* Did you know *cuando tu madre te dejó,* I wanted you and Julio to come live with me?"

My jaw drops. I shake my head, sketchbook forgotten. Wait, I could have had Aunt Mari as my mother figure, lived here my whole childhood? How different would it have been from being raised by my uncle, a single dad, in Los Angeles?

"*Pues* Gustavo was too sick, he needed care and he needed peace and quiet. But once he passed, I told Miguel to bring you for the summer."

Summers at Aunt Mari's were the highlight of every year when I was growing up. I remember her house as cool, spacious, and finely furnished, and the fridge had a water dispenser that would give you ice two different ways: cubed or crushed. The icemaker was a distinct marker of Aunt Mari and her fancy house.

Julio and I were always spoiled rotten, and for the first few years, I assumed we were the most exciting part of Aunt Mari's year. But as we got older, I realized she had her own life and social calendar, full of jetting off to Latin literature retreats, Spanish film festivals, and a smattering of international dates with widowers who adored her. But she never made us feel like an inconvenience, and we were always celebrated.

"Thank you for letting me stay here," I say as respectfully as possible.

"Christiana," she replies, not looking at me. "I worry about you painting because I love you. *Nuestra familia*, we were raised to be afraid of failure, to not like risk. You know I enjoy the arts, but it is a vulnerable thing. For someone outside of our family to try to create art that will be enjoyed, *sí, está bien*."

"But you left Mexico to come to America," I say. "I feel like that is way more vulnerable."

Aunt Mari looks up at me, pointing her chef's knife to accentuate her points. "It was a calculated, well-planned move. I had a job waiting for me, Gustavo had a job waiting for him, we had visas, it was all very carefully arranged. And the rest, we learned to be brave about."

"I can be brave too, about painting."

"Christiana, it will not be easy," she says, glaring at me over her reading glasses. "*Te lo prometo*."

———

AUNT MARI'S promise is sobering, but by the time I head into the next soccer game, I've taken on her appropriate concern and jettisoned anything that would make me too fearful to keep going.

We end up dominating in our game, and the whole team is fired up. Cole scores two goals with moves so slick, I literally do a double take. His last goal he scores with a series of step overs into a freaking rabona, planting his left foot and hooking his right foot around behind his leg in a kick that sends the ball sliding across the goal line in style. Where did he come from? He jogs back to our half of the field flexing his huge biceps and yelling, "Don't sleep on Slaeden!"

"I see you, Cole!" I shout.

"Let's go, Lopez!" he chirps back.

We win easily and celebrate like we struck gold. Anisha is especially enthusiastic. "Mick is gonna be thrilled," she says with a gleeful smile as we stretch after the game.

"How long has he been gone?" I ask.

"Uh, three months in, so four to go?"

"Oh, shoot," I say, my mouth falling open in shock. "He's just...gone? For seven months?"

"Yup. Navy life is so great, it's the best," she says with fake enthusiasm.

"Yo, let's go hit up In-N-Out," says Denny, tapping Anisha on the shoulder. "Chocolate milkshakes make everything better."

"That does sound good," she says. "Carpool?"

"For sure. Tia, come with?"

"Yeah, definitely. Cole," I yell, turning to find him slinging his soccer bag over his shoulder. "Cole, I'll buy you a milkshake for your goals."

His face clouds over. "Can't. Ripley booked us surfing lessons."

"Dude. You hate surfing," says Denny.

"And you have to study for your pin," says Luko, as he hovers nearby.

"I know what I have to do," Cole snaps. "I am studying for my pin, I'm holding it together, quit nagging."

We all go silent.

"I gotta go," Cole mutters and storms off to his car.

As he drives away, Anisha sighs loudly. "He's not happy. She's always been awful to him, but I feel like it's gotten worse."

"What did he ever see in her?" I mumble.

"It wasn't always like this," says Luko. "He said in the beginning she was unassuming and nice, treated him well, and kind of took him under her wing. But by the time Denny and I got stationed here, all I saw was her being controlling."

"Our theory is she's just a really insecure person with a jealousy problem," says Denny.

My heart hurts for Cole. I think he knows it's getting bad, but he's going to do the same thing I did—overlook as much as he can and hope for the best.

"He has to realize it for himself," I say, loosening the laces on my cleat. "I just got out of that and he won't know how bad it is until it's over."

"How did it end for you?" Denny asks.

"I found out he was basically lying to me the whole time. I thought we were going to end up together and he was just using me until someone better came along. Now I can see he was pretty toxic."

"I'm sorry. That sucks."

It does. It sucks that it's part of my story. I know everyone has bad experiences in dating before they finally settle down with someone, but it doesn't take away the sting of being played for a fool.

"Okay, I'm buying milkshakes for everyone," Denny says, twirling his keys around his finger.

―――――

I FINISH my fantasy romance novel a few minutes before midnight and set it on my bedside table with a sigh. The romance was a beautiful, sweeping love story for the ages, full of sacrificial choices and selflessness combined with passion and longing. I adored it, even though it brought a sobering truth to light.

I don't think I ever truly loved Bryce and I don't know that he loved me.

So why was I ready to settle for him? I think my pride kept me from waving a white flag and admitting I was with someone who was wrong for me. I didn't want to deal with a breakup. I think compassion for Bryce in his moments of vulnerability went a long way. I never felt insane fireworks with him, but I had convinced myself that wasn't a significant factor. I don't know that either of us would win an award for "Most Selfless."

We never fell out of love because we were never "in love." There were bits of friendship and kindness. There were times we genuinely had fun together. But the kind of love I've just read about, a life-altering love, the kind of love I dismissed as too idealistic—we definitely did not have that.

And I don't know if I ever will.

CHAPTER 10

I START the day with a burst of inspiration from Mr. Longfellow, this time the middle stanza of his poem, "The Tide Rises, the Tide Falls" with its glorious depiction of the sea at night.

> *Darkness settles on roofs and walls,*
> *but the sea, the sea in the darkness calls;*
> *the little waves, with their soft, white hands,*
> *efface the footprints in the sands,*
> *and the tide rises, the tide falls.*

Which leads to my plan of the day to work an opening shift, go home to an empty house (Aunt Mari is on a weekend trip to Santa Barbara), have some ice cream, and take a late-night walk on the beach to watch the soft, white hands of the little waves in the darkness.

And that's how I find myself sitting under the stars in wet sand, whimpering, with a massive sting from a freaking stingray wrapped across my foot. I rescue my phone from my damp shorts and try to think of what to do. I clench my jaw and try to breathe evenly through my teeth while I google if stingray stings are fatal.

They burn like they should be fatal. Why did I decide it would be a good idea to wade through the tide at night? Who does that? You know what, I blame global warming for a stingray showing up on this beach. There weren't stingrays here when I was a kid.

Great, Google says it's not usually fatal unless you have an allergic reaction, but stings can cause all sorts of nasty side effects if not treated, including seizures. And I have to remove the spikes with pliers? I might throw up.

The options for getting home are limited. The lifeguard shack was closed up long ago, and of course Aunt Mari is gone. I'm going to have to suck it up and hobble across the sand. But wow, this thing hurts so, so bad.

I do have one lifeline, my last resort—I know a corpsman. I dial Cole's number. I need to know how bad this is and what I need to do next.

"This is Cole Slaeden."

"Hey, it's Tia," I say through clenched teeth.

"What's wrong?" he asks, his voice calm, but commanding. "You okay?"

There's jazz music filtering through as a feminine voice in the background demands to know who's on the phone. He's on a date. With Ripley. Of course he is.

I hang up and groan, half out of frustration with Cole and half out of pain. I'm going to have to figure this out on my own. I'll make it work somehow.

My phone lights up with an incoming call from Cole. I hesitate, but he is a medical professional and I don't know what else to do. I swipe to answer.

"Tell me what's going on, right now," he says.

I throw myself on the mercy of the corpsman. "Well, I was wondering how much you know about stingray stings?"

"Seriously?"

"I'm on the beach, on Crown Island, and I'm almost positive I just got stung by one. I was walking in the water and then there was this smack and a sharp pain, like stepping on a ton of nails." I fight back tears.

"Okay, first of all, it's probably going to be okay. Where are you?"

"Probably?!"

"I never promise, just in case. How are you?" he asks. "Are you dizzy, nauseous, feeling faint?" I definitely can hear the hum of a restaurant and a band. But it's fading away, and judging by Cole's breathlessness, he's walking or even running. "Where are you? Tell me where you are."

"Are you on a date right now? You can hang up," I say, equally demanding.

"I was," he admits. "It's over now."

It's over? Like the date or the relationship? It feels wrong to be holding out hope it's the latter, but oh man, how great would it be if Ripley was out of his life forever?

My silence asks the questions, and he starts talking, explaining everything. "I got dumped." He clears his throat. "Freakin' tired of hoping I've found true love and being disappointed every time. What a joke." His breath starts to pick up, the sound of the ocean becoming more prominent in the background.

"Are you running?" I ask. "Are you okay?"

"Tia, you're the one who got stung by a stingray. How far from the lifeguard shack are you?"

"It's closed. There are no lights on."

"No, I'm coming to you. Where are you?"

"You're on the beach?"

"Yeah, my date was at the resort. Lucky I'm close."

I look down the beach, at the lights of the resort at the far end, about a quarter mile away. And sure enough, between here and the resort I can just make out the backlit form of a man running towards me.

No way. No freakin' way.

I stick my phone in the air, so he can see the lit-up screen.

"I see you."

He hangs up, and it's only a few more paces until he drops down to one knee next to me.

"Okay, the sting is where?" he asks.

"On my foot," I say, pointing down my left leg.

Cole turns on the flashlight on his phone and sticks the phone between his teeth, gently using both hands to turn my leg side to side and check out my injury under the light. He's gone full corpsman mode, calm and in control. Letting him take charge of the situation is a relief.

The flashlight illuminates an inflamed ugly mess that wraps from the sole of my foot near my heel to the top of my foot near my toes. He grabs his phone from his mouth and navigates to the stopwatch.

"Little sucker really didn't like you," he says. "I'm going to check your heart rate."

He presses three warm fingers to the side of my throat, sliding them back and forth and gently putting pressure until he finds my carotid artery. He starts the timer and counts my pulse, quietly whispering the numbers to himself.

Cole Slaeden is touching my neck. Very professionally, very caring. Be cool.

The timer rings. He nods, seeming content, and slides his phone back in his pocket. "Your BPM is in the normal range for being in pain. How far are we from your house?"

"About a ten-minute walk."

"It's about the same to my car. What do you want to do? I can carry you home or carry you to my car."

He's really about to pick me up in his arms? My brain trips over itself trying to put it all together.

"Tia? We need to get this foot soaking in hot water and check for spines."

"I feel bad," I admit.

"Bad how? Nauseous, dizzy, hot?"

"No, just about how your night is going. You don't need to rescue me, you can take me to urgent care."

"Urgent cares are closed, it's ER or nothing. You really want the bill for that?"

Pain radiates up my leg, and I clench my teeth, grabbing at my left thigh.

"Okay, let's go," he says. "On my back."

He does some cool maneuver they must teach in corpsman school that gets me on his back without jarring me too much, his arms looped around my thighs and my arms wrapped around his shoulders. But I can't hold back a groan when he does a little hop to adjust my weight and my foot shifts.

"You got this," he says. "We're going to walk now."

I'm not a light-framed woman, but he makes me feel weightless as he moves easily across the sand. When we get to the sidewalk and approach the steps up to the road, I'm ready to insist I can use the railing to hobble up. Like he's sensed my thoughts, Cole tightens his grip on my legs, his hands splaying out against my skin. I hope he can't tell that the pressure of his fingers is giving me goosebumps. I'll blame it on the night air.

Under the yellow glow of the streetlights, I can see now he's wearing a long-sleeved white button up dress shirt, navy chinos now dusted with sand at the knees, and brown Oxford dress shoes. I even pick up a hint of a masculine spiced vanilla cologne from his collar. It's a completely different look from his soccer uniform...the kind he wears for date night.

"I'm sorry about your breakup," I say, my mouth near his ear.

He sighs. "Yeah, I just feel stupid. Like...what a waste of time."

A waste of time...how aptly put. There is so much more that could have come from the past few years if I had known to avoid Bryce, to ignore him altogether.

"I understand. I'm sorry."

"Thanks," Cole murmurs. "Where to?"

"Right at the big white mansion."

"Which one?" he says with a laugh. I point out where the turn is.

The pain hits harder, making me nauseous as we walk, and I don't talk the rest of the way home, afraid I'm going to throw up all over Cole's neck.

We make it to the house, and I tell him the passcode to unlock the front door. He doesn't put me down until we're in the bathroom, then he sets me down with my feet in the tub, puts in the stopper and cranks the water on at the hottest setting. As the bathtub fills, I scoot down to the far end to rest my back against the wall. The hot water offers sweet relief and I can't hold back a deep sigh.

I can't believe he carried me home. I felt like a backpack, not a burden. He's not even breathing hard anymore.

Cole swipes the hand towel off the counter and gets down on one knee next to me, his thighs testing the stretch factor of his pants.

"All right, let me see that sting again," he says.

I wince as I put my foot in his hands and he props it up on his thigh to inspect it under the bright overhead lights. It's not pretty, and I don't mean the injured area. That'll teach me to skip pedicure day.

"I don't see anything that looks like spines. I'm going to turn down the water temperature, but go ahead and let your foot soak. I'll sit here for a bit and you tell me if you feel anything strange—your heart starts racing, you feel feverish, a little dizzy."

If he kneels down next to me again, I might feel all those things at once.

"I'm sure I'll be fine," I say, dunking my foot back in the tub. "Thank you."

Cole nods and smiles to me as he sits back against the cabinets with a sigh, extending his legs out in front of him, and brushing the sand off his pants.

It's not the first time we've been alone together, but the

context is totally different. Now we're alone, in a narrow bathroom, showered and dressed, not sweating after a soccer game.

He carried me home. He's single. I'm relieved for him, but I know first-hand that getting dumped, even by an awful partner, still sucks.

"Are you okay?" I ask.

"I'm fine. No worries."

"No, I mean about...how your date went."

He runs both hands over his head, dragging them down his face, and his next breath is rough. "Ugh, not quite ready for all those thoughts. And there's a lot there. Like, why did I think the way she treated me was okay? Why was I with her for so long? What a joke."

All too familiar questions. "I hear you."

"I don't...I don't know. Like, it'll feel better to not have her voice in my head all the time, all negative and cutting. But then it's just me. It's not that I mind being single, I just...it's this sudden void. There's emptiness now."

"Yeah."

Cole leans his head back against the cabinets and closes his eyes with a deep sigh.

"It feels weird right now," I say gently. "But it does get better. I know you know that."

"Does it?" he asks, his eyes meeting mine with heart-wrenching sadness. I feel a sudden urge to hop over to his side and hug him. I hope he knows it's okay to cry if he needs to.

My phone vibrates in my back pocket, echoing loudly against the tub and breaking up the moment. Who would be calling me right now?

"Oh, crap," I say, looking at the screen.

"What?" Cole asks.

"My ex."

"Bad dude?"

I nod, fixated on the name on the screen. Bryce McFourne. My stomach clenches. We still have not had the breakup conversation. I've been avoiding it for too long, I know I need to be brave and get it over with, once and for all. Just not right now. Cole doesn't need this right now.

"Why's he calling?"

"We never really had a final conversation. I left quickly and I don't think he's satisfied with that being the end of things," I say. I look over at Cole as a strange sense of panic rises in me the longer the call rings.

"Are you scared?" he asks, sitting up straighter, his brown eyes fixated on me.

"A little," I whisper.

It's not because I'm scared of Bryce. It's because once we talk, no matter how good or awful the conversation goes, it's over. The end. I'm moving forward, cutting the last remaining string to my old life. Change is scary, no matter how healthy it is.

My finger hovers, hesitating to swipe and answer it.

"I can stay or leave," Cole says as he gets to his feet. "Whatever will help you."

"Please stay," I say quickly.

Cole nods, standing in front of the sink in a wide stance. His shoulders are thick as he crosses his arms and his eyebrows pinch together with an unreadable emotion, possibly concern.

He looks intimidating, but he's on my side. He's here for me.

I answer the call on speaker phone. "Hello?"

"Where are you?" Bryce's voice is strangely calm and non-threatening. Maybe I've worked myself up for nothing.

"I'm fine, thanks. I'm in California, spending some time with my great aunt."

"I heard you're not coming back. From Sutton. I'm disappointed I had to hear it from her."

There it is. My fingers massage my temple and I fight to remind myself that this is the last time, the last call, then it's over, no more.

Bryce takes my silence as consent to carry on. "I was worried about you, how come you didn't respond to my texts?"

"I needed some space," I say lamely.

"I lost sleep over you, which meant I wasn't on the ball at work. Your rashness affects other people, do you realize that?"

"Bryce—"

"You know, the more I think about it, the more I wonder if we're equally invested in this relationship. You really showed how little you value me when you didn't so much as reply to my texts and—"

"Bryce—"

"I think we are incompatible in terms of diligence and maturity."

"Bryce!" I shout incredulously. How is he turning this into him breaking up with me?

"What are you going to do now? Ooh, let me guess, you're going to pursue your dreams, be all you can be, see the world. Tia, I'm honestly shocked you made it from D.C. to California without someone holding your hand and reading the signs for you."

I'm speechless. I look up at Cole, and he is waving his hand across his throat, mouthing the words, "Cut. Him. Off."

"We're over, Bryce. Done. Don't call me again. I look forward to having—"

"Are you saying we're over as a couple?"

"Yes," I say with a harsh laugh and all the emphasis of my entire soul. Hallelujah.

Bryce scoffs and it's a loud whoosh of air through the airwaves. "Oh, boy, Tia. You think you're going to be anything without me? You're going to wake up tomorrow and be nobody with nothing. This is your biggest mistake yet. Don't come calling and crying, trying to beg me back, I'm not answering."

Cole shifts and seems like he wants to say something. I shoot him a quizzical look.

"Fight back," he mouths back. He shoves his fist against his palm for emphasis. "Don't take his crap."

I usually do what I can to make people feel as comfortable as possible. But Bryce doesn't deserve that. Digging deep, I give him my truest thoughts.

"Thanks for making things clear. I wish you the worst. You are a small, narcissistic, self-centered, mean, limp noodle of a man, and I hate that I wasted my time and energy on you. I look forward to having nothing to do with you for the rest of my life."

Bryce launches into a tirade, and I give him enough time to get going into a full meltdown before I hang up and immediately block his number.

"I hate that guy," Cole says, and when I glance up, his eyes are dark and furious, and he's clenching and unclenching his fists.

"You and me both," I mutter.

"Why did you ever let him into your life?" he asks.

"Oh, that's rich, coming from you," I retort. Is he for real? I roll my eyes and pull my foot out of the water, grabbing a towel off the nearby rack to gingerly dry it off.

"Is that what it sounded like?" Cole asks, his tone much more humble.

"Yeah, maybe worse," I answer honestly. I swing my feet to the bathmat and ease myself upright.

As soon as I stand, Cole comes over and wraps his arms around me, hugging me tight. My hands are trapped against his wide chest as he squeezes the breath out of me. For a second, I'm shocked. But a hug is a good idea right now, especially with someone so warm and strong and safe.

"Don't let it happen again, being with a mean girl," I murmur, my cheek pressed against his dress shirt.

"I won't, I promise," he says, resting his head on top of mine. "Promise me you'll never let a guy treat you like that again."

"I won't," I say with a sigh. "One day, I'll be ready for love again, but I'm determined that the next guy I'm with will be the last. One more good guy, that's all I need."

Cole eases back and squeezes my shoulder. "Good for you. And if someone's mean to you, you don't have to let them be mean to you without standing up for yourself. I don't know if that's the grand life lesson here, I just want you to know it's not normal or okay for people to treat you like that."

I laugh in disbelief. "You talk a big game, buddy. But pot, meet kettle."

"No more," Cole says, shaking his head. "I swear. Also, I need to teach you some real insults."

"Yeah?"

"You want to comment on someone's looks? Tell them they look like the east end of a horse headed west."

My brain pieces the diss together, and I smile.

"Someone's in your face and you want to take them down a notch? Tell them to shut up 'cause their breath smells like unsalted Wendy's fries. Someone's being a complete idiot? Tell them to apologize to nature for taking up its valuable oxygen."

"What in the world? That's so rude."

"Yeah, that's why they're called insults, Tia," Cole says with a smirk. "There's a lot more, but most of them involve foul language and even fouler sexual innuendo, so we'll leave it at that. But you have to go for the shock-and-awe factor."

"What's one of your go-tos?" I ask.

"You suck."

I chuckle and Cole eventually joins in, his face flushing red.

"Alright, you seem fine, I'm gonna go. I'll send you some articles on how to take care of that foot and hopefully you'll be back on defense by Saturday."

"Thanks, Cole, for everything. What a night."

"Yeah, what a night," he says, giving me one more lingering smile before he heads out.

CHAPTER 11

It's a cloudy but humid Saturday morning, and my foot has healed well enough for me to play in our next soccer game, thanks to Cole's attentive care and follow-up instructions. My heart feels better too, after formally ending things with Bryce. Maybe I'll be ready for hopes of romance and love soon, but right now, I'm just hoping for a Goal Digger win.

The team is working well together, but I feel like we have untapped potential. Even though we have great energy, we're still behind a few goals at the half. Frank and Anisha have a quick side-bar, then come join the rest of us as we sip water and stretch.

"We need to switch positions," announces Frank. "I want to see if we can get more forward momentum on offense if we switch Anisha and Tia. Tia, you're pushing forward anyways, so you and Cole can play mid-field. You good with that?"

Cole and I look at each other, his brown eyes asking if I'm up for this and I nod. I've been playing my butt off, and so has he, but I think we'll do even better together. He nods back.

"Let's do it," Cole says, his upbeat response echoing my thoughts. The whistle tweets and I jog onto the field, my pulse picking up from more than running. There's something about a silent conversation, communication with a glance, that makes me feel seen, noticed, trusted.

When the other team kicks off, Cole and I move up the field in sync, making smooth, calculated moves as we trail behind Sarah and Denny. As soon as the other team gets past them, my adrenaline kicks in and it's my time to shine. This is what I'm good at.

My brain zeroes in on scoring the next point, and I focus on getting the ball. When the striker jukes left, I follow him and snag the ball with my toe. I get a clean breakaway and dribble like mad up the field.

Denny sets up a play, blocking the defender in front of me, and with a few slick step-over moves, I get clear space and line up a shot. At the last possible second, I suddenly hesitate. Should I pass? Should I let someone else take this goal?

"Shoot!" shouts Sarah, and I go for it, sending the ball sailing in a gorgeous cross into the upper left corner.

Goal.

My brain floods with more dopamine than I know what do with. Holy crap, that felt *good*. I did that. I scored that goal. I pump my arm in the air, shouting, "They don't call me 'Queen of the Field' for nothing!"

"Hell yeah!" Denny swoops up behind me, shaking me by the shoulders. We jog back to our side of the field and Cole comes over with a stunning mile-wide grin I've never seen before, his face is all white teeth and sparkling brown eyes.

"'Queen of the Field?'" he says, holding his hands up.

My face is flushed as I high-five him, both of us breathing hard. "That was my nickname on my last team."

"All right, Queenie, let's go. I'm here if you need me, but if you have a shot, don't hesitate again."

"Deal," I respond. I can't stop smiling as we quickly fist-bump before going back to our positions on the field.

Sarah takes the kick-off, and Cole locks eyes with me as she sets up the ball. Time freezes for a second and in that brief moment, it's only him and me, and we're in this to win it, together.

My stomach flips. His brown eyes hold my gaze, and surprise, surprise, butterflies show up to the party. What in the world?

We pick up the win, thanks to a goal from Denny and another from Sarah. We're climbing one step closer to that championship game and each victory feels so sweet.

But what about those butterflies? There is no need for that. Just because Cole and I are single twenty-somethings does not mean we are victims to some unspoken law of attraction. No, no way. I'm saying no to this before it's even a thing.

Besides, I need all my focus on me right now. I have an art career to launch.

———

I STOP by Lorraine's gallery after work and find her alone. I want to show her my current work-in-progress and I pull up a photo of the painting of Aunt Mari on my phone to get her feedback. She looks at it for a second too long, and I just know. She hates it.

"Okay, so I like the colors," is where she starts, and I want to sink through the floor. "I think your style is unique."

"You can say it's not great," I offer, setting my phone on the counter and stifling a sigh.

"I think you need practice. And I think you need a different subject."

"How so?"

"I feel like it lacks connection. Or purpose? We see her cooking, yes, but there's no context. Ah, context, that's it!"

I see her point. With Aunt Mari's back to the audience, there's not much personal connection. It means something to me, but mostly because it's a memory and she's my family. I think a lot of families could relate to the idea of a matriarch cooking late into the night, but it's probably not going to resonate or find a home with most of the clientele who come through Crown Island.

"Look, whatever you do, don't abandon it. This will be part of your portfolio, and you can start working on a small grouping to have on your own website. I think the theme is good, so keep at it, okay?"

IT'S MY DAY OFF, but I'm set up opposite the register at the coffee shop with a sketchbook and some pencils, ready to practice some more.

"You know I can't stand still for long," Jules says, her back to me while her hand pauses on a lever on the espresso machine. She's been going through the motions of making a latte at an eighth of her usual speed.

"Oh, yeah, do it how you normally do it. I'll capture you in action."

She resumes her quick pace, and I do my best to add lines here and there whenever she does pause for a few moments. It's still feeling flat, like Lorraine said, basically a still life.

But then Jules turns with a smile towards one of our regulars who's picking up a tea for his wife, and I catch hold of a vision. It's her profile, her hands at work, her head engaged with a customer. That's how the emotion flows forward and makes her more engaging as a subject.

I play with different lighting angles and eventually whip out my watercolors to feel like I'm doing justice to the setting. I've been learning more about offsetting the subject with a contrasting background, and I play around with some colors that warm Jules and make her seem like sunshine is radiating through her.

"How's it coming, chica?" she asks about an hour later.

"Don't look at your face. Well, there actually isn't a face right now. But I'm working on getting body proportions right and making the colors work well together."

She comes and looks over my shoulder. She pinches her eyebrows together and tilts her head sideways.

"I think I like this one the best," she says, pointing to a cool, bluish gray that makes the golden skin tone I gave her look more dimensional and sun-kissed. Even her dreadlocks have a glow to them.

"I like that one too."

"What are you going to do for my face?"

"Actually," I say. "Can you sit for a second? I could do a quick profile sketch, in like five minutes."

"Joe, cover the register," she says to one of the guys in the kitchen as she sits sideways in the chair opposite me.

"Can you smile, kind of a laughing smile?" I ask.

She gives me a cross-eyed goofy smile, making us both giggle, before settling into a more natural enthused expression. I do my best to get the more intricate facial proportions correct, but Jules is on the clock, so I try to keep it quick and simple.

"Okay," I say to Jules. "Thanks so much."

"Can I see?" she asks.

I hesitate, trying to decide if this is one of my better drawings. It's not terrible. It helps that it's not a forward-facing sketch, so I only have to get one half of it right. Her nose looks too short and her lips look overly full, but it's not the worst thing ever. I twist the sketch book around so she can see it from her seat, bracing myself for her reaction.

She starts to say something, then pauses. "It's good," she says. "Practice is good."

Again, not the kind of feedback I was hoping for. My shoulders sink.

"Sorry," she says, with a cringe. "That probably wasn't the right response."

"No, honesty is always the best response," I say, pulling the sketchbook back to me. I know I'm starting at the beginning, but my drive to succeed at this and the stakes behind it mean each time I miss the mark, I'm flattened.

"Art doesn't happen in one day," she says, trying to encourage me. "Just like everything, making lattes, even, practice is good."

"Thanks," I say with a forced smile. She gives my shoulder a squeeze as she heads back behind the counter.

I stay and keep practicing, even though I'm gritting my teeth as I do it. The rough reception my attempts have had so far are bringing up too many questions, making me wonder if I'm choosing the right thing. If I can't paint something worthy of Lorraine's gallery, what am I doing? I can't make a living from art no one wants to display.

I go home in a funk, quickly dropping off my art supplies and changing into running clothes. A long, punishing run around the island does little to burn off my negative thoughts, even after I add a second loop.

This whole move to sunny California was going so well, but maybe I was in a honeymoon phase. I know artists go through seasons of doubt, but there's a difference between self-doubt and being objectively bad. Is that the reason my subconscious never allowed me to break out of the career-and-job mold? Because deep down, I knew I don't have what it takes to be a professional artist? Maybe it was self-preservation this whole time, not a lack of initiative.

When I finally slow down and do a cooldown walk to Aunt Mari's front door, dripping sweat, I'm even more confused than when I left.

———

AFTER SHOWERING AND DRESSING, I braid my hair over my shoulder and text Anisha.

TIA

How did you get over feeling like you weren't good enough as a graphic designer?

ANISHA

Good question! Um, practice, feedback, and more practice. Confidence grows with time.

Not entirely what I wanted to hear. I'm impatient and I want answers and results and praise right now.

TIA

Why is there no immediate gratification with art and design? *laughing emoji*

ANISHA

That's kind of another question. You should feel immediate gratification in your work even if no one else does. You have to keep going until you love it. Then you'll be satisfied, even if no one else connects with it like you do.

TIA

Yeah…good point. I think that's the part I haven't hit yet. Still not good enough to love my attempts.

ANISHA

You'll get there! You got this!

I'll get there. I just have to settle in for the journey, ignore the doubts, and keep going.

CHAPTER 12

IT'S another sweltering afternoon as summer heats up, and I picked up a last-minute closing shift, wrapping up around four. Even though my ego is still recovering from the last time I stopped by, I decide to go see Lorraine on my way home.

She calls out to me as soon as I step inside. "Tia! Perfect, I was hoping you'd come by today. I was wondering if you'd like to talk shop, maybe get you a spark of inspiration."

She pulls a thick stack of hardbound books out from under the register and sets them on the counter with a thud, giving them a nudge towards me. They're all coffee table books of portraits: *The Art of the Portrait*, *Women Painting Women*, books from The Met and the National Portrait Gallery.

"Take a long browse, and let's talk about some of them," instructs Lorraine.

I leisurely peruse through the pages, taking my time to study each full-page illustration before turning to the next. "Think of the myriad decisions that have to be made when painting a portrait," I murmur. "The angle of the nose, the curve of the eyelid, the bow of the lip. So many minuscule choices. And you change one little thing and it becomes a picture of another person entirely. It must take forever to do one of these paintings."

"How long does it take to do one of your nightscapes?" asks Lorraine.

"Mm, four or five hours of painting, lots of time spent prepping and sketching before that. I paint alla prima, adding in all the layers before letting it dry."

"Good. And how long do you think a portrait would take you?"

"I have no idea. With my usual style, I deal in shades and shadows and shapes that meld together to meet a vision. There's less precision involved. But with a portrait, I'd have to think about each move I make before I make it."

"I wonder though. Really, I think if you close your eyes and trust your mind's eye, it's more intuitive than you think."

"Have you painted portraits before?" I ask, glancing over at her.

"A few."

"Do you do them from photographs or live models?"

"I prefer to have a living, breathing person in front of me. It helps me remember that what I'm painting isn't simply a memory or a moment, it's biographical."

"Oh, I like that word. A visual biography."

"There's a point of inspiration for all these artists," Lorraine says, flipping through pages. "Something that clearly represented their subject so well, they knew that's what would make the best portrait. And then adding in the details to tell the story behind the person."

"Well, I thought I had that with the painting of Aunt Mari."

"I think you need a true portrait, someone's full facial expression combined with the right setting. Trust me, when it happens, it'll feel like someone ringing a bell, like you just won a prize."

She sends a few of the books home with me and after depositing them in my mini art studio, I grab my soccer ball and head straight for the beach with a backpack full of art supplies and a towel.

Once I get to the packed wet sand of low tide, I stash my flip-flops in the outer pockets of my backpack and roll my ball out in front of me. Dribbling slowly down the beach gives me something to do while I think. I tap the ball again and again, watching the way it picks up little drops of water as it rolls closer to the edge of the waves. My mind wanders to how I would paint that, but instead of focusing on the details, my worries drift to the surface and crowd my thoughts.

I have no inspiration for what to paint. Am I doing the right thing? Should I quit this little painting side quest and get a more career-oriented job? Or should I do the opposite? Find a shift-work job that pays better and go back to school for art?

I got into painting because of Ms. Staten's art class in high school. I always doodled in my notebooks growing up, but when I saw the elective, I jumped at the chance to really *learn* art. She's the one who taught me how to work with different mediums and encouraged what she called my "natural talent." I doubted those words then, still doubt them now.

Ms. Staten was tough, and she taught us well, always keeping us fueled with inspiration and supplies. One time I overheard her and another teacher bartering to exchange resources so she could get more paint and brushes. The way she fought for her art students combined with lectures on art history showed me art was invaluable. It held inherent worth for both the artist and the viewer.

She also showed me how my thoughts could be processed out into a painting, how art could be a form of therapy. I loved every minute of being in front of an easel with paintbrush in hand, but art was always just an elective, something on the side, never the main thing. I never thought it could be a career, and no one in my life told me anything different.

I shake my head, clearing my reverie. At this point, I just need to keep going. There's no fallback because I'm in the fallback and I won't let myself stay here forever.

I lift my eyes off the sand and take a deep breath, looking down the beach. The sun is bright; kids are splashing and dragging boogie boards through the shallow tide. Someone's playing country music on a speaker and cracking a drink open. There's a runner coming towards me in a white shirt, black running shorts, and a blue baseball cap on backwards. His gait looks a lot like Cole's, and his build is the same, a mix between a soccer player and a rugby player. Yep, it's him.

I line up my kick and send the soccer ball sailing down the beach in a low arc. Cole traps it with ease.

"Hey, I thought that was you," he says, dribbling the ball closer, then passing it to me. "What are you up to?"

"What does it look like?" I say with a smile.

"Right," he says, falling into step next to me.

"You don't need to interrupt your run for me," I say as I pass the ball to him.

He dribbles ahead of me, does a few step-overs, looks like he's going to pass it, then pulls it back. "Eh, I already did five miles, I think I'm good for the day."

I lunge towards him and follow him when he jukes right, earning the ball back, and a smile from him. "You don't want to go for an even six? You're one of those people who can do things that end in odd numbers?"

"I guess so," he says. "Can you?"

I shake my head, keeping the ball close between my feet. "I go for even numbers every time, if I can help it."

"Good to know. Are you going to walk the whole beach?" Cole says, suddenly shouldering his way into my space and trying to throw me off balance to get the ball back. I push hard against his shoulder, but his upper body is one solid mass of carved muscle.

"What are you doing, you sweaty beast?" I say with a laugh,

trying to shove him again. He goes nowhere, but he lets up with a grin, leaving the ball in my possession.

"Yeah, I'll walk for a while. I have a lot on my mind, some things I need to work through."

"Want to talk about it?" he says, our little soccer game now over. "Always helps me."

A laugh bubbles out of me. Cole's always ready to talk, especially now that he's post-breakup.

"What?" he asks, his face reddening.

"Nothing," I say.

"No, really, what?"

"You're cute." I pass the ball to him.

"You're cute."

He kicks the ball back to me, and I pop it in the air and knee it a few times before letting it fall back to the sand.

"Want a burrito? C'mon, let's go to Mexican Take Out and get burritos. I'm starving, and it'll fuel you up for your contemplation."

I feel like I should object, but I can't even remember what I ate for lunch. And I never pass up a free burrito from MTO, the best hole-in-the-wall on Crown Island.

"Let's do it."

———

A PERFECT BREEZE kicks up from the ocean, brushing my hair away from my face as I sit cross-legged on top of the sand dune, my soccer ball cradled in my lap and a California burrito in my hand. Everything about this is a slice of summer heaven. This is what I want for myself—for my future to have more of this than I can imagine.

But what if luck turns against me? What if life requires that I work in a concrete jungle with my feet in court heels instead of flip-flops, a hurried lunch break in a small kebab shop instead of a burrito on the beach? No, I'll fight for that to never happen again.

"What are you thinking about?" Cole asks.

"A lot about the future, some about the past."

"Don't tell me you're thinking about your ex," Cole says.

I shake my head. "No, not him. But sometimes I do wonder how exactly I wound up in D.C., a place I don't love, with a jerk of a boyfriend. Like, what was the specific series of events that made that happen?"

Cole nods in understanding. "Yeah, I get that. With Ripley, we matched on an app and I thought we had this instant connection. I was new to San Diego, didn't really have anyone. Luko wasn't here yet, Denny was deployed, and I didn't like how lonely I felt. She took me around, showed me the best food, the most beautiful beaches. I thought she was pretty, she said I was hot. She kept her crazy hidden well for a while." He pauses to take a bite, then adds, "Why do you think you were with him?"

I shrug. "It was exciting, people looked at me differently. I was someone because I was with him. He could be really attentive when he wanted to be. And he was...subtle in the way he wore me down."

I wonder how much more of myself would have been eroded away if I hadn't left when I did. If I had married Bryce—well, I guess that never would have happened. But it wasn't just staying with him that was wearing on me. It was everything around me: the shallow friendships, the way the city made everything feel too close all the time, the unnecessary stress, the loneliness.

"The other night, you said you're ready for marriage."

"What?" I shriek, laughing, then choking on a bit of tortilla. "No, no, I did not say that."

"You said you wanted to marry the next guy you dated," Cole protests with a smile. His neck is flushed red.

"Yeah, but I'm not necessarily ready right now," I say, digging my feet in the sand. "If I let someone into my life again, it will be after a lot of time and there would have to be a ton of trust."

Cole crumples up the wrapper of his burrito and tucks it under his leg so it doesn't blow away.

"What about you? You going to be single for a bit?"

He shrugs. "So, Denny and Luko and I have been friends for years, like, way before San Diego. Denny says I'm a hopeless romantic. Luko says I commit to relationships too easily and quickly. I guess I am kind of a romantic, always believing any bit of chemistry with someone could turn out to be true love."

"Really?" I ask with a laugh and a questioning look. "True love?"

"Why is that so hard to believe?"

"I've never known a guy to be a romantic. And I don't really believe in true love anyway."

"Wait, what? Then what *do* you believe in?" Cole asks, his eyebrows furrowing. "Like, how would you know you wanted to commit to someone?"

"I think you just make a decision. There's logic involved, you decide that it's going to be the right thing, and then you go all in on that. That's where you put all your effort."

"Effort?" Cole says incredulously. "Love is not effort."

My cheeks heat as I defend my position. "It is, at least to some degree."

"Commitment takes effort, sure. But falling in love...there's the initial free-fall of not knowing how you could ever stop yourself from loving this person to the point of being willing to do anything for them. There's a crush, there's obsession, there's lust even. They take up your entire mind and your heart. That's falling in love. And then you do whatever you can to help them, encourage them, be there for them. You give up anything and everything to be by their side and try to spend every waking minute with them. The feeling ebbs and flows, but it never leaves.

And to have that with someone who feels the same way about you, to love and be loved...it's magic. That's true love."

I don't think I've ever put into words what love looks like to me. What Cole's talking about is...beautiful. Poetic, even. I didn't know guys spent this much time thinking about love.

Cole blushes and clears his throat, shaking his head. "That was a lot, I'm—"

"No, don't apologize," I say, nudging my shoulder against his.

Cole grins sheepishly, then looks out at the waves for a while. I glance over at his profile.

"What you're talking about...I've never had that," I say softly. "And I don't know if I will. Maybe it's easier to not believe in it, if you don't think you can have it."

"You'll find your soulmate one day and fall so madly in love—"

"I don't know..."

"That's like saying why believe in unicorns if you can never have your own. I say you might as well believe in something beautiful."

"Okay, but why would you believe in Santa Claus if he never brought you any presents?"

Cole moves his head side to side, weighing my counterargument. "Okay, touché."

We listen to the waves for a while. "But the one Christmas where Santa got you everything on your wish list would be all the more magical, right?"

I laugh and turn my gaze to him, tucking my chin against my shoulder. "I like that you believe in true love."

He adjusts his hat, still flipped backwards, then mirrors me, looking over his broad shoulder at me with a smile. "One day, you'll get hit over the head with it, and you'll remember this moment on the beach. And I'll go ahead and say it now in case I don't get to say it then. I told you so."

I grin as I stare into his brown, twinkling eyes. "You know what? I hope you're right."

And those darn butterflies come back with a vengeance.

———

I GO HOME and put the finishing touches on my painting of Aunt Mari. Lorraine had a point about building up a collection, so I'm not going to leave it unfinished. The brush strokes grow less precise towards the bottom which makes it seem a little slapdash, but the end result surprises me by being more dynamic with brighter pops of color. I kind of love it.

It takes me a while to tidy up my space and put away my supplies, and while I'm cleaning my brushes, I cycle through my situation again. Am I doing the right thing? Should I be somewhere else, somewhere with a lower cost of living, or nearer to my dad? Am I really, truly meant to stay here on Crown Island? I'm happy. Doesn't that mean something?

By the time I'm done, I'm groaning with exasperation. I'm here. The end. I need to stop overthinking it. I flop backwards on my bed with a sigh and open my phone. Some mindless scrolling should give me a break.

I'm watching reel after reel, smiling at some, laughing internally, but nothing really grabs my attention. Until a Navy recruiting ad about becoming a corpsman fills my screen.

I sit up and watch a montage of guys in uniform doing training, something called Field Medical Training Battalion. They're inserting IVs, carrying stretchers, bandaging fake wounds. One guy shoves a breathing tube down a dummy's throat, and my gag reflex is triggered.

The whole video is over in sixty seconds with a fair sprinkling of motivational quotes and people in green camouflage and blue medical gloves working together, and it ends with the words "America's Navy" and the slogan "Forged by the Sea." Impressive. I wonder if this is the kind of thing that caught Cole's attention and made him want to join the Navy.

I tap the "#corpsmanup", and so begins my tumble down the rabbit hole. For the rest of the afternoon, I'm learning acronyms and terms I've never heard before. Parts of it sound familiar, like Cole being Navy but working with Marines, but a lot of it I have to pick up in context.

It's wildly interesting to me. These individuals sign up to join the Navy, get a contract to go corpsman, go through training, and then they're out in the world taking care of other Navy and Marine Corps personnel. Most of the videos are about training and faux combat scenarios, but there's this unspoken reality that all the training is in preparation for actual conflict. Something harmful, deadly.

I suck in a breath, and my mind plays it out before I can stop it.

Cole on a battlefield, putting pressure on a bleeding wound, carrying a Marine, putting in an IV, shouting instructions as Marines lift a stretcher, all while dust kicks up and mortars explode in the distance. That's what he trains for. That's the mission. And should the need arise, I know he would be the best corpsman out there.

I'm kind of proud of him.

I click my lock button, and the screen goes dark, mirroring my own face back to me. My thoughts float back to my conversation with Cole earlier, the butterflies that came when we looked at each other. Those warm brown eyes, that gorgeous smile, his sharp haircut and solid, muscular build. He's...interesting, dimensional. I wonder what it would be like to see him in action as a corpsman. I wonder what he looks like in uniform. I wonder if I'll ever see that side of his life.

I wonder if I need to stop thinking about him as much as I do.

CHAPTER 13

Hey, not to be like that lonely, clingy friend, but any chance we could hang out today? Just really tired of listening to the empty spaces in my house.

TIA

Yeah, I'm free after my shift ends at four. What's your drink of choice?

ANISHA

A Negroni, sbagliato. Lol, just kidding. Iced latte with coconut milk. Thanks, friend.

———

ANISHA SHOWS up at Cafe 22 right as I clock out. Her iced latte and my iced tea are waiting at the end of the bar for us.

"How's it going?" I say, taking in her oversized gray Navy shirt, blue work-out shorts, and messy bun. She looks cute, but her expression is annoyed.

"Oh, you know, not good. Deployment's kicking my butt, Murphy's Law is hitting today, the usual."

"What's Murphy's Law?"

"Anything that *can* go wrong, *will* go wrong when your person is gone. Like, our dishwasher flooding the kitchen this morning and my dog splashing through it with mud on his paws. Awesome start to the day."

"Oof. You want something stronger than a latte? We can go down the street to The Seal Pub, if you want, get you that Negroni."

She chuckles. "Nah, some fresh air will do me good."

We grab our drinks, and I wave to the chefs before I leave. They'll lock up for me when they're done shutting down the kitchen. The sun is beating down with unreasonable heat, and I'm sweating in my white tank top and black linen shorts by the time we turn towards the beach.

The faint chop of helicopter rotors sounds from behind us. It grows louder, and Anisha and I both look up to watch two Navy helicopters fly over us and down the beach towards North Island. I wonder if that's Luko. It's crazy to think one of my friends does something as cool as flying Navy helicopters.

There's two women about our age standing on the boulders of the sea wall ahead of us cheering and waving at the helicopters, taking a video with their phones.

"First squadron flight?" Anisha calls out to them.

"Yeah!" They're hugging each other and laughing, and Anisha gives them a thumbs-up as we walk by.

"Oh, to be young and happy like that," she murmurs to me. "That was me waving to Mick like five years ago. I'll tell you what, those moments of pride can carry you a long while in this Navy journey." She sighs, and her exhale is ragged. "Sorry," she says, sniffling. "I might cry. It's been an emotional day."

"That's okay," I reply softly. "You're really strong, but you don't have to be all the time."

"Aww, thanks, girl," she says, giving me a side hug. "Man, it's sweltering today."

"Want to come to my great aunt's house instead of the beach?"

"Sounds good to me."

We make our way to the back patio and it's significantly more comfortable in the cool shade offered by the overhead awning.

"How did you meet Mick?" I ask as we sit opposite each other on the outdoor sectional.

"At a bar in Pensacola when he was in flight school. Have I ever shown you my favorite picture of us?"

I shake my head, and she pulls out her phone. She scrolls a bit, then pauses with a smile, handing the phone over to me to take a look.

Mick is in a black uniform with gold buttons and gold trim on the cuffs of the jacket, standing in front of a giant American flag that hangs from the ceiling. Anisha is pinning gold pilot wings onto his uniform jacket, and they're both laughing as they look into each other's eyes. It's obvious they are overjoyed.

"You look so happy," I say, handing the phone back to her.

She nods, a smile of nostalgia on her face. "It was such a special moment. Mick struggled hardcore in flight school, it was like pulling teeth. Dates turned into study dates pretty quickly, but he hung in there and kept grinding and he made it. Pinning those wings on him was the culmination of all that. Couldn't be more proud of him."

"Where are you from originally?" I ask.

"New York. I was down in Florida for grad school, trying to escape the cold weather for some beach living. Mick's lucky he's Navy—it means we're usually stationed near the water and some semblance of a beach."

"Did you know anything about Navy life? Like, did you already know he would usually be stationed near water?"

She shakes her head. "I had no idea what I was getting myself into. I knew nothing. I only knew I loved Mick."

"Is it dangerous where he is now?" I ask, then cringe. "Sorry, if that's a taboo question. Deployment sounds dangerous, but I don't really know what I'm talking about."

"No, he's not really in danger, but it's still not easy. Nothing can magically make deployment easy."

She looks down at her wedding ring for a second before shaking her head. "Sorry, I did not mean to make this all about me. I haven't had anyone to talk to about Navy life in a long while," she says with a self-deprecating laugh. "But why do you want to know? Is it because there's a certain hot corpsman who's now single?"

Blushing is too gentle a word for how my face instantly heats.

"What? No, definitely not. I don't know what you're talking about." Anisha giggles and points a finger at my blush as I sip my iced tea. "I don't mind you unloading your thoughts a bit though. Tell me about the worst-case scenarios you've been in. Like, what's the ugliest it's gotten for you?"

Anisha arches an eyebrow but chooses to move on. "Well, for one, we hate moving. It really takes its toll on both Mick and me. There's so many logistics, so much paperwork you have to do with the Navy, and so many details—it's overwhelming. And then there's the emotional goodbyes and the starting over. Last time we moved, we fought so bad, I left him at a gas station for an hour. I literally just drove away, and it took me a good thirty minutes to cool down and turn around to go get him."

"Oh my gosh, Anisha," I say, putting my hand over my mouth. "I'm sorry, I know I should not be laughing, it is not funny."

"No, you're fine," she says, chuckling to herself. "I've been known to be a bit of a drama queen. We move as frequently as twice in one year, but it's most common to move every three years."

"That sounds...not fun."

Anisha nods in agreement with a tight smile. "And how about when you PCS to a new duty station and you know no one and your family is hundreds of miles away and your husband says, 'I'm flying out to meet the carrier in ten days.' And your stuff hasn't even arrived to unpack, so your last few days together are spent on an air mattress in an empty house, and then he leaves and you're all alone in a city where you know no one and there's not even a name to put on a form asking for an emergency contact."

"Yeah, nope. No, I'm out." I sigh and drain my iced tea. I'm never going to be signing myself up for that. "It's a miracle anyone is married in the military."

"It's called love." Anisha smiles, then leans forward. "Look, it sounds bad now, I know. But if you and a certain person whose name starts with 'C' and ends in 'O-L-E' were to become...more than friends, my advice to potential Navy girlfriends is always the same. Don't get with someone in the military because it sounds like a good idea or it checks some boxes or you like the uniform. Do it because you can't imagine life without them. You have to be madly in love to make it work."

"Well, I think you're incredible," I say.

She waves off my praise. "I know I trauma-dumped the worst of it on you, but on the flip side, it really does have its days of being amazing. And military spouses carry a lot of pride. I'm freakin' proud of Mick, he's done some really cool things as a helicopter pilot. The Navy does so much that people don't realize— protecting sea lanes, guarding communication lines, anti-piracy, and humanitarian rescue and support. The actual job is very unique from most people's idea of the military."

"And you're going to keep doing this for what, the rest of your life?"

"Oh, no," Anisha says laughing. "That's one silver lining. Most people try to do twenty years active duty so they get full retirement benefits as soon as they get out of the Navy."

"Twenty years is a long time."

"The handful of years we've been in have gone by like a flash.

Filled with traumatic life events, but then you look back and only remember the best parts. Like how you and your neighbors sat on your front porch with drinks every night in the summer time and you all went on a giant ski trip in the winter and you made a meal train for every new baby and cried together at every hail and bail. We find the best family wherever we go. Takes time, sometimes, but we love our forever friends. I have a feeling we'll be friends for a long time," she says, drawing out the long and adding a wink.

If I had people like Anisha in my corner, maybe not in the same city as me, but at least on speed dial, I could conquer anything. She's so real and genuine, not shying away from the harsh realities of her life, but not letting them drag her down either.

"I'm so glad I met you," I say.

"Me too," she says with enthusiasm. "Now tell me about you."

She reciprocates all my interest in her life by asking me about my art and listening to me talk through my latest wobble of indecision. She's supportive without being placating, which is exactly what I need.

"I totally see how it would be so intimidating to start a new career with something so subjective," she says, finishing off her coffee. "You're really brave."

"Ha," I say, rolling my eyes. "I am not. I was just backed into a corner and kicked down a wall to make a way out."

"Don't sell yourself short. I think it's hard to recognize bravery in ourselves, so I'm just going to tell you, you're pretty stinkin' brave for ditching a bad life and trying a new one, Tia."

"I'm privileged," I say in protest. "I had savings and a great aunt with a spare bedroom."

"Girl, own your bravery, okay?"

I haven't even started a painting for the gallery, I haven't done the hardest part of conquering a new subject, the only dent I've really made in my new life is playing soccer and working at a coffee shop. Big whoop. We'll see what I'm made of when I finally start painting. My bet is on discovering how little bravery I actually have.

CHAPTER 14

I AM NOT A MORNING PERSON, so the hardest part about morning shifts at Cafe 22 is our opening time. We have a handful of regulars who are as consistent as Old Faithful and like to roll out of bed at five in the morning to get their first sip of coffee straight from our hands. I have to be walking in to open no later than half past four, and it's...a struggle.

It's barely dawn and freezing out. I'm yawning while twisting my hair in a high messy bun and slipping gold hoop earrings on as I trudge from Aunt Mari's to work. One of our line cooks has already unlocked the front door and is warming up the kitchen, so I set the sandwich board out on the sidewalk, turn on the iPad, tie on my apron, and check our stock of baked goods in the display. Jules is off, so one of our other baristas, Sal, is filling in for her, and he's running late.

A tall guy walks in arguing loudly into his AirPods. My generation would call him a "finance bro," identifiable by his Patagonia fleece layered under a North Face vest that's supposed to read as an outdoorsy look, but actually means he spends 18 hours a day in an office that blasts the air conditioning.

He steps up to the counter to order, then backs up to berate whoever he's talking to. "I'm in California, on my honeymoon, and you're supposed to be doing your job, but tell me why you got three hours of work in before I woke up, and yet I'm still looking at a complete crap show. Fix it."

He hangs up and steps up to the counter again. He takes one look at me, then gives me a tilted smile, followed by an up-and-down perusal of my shape and size, his eyes narrowing. I wilt, alarm bells going off in my head.

"Hey, how about a black coffee and you forget you heard I'm on my honeymoon?" he says.

Gross, gross, gross. My hands are shaking as I tap the screen, not looking up.

"Black coffee," I say, my voice near cracking. "What size?"

"Large, honey, large." He winks. "And you could throw your number on that coffee cup, too."

I'm livid, but I'm too scared to engage with him. The audacity, the way I know this guy's poor wife is now attached to him by marriage.

"Hey!" A deep male voice shouts from behind the guy. "How about you order your coffee without sexually harassing someone?"

Cole is here.

In the cafe.

In his hunter green digital camouflage uniform and tan boots, looking every bit a warrior, intimidating and strong. He makes eye contact with me, checking to see if I'm okay. I give him a nod and turn to get the coffee so I can get this finance bro out of here.

"How about you mind your own business?" asks the bro.

Cole raises his voice to thunderous levels. "How about you stop being a d—?"

"Large black coffee!" I call out, practically shoving the searing hot cup across the counter.

"What's it to you, Rambo-lite?" The bro's tone is threatening.

I make eye contact with Cole and shake my head, ready to let it go if he is. His hands are flexing at his side. He doesn't like what that guy said, and he's ready to do something about it. Even though he's the shorter of the two, Cole has a much bigger presence. He's...hulking. His sleeves are cuffed high on his arms, and they're straining to handle the flex of his biceps.

"You can't talk to my girl like that."

I'm rooted in place, my heart pounding against my ribs.

My girl. My girl.

But Cole's not done. His face spells anger, and now his hands are forming casual fists, until one hand goes flat, fingers together, and aims right at the guy's chest.

"In fact, you can't talk to any girl like that. If I see you in here again, I'll break your nose faster than a bullet and put it back together like an abstract Picasso. I know you've only got a soup sandwich for brains, but you'd better try to remember that."

The finance bro scoffs and mutters, "Okay, tough guy," grabs his coffee, and jabs his phone to answer a call as he walks out. I can hear him talking down to someone again as his voice fades.

Cole steps up to the register flustered, his face flaming red, a muscle in his jaw twitching.

"Sorry, I don't normally blow up like that," he mumbles, and any trace of casual, funny, good-natured Cole is gone. Instead, there's just Cole who defended me and called me *his girl* while looking exceptionally attractive in uniform. I'm...in awe.

He takes off his uniform hat and sets it on the counter, rubbing a hand over his buzzed blond hair. "I hate those kinds of guys," he says emphatically.

When I can finally pull my words together to form a sentence, I clear up one detail. "I'm not your girl."

"I know," he replies, staring at his boots. "I was going to say 'my friend' but it just...came out."

He finally stands up straight and looks me in the eye. "You good?" he asks, his gaze shifting from heated anger to comforting.

Butterflies riot in my stomach. I nod, only able to utter one word. "Usual?"

"Yes, please."

My hands shake as I pull a cup off the tower next to the register and try to remember what I'm doing. Deep breath. Right, make his coffee, give him his coffee, don't make things more than they need to be.

I ring him up while the espresso drips into the mini pitchers, and he tips a ton but doesn't say anything else. When his drink is ready, topped with whipped cream, I carry it to him.

"Thanks for sticking up for me," I say with a smile.

He fumbles to get a lid and snap it on. "If anyone starts bothering you like that, or if he comes back and gives you a hard time, call me."

Tempting. Very tempting. That red-blooded show of force was...attractive.

"Cole, I'm sure you have a job to do, and it's not threatening guys who talk to me."

"I'm working out of North Island today, I'm less than a mile away."

"I'll be fine. Have a good day, okay, friend?" Gotta throw that last part in so we're clear where we stand.

He looks up at me, and I give him enough of a nod and smile combination that he softens his expression and smiles back. "Okay, see you soon."

He goes to leave, crossing paths with Sal, who's finally showing up for his shift, but I quickly call him back.

"Cole, your hat," I say, holding it up for him.

"That's called a cover," says an older gentleman who's sidled up to the register with a Gulf War Veteran ball cap on. "Not a hat, a cover."

"Sir," says Cole, putting his cover under his arm and snapping to attention.

"Navy corpsman, son?" says the man, pointing to Cole's uniform. On the left side, over the pocket, there's a strip of fabric with the words "U.S. Navy" embroidered on it in thick letters.

"Yes, sir."

"The only squid worth a damn."

Cole's face flares pink, but he smiles and nods. "Yes, sir."

"Good, good," says the man, turning back to face me.

Cole winks at me in farewell and heads out the door while the man orders a cappuccino without further comment.

"Were you a Marine, sir?" I venture to ask as he pays.

"Sure was, but why are you all calling me 'sir'?" he says with a laugh. "I did one tour and got right on out. I was on the bottom of the enlisted food chain."

"But you served," I say as Sal hands him his drink. "Not everyone can say that."

"Thank you, that I did," he replies with a smile, taking his to-go cup.

"What's a squid?" I ask quickly. "You said 'only squid worth a damn'."

"Oh, it's a kind of slight towards the Navy. Derogatory term for sailors, if you will. But corpsmen are different, they'll run into gunfire to save you and we respect that. They're the real heroes."

He raises his coffee in my direction as he leaves.

The rest of my shift goes by quickly as tourists and locals continue to stream in and out of the coffee shop, but the events of the morning have altered my perspective. Now I notice anyone wearing military-related apparel. Older men in blue and gold golf polos with an "N" for Navy embroidered on the chest , women in t-shirts with the words "Chief Petty Officer" and an anchor design on them, and even an elderly couple who comes in for a later breakfast wearing matching Air Force letterman-style jackets.

As I head home, I keep replaying the moment when I first saw Cole in uniform. I know he's good and kind on the inside, but he looked like a beast when confronting that awful guy. He was so intimidating. And powerful. And handsome. And stunning.

"It's not for you, Tia," I remind myself.

———

I'VE NEVER BEEN SO grateful for air conditioning. It's rare to find it in island homes, but Uncle Gustavo made sure Aunt Mari had it, a luxury I don't take for granted as I come back from an afternoon run and grab a quick shower.

I get a glass of water from the kitchen, and flop down on the cool leather couch while Aunt Mari reads in the armchair near me.

"How was work?" she asks.

"Eh, fine. Started off bad."

"Oh?"

"A finance bro came in—"

"What's that?"

"It's a guy you can tell works in the financial or banking industry because he wears like button down shirts with fleece vests or puffer jackets and outdoorsy brands with office wear."

"That is a very specific description."

I have to laugh. It really is.

"Anyhow, he was being really slimy to me, and then this other guy was nice and stood up for me."

"Oh?" Aunt Mari's book goes down, and she pulls off her reading glasses and stares me down as I bite my lip.

Either Cole is nothing to me and I don't tell Aunt Mari about him, or I tell her his name is Cole and I've seen him around the island and suddenly it's going to be a thing. A big thing. But after all my run-ins with him and the way he helped me the other night, it feels disloyal to act like he's nothing. But he doesn't have to know I didn't stick up for him with Aunt Mari. Why do I care so much?

"His name is Cole. I play soccer with him."

"You met a boy, and you know his name, and you didn't think to tell me?"

"He's in the Navy," I say, like that's an excuse for not telling her. It makes things worse.

"Christiana!" Aunt Mari's scolding tone tells me I've been caught red-handed. "What did I tell you?"

"It's not like I'm running off with him to get married," I say in my defense.

"I bet he's nice and kind and hot," she says, pointing a finger at me.

"He is, okay? Are you happy?" I argue with a blush and a smile.

She inhales sharply, giving me a look that should send me straight to my grave with its ferocity.

"I'm not dating him or anything, okay? We're just teammates. And we sometimes run into each other on the island." I don't tell her that he saved me in the liquor store or about the time I called him like he was my personal EMT or that he gives me butterflies. The more I think about it, the more my cheeks heat up.

All those things strung together are incriminating. Are we friends? Like I said, friends are good and necessary, but that's like... a really, really nice friend.

"Are you ready for another man after that boy in Washington was so bad to you?"

I could try to explain how different Cole is from Bryce, how I know for a fact that Cole would never hurt someone the way Bryce hurt me. How he's in the medical field, providing care for Marines, about as far away from Bryce on the selflessness scale as you can get. How he's never, ever made me feel small.

"I can't let one bad guy overshadow my whole life," I say. "I'm allowed to be happy again, I'm allowed to want a relationship with someone who's good and kind."

"You will need to trust someone in order to find what you're talking about. Because I think you mean love. You're telling yourself you're allowed to love again."

I don't correct Aunt Mari, but the truth is I have never loved anyone, so there's no *again*. After thinking more about my talk with Cole, I recognize now that my relationship with Bryce was never about love. It was about interest and maybe a bit of selfishness, but not genuine and reciprocated care, compassion, or kindness. Definitely not love.

"Don't worry," I say to Aunt Mari, but it's more for myself. "I'll be careful."

It's a promise I make to myself—to be careful with my heart and my choices. I've learned my lesson the hard way and it's not a lesson I need to learn twice.

CHAPTER 15

I'VE PAINTED AUNT MARI, Julio, Dad, and they have all turned out...middling at best.

Painting sucks. Art is stupid.

I can't understand why I haven't had a breakthrough. I blow out a deep breath as I walk to work. What happens if I can't hack it as an artist? Art won't go away; it doesn't need to be my profession to remain in my life. I don't know. Giving up now feels like giving in and proving all my naysayers right. I'm not out to have a "Gotcha!" moment or put people in their place. I just want to be proud of doing something on my own, by myself, making my own way in the world. Why does painting have to be so annoying all the time?

I stop by the gallery after work to have a little pout with Lorraine, but she's busy with another customer. She sees me and waves for me to stay.

I wander around a bit, wondering why I'm so stuck on this gallery. I could be painting my normal nighttime paintings and leveraging them into printed merchandise, like notecards, wrapping paper, framed prints to be sold on home goods sites.

Lorraine sidles over with a "Sold" sticker to put by the boat captain's portrait. "I can tell by your sour expression it's not going well."

"I'm considering going back to what I'm comfortable with. I don't know if I need to push myself to do this portrait."

"No, don't say that yet. Just keep practicing. It takes endless patience." She gives my shoulder a reassuring squeeze. "Have you tried doing a self-portrait yet? A lot of artists start there."

Which is how I find myself in the bathroom with an easel and canvas set up in front of the long mirror. I stare into it and take notice of my shadows and highlights, the overall shape of my face. I play with raising the blinds at the end of the room to let in natural light, then turning on the vanity lights versus the overhead lights.

And then I look into my own eyes for a while.

What do you want?

The longer I study myself, the deeper I fall into reflection, as if I'm viewing myself in third person. What does she want? What does the future hold for her? Where will she live, what will she do, what are her goals, her hopes, her dreams?

The future? In ten years, give or take, I'd like to be an established artist, painting collections of fine art. I'd like a small family, a husband and a baby or two. I want to feel confident in my choice to be an artist, secure in my marriage, and happy in my community. I want love, both the soul-splitting romantic love and the steadfast love of friendship.

I don't need to travel the world or discover new places. I don't need an illustrious title or a job in a renowned city. I want to use my creativity to plumb the depths of my heart and soul, to share the things I'm passionate about with the world, and to help others along the way. I want to know at the end of the day that I'll crawl into bed and feel safe and cared for.

I exhale and drop my gaze. That's what I want, but it feels unreachable, too far to fathom. Am I going to be able to support myself on coffee shop shifts and selling art, or is there some other job in my future, like running a gallery? Should I go back to school, get more training in art?

I look up again. "I just want to be brave," I whisper to my reflection.

———

THE GOAL DIGGERS are on a roll, and we're letting the league know we're here to win. After we add another "W" to our record, the Navy guys decide it's too hot to go to the beach and we should all go to Luko and Denny's place for a Mario party.

When I walk into the guys' townhouse, I gawk at the sheer quantity of couch dominating their living room. A massive, over-stuffed U-shaped sectional lines the wall with a huge ottoman in the middle. All seven of us on the team could easily fit on it without needing to touch each other.

I'm nudged out of the way by Sarah and Anisha, who take a diving leap onto the couch and claim the middle cushions. Denny opens the long entertainment console under what must be an 80" TV screen and starts tossing video game controllers around the room. He glances at me, about to frisbee one my way, but I hold my hands up in protest.

"I'll watch. I suck at video games."

"No worries," he says, chucking it to Frank instead.

Luko and Cole head towards the dining room table across from the kitchen and I follow them. Cole dumps a heavy backpack on the floor and sinks down on a chair on the far side of the table.

"Make yourself at home," Luko says to me. "Drinks are in the fridge, but no food or drinks on the couch."

"Noted."

The lack of color, the absence of anything hung on the walls, and the fact it smells like car air freshener screams bachelor pad, but it's also mature and comfortable. There's real furniture, however mismatched, and when Luko opens the fridge to grab a beer, it's well-stocked with ingredients and meal prep containers stacked up in neat rows.

"Beer? Soda? Sparkling water?" Luko asks.

"I'll take sparkling water," I reply.

He grabs a can and tosses it to me.

"Cole? Beer?" he asks.

Cole is unzipping his backpack and pulling out some hefty notebooks and binders. "No, I gotta study. I have so much to catch up on."

"Told you Ripley was dragging you down," Luko says on his way to the living room.

I'm stunned Luko would toss that out so casually. I sling my purse over the back of a chair and sit down across from Cole. His eyes are glued to his notebook, but his pen is hovering over it, not writing anything.

"You okay?" I whisper to him.

"Yeah, fine." That's far too curt an answer for him. He sighs and drops his voice. "I'm on a deadline for this, and I'm behind. Luko isn't wrong. I did get distracted for a bit, stopped studying for my pin like I should have been. It happened, I need to move on. But not gonna lie, I'm worried."

"What are you studying?" I ask.

"I'm working on my Fleet Marine Forces pin. This"—he points to the two-inch thick binder—"is my study guide. Gotta know everything in it, from why the Marines have the shores of Tripoli in their hymn to how to disassemble and reassemble a rifle to how to do basic land nav, and more. Plus all my corpsman stuff."

"Land nav?"

"Land navigation, using a compass and map. And then once I think I know it enough, I have to go around and get signatures from different people that confirm that I know it. They want to make sure that even though I'm technically a Navy enlisted sailor, I can operate on the same level as a Marine when I'm with them." He slides the binder towards me. "Take a look."

I start flipping through page by page, then chapter by chapter, turning chunks of paper at a time and still not getting to the end. The sheer volume of information is overwhelming.

"You have to know all this?" My brain is panicking on his behalf.

"I can do it. I just have to focus."

"When they test you, they can ask you anything?"

"Yeah, gotta be ready for any question they throw at me."

It's section after section after section of information on a myriad of topics. Guns, tanks, maps, structures, terminology, history. It's completely daunting. The last page is about the structure of dental battalions, and it's so unexpected I laugh out loud.

"Dental battalions?"

"Yeah, dental battalions," Cole says with a chuckle.

"You want me to leave?" I ask. "I'm not big into video games, so I was going to do some sketching, but I can leave if you want to be alone."

"No, stay. If you want to. It does something to my brain, helps me stay focused to have someone nearby."

I nod. "It's like silent accountability."

"You get it," he says with a grin.

I reach in my bag and pull out my mini sketchpad and pencils, setting up my own little space on the table.

"You seem so calm," I say. "I would have taken one look at that study guide and said no, thank you."

He looks down at his hands, rubbing his thumb over a callus as he laughs to himself. "Well, it's a requirement, can't really skip it. But I also want to prove to myself that I can do it. I once heard this interview with an older corpsman, from the Vietnam War era. He said this line that I'll never forget, something he was taught by an even older corpsman. 'Be the job big or small, do it well or not at all.'[1] And that's kind of become my mantra. Just trying to do my job well."

"It's weird that it's one of those things where we'll never get to see you on the job," I say. "It's not like we can sit in the back of your classroom and watch you teach or go eat in your restaurant and enjoy your cooking skills. But I imagine you're really good at being a corpsman. I mean, look at how you were the other night. You were so calm and ready for anything."

Cole's cheeks flush, and the blush travels down his neck, sliding under the collar of his t-shirt. "Look, don't go glorifying what I do," he says. "I'm not a hero or anything. Marines don't always think the best of corpsmen, especially when we haven't had a chance to prove ourselves in combat."

I shrug. "You're never going to convince me it's not a cool job."

He may be red in the face, but he has no problem meeting my gaze. I love that his eyes are so warm and inviting and deliciously brown. The butterflies are back again. What are they doing here?

When he looks away and starts quickly flipping through the binder, I take a deep cleansing breath and shift my brain into art gear. I scan my lines of sight, trying to decide what I'll attempt to sketch. It's just for fun, just for practice.

I glance over to my right, towards the living room, right as Denny and Frank explode off the couch with fist pumps of victory and everyone else leans forward, groaning. I can capture that, the juxtaposition of elevated winners and sinking losers.

Sketching out the beginning lines is easy. Keeping my eyes off Cole as he studies is not.

There's an intensity to the way he fixates on each page, running his finger across the text, jotting down notes in a note-book, subtly whispering to himself. He's locked in, oblivious to the cheers and jeers coming from the living room. His forehead furrows every so often as he pops the cap off a highlighter and slides it across the page.

I keep sketching, adding color, shading, and detailing, all the while sneaking glances at Cole. I admire his dedication, how seriously he takes his job. People drift in and out of the kitchen to grab snacks or drinks, patently ignoring us so Cole can stay focused.

After about an hour, I finally set my pencils down and stretch my arms, shaking my hands out. Cole looks up, and when he sees me taking a break, he leans forward with a groan, rubbing his hands over his face.

"You good?" I ask.

"Brain fried." He smiles at me. "Can I see what you've been up to?"

The little scene I've drawn is neither my best nor my worst work, but the prospect of showing it to him makes me nervous. What's there is there, it was the best I could do in the moment. But it's just Cole asking to see it, not an art critic.

"Sure," I say with a shrug.

He comes over to my side of the table and leans one hand on the back of my chair and one hand on the table. I angle my sketchpad towards him. He looks at it for a long while, tilting his head back and forth. He's close enough for me to catch the faint scent of laundry detergent emanating from his shirt and feel the heat of his body. My legs get goosebumps, and I run my hands over my thighs to make sure he knows it's because I'm cold in the air conditioning, not because he's so close to me.

"You drew that?" he asks.

"Mmhmm." He might not get it. To the untrained eye, it could look like weird shapes and blobs.

"Tia, that's incredible." He looks over his shoulder at the scene in the living room, everyone yelling and cheering and taking Mario Kart way too seriously, then back to my sketch pad. "That's so cool. I've never known anyone who could draw like that."

A thrill runs down my spine, and I can't hold back a grin. "Thanks," I say.

"Can I see what else you've drawn?"

I mentally flip through the pages, hoping and praying that there's nothing in there that would be embarrassing. It's mostly nightscapes, some seaside sketches, some of the island's main avenue, the trees in the park, a few of Aunt Mari in the kitchen.

"If you really want to," I say, sliding the book over to him. He sinks down in the chair next to me, his knee brushing against mine.

Cole turns each page slowly, taking it as seriously as his study guide, his eyes roaming over each sketch and drawing. I have to remind myself to breathe like a normal person, in and out, in and out.

"I love your style," he says. "It's like you're barely capturing the scene before something shifts. Like you don't have enough time to do all the details, you're just putting down the basic shapes and shadows, and yet it's all there. That's so cool."

I blush. No one has ever talked about my art that way. It's filling a cup I didn't even know was empty, my cup of reassurance, of confirmation. My logical brain says he's simply being complimentary, but my heart is already melting into a letter mold that spells C-O-L-E.

When he looks up and meets my eyes with his brown, earnest gaze, my heart stops.

"Thanks for showing me this," he says, looking beyond my eyes and into my soul.

"Yeah, anytime." I say, the words coming out in a dry whisper.

He gets up and heads to the kitchen, then comes back to the table with a Coke in one hand and a sparkling water for me in the other.

When he settles back in his seat and resumes studying, I can't stop watching him. He's intent, persevering through the mound of information in front of him with a furrowed brow that illustrates his diligence. I have a revelation of a thought.

This is the painting you need to do.

"What?" Cole asks, catching me staring.

"Nothing," I say, shaking my head with a smile and a heated blush.

No. Absolutely not.

But even as I protest, my mind's eye starts to sketch out how I would arrange the notebooks and the spill of pencils and where I would put the light to catch the intensity of his eyes and the little pinched lines between his eyebrows and...

No, this is ridiculous. I'm not painting Cole. There are about a trillion things in this world that can act as inspiration for the subject of my painting, and it's not going to be him. I refuse.

Because I like him too much.

No. It's because I would be taking up his valuable time. He obviously needs to stay in the zone with his studying. There's no way he'd have time to sit for a painting. Can you imagine? Me, asking him to sit for a portrait? Crazy.

Maybe not so crazy. Maybe the smartest thing you've ever done.

No, I will not be painting Cole Slaeden.

---

1. All Hands Magazine, "Between Two Corpsmen" YouTube, June 29, 2018, video, 6:29, https://www.youtube.com/watch?v=q9DjwKFQuLA

CHAPTER 16

I set my paintbrush down and take a step back to critique my portrait of Lorraine. It's a different concept, a portrait of her painting a portrait, a choice I made because I need to practice more than just a face. Turns out hands are hard too.

Something is off about the perspective, probably because the arm holding up the paintbrush is thin as a twig, but everything else seems right. It shows improvement, which is heartening, but there's no way I can fix that arm easily. I'm done for the day.

Aunt Mari is in the living room watching *Downton Abbey*, and I flop down on the couch, across from where she's ensconced in her overstuffed leather chair.

"*¿Estás bien?*" she asks.

"Yeah, just need a break."

"You've been painting since lunch, and you skipped dinner." She doesn't look at me as she says it, but her voice carries a hint of interest. "What are you working on?"

"I can't figure out what I'm going to paint for the gallery. Nothing is working."

"Maybe it's a sign."

Of course she would say that. I barely keep myself from rolling my eyes. Even though she's fixated on her show, she would know if I was disrespecting her.

My phone vibrates in my back pocket, and I pull it out to see Cole is calling me. Why is he calling me on a Friday night?

"Hey, Cole."

Aunt Mari immediately pauses the show and shoots me a look, which I patently ignore.

"Hi," he says in his perfect manly voice, paired with a huge sigh. "Um, are you busy right now?"

"No, just watching a show."

"Can I ask you a really big favor? And you can say no. Absolutely say no if you don't want to."

"Okay..." I get up and wander back to my room to let Aunt Mari resume *Downton Abbey* in peace.

"Denny and Luko are both either gone or on duty, all the guys here are out partying, and I really need someone to help me study. Would you be down for getting on FaceTime and going over some stuff with me?"

I grin. "Geez, Cole, buy a girl dinner first."

He laughs. "I'll take you out anytime, but tonight, I need to study. Look, you can say no and I'll totally understand. No hard feelings."

My mind runs through a quick checklist of whether this is a normal friend thing. He's asking for a study partner. I'm his last resort, he's made that clear. It's not like he's calling to flirt, he simply needs some help.

"Tia, you're allowed to say no because you'd rather relax and watch a show. That's totally okay."

I can help. Better to help a corpsman than watch a show, and it will definitely take my mind off my art. Win-win.

"No, Cole, it's fine, I promise. What do you need me to do?"

"For real?" I can tell through the phone that he's smiling as he says it.

"For real," I say, with a grin on my face.

"DIVISION,   REGIMENT,   BATTALION,   COMPANY,
PLATOON," I recite into my phone that's propped up against a
coffee mug next to my laptop. My knee is tucked up next to my
chest as I sit in an office chair at the little desk in my mini art
studio.

"No, I know that, we're talking about something different
now, we're talking about the combat elements." Cole's sitting at a
desk in his barracks room in a navy-blue t-shirt. He runs his hands
over his short hair and I get an eyeful of his defined biceps.

"Hmm, what? Oh, the flowchart thing?" I ask.

"Yeah, can you find it again?"

I scroll through the three hundred-plus page PDF Cole
emailed me, then quickly type in "GCE" to find it. The search
brings up a bunch of sketches of a guy demonstrating hand signals,
definitely not what I was looking for. What are these?

"Have you learned Tactical Measures yet?" I ask. "They look
like mimes in uniform."

Cole rolls his eyes at the camera. "Ground. Combat.
Elements."

We've been studying for over two hours now, and someone is
getting more and more grumpy. I'm just getting more and more
punchy.

"What do you do to tell the team there's a hasty ambush?"

"Tia..."

I make a fist and punch it out to my side, a goofy smile on my
face.

"You know what? Laugh away. That probably saved someone's
life in Vietnam or Afghanistan." He says it lightly, but the weight
of it sinks in and sobers me.

"Sorry. I'll find the ground combat elements, hang on."

"Did you even know that term before tonight?"

"Nope."

"Guess it's my job to teach you the most important things in life."

"Yeah, hope for true love and understand the structure of the Marine Corps."

Cole laughs out loud, deep and powerful, and it's an absolute delight.

"Is this all part of a greater plan to try to indoctrinate me and get me to join the Navy?" I ask, wondering what I can say to make him laugh again.

"Oh, definitely. We'll make a new rate for you—Art Specialist. Actually, wait, that's a real thing, it's called Combat Artist. You could paint incredible pictures of me lecturing Marines about hydrating and changing their socks."

I shake my head with a smile. "I'm sure we could come up with something much more heroic."

"I'm not a hero. Probably the most heroic thing I've done is vaccinate against smallpox," Cole says, dragging a hand down his face. "Oh, man. We should call it a night. I'm useless this late. It'll be better for me to get some sleep and then wake up and start again in the morning before our game."

"You sure?" I ask.

"I think so." He rests his head in his hand and smiles in the comfortable silence. It's the kind of silence that lets me study his face for too long, growing too curious.

"Hey, can I ask you something?"

He nods as he yawns.

"What makes you want to be good at this? Like, why do you care so much?" Maybe he's not as bold and courageous as I've made him out to be. Everyone's human, no one's that altruistic.

"Oh boy, that's another conversation for another time," Cole says, looking up at the wall above the camera, his eyes serious. "But family, mostly. Yeah, I'd say family and a desire to help people. I always knew I'd be in the medical field, but I didn't think it'd be as a corpsman. We'll talk about it one of these days," he promises.

"Hey, would you be up for helping me study like this regularly? I know it's a big ask, but I'll buy you as many California burritos as you want. You're so helpful and I feel like we make a great team."

We do make a great team. My heart starts thumping so loud, I'm worried FaceTime is going to catch the sound of its rapid beating.

"Yeah, I'd be down," I say, striving for a casual tone.

"Thank you." He has the cutest grin in the world.

We stare at each other for a long moment, a smile growing on my face as a link solidifies between the two of us. Something special, just him and me.

"Good luck, Doc," I say in a soft voice.

"Thanks, Queenie."

I love hearing him say that.

After he hangs up, I immediately start googling more poems from Henry Wadsworth Longfellow to try to forget about Cole's winsome face and the nagging idea that I need to paint him. Poetry will give me something else to inspire me.

I click on "The Arrow and The Song" and for the first time, my poet muse betrays me and only makes me think about Cole more.

I shot an arrow into the air,
it fell to earth, I know not where;
for, so swiftly it flew, the sight,
could not follow it in its flight.

I breathed a song into the air,
it fell to earth, I knew not where;
For who has sight so keen and strong,
that it can follow the flight of song?

Long, long afterward, in an oak
I found the arrow, still unbroke;

And the song, from beginning to end,
I found again in the heart of a friend.

———

"WHERE'S YOUR BOYFRIEND THESE DAYS?" asks Jules as she holds a pitcher of milk under the steamer.

"What boyfriend?" I say with a laugh.

"The blond guy from your soccer team."

"Oh, Cole? It's not like that. I told you, he's in the Navy, I'm not interested. We're just good friends."

Cole usually pops into Cafe 22 on Sunday afternoons, so Jules has seen her fair share of him. I've spent almost every weeknight with him on FaceTime, quizzing, reviewing, and learning right along with him. In fact, I think I've seen him every single day this week. We've mostly stayed on task, working our way through the Fleet Marine Force study guide, but we've also had some side conversations about food and music and soccer.

A tiny little crush is desperately trying to gather evidence for its case, but every time I start to paint Cole into my picture of the future, I remember my talk with Anisha and how awful Navy life sounds. Crush closed.

Jules looks at me with wide eyes for an uncomfortably long moment.

"What?" I ask, raising my eyebrows.

A customer comes in with a couple tea orders, and I stay busy scooping the loose leaves into little sachets and dropping them into to-go cups. Jules deposits some coffees at the bar and comes over to me. "What does he do? He looks like a Marine."

"He's in the Navy, but he works with the Marines. An infantry unit, if I remember correctly."

"He lives in the barracks, on base?"

"Yeah?"

"And he comes here for coffee?" Jules asks.

"Yeah, what's so weird about that?"

"Well, what's weird is we're an hour away from Camp Pendleton, the nearest Marine Corps ground base. Why would he drive an hour to get coffee? Unless...he really wants to see the cute girl who takes his order?"

In my head I knew he lived on Camp Pendleton. I knew it was not close by, but now it's coming into stark focus. Why is Cole always down here? My hands pause mid-scoop as my stomach flutters. "He could really like the coffee here," I say, going back to fill each cup with scalding hot water.

"No, he doesn't really like the coffee here. He really likes you. You know how I know? Because he never stops smiling the whole time he's here. He's always grinning and happy."

My mind pulls up the image of Cole laughing over FaceTime last night, head thrown back, all sunshine and white teeth.

"See, now you're smiling all cute and goofy thinking about it," Jules says in triumph. "That's why I asked if he was your boyfriend."

I pop lids on all the cups and shake my head. "We both just got out of bad relationships. We're happy to have someone to hang out with who's kind and caring. Even if he was interested and I was interested, I am not up for the whole Navy life thing. We're never going to be anything more than friends."

I'm going to choose not to read into the fact that maybe (and it's pure conjecture at this point), *maybe* he drives an hour to come to this coffee shop for reasons other than the coffee.

Definitely won't think about how he pulled his jersey off after the soccer game yesterday. I glanced over at him right as he reached behind his neck and yanked his jersey off in one smooth move. He just stood there, all hot and studly in the baking sun, solid torso muscles and tanned skin for the whole world to see. I stared so long Anisha finally elbowed me. It would have been a crime to let his shirtless moment go unappreciated. His shoulders...I bet he could throw a two-hundred-pound Marine over his shoulder and march through the desert without breaking a sweat. He has alpha-male strength in that body, the kind that could make a girl reconsider her priorities in life.

"So, you would say no if he asked?" Jules adds.

I blush and shake my head. "Definitely. I don't think it would be a good idea," I say, sliding the cups into a drink holder and delivering them to the bar.

Jules sighs. "Okay. But I reserve the right to do a gleeful dance when you finally tell me you're dating."

I roll my eyes, but I'm smiling. "Sure, all rights reserved, Jules."

———

IT'S JUST A BARBECUE. A team barbecue. Some drinks, some burgers, some cornhole on the tiny back patio. Friendly activities. No one is going to interrogate me over whether I have a crush on Cole. And he's not even going to be here, so it's perfect, just time with friends.

I grab the case of seltzers I picked up at the corner liquor store and try to seem breezy as I sail in through the front door.

"Hey, Tia's here!" shouts Denny with a quick side hug. He's wearing a handsome pair of clear-framed glasses.

"I didn't know you wear glasses," I say as I hand him the drinks and follow him into the kitchen.

"They're new," he says. "Navy life is aging me already, stressing my eyes out. I really only need them when I'm looking at stuff close up."

"You look good in them."

He grins. "Yeah? Okay, cool. Thanks, Tia."

Someone short sneaks up behind me and hugs me around the waist. "Hey, you," Anisha's voice says over my shoulder.

"Hey," I say, turning around to hug her back. "How are you?"

"Oh, you know, surviving, not thriving. Work is meh, Mick's stressed, things are breaking around the house."

"Oh no, what now?"

"The dryer stopped drying and the washing machine somehow got off-balance. I've been going to my neighbor's to do laundry until we can get the repair guy out."

"That's so lame. Murphy's Law."

She makes a snarling face of annoyance. "Yeah, Murphy sucks."

We ease towards a massive bowl of chips on the counter alongside a store-bought container of guacamole. Anisha loads up a chip and right before popping it in her mouth says, "Let's talk about something else. Tell me something fun."

Anisha is quickly becoming my closest friend, and I trust her insight, so I lean towards her and whisper, "Do you think Cole maybe kind of...likes me?"

A laugh snorts out of her nose as she covers her mouth to keep the chip and guacamole from spewing everywhere.

"Don't laugh at me," I whisper, even as I chuckle along.

Anisha is still trying to not choke on her chip, but she waves Luko over with a series of sounds and gestures. Something about pointing to me and an invisible person next to me and somehow, Luko gets it immediately. He comes over from the fridge, sliding cans of sparkling water to Anisha and I.

"Oh, does Cole like her? Where is he, by the way?"

Now it's my turn to cough on my first sip. How is this a thing, that Luko already knows what Anisha is gesturing about?

"He's studying for his murder board," I say, once recovered. "It's on the schedule now."

Luko goes wide-eyed. "Did you say murder board?"

"Yeah, like the practice exam for his pin. The whole point is they try to murder you with questions."

"I know what a murder board is, I've had to do them too," Luko says with a grin. "I'm surprised you know what it is." He holds eye contact with me for a knowingly-long moment.

"What? I've been helping him study," I say while loading up a chip, trying to remain resolved under Luko's gaze. It's none of his business what Cole and I do. "You were on duty the other night, and I helped him, and we kind of fell into a routine."

Luko chuckles to himself. "How do you even know what duty is?"

I hold up a finger for him to wait while I finish my mouthful. The things Luko doesn't even know I know. Enough of his passive judgment.

"I know the difference between an LSD, an LPD, and an LHD, I know the Marine Corps hymn, the place where the Marines was founded—Tun Tavern, baby—, battle formations, how to dig a foxhole, and the fact that Opha Mae Johnson was the first female enlisted Marine."

Luko's jaw is hanging open.

"I know things now," I say with pride. Anisha rewards me with a golf clap.

"Well, then," says Luko, crossing his arms over his chest. "You and Cole studying, huh? And you want to know if he has a crush on you?"

"I'm not here to talk about him behind his back," I say quickly. "It was just a bit of girl chat."

Luko sighs and rubs his cheek. "Cole falls hard and fast. If he has a crush on you, he's gone already, there's nothing you can do about it."

It's one thing for me to have a crush on him, it's another for it to be possibly reciprocated. It throws my sweetly-spinning world off its axis to think of what could result from Cole and I both having a gravitational pull on each other.

"What?" Luko asks, watching my face fall.

I blush and stammer, trying to find my words. "I...I think the world of him, we've become great friends, but I can't..."

"Do the Navy thing?" Anisha chimes in.

I nod. "No offense," I say to Luko. "You and Denny and Cole are awesome, I love you guys, but I would not sign up for life as a military girlfriend or whatever."

Luko shrugs. "I understand. It's a tough gig. Look, you don't have to go out of your way to protect him or anything, just keep being you. You're not responsible for his feelings. He's a big boy, you're a grown woman, things will figure themselves out."

"One way or another," Anisha adds under her breath.

CHAPTER 17

THAT'S the second time I've flung my pencil across the room while trying to start this sketch. I crawl under the desk to retrieve it, my heart pounding, and of course I bang my head along the way.

If everything has happened on schedule today, Cole should be finishing his murder board right about now. I'm on pins and needles waiting to hear how it went. He said he could fail it, in which case he'll have to do it all over again in a few weeks. But I'll be shocked if he fails.

He's studied well for this, and I've had a front row seat to how seriously he takes this qualification. I have no doubt he'll pass with flying colors. And then it'll be on to the final board, then his pinning ceremony. He'll have victory in his grasp.

But there's always a chance something could go wrong at the last minute. He could've slept poorly or forgotten to eat breakfast or tripped in the shower and hit his head and now has amnesia.

He'll be okay. I know he will.

On the other hand, I am floundering. Nothing—no one—has inspired the spark I need to paint well, and I'm caving to my last resort. I've ignored the glaring, blinking signs with Cole's face on them, telling me to "Exit here" on the highway of creativity, and I've been metaphorically driving through the night for as long as possible. Now, I'm running on empty.

The small canvas is finally situated on the easel. With a pencil in hand I close my eyes, and imagine something I've become more and more familiar with: Cole Slaeden's face.

His jawline has a soft curve to it. His nose slopes gently, not sharp or pronounced. His eyes—I'll need more time and practice to get them right, so I rough them in, then give him smoothly arching eyebrows and barely detail his ear shapes. He has the hint of wrestler's ear on his left side. I wonder how he got it.

I set the pencil down and go back with a piece of charcoal, bringing out his cheekbones, then slide the charcoal down the canvas to give a sense of his upper body build. He has a thick neck and solid, muscular shoulders.

Taking a step back, I squint and look sideways at it. Okay, not bad. I got the width of his nose wrong so it kind of looks like someone stepped on his face, but still, the essence of *him* is there. I actually can't believe it. All those hours of practice might be paying off.

A bubble of pride rises in my chest, and I smile to myself.

My phone vibrates in my back pocket, and my heart leaps out of my chest. Cole is calling. My hands are shaking as I answer.

"How did it go?" I ask quickly.

"I passed."

I scream into the phone and do a happy dance. He did it. He passed. The phone chimes with a FaceTime request and I accept the video, setting my phone against the coffee mug on the desk.

Cole's sitting in front of a tan cinderblock wall, in his green camouflage uniform, a massive grin on his face. But he looks absolutely wrung-out. His eyes have dark circles under them, and he keeps rubbing his hand down his face.

"You did it! Ah, I can't believe it!" I squeal with delight and do another dance. "How do you feel?"

"I'm so brain-dead, I can't even think. I just walked out and called you right away."

He called me *first*. I don't know if my heart can take how special that makes me feel. Out of all the people in his life, he wanted to tell me first. I'm so happy for him, I want to wrap my arms around his tired head and hug him forever.

"It's over! You did it!" I say in awe.

"I still have my final board."

"You said it's a formality. You'll be fine."

He nods. "I need to sleep for like a week."

"Cole. I'm so proud of you. I want to hug you or something."

"Tomorrow," he says with a grin.

"You're still going to play tomorrow?" I ask. "You look like a zombie."

"I have less brain capacity than a zombie, but I'm not missing a game. We're going to the championship."

I laugh and shake my head. "I don't know how you do it."

"Haven't you heard? I'm about to be a full-fledged Devil Doc," he says, winking at me. I ache with the need to hug him, to give all this pride an outlet. Maybe even kiss him on the cheek or something. A friendly gesture, not crossing any lines.

"I hate that I don't have my own place," he says. "I'd ask you to come watch movies with me for the rest of the day. Well, you'd watch the movies, I'd sleep. Actually, you probably have stuff to do. Did I interrupt you?"

"Just working on a sketch," I reply, hoping my furtive glances to the corner don't give me away.

"Can I see?" he asks.

"No, it's not ready. It's just a sketch," I say.

"Okay, well, I'm going to go stumble to my room, but I wanted to call you first. Thanks for everything, Tia. Can't wait to see you tomorrow," he says with a sleepy smile.

"Me too," I reply with a goofy grin on my face.

The call ends, and I go back to the canvas. After talking to him,

I can see I got the shape of his temples wrong, and the curve of his bottom lip is fuller in real life.

When I close my eyes and picture him again, a fountain of emotion wells up in my chest—pride, happiness, joy, awe.

You have to ask him.

If I paint Cole studying, it's going to have meaning and feeling behind it, the thing that's been missing from all my other projects. I need to go for it. I'm going to ask him.

"What was that?" Aunt Mari asks, from very close behind me, and I jump with a shriek.

"Oh, my friend Cole passed a test," I say with a nervous laugh as my adrenaline dies down.

"Your friend," she says, looking at me with suspicion over her reading glasses.

"Yes."

"Just a friend."

"Yes," I say, determined to stay strong under her all-knowing gaze. "What?"

"Okay, I'm going to San Francisco for a small film festival, then Arizona for an art festival. When I get back in two weeks, you will introduce me to this boyfriend." She leaves before I have a chance to find my words.

———

I PARK FACING THE FIELD, take a deep breath, and remind myself why this is a good idea. We're just friends. This isn't going to lead to anything else. I'm simply asking Cole for a favor—like the favor I did for him when I helped him study. Plus, if the image comes out on canvas as well as I'm picturing it in my mind, it's going to be exactly what Lorraine is looking for and it will fit the vibe of the gallery perfectly. It's almost a selfish request.

I get out of the car and sling my bag over my shoulder, casually scanning the parking lot for Cole. I spy him and Denny standing close together by the Camaro having an intense conversation. Today probably isn't the day to ask Cole to sit for a portrait.

I sink down to the grass to put on my cleats and focus on getting the lacing right. No, not asking him is chickening out, making excuses. I can do this. The worst he could say is no. What if he thinks I'm silly? Or worse, what if he takes it the wrong way and thinks I'm slyly trying to spend more one-on-one time with him? Like I'm subtly trying to seduce him. Okay, even that is a bit far-fetched. I finish with my cleats, giving each of them a quick pat.

"Hey, Tia," Denny calls from behind me. "Can I talk to you for a minute?"

"Yeah, of course."

Denny comes over with Luko and Cole trailing behind him, like a pack of ducklings. The three of them sink down to the grass to quickly put their cleats on.

"Luko, I love you man, but keep your mouth shut while I talk," says Denny.

Okay, then. I look over at Cole with raised eyebrows and he shrugs in response. I look back at Denny, and his expression means business. I bet this is what he looks like when he's doing his job on his ship—focused, collected, intent.

"Here's my question," he says. "If I got butt-dialed by an ex-girlfriend, but I kind of had this one-sided conversation with her and I heard her listening and she only ended the call after I said my old nickname for her, does that mean she still has feelings for me and I should call her back?"

I'm reeling trying to put together a mental image of what Denny's talking about. I think the gist is he thinks he might have a shot with his ex-girlfriend? Because she didn't hang up when she saw she'd butt-dialed him? Denny finally looks up at me with sad and pleading blue eyes, like a lost puppy begging for a home. Poor guy.

"Why can't Luko chime in?" I ask. After our conversation about Cole, I've grown to appreciate his thoughts.

"He's protective of Denny," Cole offers. "He doesn't like Ellis for what she did to Denny, just like he hated Ripley."

"Oh my gosh, it was high school, man," Denny says, raising his voice in frustration. "And Ellis is nothing like Ripley!

"No, no, you're right," Luko says defensively. "Ellis isn't mean, at all. She's great, she's sweet." He sighs and throws his hands up in defeat. "She has a lot of walls up and you're never going to get over them and I want you to stop hurting yourself trying."

Denny nods, then looks at me with waning hope.

"What do you think, Tia?"

I feel like there are years of history between Ellis and Denny that I need to be caught up on before I'm qualified to give any advice. But the other team is arriving and warming up and I don't want to leave Denny hanging. "Maybe the pocket dial put your name back on her mind, so...try to be patient? See if anything comes of it?"

Denny nods, his hands picking at the grass. Luko stands and reaches a hand down to him. Denny takes it and they walk onto the field together with their arms around each other's shoulders.

I look over at Cole and he gives me a sad smile. "Thanks for letting him down gently. I don't think he'll ever get over her."

"That sucks," I say with sympathy, watching Denny lay into a soccer ball and send it shooting into the goal like a cannon.

Cole gets up and I lock eyes with him as he walks over, then pulls me to my feet. We're standing only inches apart and he's not letting go of my hand.

"Oh, hey, congrats on passing your murder board," I murmur, quiet and close, matching the distance between us.

"Thank you," he says, his voice dropping lower to meet mine. His thumb brushes over the back of my hand, and combined with the intensity of his stare, I'm forgetting how to breathe. I'm forgetting everything. All I know are Cole's brown eyes, looking at me, never leaving my face. I have to look away, otherwise I'll be lost in those eyes forever. I pull my hand out of his and clear my throat.

This can't be a *thing*. It can't.

"I have a favor to ask," I say, gathering my thoughts, looking beyond him so I don't have to look him in the eye.

"Yeah?" His voice rises in interest.

"Um, so, you know how I paint sometimes?"

"You mean how you're an amazing artist?"

My face flushes, and I stammer, trying to find my next words. "Tha-thanks you." Thanks you?! My brain and my stomach are tied in knots. Quick breath, be professional. "Um, I have a chance to have a painting displayed in a gallery on Crown Island, but it has to be a painting of a person. I was wondering if, uh…"

I can't finish this sentence. I can't think of the words I want to say. I'm blanking out and simply staring at Cole. His haircut is fresh, a sharp fade. I have a weakness for fresh haircuts.

"You want to paint a portrait of a person?" he asks, trying to jog my memory.

"Yeah," I say. I can't ask this of him. I want to run back to the car and drive straight home and dive under my comforter and stay there until my embarrassment fades, two hundred years from now.

"Just ask," Cole says gently. "Whatever it is, I'm not going to make fun of you."

I inhale and puff out my cheeks, blowing out a breath.

"Would you let me paint a portrait of you studying for your FMF pin?"

Cole raises his eyebrows and tilts his head to one side, considering it. "Gonna be totally honest, that was not what I was expecting."

"It's fine, ignore me. Don't worry about it. It's no big deal," I say, speed-walking onto the field. I snag a ball and roll it in front of me, dribbling towards one of the goals to do some warm-up kicks. My cheeks are on fire, and I'm struggling to breathe correctly. There's a voice in my head—a mean, laughing voice that sounds an awful lot like Bryce.

You're an embarrassment to yourself.

No, that voice doesn't get to have any power over me anymore. Absolutely not. Out of my head, loser, you suck. I kick the ball extra hard, then dash to go get it out of the goal. No, I'm not embarrassed.

"Tia," says Cole, jogging up to my side as I look straight ahead, line up my next kick, and launch the ball straight into the upper right corner of the goal.

"Tia," Cole says again, this time gently putting his hand on my arm. "Come on, Queenie."

I turn towards him, studying our cleats lined up across from each other in the grass.

"Don't be embarrassed. We're friends. Friends ask each other for things like that."

I don't know if we're really friends. I don't know how to explain it. We are friends, but friends don't have chemistry, they don't have that unique pull that makes you look for each other in a room full of people. Friends don't notice the shape of each other's lips or wonder what it'd be like to kiss them.

But it's more than that. It's not just my attraction to Cole that's made me incredibly self-conscious.

"I've never had friends who were supportive of my art," I say, doing little ankle circles with my toe in the grass. I look up at Cole to see him staring at the goal, his face in profile.

I want to paint that face so badly. Now it's an ache, a thorn in my side that won't be removed until I allow my brush to sweep over the canvas to shape the contours of his forehead, his gently sloped nose—

"I'll do it. I want you to do it," Cole says.

"What?" I ask.

"Can we do it after my final board, though? It's in a week, and I have to stay focused. After that, I'm all yours."

Frank calls us together for a pre-game huddle before I can do any more than nod to Cole. The Goal Diggers barely eke out the win. Not surprising, given the way I lost focus every time Cole locked eyes with me on the field.

I'm all yours. I've never had such simple words leave me shaking inside. He pulls at my resolve, like a high tide tugging a piece of driftwood back into the sea. I'm going to be swept away if I'm not careful.

CHAPTER 18

THE SAN DIEGO skies are playing a coy game of being windy and gray right now, but they'll eventually give in to the sun, and the air will turn stiflingly hot later in the day. I throw on a tan hoodie and some loose jeans cuffed at the ankles, make sure my phone is charged so I can type out any notes I want to remember, and drive Aunt Mari's Mustang north to La Jolla to meet Cole.

If I'm going to paint his portrait, I'm going to do it the way Lorraine and I talked about— biographically. I need to know more about Cole, his life, his backstory, so I can make sure I represent him well. Thankfully, he's on board with my plan.

I'm all yours.

I wait by the lifeguard stand for Cole's black Camaro to come growling into the parking lot. The wind is making my bangs dance around, and I twist my hair up into a messy knot to keep it from whipping across my face. I'm tempted to pull out my phone and browse the art side of Instagram while I wait, but I know it will only stifle my creativity. I need to fill my mind with my own ideas of how to paint Cole, not other people's drawings and paintings. But thinking about Cole gives me butterflies, and Instagram would distract me from those feelings.

My phone buzzes with a text.

COLE

Base is locked down, someone tried to run the gate, I'll let you know when they finally open back up and I get on the road. Sorry.

TIA

No worries!

Oh. He's well over an hour away, then. Boo. I sigh and tap my phone against my chin, wondering what to do to kill an hour. I could go get some tea, or I could do a sketch.

I should call my dad, check in and say hi.

I dial the long-distance number and wait for him to pick up. After the phone has been ringing for over a minute, I give up and push the send to voicemail button so I can leave him a message.

"Hey, Dad, it's Nina. Just wanted to say hi and let you know that I'm doing great. I got a job at a coffee shop owned by some friends of Aunt Mari and I'm playing soccer again." I hesitate for half a second, then get annoyed with myself for hesitating. "I've been painting more, and I hope to get my work displayed in an art gallery here. Anyways, just wanted to let you know I'm good. Okay, *te amo, adiós.*"

Next time, next time, I'll call to tell him my portrait is hanging in the gallery and I'll say it with pride. I go to the Mustang and grab my soccer ball and walk out onto the sand.

––––––

"Hey, while you were stuck on base, look what I learned how to do," I say, kneeing the soccer ball into the air four times in a row, then kicking it up high enough to head it.

Cole laughs and shakes his head as he walks across the sand towards me. He's wearing a black hoodie with USMC across the front in red letters, and he has his hands in the pockets of his tan pants.

"Sorry I'm late." He's quiet, looking out at the horizon.

"What does it mean to run the gate?" I ask, kicking the ball in his direction.

"An unauthorized person tried to drive past the gate guards to get on base. They have to lock down people leaving and coming onto base until the situation is resolved," he says, popping the ball into the air by kicking it behind his back, then heading it twice in a row. He traps it back on the sand and passes it right to me with ease. I want to call him a showoff, but the man has skills. I'm impressed.

"Hey, can I ask you something kind of random?" he says.

"Sure." I pick up the ball and roll it between my hands as we start walking towards the water.

"If I said I liked you, and I meant it, how would you feel about that?"

The ball drops onto the sand. What?

I venture a glance at him. He stops a few feet away and turns to look at me. He's standing firm, not backing down, not adding anything. His question hangs in the air between us. Did he just say he likes me? Like, *like* like?

"I mean..." I don't know where I'm going with the rest of my sentence.

"I think I have my answer," he says with a nervous laugh, running his hand over his hair. His neck is flushing red, and he keeps walking towards the ocean.

What just happened? We were supposed to hang out and talk before I start prepping for his portrait, and now the portrait is the furthest thing from my mind. I grab my ball and jog to catch up to him. When I fall in step alongside him, he keeps his eyes fixed on the sand.

"You caught me off guard."

"It's okay. We don't have to talk about it," he says quickly.

On the one hand, he's put it out there. Maybe now's a good time to talk about it, when we can still go back on the painting thing. On the other hand, I'm terrified of answering badly. My mouth is moving like a fish out of water, but no words are coming out.

"I like you," I offer, when I'm finally able to talk. "But anything more...well, you're in the Navy."

"Really?" Cole says, wheeling around and giving me a quizzical look. "I didn't expect that from you."

"What do you mean?"

"You're tough. I didn't think me being in the Navy would faze you."

I huff a laugh and shake my head. "You don't really know me."

"Then tell me. Isn't that why I'm here—for you to get to know me? So, let's talk about you too."

"You first."

He plants his feet in the sand and squares his shoulders, facing the waves. This is our spot now. I let the ball drop to my feet as I wait for him to start.

"Well, I'm from California, born and raised in a mountain town up near Bearstone Lake. I have an older brother, Carson, and a younger brother, Cillian. My mom is a midwife. My family's great, we love each other a ton. For a family of all dudes, my mom's kept us from being total meatheads."

He pauses and takes a deep breath. "I went to college to study kinesiology and sports medicine and—" He's about to say something, but the words don't come out. "Sorry." He tries again. "My dad died when I was in college, about five years ago now."

He rubs his chest, and I take a step closer to him.

"Cole, I'm so sorry."

He nods, his eyes glistening. "He had a heart attack when he was out hunting. I love my dad. He was a great guy, a fantastic dad. We all miss him a lot."

He takes another deep breath and exhales slowly. My heart

goes out to him. I can't imagine losing my dad. I would be devastated, and I would struggle to talk about him, even though I would also want to talk about him, to remember him.

"It was the end of my junior year of college. Denny and Luko and I had been roommates since day one, and they really helped me through the worst of my grief. My dad passing away meant our family's primary breadwinner was gone. My mom could make good money as a midwife, if she charged people and actually collected her bills. But she helps a lot of poor families way back in the mountains and she usually does it for free or just the cost of supplies. Carson took on the mantle of bringing in more money, but I didn't want him to have to bear that alone, so I dropped out of college and enlisted. That way Mom could keep doing things the way she's used to."

He pauses to clear his throat and seems unsure of where to go from there.

"What made you enlist instead of getting some other job?" I ask.

He nods. "I always wanted to do something with medicine, but my dad passing away left me wanting to do something to honor him, something he would have been proud of. He was a Marine, did one enlistment, but never let anyone forget it. He always reminded us boys to be proud of our military, but especially the Marines. Being a corpsman meant I could do it all, be kind of a first responder and serve with the Marines."

"You weren't intimidated by the idea of being in the military?"

Cole shrugs. "I've always wanted to be challenged, to see if I have what it takes to help save lives in the most stressful situations possible. I want to see what I'm made of. The military shapes you and forces you to confront yourself and your weaknesses in a way that not many other organizations can. There's also a legacy of being brave and sacrificial, being part of something bigger than yourself. I want that to be part of my life story too."

He studies the sand as we listen to a seagull caw, the roar of waves, a distant dog bark. I stand in the quiet with him. Who he is and what he does is so much bigger than I thought. It's his dad and his family, it's corpsmen who came before him and the Marines he'll serve alongside. Cole constantly talks himself down, saying he's not heroic or inspirational, but he is. He represents resilience.

"How do you handle your grief?" I ask.

He gives a rueful laugh and runs his hand over his hair again.

"Well, I got a black belt in MCMAP, the Marine Corps Martial Arts Program, if that's any indication of how things went initially. I was...consumed with fighting and training. My whole life was basically fight, study, work, and sometimes sleep. But I was in this drowning darkness, where it was a battle to go to sleep and then a battle to get up. It got to a point where my brothers made me text them a thumbs-up every morning to let them know I was going to get up and go through my day. I don't know, it was a dark time."

Unexpected emotions rise in my chest. It's hard to think of Cole going through darkness like that, alone and angry. I wish I could rewind time and go to him, be there for him.

"But eventually, with some time and a few counseling sessions with the base chaplain, I grew around my grief. I think everyone felt relieved when I drove home in my Camaro for the first time. I made a classic enlisted move and got it straight out of boot camp. Felt pretty guilty about it at first, since we were all trying to keep our family afloat, but then my brothers were so jealous, I had to keep it."

His logic makes me chuckle. "For what it's worth, I have a crush on your Camaro."

"Oh yeah?" He smiles, sad and sweet. When I take a step closer to him, he holds his arm out in an unspoken invitation. I go to him immediately, wrapping my arms around his waist. I stay quiet, letting him choose whether there's more to his story that he wants to share.

"Yeah, losing Dad hit me hard, but just growing, maturing as a person over time has been good. Hard but good. I try to stay active and be with friends a lot. I don't love being alone. Every so often I make dumb mistakes—like dating someone I should never have been with—and it brings me down." Cole looks down at me with a gentle smile and adds, "But then you came along. And these past few weeks, I feel like I'm breathing again."

I meet his eyes with recognition. I know that feeling, because he's made me feel it. He just quietly walked into my life, all full of genuine care and kindness. The kind of guy that becomes your best friend, the teammate that you always know is in your corner, and then...I don't know. He's the song from beginning to end, the one I've found in the heart of a friend.

"What about you? What's your story?" he asks, running his hand across my back before letting me step away.

"Well," I say, taking a deep breath and letting it out slowly. I don't love talking about myself, but I want to meet Cole in his honesty, be as vulnerable and open as he has been. "My mom got pregnant with me from a one-night stand. She didn't know anything about my dad, just that he was some white dude. After I was born, she took me straight from the hospital to her brother Miguel's house and left me there. My dad—technically he's my uncle but I call him Dad—was already a single dad, raising his own little boy, Julio. I call Julio my brother, even though he's my cousin. He was like two and a half when I came along, and we don't remember life without each other. So then Dad had a two year old and a baby. My grandparents had already left to go back to Mexico, and Dad was basically a superhero at that point."

"And your mom never came back?"

I shake my head emphatically. "No. She had addiction problems. In a way, it's kind of okay. I was safe and loved."

"Oh."

I can feel his hope deflating in one syllable, the hope that I would have a happy reunion story to share at the end. Honestly, it's not something I've ever wished for.

"But, like, how are you okay with that?" he asks.

"It's just part of my story, not my identity," I reply, crossing my arms over my chest. "When I was old enough to question it, when I wondered why my mother hadn't loved me enough to stay in my life, Dad talked about it openly with me. He would remind me that she was sick and lost and blind to everything but the things she was addicted to. If she could have seen me, the real me, she would have loved me and been proud of me. He promised me that and I believed him."

I didn't get to choose my childhood, but as an adult I think it was all for the best. I had a home, a family, and love.

"Are you still close with your dad and your brother?" Cole asks.

"Yeah, although not as much as we used to be. We're all adults with our own lives. It's been too long since I've seen them. And you want to know what's funny? The only thing I would change about my whole life story is I wish I would have had their support for my art at a younger age."

"Really?" Cole says, his eyes wide. "That's the thing you would change?"

"Yeah. Well, and maybe the whole Bryce thing. But I think if I would have had my family's encouragement to pursue what I loved, I wouldn't have fallen into that hole of living in D.C. I loved doing art in high school, but no one cheered for me. I just kept playing soccer and getting good grades, and that's what they were proudest of."

I don't know if I'm being entirely fair to Dad and Julio, but whenever I think back to the moments where I was excited and on the cusp of taking the next step in studying or making art, I remember being totally deflated by their comments. "You know you have to be really good to make money as a painter, Nina." Or, "You can't study art in college, that's no way to make a living." Or, "Your art is fine as a hobby, but don't count on it for more."

Maybe that was as much my fault for not believing in myself, but if there's no one to encourage you, perseverance is doubly difficult.

"College was rough. I wanted to study art, but that would have been a...a thing, you know? I needed to major in something that could lead to a traditional career. I had a hard time fitting in in college, finding my place. Being bi-racial and raised here in the States is weird sometimes. I look Hispanic, but I can't speak Spanish, I can only cook like one Mexican thing, I didn't have a traditional Mexican upbringing, no *quinceañera* or anything like that. Even though my mom and my uncle are first generation Americans and full Mexican, I'm culturally pretty white. And it's not a huge deal, it's not something I necessarily need to find my identity in, but it always feels like I'm the one puzzle piece that sits a little awkwardly in the puzzle."

I smile to shrug off any pity Cole might be tempted to send my way. My story is mine and I'm proud of it, the good and the bad. I don't need sympathy or pity.

"I struggled to land on something I loved all the way and that loved me back. I've never felt like I found my landing place, but these last two months have made me feel like I'm nearly there. It's not easy, but I love what I'm doing now."

"What did you study in college?"

"Public policy."

"Oh wow, that is...not even close to art."

I laugh as I nod. "I did enjoy learning about government and legislation and policymaking. It can be exciting—a great way to learn how to help make a change. I had this idea I would work towards promoting the arts in schools through policymaking and budgeting. I do have some patriotism in me, maybe not enough to make me join the military, but I do like the idea of influencing change, making things better, helping people through the things I love. Right after college, I got an internship with the House Ways and Means Committee, and it turned into a job that I liked initially, but quickly realized was going to get me nowhere and was going to influence no one."

"That's what you were doing before you came here?"

"Yeah." Taking a deep breath full of ocean air brings cleansing relief. "You know, I don't share my story with many people. Bryce knew a bit, but never the whole thing."

"Because you knew. Deep down, you knew to still be guarded," Cole says softly, looking down at me. His words could sound accusatory, but they don't make me feel that way. Instead, they make me tear up for the past version of myself, the Tia who was with someone she couldn't fully trust.

"I know, because I did it too. I never told...her...what I just told you."

Cole moves closer and his fingers brush a few stray hairs back from my cheek. I haven't cried in weeks, but all my emotions come rushing forward with a vengeance and my lip wobbles when I try to talk, when I try to piece together and verbalize what exactly happened with Bryce.

CHAPTER 19

I START at the beginning and I can see the fault lines already, the warning signs I should have recognized immediately. "Bryce and I met in the House cafeteria; our mutual friend Sutton introduced us. He was the hottest item on Capitol Hill, a rising star. He was quite the conversationalist and he knew how to influence people to get his way, so he was on the golden path to power. I was starstruck from the first moment he made eye contact with me. I felt like I knew all about him from the gossip, but the fact that he looked at *me*...it was different, you know?"

Cole nods.

"I was so flattered. He asked me out a few months later, after weeks of flirting and teasing me. I had waited so long for him to ask that I was dying to say yes. He was kind and attentive. Our first holiday season, we'd only been together like a month, and he took me to see The Nutcracker. He didn't even know it was on my bucket list, and it was so beautiful I cried."

It's cathartic to verbalize the things that I've shoved down the last few months. Even in knowing it was right to leave, even in the relief of all of it being behind me, there's still a tinge of sadness.

"When I was with him, on a date or at an event, I felt like I had a place. It gave me a sense of belonging to be Bryce McFourne's girlfriend, because he was a big deal, and I became a big deal too when I was attached to his name. But he was always subtly asking me to be more or different or less. I never knew what he was going to ask for, if I could be enough for him. I didn't realize it was all about him being in control."

Shame burns my chest. Why did I let myself be so devalued? Why did I let him wear me down like that? Tears prick at my eyes again.

"He laughed at my art and I still thought I could see a future with him. I just kept adapting to his whims. Earlier this year, I thought we were getting to a place where things were good. I felt like we were on an even playing field. Which was stupid of me. Bryce would never let anyone be equal with him."

I press my hands to my cheeks, trying to get them to cool down.

"I should have known that..." I stop mid-sentence to take a breath as I cry. "Ugh, I should have seen it coming. I overheard him on the phone, telling one of his old fraternity buddies that he would never marry me. That his family didn't even know I existed."

"Oh no," Cole says, his voice dropping low and incredulous.

"So, I left. Packed my bags and quit my job and never looked back. I won't be going back to the East Coast ever again. I'm going to be building a new life here. I'm ready to create my own stability, for myself."

I wipe my face as Cole gently puts one arm around me.

"You've been through it," he says. "I don't know what to say. I'm sorry isn't enough."

"It's not anything to be sorry about. It's just life," I say, digging my foot into a mound of sand, letting the damp chill press against my skin. "And I'm not the only one who's been through it. I'm so sorry you lost your dad."

He turns to face me and wraps his arms around me, letting me lean into him at my own pace. I'm scared to let go, to hug him back, worried I'm going to like it too much. He's told me his story and I've shared mine and there's more between us now than ever before, more meaning and respect and understanding.

But I go ahead and hug him.

I wrap my arms around his solid waist and rest my cheek against his sweatshirt. One of his arms drops down to circle my waist, his other hand warm against my back. I let go of everything holding me back and commit all the way, completely hugging him and being held in a way I've never experienced before.

We fit together. He's steady and warm and he holds me like I'm something to be treasured and protected.

"Thank you," I whisper to him.

There's another conversation waiting to happen, where we talk about what it means that he likes me. But for now, this is us meeting each other, soul to soul, heart to heart. Everything about it feels safe, like I'm where I'm supposed to be.

————

ONE WEEK LATER, Cole has passed his final board for his FMF pin and, as promised, shows up at Aunt Mari's house at eight at night for our first portrait session. I could have faked painting him in the dark, but I want everything about this portrait to be authentic, including the lighting. He brings burritos for dinner, the perfect move because I forget to eat when I'm by myself and there's no one cooking food.

Aunt Mari left for her trip earlier in the week, and I love the freedom it gives me to do this portrait on my own, without her comments and ever-watchful eye. I've rearranged things a bit so that I have a bright lamp set up across the dining room from where Cole will sit, and I can leave it like this for this session and the next. I'm hoping to have the confidence to get it done in two sittings so Cole only has to give up two of his evenings.

Céline Dion is playing quietly from a speaker in the kitchen, per Cole's request. He's sitting at the dining table with his notebook, study guide, and an array of pens and highlighters fanned out in front of him. He's wearing his black sweatshirt, USMC in bold red letters across the front, and his forearms rest on the table as he leans forward, looking intently towards the light streaming from the lamp across from him.

So far, he seems content not to revisit his admission of liking me, and since I've now taken on the role of professional portrait painter I'm definitely not going to be the one to bring it up. Compartmentalization is the name of the game, and tonight is about art and art alone.

He's a willing subject, listening to all my cues. I decide I'm going to paint him in three quarter view, with his eyes looking up into the light, his shoulders leaning forward, and his arms and hands braced across his study materials.

"Tilt your head, no, sorry, turn your head towards the light more. There! There we go." I snap a few pictures with my phone to reference later.

"Do I have to stay still like this the whole time?"

"No, we can take breaks. But give me a few minutes or so like this."

"Are you going to do the whole portrait today?"

"Definitely not. I'm just trying to figure out the lighting and shadows, what background I'll do, and then hopefully do a blocking sketch with all the lines."

"How did you learn to do all this? I wouldn't know where to start."

"Art class in high school, YouTube, and a lot of books from the library," I say, focusing on the contrast between Cole's blond hair, freshly cut, and his fair skin. "How often do you get a haircut?" I ask him as I look back and forth from him to my canvas, judging what the scale of the painting will look like.

"Every weekend."

"Seriously?"

"Yeah. Since I opted into wearing a Marine uniform, I abide by Marine regs, which includes getting a skin fade every six to eight days."

It's going to be tricky to create enough contrast to accurately portray his hair in the light. And then the black of the sweatshirt is going to need to be mixed right to not be too cool. It's supposed to be a warm painting, despite the nighttime setting. I'll probably go for a warm, reddish gray background, mixing cadmium yellow and dioxazine purple, and make sure there's plenty of depth between his sweatshirt and the background. His face and head are the focal point, and the real test will be getting his gaze right. His eyes are such a gorgeous brown, nearly hazel, and I need to convey a sense of forward movement and urgency, a drive towards something.

But how? How do I do that?

Negativity and insecurity rush to the forefront of my mind. I am in way over my head. I don't have nearly enough technical skills. It's going to be a miracle if I can pull this off. And what if I can't? What if I show Cole and he hates it?

The first time I showed Bryce a painting of mine, he gave me this sneering, pitying smile with a little chuckle, like I was a cute kindergartner drawing a stick-figure family. After enduring the waterfall of shame that followed, I kept my art to myself—with the added burden of doubt. Was I really not good? Bryce had taste, and he would know, right?

I close my eyes and take a deep breath, pulling in the full scent of the Turpenoid and linseed oil mixture I use to dip my brushes, along with the subtler scent of oil paint.

That was the past. I have to put all that behind me.

"You good?" asks Cole.

"Yeah," I say, keeping my eyes closed, trying to quell my nerves.

"You don't look good."

"This is a big project for me," I admit.

"You'll do great," he says. "I've seen your drawings. I mean, granted, I haven't seen any paintings you've done, but I believe in your artistic abilities. You'll be fine."

"I can't settle for fine this time. I need it to be fantastic, stellar, incredible, amazing."

One more big inhale, one more big exhale.

I open my eyes, pick up my palette and palette knife, and start mixing my background shade and spreading it on the canvas. A blank canvas will get us nowhere, but panic is rising in my chest. I don't know what I'm doing.

Céline Dion is gently singing about being forever thankful, and to my surprise, Cole starts singing along under his breath. My hand pauses in mid-air. When he catches me watching him, he doesn't stop. Instead, he sings louder and gives me a cute grin, leaning into the lyrics with feeling.

"You know all the words to this song?" I ask.

Cole nods. "My mom absolutely adores Céline Dion, so my dad learned all the lyrics to sing along with her. Taught us boys too. We always belted out love ballads on family car rides."

The thought of all the Slaedens singing this makes me smile.

"That is adorable. And very thoughtful of your dad," I say.

"Yeah, he was an awesome husband."

The song changes key, and I go back to focusing on the canvas. I can do this. I just...argh, where has my confidence gone? I am wasting time with all this wavering.

Cole gets up from his seat and comes around the table. He gently takes my palette and palette knife from my hands, sets them on the table, then spins me around while dramatically singing the lyrics.

"What are you doing?"

He pulls me back towards him and starts rocking back and forth, slowly dancing with me in the little space between the dining room and the kitchen, singing every single word of "Because You Loved Me."

"Just breathe," he says. One of his hands settles on the small of my back and he interlaces his other hand through mine as he guides me in a small, swaying circle.

"You can dance? Who are you?" I say with a laugh.

He grins. "My dad would do this whenever my mom had a hard day or was overwhelmed with us boys. Anything remotely romantic, I learned from him."

"That's really special," I whisper as I lean my head on his shoulder.

He goes back to focusing on the lyrics, a hint of extra drama to his singing, not taking it too seriously. I find my shoulders relaxing as we sway.

"We got my pin together, as a team," he says in a low voice. "We're going to do this painting together, and we're going to win the soccer championships as the best midfield team in the world."

"You've got a lot of faith in us," I say, looking at our stuff spread across the table. My palette and palette knife next to his Fleet Marine Force study guide, our passions uniting.

"I do," he says, giving my hand a squeeze. "You're up for this. You can do it."

My heart is demanding that I notice the way Cole reassures me, the way we work together, the way we can read each other. I don't know what to make of it, and I find it frustrating how incredibly thoughtful he is. I really need him to have some disgusting habit—anything to stop me from caring about him more than I should. But...he is so worth caring about. And the time I've spent with him has been my favorite part of being in San Diego.

"You have to listen to the kindest words in your head," Cole says, shifting my thoughts. He's holding me so close, my face nearly against his, his voice in my ear. "Is there someone's voice you can imagine being encouraging to you?"

Yours, Cole.

"Maybe," I say softly.

He spins me again. Calm and peace are settling in my body simply from letting Cole lead us in little circles and spins.

"There's a voice in your head that's good and encouraging, you just have to listen to it. Give it some space to get louder."

I nod. "Say something nice, something positive."

He thinks for a moment, then he murmurs in my ear. "Tia Lopez is my favorite artist."

My knees go weak and my breath shudders as I press my cheek to his. Cole's grip tightens on my waist. I close my eyes, drop my hands to his side, and I end up grabbing his sweatshirt in my fists. That kind of kindness, support, that love...I want that in my life forever. I want to hold on to it and never let go. I press my forehead to his, everything inside of me at war and peace at the same time.

He doesn't move until the song ends, then we wordlessly step away from each other. I don't know how I manage it, but we fall back to our positions as painter and model. My pulse is pounding in my ears and it takes a few minutes for me to be able to focus on the canvas again. I can't look at him, can't meet the look I know will be in his eyes.

Tia Lopez is my favorite artist.

I like him way too much. I like him in a way that puts our hearts in danger. And it does not help to know he likes me too. There's too much at stake here.

And yet...there's a part of me that's ready for the thrill of the roller coaster, the highs and lows of the beginning of something, especially with someone I trust. I don't know what will come of it and it's scary and exciting.

No. I shake my head and finally put my palette knife back into some paint. No, we're not doing that. Neither of us deserve to be taken for a ride. I can't be with him, I can't have him, he is not for me.

CHAPTER 20

THE SAN DIEGO-NORTH Recreational Soccer League championship comes down to penalty kicks. The field is not in great condition which has impacted the game in big and small ways, from me tripping on a big drive, to Anisha wrenching her ankle and hobbling her way through the last few minutes of playing time. Huge patches of missing grass have again turned into mud pits from the overactive sprinklers, and everyone is sporting stain-covered jerseys and shorts. The sun finally comes out, blasting us with heat as we start to organize the rounds of penalty kicks.

The Goal Diggers are in a huddle, all sweaty and breathing hard. Cole runs his hand over his blond buzzcut, sweat spraying into the air. Why is that so attractive? A primitive part of me is slowly being seduced by the sight of his damp jersey clinging to his muscular chest.

"Okay, they're kicking first," says Frank, jutting into my thoughts, reminding me to keep a clear head. "I'm going to do my best on goal, but I'll really need you guys to pull through if I can't catch them all. Let's do this."

We nod, making eye contact with a seriousness I imagine

people take into battle. We're not going down today. Today, we're warriors on the soccer field, laying it all on the line.

"For Mick," whispers Anisha, then louder, "Goal Diggers on three."

"One, two, three, Goal Diggers!"

The opposing team makes every single penalty kick except the last one. Frank is a tank and a beast of a goalie, but today, luck is not on his side.

The goalies switch and we go through our roster. Cole, Luko, Denny, Sarah, Anisha and Frank all sink their shots, and somehow it's down to me. I have to make this goal to win us the championship outright, and to do that, I have to get this ball past The Nemesis, the goalie we lost to in our first scrimmage of the season.

Crap. Crap. Crap.

The team huddles around me with echoes of, "You got this, you got this."

Cole comes in front of me, taking up my whole field of vision.

"Bring it home," he says, giving me a fist bump and a long, lingering look. I nod to him with confidence and head to the line. Forget Mick—I'm winning this for Cole and me.

My nerves are through the roof as I twirl the ball between my palms, place it on the faint white marker, and plan my kick. I'm going to sink a shot in the upper right-hand corner. I could go for the slow, easy cross to the left, but I think it's too predictable.

If I miss...I can't miss.

My heart is pounding. I wave my hand in the air behind me to get some hype going and Sarah starts a low, "Ohhhhhhh," and everyone joins in, growing louder and louder. I stare into The Nemesis's blue eyes and give him a smirk that makes me seem cockier than I feel. I think I've got this, but nothing is for sure until the ball crosses the goal line.

"You got it, Queenie!" shouts Cole.

Step, step, step, plant my left foot, kick through the ball with my right.

Boom.

Goal.

The team erupts in cheers behind me.

A euphoria I've never experienced before sweeps over me, and a roar of victory rips out of my chest. I pull a Brandi Chastain, whipping off my shirt, whirling it over my head, and doing a dramatic victory slide across the mud on my knees.

"Let's go!" I scream, jumping to my feet.

Cole and Denny whip their shirts off and whirl them in the air, then Cole scoops me up around my legs and hoists me up on his shoulder while I pump my fist in the air. My muddy legs are slippery against his sweaty chest, but his arms are strong and sure around me.

He parades me around the field, and everyone is cheering like I just won the World Cup. Our team secured the championship, but the quieter victory for me is that I did something I loved, I saw it through to the end, and I succeeded at it. I'm so freakin' proud. I did that.

By the time Cole sets me down, I'm teary-eyed and holding one hand over my mouth to keep a happy sob from bursting out.

"You good?" Cole shouts, and I nod. He sees my glistening eyes and he pulls me to him in a big hug. I'm hugging his bare, muscular torso and we're both so sweaty, but so happy. Butterflies in my stomach are joining in the pandemonium of celebration, and my endorphins are through the roof. I'm elated and I love that I get to share it with him.

Which is why I do something slightly silly and press a kiss to Cole's chest, right below his collarbone. He pulls back and looks down at me with a surprised grin as I smile sheepishly.

Then his eyes look to my mouth, and a visceral spark passes between us, like electricity crackling in the air before a lightning storm. His head dips and my heart stops. He could kiss me. I'm half terrified, half thrilled, but the terrified part wins out.

I turn my head away.

When I take a glance back at him, his neck is flushed red, but he's not done. He puts his arms around my shoulders and squeezes me tight, then whispers in my ear. "You're amazing. Freakin' proud of you, Tia."

I lock my hands behind his back and hug the breath out of him in reply. "Thanks, Cole."

Anisha catches my eye and arches an eyebrow at me, coming to my side as I separate from Cole.

"Okay, team," shouts Frank. "Shower, clean up, change, we'll meet downtown in front of the bar in an hour and a half." We start to disperse, but Anisha stays next to me.

"This is the part where you can choose to let go and have fun," she whispers to me. "Your first step in letting go of the need to be in control."

"He can't be my forever," I whisper back. "I don't want to mess him up with false hope."

"Then don't promise anything. Relax and enjoy the moment."

———

EVERYTHING IS FINE. My butterflies are fluttering down as I shower, quickly blow-dry my hair straight, and flick on some makeup.

But then I'm faced with the decision of what to wear to the bar. And Anisha's words are echoing in my head.

It's casual, just celebratory drinks. If it weren't for the painting, this would be the last time Cole and I would naturally cross paths. But it's not the last time, so I can wear whatever I'm comfortable with. I won't make it flirty. Cutoffs, a cute white eyelet top with puffy short sleeves, flat sandals, and some gold jewelry should communicate the message, "I'm dressing cute for me, not you."

I think. I hope. I don't know anymore. This weird whirlpool of feelings is messed up, and I want to go back to when Cole and I could walk and talk on the beach as friends.

Do you though?

───────

THE BAR IS PACKED. There's a European soccer game on, broadcasting over multiple screens. It's only in the first few minutes, but raucous cheers and sloshing beer indicate people have been here for a while.

A bachelorette party joins in the surge to grab a table, and Cole meets my eyes through the crowd, immediately coming to my side. He takes my hand, laces his fingers through mine, and tucks our combined fist into the small of his back as we jostle forward. It's a protective gesture that forces me to walk close to him, just behind his shoulder.

There's warmth and a spiced scent of masculine vanilla cologne coming from his black t-shirt. It smells so good, so inviting, I could press my nose to him to inhale deeper. If he caught me, I'd blame it on the crowd. Tempting.

Cole runs his thumb over the back of my hand as he guides us through the crowd, and my heartbeat starts to pick up the pace, pounding in my chest. My eyes flutter closed for half a second and I will him to do something, anything, that's going to counteract his effect on me. A protective man is my weakness.

I should stop letting him do things like hold my hand. Not even Frank and Sarah are holding hands right now. But I don't want to take my hand out of his. I want this, this feeling of being looked after and cared for. And I'm not going to tell myself it's wrong anymore. I can enjoy hand-holding or hugs or whatever and not make it all add up to more than it is. I'm going to let go and stop being so uptight—for now.

"You want a Jack and Coke?" Cole asks, tucking his mouth against my ear so I can hear him over the next roar of cheers. I nod and he gets the attention of the blonde bartender in no time. She's more than happy to sidle over to him and lean close to his neck to hear his order. He quirks a grin at her when she looks up at him from under her eyelashes, and I swear she blushes.

Cole turns around and smiles at me, then scans the crowd around us. My shoulder is jostled as someone else goes to order a drink and Cole's warm hand settles in the small of my back, pulling me closer to him. He smiles down at me, inciting a riot of butterflies. He doesn't even know he's doing it, he's just being Cole, cool and handsome.

When the bartender comes back to hand him two Jack and Cokes, one has a black cocktail napkin and the other has a white napkin with black scribble on it. He hands the one with the white napkin to me, and his free hand settles low on my hip as he steers us towards the corner where the Goal Diggers have commandeered a table.

He's attentive and protective, shouldering our way through the crowd, and I'm very aware of every time he touches me. Which he does a lot. I bite my bottom lip and remind myself to stay cool.

We tuck into a booth, and Cole gets Denny to move out of the way so he can slide in next to me, his jeans pressing into the side of my bare leg.

"Do you want this?" I ask, sliding the napkin towards him. Here's hoping his response will do something to break the unbearable tension and my rising desire.

"What?"

"The bartender gave you her number."

Cole grins and shakes his head at the bar, and my heart drops. Maybe he does want her number. And who am I to stand in the way? We're just friends.

"She's cute," I say, offering a concession.

"Eh," Cole says, taking a long sip of his drink, the ice clinking as it settles.

"C'mon," I tease. This feels more like us, friends again. "Could just be a drink and a kiss."

"We don't do casual," Cole says. "Not anymore. We talked about this."

"*We*? We don't do casual?"

He suddenly swings one arm over the back of the booth and behind my shoulders, heat washing over me. "You know I like you and you're the one who kissed my bare chest today. Don't play with me, especially not the jealousy game."

"I'm not jealous," I scoff, blushing furiously. But he's staring me down like he knows every secret in my head.

"You want me to say if I'd rather kiss her or you?"

"No, that's—"

"You. You every time, Tia. And I'll tell you a secret." He leans forward and whispers in my ear. "I've kissed you in my dreams, and I'm patiently waiting to see if I'll get to do it in real life."

Breath is a luxury, and my heart is running away from me. He's dreamed about me. He's dreamed about kissing me. Cole Slaeden wants to kiss me.

If I thought I wanted just friendship with him, my body and my heart are now informing me I have been sorely mistaken. My lips part as I exhale, and I'm about to grab Cole's fitted shirt and drag him to me. His wide lips are curved ever so slightly, ready to meet mine, if that's what I want. What do I want?

Denny and Luko are at the bar taking shots, and Anisha, Sarah, and Frank are waiting to order at the far corner, leaving Cole and me alone at the table. Everything about this is so tempting. A deep need in me combines with my curiosity. What would happen if I kissed him?

"One kiss," I whisper.

His eyes go dark and his gaze drops to my lips, then back to my eyes, then back to my lips, flirting with me, pulling me closer without even touching me. It'd be just a kiss, it's nothing serious. We're young and we've got our whole lives ahead of us to be patient and plan each move. Who says a kiss is reckless?

It's just a kiss.

I take his chin in my hand, pull him close, and kiss him.

We share a sharp inhale the second our lips press together. Everything about him—the fresh smell of his skin, his hand gripping the inside of my leg just above my knee, his warm mouth against mine —takes over and floods my senses with a thrill. It's only a few seconds long, but it is the most addicting thrill in the world, the kind you get from jumping off a cliff into a deep, refreshing pool on a hot summer day, and you want to keep doing it over and over and over.

Cole lets me have full control over the kiss, but the way his fingers flex against my skin tells me he's fighting to hold back. I bet if I let him kiss me, I wouldn't survive.

Shoot.

I push his face away and stare into his dark and hungry eyes, my whole body humming with awareness and desire. I've never had a kiss that resonated in every cell.

"This could end so badly," I whisper, a warning to myself as much as him.

"Doesn't have to." His voice is a blend of optimism and conviction that I can't share, and his eyes roam over my face like he's waking up and seeing me for the first time.

I glance around to see if anyone else saw us. I'm not ready for anyone else to notice or comment. Whatever that moment of sheer incandescence was, it's for Cole and me.

"Keep it between us?" Cole says.

"Yes, just us," I say, quickly taking a big gulp of my drink. Whew, that's strong.

"Are you going to make me throw pebbles at your window in the dead of night to beg for another secret kiss?" he asks with a wink.

I nearly do a spit-take. "Would you do that?" I ask, grinning as I wipe the corner of my mouth with the back of my hand.

"For you? Anything." There's a glint in his eyes that makes my blood feel like fireworks. I finish the rest of my drink in a few long sips and keep my eyes on him the whole time. His gaze makes me tremble with newfound want. I have no idea what to do or say now.

I could kiss him.

"You want another?" Luko roars across the table, making me jump. He points to my empty glass, and I shake my head. Right, the whole team is here now.

Denny slides in on the other side of Cole. "Check out that score. Geez Louise!"

Frank and Sarah bring over pitchers of beer, and I pour myself some as a distraction from the way Cole's muscular, jean-covered leg keeps brushing up against me as he and Denny start an animated running commentary on the offense's strategy. He doesn't turn towards me again, and when Anisha and Sarah say they're heading to the restrooms, I eagerly slide out the opposite side of the booth and go with them.

As soon as we're ensconced in the tiny bathroom waiting for one of two stalls to open up, Anisha gets distracted texting Mick and Sarah leans into me with a nudge. "I saw that, Lopez."

"What?" I ask, my cheeks betraying me with a blush.

"You and Cole and that hot little kiss you gave him."

"No comment," I reply, shaking my head.

"I get it. The Navy thing is too much to handle. But even I know Cole's not wired for flings. I think you'd both be a lot happier if you didn't mess around."

"Trust me, I'm entirely of the same mindset."

"You guys do have a lot of chemistry. Shame to let it go to waste."

It would be a shame. "Yeah. But I still think we're better off as friends."

"So that was like a 'kiss and get it out of our system' thing?"

"Yeah," I say, way more confidently than I feel. Cole and I still have to get through another portrait session, another chance for us to grow even closer in an intimate setting. I fan my face. I need to remind myself why being a Navy girlfriend would be such a bad thing.

"Is Mick okay?" I ask Anisha.

She startles and locks her phone screen. "Yeah, sorry, what?"

Even with her dark skin, I can tell she's blushing.

"Oh my gosh, are you sending your husband dirty texts right now?" Sarah asks with a grin.

"Whatever," Anisha says, rolling her eyes with a grin. "He started it, he sent me a picture of him in SDBs. I go feral for him in that dress uniform. The double-breasted black jacket, white shirt, black tie, the gold trim on the sleeves—we're so going to have a deployment baby. Mark the day he gets home, my due date will be nine months later."

"Tell me again why I don't want to get with a Navy guy," I say with desperation.

"Girl, you go on with your bad self and get with Cole Slaeden," says Anisha. "You two are good for each other."

"I disagree," says Sarah. "You know Tia doesn't like the Navy life thing."

"Oh, you can do it, Tia. You've got guts, you're brave. That's all it takes. A whole lot of love, some bravery, and a weakness for your man. By the way, Mick says great job on the PKs today."

Anisha goes back to looking at her phone and a part of me is happy for her, but a bigger part of me grows increasingly jealous. Maybe that's a sign—jealousy. I want what she has. I want the flirty texts and knowing who your person is and settling down and having a wedding picture as a lock screen.

Maybe I should download an app, go on some first dates, start meeting some guys. Maybe I should find a way to ease myself away from Cole, to let him move on as well, put some distance between us. If I can't have happily ever after with him, it's time to find someone I can have it with. Maybe I'm ready for that.

I walk back out to the table; Cole's gaze snaps to mine, and I instantly melt. Anisha says I need a whole lot of love, some bravery, and a weakness for my man. I do have a weakness for him now, now that I know what his lips feel like on mine, how his hand feels wrapped around mine or pressed to my skin. I think he's an amazing person, an outstanding guy, but love...I don't know. Bravery? No, I'm running on empty when it comes to bravery.

And nothing changes the fact that I want to kiss Cole again.

CHAPTER 21

CRICKETS ARE CHIRPING in the cooling night air as I open the door for Cole for what should be our last portrait session. For some reason, I'm whispering when I say hi.

"Hi," he whispers back with a knowing grin as he follows me into the house.

"Fancy seeing you here," I say, trying for friendly banter as we both pause next to the kitchen. I will be a professional about this. I will be.

"Where do you want me?" The way he asks, in that velvet whisper with that cute grin, makes my blood heat. We're going to be twelve feet away from each other and yet it feels like I'm choreographing something much more intimate.

"Um, the same place at the dining room table," I reply. Come on, be professional, Tia. "I have everything set up already, and I made really good progress last weekend. I think I should be able to focus on the details of your face and finish up this time. Do you need anything to eat? Some water?"

"No, I'm set."

"Since I'm working on your face, we're going to have to not talk. Can you do that?" I tease.

"Sure." He smiles, settling down in his chair.

"Really?"

"Yes, Tia, really." He chuckles. "I'll set an alarm for when I have to start driving back, and we'll see how far we get."

I remember Lorraine saying if I trust my instincts, I can paint more intuitively, instead of trying to keep every detail perfect. This may be me painting the hot corpsman I have a massive crush on, but I need to set that aside and be Tia Lopez, artist and portrait painter. I take a deep breath and dive in.

―――――

TWO AND A HALF HOURS LATER, I set down my palette. Two and half hours of painting Cole's face, mostly focused on his eyes, but also filling in the details of his lips, his chin, his ear, and his expression. I wanted his eyes to show his determination, but also the hint of weariness that I see in him tonight especially. You can't show courage without showing the cost, the sacrifice. I take a small step back and study it.

"Do you love it?" Cole asks, breaking the silence.

"I do."

It's so good. It looks just like him and I love it. My breath is shaking as I exhale. Holy crap, it's good. In my eyes, the story I'm trying to tell translates into the final portrait and I'm so proud of it.

I'm so drawn in by all the details I've painted. I am dying to run my fingers over his nose, his forehead, his lips and feel them in real life. Feel the warmth and the life that's coming through in the painting, but in flesh and blood. I want to hug the painting, then hug him.

"Can I see it now?" he asks.

I haven't let him look at any part of it in case it turned out horribly and I needed to start over. Plus, a painting in progress never looks right. But this end result...this is everything I ever dreamed of painting.

I nod. "It's done."

I take a big step to the side as he comes over. I want him to have the space to see it without feeling pressured to say anything right away. My heart thumps, and I can't help biting my thumbnail. I want him to love it, but I also want him to be proud of himself, to feel like it's a strong portrait, not tacky or overly sentimental.

Cole comes around and stands in front of the easel, his hands on his hips as his eyes take in the painting. I hold my breath, waiting for the first reaction, a word, a look, a gesture.

The Cole of the portrait has his head turned and looking up into the light. There's a warm darkness all around him, to where the books and notebooks on the table are fading into the darker edges of the painting. But his face is lit up and unbowed, his eyes are determined and focused, his mouth is set with enough of a hint of a smile that you can tell he's eager and motivated for whatever comes next. I figured out how to paint his fade and buzzcut and he looks sharp, even in his USMC hoodie.

The living, breathing Cole laughs, a soft chuckle as he shakes his head. He turns and looks around the living room still shaking his head, his back to the painting, like he can't quite process it all in one moment. It's quiet, the subtle tick of a clock in the living room the only hurried sound.

He comes back around and studies the painting again, taking a step further away, then tilting his head side to side. He finally looks at me, and the lamp light catches a watery shine in his eyes. "Is this how you see me?" he says in a hoarse whisper, pointing to the painting.

"How does it make you feel?" I ask with a soft smile.

He runs his hand over his hair. "I ...don't know. I don't even know how to say it. It's the expression, the way you can tell he—I, I guess—wants this thing that he's working towards, no matter how hard it's going to be. And it's a worthy goal, worth the drive and the purpose. He's...someone to be proud of."

"He's brave," I say gently. "I couldn't have painted you any different, because this is who you are. Yes, Cole, this is exactly how I see you."

In two strides, Cole crosses the space between us and wraps me up in his arms, one low and squeezing around my waist, his other hand pressing my head to his heart. As quickly as he hugs me, he lets go and takes my face in his hands.

"You are incredible," he whispers, his eyes flickering with emotion. "Do you know that? You are incredible."

I want to argue, to remind him that he is equally, if not more, incredible. But instead I grab big fistfuls of his sweatshirt, pull him to me, and tilt my chin up as he drops his mouth to mine.

There's wonder and awe, gratitude and desire in each press of his lips. His hand slips around the back of my head and into my hair as he pulls me closer to him, deepening our kiss with desperation, like he needs more than kissing, he needs *me*.

My hands grip his biceps, matching him kiss for kiss. Feeling wanted like this, desired—it sweeps my feet out from under me and takes me somewhere I've never been before, into a swirl of emotion that goes deeper than the physical relief of kissing him again. My hand slides up the back of his neck and over his short, velvety hair. I kiss him back, unashamedly, with wild abandon.

Being kissed by Cole makes me feel like the entire world was created solely for the ultimate purpose of love, that there is nothing more worthwhile than truly loving and being loved.

His body is sure and strong, and his muscles flex around me as he holds me close, gradually slowing down each press of our lips until his forehead is resting against mine and his chest is rising and falling as we both try to catch our breath.

Cole's alarm blares out, jarring us, bringing a sense of reality back into focus.

"I have to go," Cole whispers.

I'm so breathless, I can only nod and watch him pack up his stuff in a whirlwind.

"Good night," he says, pressing a kiss to my neck that leaves me nearly unable to stand, and then he's gone.

I look over at the easel, at Cole's immortalized face. What have we done?

———

I CAN'T SLEEP. I'm still blushing hours later and rethinking all my life choices. There was a moment where he held me so tight, stole all of my breath in a long kiss, and I lost myself in him. Tia and Cole didn't exist anymore, there was only *us*. I've never known anything like it and all I want is that, over and over and over again. But as the feeling fades in the dawn light, I know that I can't have that, unless I want it all—the good, the bad, and the Navy life.

As I drink my tea on the back patio in the subtle heat of the morning, my phone vibrates with a text from Cole.

COLE

Hi. Will you come to my pinning ceremony? I'm not forgetting about last night, I just wanted to invite you before I forget. It's on Friday, we just found out. Would you want to come?

A thousand conflicting feelings running through my head. Ultimately, I have to smile at the way he's compartmentalized everything.

TIA

Are you sure?

COLE

I really feel like we got the pin together, I couldn't have done it without you. Will you please come? I want you there.

Want is such a powerful word. He wants me there. My heartbeat thrums with *want, want, want.*

> TIA
>
> Okay. What do I wear? Is it like a formal ceremony?

COLE

Not formal.

> TIA
>
> Are jeans okay, or should I wear a casual dress or something nicer?

COLE

Probably the dress option. You coming?

> TIA
>
> I'll come.

COLE

Thank you. I promise we'll talk soon, but we're about to start a meeting. I swear, don't date Navy guys, they're the worst, they're always texting or calling, never showing up in person. So lame.

> TIA
>
> Lol, then explain why you're always down on Crown Island on the weekends. You live over an hour away and there's plenty of beaches and coffee shops between here and Oceanside.

COLE

I said don't date Navy guys, not don't date me. I'm always down there so I have a chance of seeing you and your cute little smile and your pretty brown eyes.

I gasp. Look at him, flirting and making me blush via text.

TIA

I see you trying to flatter me, Cole Slaeden. Why not just ask me to come hang out in La Jolla or something?

COLE

Because then it'd sound like a date and you'd get worried and you'd say no.

TIA

You've got Christiana Josefina María Lopez all figured out.

COLE

Is your full name really Christiana?

TIA

Yeah...

COLE

Holy crap.

TIA

What?

COLE

Nothing. Btw, work is getting wild, so if I don't text or call for a bit, I'm not ghosting you. Meetings about to start, I'll see you Friday.

TIA

Sounds good. See you then.

———

SUMMERTIME MEANS people are traveling and visiting family and Lorraine is no exception. She's spending time with her sister in Michigan, so I have to wait a whole two days and a morning shift at Cafe 22 before I can show her the painting of Cole. I'm giddy as I hang up my apron before leaving work.

"What've you got going on the rest of the day?" asks Jules.

"Oh my gosh, I almost forgot to show you! I finished my painting for the gallery while you were in Portland." I pull up the photo and hold my phone up so she can see it while she stirs an iced latte together.

"Holy crap, girl!" She gasps as she leans in to study it closer. "Oh my gosh, you made him look so hot. Is it bad I kind of have a crush on him now? Oh, Tia, you did an amazing job."

"Thank you," I say with a blush, pocketing my phone. I come around the counter as she delivers the iced latte. "I'm going to go show Lorraine now and see if she'll accept it to go on display at the gallery."

"No doubt she's going to be thrilled," says Jules with a grin.

As soon as I step into the gallery, Lorraine and I give each other a big hug. She's only been gone a few days, but I find I've missed her like a dear friend.

"I've been thinking about you," she says with an emphatic squeeze to my shoulders. "How are you getting on?"

"Well, I think I have something for you." I pull out my phone with shaking hands and everything starts to feel surreal. My limbs feel like they're floating as I tap the photo, then set the phone on the counter in front of her.

Please love it so much.

Lorraine gasps, then grabs my arm, her bangles clacking together. It takes her a good minute to form any words. She picks up the phone and zooms in on different parts, every so often letting out another audible gasp.

"Tia, I am blown away. Oh, it is incredible. I love it! To think of all that you put into this...sweetheart, I am so, so proud of you."

Happiness doesn't begin to describe the elation I feel at Lorraine's praise. Not only that she's impressed with the painting, but she loves it, and she's proud of me.

"Then you'll accept it to the gallery?" I ask, shaking on the inside.

"Absolutely! How much are you going to price it for? Keep in mind I'll keep a small commission."

"Um..." My brain's excited race of happiness is not slowing down to think of something like prices. "I really don't know." Numbers, money, what are they in comparison to love and art?

"Do a thousand," says Lorraine.

"What? No, I couldn't."

"You want someone to come in off the street and buy this masterpiece for two hundred dollars?"

"No, definitely not. Five hundred?" I shrug.

"But it's him," Lorraine says, pointing to Cole's face on my phone. "He's your breakthrough, your muse. Artists get a special touch when they paint something they love, I see it here. He is someone special to you, he holds your heart."

Cole is someone special to me. I don't think either of us holds the other's heart, per say, but there is a part of me that wants to bottle him up and keep him all to myself, to not let him share any laughs, glances, or kisses with anyone else, ever. But there's another, more rational part of me that knows I need to let go, back up, step away.

He holds your heart.

We settle on the price and talk through a few more details, but I keep thinking about what Lorraine said as I walk home.

This feeling of knowing someone and being known on such an intimate level, the trust and peace and friendship combined with the swirling desire and heady passion—now that I've felt what it's like, I want it to have a permanent part in my life. Cole once asked how I'll make a decision about who to commit to in the future and I know my answer. If they make me feel the way I do now, I'll be ready to marry in a heartbeat.

As long as they're not in the military.

CHAPTER 22

I'VE NEVER BEEN to a military ceremony. I have no idea what to expect, I want to do everything right, oh, and Cole is going to be there in uniform. The urge to either throw up or run a mile fights for dominance as nervous energy shoots through my body. I have about twenty minutes before I have to leave. As I slip into a red linen sundress with a square neckline and wide straps, my phone starts vibrating on the bedside table. It's Luko.

"Hey, Luko," I say, breathless.

"Hey, come park at our place and we'll carpool to the cere-mony. It'll be easier to drive you and Carson onto base."

"Carson?"

"Yeah, Cole's brother. We tried to get his whole family to show up and surprise him, but only Carson could come."

"Wait, I'm going to meet his brother?" I start sweating just asking the question.

"Yeah, I could have thought this through better." Luko pauses, like he's now seeing what I'm seeing, in big flashing lights. "Girl Meets Crush's Brother With Zero Warning." He clears his throat. "Actually, no, it's not a big deal. Be cool, Tia. It's not a big deal."

"Not for you!" I nearly shriek.

"Tia. He's chill. You'll like him."

"Luko—"

"See you soon."

After Luko hangs up, I run to the bathroom and press cold water to my face. I don't know what to think about meeting Cole's brother. I did not plan for this, this is a curveball. It takes a lot of deep breaths before I can look at myself in the mirror. But as I pull my hair into a small half-ponytail and re-blow-dry my bangs, swipe on some eyeliner, mascara, and lipgloss, I remind myself this is not about me. Nothing about this day is about me—it's about celebrating Cole and his accomplishment. I can do that.

———

THE GUYS ARE ALREADY SITTING in Luko's 4Runner with the windows down by the time I park, and surprisingly they're both in uniform. Denny is wearing a lighter green digital camouflage with flecks of black and tan and a brown ball cap with his ship's name on it, while Luko is in a flight suit and squarish-framed aviators.

"Hey, don't you have to wear a cover?" I ask him as I slide into the back seat.

"I can't believe you know that word," he says with a laugh. "You don't have to wear covers in cars."

"He's not wearing it out of respect for the female population," Denny chimes in, texting in the passenger seat. "They'd all faint if they caught sight of him in his full pilot glory."

A deep chuckle rumbles next to me. I jump, barely suppressing a squeak of surprise, and turn, making eye contact with a guy in the back seat. "Oh my goodness, I did not realize you were there."

"Hi, I'm Carson," he says, holding his hand out. He has gray-blue eyes, and unlike Cole, he has dark hair that curls above his collar and dips down across his forehead, and a trim beard that covers his jawline. He's dressed in dark boots, dark jeans, and a gray dress shirt that nearly blends into the seats of the car.

"Tia," I reply, shaking his hand. "You look nothing like your brother."

Carson laughs, and it's another subdued, deep chuckle. "Didn't he tell you? He got the recessive gene. Cillian and I both have dark hair, but Cole sticks out like a true golden boy. I used to tell him he's adopted."

Carson shows me the lock screen on his phone, and it's a picture of him with his arm around his mom, a darling short woman with a smile so big it nearly makes her eyes disappear and a long gray braid over her shoulder. Cole stands on the other side, with a tall dark-haired guy who looks fresh out of high school next to him. That must be Cillian.

"Wow, Cole really does look adopted," I say with a laugh.

"He's the perfect one for your painting though." When my eyes widen in surprise, Carson adds, "Oh, yeah, he told me all about that. How did it turn out?"

"Well..." I don't want to brag, but I'm also not going to sell myself short. It's a darn good painting. I pull out my phone and find the photo I took of the finished portrait on the easel. "It hasn't gone on display yet, so this is an exclusive sneak peek. Here it is," I say, passing Carson my phone.

He takes a long look at it, zooming in on different parts, then slowly says, "Wow. That is so good."

"Can I see? We haven't seen it yet," says Denny, turning towards the back seat. Carson passes the phone to him, and Denny goes wide-eyed. "Holy crap, Tia."

"Show me," says Luko. Denny holds up the phone for him, and Luko sneaks glances at it as he drives. "Damn."

My face is hot as Denny hands the phone back to me. "I'm lucky Cole agreed to do it. It was a big time commitment, and I know how busy he is." Absolutely no need to mention how much kissing ensued when it was done. I wonder if Cole's the kind of guy that would talk to his older brother about his crushes or keep them to himself.

"You're selling it, right?" asks Carson. "For how much?"

"A grand," I say, wrinkling my nose. It sounds like an exorbitant amount, but it's worth it.

Carson nods. "I mean, painting a picture like that can't be easy. And you have to support yourself, you know. How does someone buy it? Would it be listed online?"

"Yeah, it'll be on the gallery's website, and in the front window of the gallery on the island."

"It's so good. I feel like it shows Cole for who he is, the one who jumped out of the nest and forged his own path. We're proud of him and what he does."

"What do you do? Cole's told me a little about you guys and your mom, but he never mentioned it."

"I'm always doing something different every time I talk to him," he says with a rueful laugh. "Right now, I'm head of security for a local resort. Really, I do whatever brings in cash and keeps me local."

Denny turns in his seat to talk to Carson. "Are you ever going to go after that forest ranger job you were talking about?"

"Probably not," Carson replies, shaking his head.

"Dude, why not?"

"Just...you know. Family and all."

Denny shrugs, but his expression tells me there's more to this story.

"Cole also told me you helped him study for his pin," Carson says, deftly switching the focus back to me.

The rest of the drive, we talk about how much material Cole and I covered, how hard he studied, and how significant the pin is. Carson is easy to talk to, more reserved than Cole, but he shows genuine interest as we converse. He asks about me with some specific questions, and I give him a rough outline of my life. It doesn't feel like Cole's told him a lot about me, just enough for Carson to pick up some hints. I get the sense he planned each topic of conversation ahead of time, like checkpoints along a road map, and I find it endearing.

Once we park on base and hop out of the car, Luko unzips the upper pocket of his flight suit and hands something to Carson. "Here's the pin you're going to put on Cole's uniform. Usually, a parent or a spouse or mentor will do it, but I think Cole would want it to be you."

It's the famed FMF pin. I peer over Carson's arm as he studies it. "Pretty cool," he says, passing it to me so I can get a closer look.

Cole and I didn't go over the details of the pin design while we were studying, but I googled it later. It's a silver pin about three inches long and an inch wide. An eagle, a globe, and an anchor are layered together in the middle over two crossed rifles. A banner underneath says "Fleet Marine Force" and to each side is a design that is supposed to depict rolling waves folding over onto the sand.

It doesn't feel all that significant in my hand, but what it represents bears a lot of weight. When Cole wears this on his uniform, it shows the world that not only is he a Navy sailor, he is an asset to the Marine Corps. He'll join a long line of corpsmen known as "Devil Docs," and who knows what heroic deeds he might do in the future? Lots of corpsmen have been awarded the Medal of Honor.

I hand the pin back to Carson, and we all follow Denny as he scans the buildings around us. "Sand brown everywhere, and the number system makes no sense," he grumbles.

"There," says Luko, jutting his chin across the way to where some Marines in hunter green digital camouflage are starting to congregate.

I don't know what I thought a pinning ceremony would look like, but I didn't think it'd be something that takes place on a small courtyard of concrete outside a tan cinder block building. A picnic table sits off to one side across from a roped-off smoking area. I think we may be the only onlookers today.

A few dozen Marines in uniform have gathered, and I try to

pick Cole out of the crowd. As we approach, a female with a perfect bun at the base of her cover marches out of the building with two other Marines. She yells a series of commands that has the milling group, including Cole, forming straight lines and rows, their hands fisted by their hips, eyes staring straight ahead, covers low on their foreheads.

"Stand off to the side with us," Luko says quietly.

"See him?" Denny whispers, pointing to the end of the back row as Luko takes a quick picture before putting his phone away.

It's hard to identify Cole in the sea of uniforms, but the second I do, my heart squeezes with pride.

He is fierce. He's not looking to the right or left, his eyes are focused straight ahead, and his neck is thick as he bunches his shoulders and stands at attention. His face is set and stoic. His folded sleeves make his arms look like they're made of iron.

It takes my breath away, seeing him in uniform, in this context. He's not showing up to a basic office and working a nine to five, he's a trained corpsman with a black belt and a dedication to something bigger than himself. Each of these Marines have chosen to serve in the military with the knowledge that they might be called on to sacrifice everything and Cole is a part of that warrior ethos.

"Personnel to be awarded, front and center, march," the female Marine calls out. Luko and Denny straighten up and stand at attention.

Cole leads a row of corpsman, turning on a dime and marching with precise steps and sharp corners to stand in front of the Marines in charge. His face doesn't flinch or show any emotion. If he sees Carson and me, he doesn't give any indication. He salutes the Marines in charge.

"Know ye all by these present that HM2 Cole Slaeden..." the female Marine shouts in a commanding voice, listing other names in addition to Cole's and making other statements, but it's hard to catch every word, "...has qualified as an enlisted Fleet Marine Force warfare specialist, Ground Combat Element."

A thrill goes through me. That's the coolest string of words I've ever heard. He did that.

"Personnel to pin the awardees, center, march."

Carson pulls the silver FMF pin out of his pocket and goes to stand square in front of Cole. He whispers a few words, brother to brother, as he fastens the pin on Cole's uniform.

It's official now.

I'm beaming ear to ear, but tears are threatening to fall, and my breath is shaking with overwhelming pride. This is so cool, so special, so unique. How am I even here, witnessing this? Nearly three months ago, I was in D.C., never dreaming anything like this would be part of my life. Now I'm getting emotional because this Navy guy that I'm so proud of and trying hard not to fall for is receiving a new pin for his uniform. Life is wild.

Cole and Carson give each other a tight nod, and Carson comes back to stand with us. The Marines in charge each shake Cole's hand and the last one presents him with his award certificate. I'm so intent on watching Cole's face that I may be the only one who sees his chin wobble.

Don't cry, don't cry, don't cry, don't cry.

Cole and the other corpsmen march back to their row, and the Marine in charge gives the command, "At ease!" then finally, "Fall out!"

Cole turns towards us to see all four of us standing in a row— Luko, Denny, Carson, me—grinning our hearts out.

He goes right to Carson and falls into his arms. He stays there for a long time, his back shaking as he quietly cries. Carson squeezes him tight and slaps his shoulders a few times. "Dad is so proud, buddy," he says to his brother.

I wipe away a few tears of my own.

"Dude," Cole says, sniffling with a smile as he finally backs out of the embrace. "I was so shocked to see you."

Carson grins. "When Luko called me, I knew I couldn't miss it for the world. Mom and Cillian wish they could be here."

"Thanks, man. I'm so happy you're here. I've been wanting to call you all week and ask you to come, but I know you don't like to leave work, and the whole ceremony lasted like three minutes, I mean—"

"Cole." Carson stops him mid-sentence. "We're proud of you."

Cole lets out a deep exhale, rubbing his hand across his face. His boots make him taller, and with his cover riding low over his eyes, he looks tough and handsome, and the traces of tears only make him more manly. I'm a little obsessed with him right now. Not a little. A lot.

When he finally turns to me, his eyes fixate on mine, and my stomach flips. My voice is shy as I say, "Congratulations."

He doesn't say anything, just wraps his arms around my waist and picks me up off my feet, taking my breath away, until we're eye to eye, nearly nose to nose.

"Dude, no PDA in uniform," Luko mutters.

"I'll break the rules for her," Cole replies, his brown eyes smiling back at me. He holds me in the air and then dips his head down to the curve between my neck and shoulder, his lips pressed against my skin for a long moment.

"Thank you, Tia. For everything," he whispers in my ear.

If he puts me down right now, I'm going to melt into a puddle. I keep hold of him, inhaling the scents of the laundered, waxed cotton of his collar, the natural smell of his skin, and a lingering hint of cologne. I cling to him.

"I'm so proud of you, Cole," I whisper back. I memorize everything about this moment. The pride, the love, the feel of his arms around me, his intoxicating scent.

This could be my future, if I was braver, and a little stronger.

He sets me down, but his hand lingers on the small of my back, warm and attractively possessive. It's only been since Sunday that I've seen him, but things have changed since then. Major life-altering things.

"Oh, I didn't get a chance to tell you yet! Our painting was accepted by the gallery."

"That's my girl," Cole says, with a grin that lights up his whole face. He looks around at where the other Marines are gathered, then he presses a quick kiss to my cheek. "Never doubted you."

Forget butterflies, forget melting into a puddle, forget any gentle analogy for being beset by feelings. Cole is like a glacier, slow but forceful, carving a new path through the mountains of my defenses, straight to my heart.

"Congrats, bro," says Luko, coming over and giving Cole a big, back-slapping embrace. "I love you." Denny joins in, and they make it a big three-man hug.

Carson asks someone to take a picture of us, and Cole gently steers me to stand alongside him, his arm around my waist. It's a small, attentive detail, but it means the world, and it leaves me with one life-altering thought.

Maybe this would all be worth it.

Later, Carson texts me the picture of all of us and I make it my lock screen background.

CHAPTER 23

Now that Cole's portrait is dry enough to not smudge, it's time for my triumphal march to deliver the painting to the gallery. I'm terrified of something happening on the trip over, but the whole goal was for it to hang proudly for others to see my name and my work. And I need it out of the house, otherwise I'll never stop replaying our kiss every time I walk past it. It makes my knees go weak and I just...don't want weakness right now.

To the gallery it goes, with four little cardboard triangle wedges at the corners that hold up a big piece of foam core and keep it from touching the paint, and tape gently holding everything in place.

When Lorraine opens the back loading door for me, I exhale with a sigh of relief. We made it.

"I am dying, Tia, dying to see it in person," she says as we go through the shipping and staging room to the front of the gallery.

"Close your eyes. I want to take off all the wrapping before you see it."

Lorraine groans but covers her eyes and faces the wall as I remove the piece of foam core covering the front of the canvas. My heart squeezes as I look at Cole again. It really is so good, but only because he is so, so handsome.

A thrill runs down my spine, and I can't keep the smile off my face as I say, "Now open."

Lorraine's jaw is on the floor and her eyes are wide as saucers. "I am speechless, absolutely stunned. Wow, Tia. What are you going to call it?"

"I don't know yet," I say. "Can you call a painting 'Hottest Corpsman in the Navy' or does it have to be something more serious?"

Lorraine chuckles as the bell at the front door gently chimes.

"Lorraine," I hear in a sing-song voice. A blonde woman in a white silk blouse, trendy jeans, and fine gold jewelry is standing inside the door to the gallery with her arms held out, anticipating a hug. Lorraine goes wide-eyed and with a shriek belying her age, she runs to the woman and they hug, swaying side to side and giggling.

"When did you get back?" asks Lorraine, leading the woman towards the register.

"Just two days ago. I've been swamped, though. Our household goods were delivered an hour after we got the keys to the house. It's been a seamless PCS and—get this—nothing is broken. Can you imagine? Pigs are flying somewhere. Only took over twenty years."

Lorraine laughs, then turns the woman towards me. "Tia, this is Heather Montclair, one of my best Navy wife friends in the world. Our husbands went to the Naval Academy together decades ago, and we were inseparable during their first few tours. Of course, her husband is admiral of the fleet now, and mine is quietly enjoying his early dementia care home."

Heather gives her an extra squeeze as they both tear up for a moment.

"Tia, nice to meet you," she says.

Lorraine continues making the introductions. "Tia is a...

protégé of mine. She lives on the island and is trying her hand at painting portraits for the first time."

"Oh, lovely! That's perfect!" Heather's enthusiasm is already making me smile. "Have you finished one yet?"

"Okay, look at this," says Lorraine, and before I can protest, she brings her in front of Cole's portrait.

Heather gasps, her hands pressed to her chest. "No. That is stunning. Oh, my word."

"Right?" says Lorraine.

I feel like I'm close to reaching full capacity of congratulations and acknowledgment of my art, something I never dreamed was possible. To feel my own pride in the painting is one thing, but to hear Cole, Lorraine, and Heather responding so viscerally to it is nearly overwhelming.

"Is he a Marine?" asks Heather, pointing to the USMC on Cole's sweatshirt.

"He's a greenside corpsman," I answer.

A sigh escapes me and Heather shoots me the most knowing look I've ever gotten from a stranger. With a small smile and prolonged eye contact, it feels like she sees everything hurtling me forward towards Cole—love, respect, pride, devotion, courage— and the inverse that's holding me back—fear, anxiety, the desire for independence.

"What an incredible painting," she says. "You know Lorraine got into painting when our husbands left on their first deployment together. It was her lifeline."

"And yours was DIY projects. Furniture flips, re-tiling bathrooms, gardening."

Heather starts laughing, "Remember the raised garden bed debacle?"

Lorraine rolls her eyes then turns to me. "Heather was trying to use a tree saw to cut a two-by-four, and she literally came over with her hand wrapped in a tea towel soaked in blood, and casually said, 'Lorraine, are you busy right now? Cause if you're not, could we go to the hospital?'"

I grimace at the mental image, but they're laughing so hard, like it's clearly a good memory for them.

Heather chuckles to herself. "And you weren't without incident, Miss Deer Murderer."

"That was a freak accident," Lorraine protests. "He jumped on my car out of nowhere! I was just trying to go see Glenn in San Diego for his port call."

"Going to San Diego for a port call was never incident-free."

"What about the Singapore trip?"

"We don't talk about the Singapore trip," argues Lorraine.

Heather leans over to me with a conspiratorial whisper. "We were supposed to meet our husbands in Singapore, but at the last minute, the fleet canceled port calls, so Lorraine and I wandered solo around the city. We got food poisoning our first night and then flew back home to face another three months of deployment all weak and exhausted."

Lorraine rolls her eyes. "The worst. The pre-baby days were something else, that's for sure. How is Ellis, by the way?"

I try to keep my face neutral, but my ears prick at the name Ellis. The Ellis? Denny's Ellis?

"Oh, you know. Strong and brave, trying to find her way in the world."

"Wouldn't expect anything less from a daughter of yours."

"Isn't that the truth. You know why they call military kids 'brats,' right? Because they're brave, resilient, adaptable, and tough. That's my Ellis," says Heather. "I'm so sorry, am I interrupting you two? Were you in the middle of something?"

Lorraine waves away her apology. "Tia and I are getting ready to hang her painting and list it online, but we're in no rush."

"No problem. I'll let you get back to it. I just wanted to come get a hug and say hi. Lorraine, lunch sometime soon, please? Tia, it was so good to meet you." She leans forward with a conspiratorial whisper. "If the guy in your painting is one of the good ones—because not all Navy men are—I hope it works out for you two." She gives me a wink and then waltzes out of the gallery with a wave.

As soon as the door closes behind her, I turn to Lorraine, my hands on my hips. "How did I not know you were a Navy wife?"

"It never came up," says Lorraine, looking at something on the computer through her reading glasses. "I'm happy to talk about it if you want. Do you want to talk about it?" She takes off her glasses and faces me. "And does this"—she points to Cole's painting—"have something to do with it?"

I ignore her last question. "How are you so easy-going about it? I mean, some of the things you were talking about sounded awful. You could write an article about why not to be a military spouse."

"I'll give you the short version," Lorraine says, pushing her glasses to the top of her head. "I loved Glenn, and I trusted him to take care of me. I had my fears, but I believed him with all my heart when he promised he would take care of me. He promised he would not quit when things got tough, he would never emotionally abandon me when I was stressed and scared, and he would refuse to give up the romance and love that brought us together in the first place."

"And did he? Take care of you, keep those promises?"

"He sure did. He is the best choice I ever made. We had so many adventures, so many memories." She smiles to herself. "I'm the treasurer of those memories now and they are priceless. I'm happy and content with the life we lived, I couldn't have asked for more."

"But you would move and he was gone and his job changed all the time and you had to go wherever he went and sometimes it was dangerous—"

"And the only thing you can count on is you can't count on anything?"

"Exactly! I can't do that. I want a life with stability and security and solid community."

"You want to live in Toledo, Ohio and marry a banker who works a nine-to-five job and live in one house for seven decades?"

"Well...okay, not exactly," I say, catching on to the teasing glint in her eye and laughing alongside her. "Although the one house thing sounds nice."

"Honey, I think you have a much bigger life ahead of you than what you imagine for yourself. Dream big and be ready for the adventure. And you want to know the best part? No matter where you go, or what you do, art will always be there too."

Her words ring in my ears all the way home.

———

AUNT MARI KNOCKS on my door bright and early a few days later, waking me up alongside the sunshine slipping through the blinds. *"Buenos días, te preparé un jugo, mija,"* she says in a sing-song voice as she comes in. She sets a blue glass of juice on the nightstand and perches on the edge of my bed in her white eyelet muumuu, a red silk scarf tied around her hair.

I smile. "This is a nice way to wake up."

"Christiana, let's go get some breakfast together. It's been too long."

As I flash back through the last few weeks, I realize there is a lot I haven't had a chance to share with her. She just got back from her trip and we've been a bit like ships passing in the night.

She hasn't even seen the painting yet. I want to be sure I'm there when she sees it for the first time. I sip the fresh-squeezed orange juice and eye her over the edge of the glass. *"Claro que sí. But there's something I want to show you first."*

———

AUNT MARI gamely follows me across Crown Island and down the main avenue, but when we pass Cafe 22, she hesitates for a moment.

"It's not something at work," I say, motioning for her to keep following me.

We're almost to the gallery, only one more curve in the sidewalk. This is my last chance to turn around, to do this another time, but we keep walking. Is she going to notice my name first or last? Will she put the pieces together? What will her reaction be? Breathing is important. If I stop breathing, I'll pass out, and then I'll miss Aunt Mari's reaction.

There's a glare on the glass, so you can't see the portrait right away, but once we can, I slow to a stop in front of it, taking it in, in all its glory.

Hi, Cole.

We've texted a few times since his pinning ceremony and he keeps saying he wants to talk, but work has been rough on him, something about him being on-call for different commands. I'm trying to be understanding, but I miss being teammates, our walks on the beach, and seeing him in person. I want to hug him and watch him smile and catch his sideways glances at me.

But right now, at this moment, I'm most concerned about what Aunt Mari thinks about my painting. I turn so I can watch her face gradually form into a look of shocking realization. The sign next to the painting says, "'Courage' by Christiana Lopez."

She studies the painting, and I watch her eyes rove from top to bottom then back up again. It takes her a few nerve-wracking minutes—and it takes everything in me to keep my mouth shut and wait for her to say something first.

"Christiana," she finally says. Her tone is full of awe, wonder, amazement, and it floods me with relief. "*Tú pintaste esto, ¿no?*"

"*Sí,* when you were gone on your trip."

She grabs onto my arm and squeezes. "Is this...him? The friend you told me about?" she asks in a slow voice.

"Yes," I reply.

"*Me encanta.*"

A grin takes over my whole face. She loves it. She can't stop staring at it.

"I didn't know you could do this," she says. "You have a gift, *mija.*"

As her words sink in, I turn away to brush off the happy tears running down my face. Years and years and years of feeling like I was walking against the wind when it came to my family and art, only to paint something that makes my heart happy and have it turn into the validation I so desperately needed. *I have a gift.*

"What is it?" Aunt Mari asks as she notices my emotion.

"You've never said that about my art," I say, laughing and crying at the same time. "You and Dad and Julio, you've never encouraged me. You know..."

She sighs as she finally turns to me. "*Lo siento.*" She hugs me as I start sobbing there in the middle of the sidewalk.

People walk by holding ice cream and carrying boogie boards, beach towels slung around their necks, while I shed tears of hurt beginning to heal, longing being met. Hearing Aunt Mari say I have a gift, that she is sorry for not encouraging me, has brought on a release that gives way to a sense of victory and accomplishment, but I scarcely believe it's real.

But it is real. I did it and I'll keep doing it. I struggled and I pushed through the hard times, and they led me to this moment.

"If someone wants to buy the painting, how much is it?" asks Aunt Mari.

"It's a thousand dollars," I say, taking a step back and wiping my face.

Aunt Mari sucks in a shocked breath, then swears in Spanish. "*En serio?*"

I nod in reply, and she starts laughing. "Is someone going to pay a thousand dollars for that?"

"Maybe. I kind of hope not. But they might, and that could be the start of something for me."

"*Mija...*" she says with wonder. "What a life you have in front of you." She squeezes my hand. "Invite him to dinner. No excuses. He will come or you will leave my house."

Okay, then.

We decide to go to Cafe 22 for breakfast sandwiches and iced tea and Aunt Mari can't stop talking about the painting and art and all the possibilities for a future career as a painter or portrait artist. The back patio tables are available and we sit under a bright blue umbrella and finally, finally, I don't have to hold back or make excuses or let any sort of shame creep in. I feel fulfilled and confident. This is what I was born to do.

CHAPTER 24

ANOTHER DAY GOES by and Cole still doesn't call. I could overthink everything for hours on end, but instead I text Anisha, and we decide to treat ourselves and go out to dinner for the night. I patently refuse to discuss anything about Cole and Anisha doesn't push me on it. By the end of the night, I decide I'm fine.

Then I dream about him finding me in a crowded bar, pulling me against him, and pressing his lips to my collarbone. I wake up missing him even more. I've never missed someone like this.

When I first went to college, I missed the familiarity of home and Dad and Julio. I would call Dad on the way to class and try to catch him on his lunch break at the mechanic's garage, but over time those calls became less and less frequent. Every so often, I would think of home with fondness and love. But I wouldn't miss it in the way that made my breath catch or my heart squeeze, the way I miss Cole. It's strange to feel how someone could have a hold on me like this. He's just a person, but it's also like half of me is missing and I don't know if it's a feeling I can shake.

I try focusing on my own plan, figuring out my next steps. I sit down at the mini desk in my art studio and start apartment hunting, something both accessible and overwhelming in the modern age. I flip through multiple browser tabs trying to figure out if I'm looking at the same listing but with different photos. It's a cute little one-bedroom place with a decent-sized living room. I think it could accommodate a studio set-up in one corner.

I'll need to pick up some more shifts at the coffee shop, or sell a bunch of paintings. It's going to make a dent in my savings to cover the deposit, first month's rent, and whatever furniture I need.

It's time, though. I've had a breakthrough with my art while being here at Aunt Mari's. Her home has been a start-up incubator for me, but now I need to make my dreams of being on my own happen. I need my own place.

But moving off the island would mean I can't walk to work anymore. I'd have to find a car too. Or I could look at a downtown apartment. Then I could take the ferry across the bay to the island and ride a bike to work or something. I need to think this through.

Maybe I should stay here for longer.

No, bravery means making more than one gutsy decision. I didn't leave D.C. and come all the way here only to become complacent and a bit cowardly again. I came here to build a life for myself, which requires a repeated response of bravery each time I make a decision. I snap my laptop closed and rest my face in my hand with a sigh. I pick up my phone and head to my room, draping myself across the bed with the intent of browsing Instagram. Instead, the Goal Diggers group chat has a notification from Frank.

FRANK

Team pictures finally got figured out, take a look.

My hands leap to immediately zoom in on the picture and see our faces closer. Cole and I are standing next to each other, and we secretly decided to smile when Frank specifically told us not to. The rest of the team have stoic, serious expressions verging on frowns, and then Cole and I are standing together with our arms at our sides with big toothy grins. I smile and want to cry at the same time.

As if he knows, Cole's name suddenly fills my screen with an incoming phone call.

"Hi!" I shout as soon as it connects. "Hi! How are you?"

"Hey, Queenie, how are you?" he says, his voice strained and tired.

"I'm good. How are you? You don't sound good."

"I think I'm getting sick. Ironic for the corpsman to get sick, right?"

"Oh, no, I'm sorry. Can I FaceTime you?" I need to see his face. Something feels off and I know if I saw his face, I could see how serious it is.

"I would if I had the strength to hold the phone up. Right now, I'm lying down on my bed, and the phone's resting on my chest, on speaker."

"That doesn't sound good. You should rest, then."

"I will." He goes quiet, and I stay on the line with him, listening for anything and everything. "I woke up this morning promising I was going to call you and we could finally talk about that kiss, but then something happened." He sighs. "I still just wanted to talk to you."

"What's wrong, *osito*?" I ask. I am flooded with an overwhelming need to comfort him. I know he's a strong, powerful, grown man with responsibilities and capabilities, but that's exactly the kind of man who needs someone to hold him in a hug after a long day.

"What did you say?"

"*Osito*?"

"Yeah, what is that?"

"It just came out," I say with a light laugh. "It's a term of endearment in Spanish, it means 'little bear.'"

"Is that your nickname for me now? It's cute, I like hearing you say it. Say it again?"

"*Osito,* what's going on?"

"This job really sucks sometimes," he says finally.

"What makes you say that?"

"Just...I have to be in a million places at once, doing ten things at a time. Some of my leadership...they're demanding, but like irrationally demanding. I'm trying to balance a lot, and sometimes it's too much." He exhales, and it's loud, like wind in my ear. "And I just want to be with you. I'm stressed and tired and...I had a close call today."

Oh, no. Alarm bells go off in my head. "You had a close call? Cole, what happened? Are you okay?"

"No, not me, one of my Marines. She started out today rough, came into sick call at the aid station, and I had a gut instinct something was really bad with her. But my senior doc thought she should push through it and kept her with the unit to go on a ruck. It's like a long marching hike. Anyways, I argued for a bit with him and he cussed me out for thinking I knew better than him. We were on the ruck when she started getting dizzy, then she passed out. I was taking her back to the aid station when she started getting incoherent and I realized she was actually in really, really bad shape. I made the call to rush her to the ER. She has rhabdomyolysis, ended up in the early stages of renal failure. They said if she had come in later, she might have died."

"Oh my gosh, Cole," I exhale.

"I've never really had that before, held someone's life in my hands like that. When the hospital corpsman called and started giving me the report, my heart stopped. You know I've never been in combat, haven't had to deal with any serious injuries. This was the first time it felt real. Life and death, you know."

"Cole...you did all you could."

"Yeah," he says, his voice a rough whisper.

"How are you feeling about it?"

"I don't know. Kind of scared. Relieved, in a way, but also scared that it was so close to going the other way."

"You did the right thing, you did nothing but the right thing."

"No, I should have done the right thing sooner. I should have just taken her without arguing with my senior doc. I'm supposed to be committed to the health of my Marines, not being afraid of my leadership."

"She's going to be okay, right?"

"Yeah, she's tough, a real badass, and the recovery prognosis is solid. I'm sure she'll be kicking and screaming to get back to the unit. It's all...I don't know. Now I'm doubting myself. I'm sure I'm going to get reamed anyway."

"I'm sure there are lots of other first responders who have gone through similar experiences."

"Mmhmm."

If I was there, I would want to crawl into his bed next to him and hold his hand and softly run my fingers over his hair and do my best to soothe him. But right now all I can offer is words of affirmation. "I'm really proud of you, Cole."

"Don't be, there's nothing to be proud of today."

"Yes, there is. You were in a tough situation, but you saved someone's life in the end. You have a caring heart, you want to help others, and you're only human. No one expects you to be flawless."

"I expect myself to be."

"Let it go, *osito*. It's over and done, there's no use imagining a different outcome or beating yourself up. Get some rest and know that tomorrow is a new day. A Marine is going to be okay because you took care of her, and you need to be proud of yourself for doing the right thing."

The line goes quiet, and I hear a sniffle from somewhere far away. Now I'm tearing up and sniffling, wanting so badly to comfort him. "I wish I could hug you. How come you live in the barracks and not out in town like Denny and Luko?"

He clears his throat, "I'm enlisted and they're officers. They get different privileges and more pay, more basic allowance for housing. If I'm married, or make E-5 here soon, I'll be able to get my own place if I want to."

"Oh...gotcha."

He goes quiet again. "My body is exhausted but my brain is awake."

I try to think of something light to distract him with. "By the way, my great aunt wants you to come to dinner. I took her to see the painting. She said either you come or she's going to kick me out of the house."

He laughs. "What'd she say, about the painting?"

"All the best things. She loved it, said I have a gift."

"Oh, I'm so happy. I'm so proud of you, you do have a gift. I'll definitely come to dinner, just have to check the calendar and I'll text you to pick a date."

"You really don't mind?"

"I want to."

He yawns, the deep exhale of air across the phone sounding like a wind storm. "I need to sleep, but I can't get my brain to chill."

I know what he needs. I pull up "The Day is Done" by my dear Henry Wadsworth Longfellow and start in the middle.

> *...Come, read to me some poem,*
> *some simple and heartfelt lay,*
> *that shall soothe this restless feeling,*
> *and banish the thoughts of day.*

"What is that?" Cole asks.

"It's a poem, by my favorite poet. Close your eyes and listen."

> *Not from the grand old masters,*
> *not from the bards sublime,*

whose distant footsteps echo
through the corridors of Time.

For, like strains of martial music,
their mighty thoughts suggest
life's endless toil and endeavor;
and tonight I long for rest.

At each break in the stanzas, I pause to hear if he's still listening. I hear rustling through the phone, like a pillow or blanket being moved.

Read from some humbler poet,
whose songs gushed from his heart,
as showers from the clouds of summer,
or tears from the eyelids start;

Who, through long days of labor,
and nights devoid of ease,
still heard in his soul
the music of wonderful melodies.

It's a very short poem and there's still three stanzas to go, but Cole's breathing drops heavier and deeper with each word. Mission accomplished. I whisper one more bit of the poem.

Such songs have power to quiet
the restless pulse of care,
and come like the benediction
that follows after prayer...

"Goodnight, Cole."

———

THE NEXT MORNING I wake up late to see a text from Cole from the wee hours of the morning.

> COLE
>
> Got called to augment to a unit in the field, so I'll be out of cell reception until I text again. Thank you for last night, I love the sound of your voice. I miss you.

I miss him. Desperately. There's another text from Denny inviting the team to come over for another Mario party and it reminds me of when Cole saw my sketchbook for the first time. I try to escape any further reminders of Cole and decide to head to the beach for a walk and some brainstorming. Which reminds me of all the times Cole and I have talked about life and love on the beach. There's no escaping him.

As I head towards the tide, my phone vibrates in my back pocket and I pull it out and answer.

"This is Tia."

"It's Lorraine, dear. Congratulations are in order, I've just sold your painting. Full asking price."

My heart stops, and I go numb. "Wh-what? It sold? To whom?"

"An anonymous buyer, through the website."

That's not what I wanted to hear. I rub my chest, trying to mitigate the aching behind my ribs.

"Okay, wow. Thanks for letting me know."

"You should be proud of yourself, Tia."

"Thanks, Lorraine. See you soon," I barely manage to choke out.

I hang up and slide my phone back in my hoodie, drag my sleeves over my hands, and burst into tears, dropping to a ball above the damp edge of the tide. My beautiful Cole painting, all my hard work, immortalized in painting form, gone. No longer ours.

I knew the painting would sell—I would have to be a fool to hope it wouldn't. But it doesn't mean as much to anyone in the world as it does to me. And it was just taken from me, by some impersonal art collector. Maybe Lorraine can give me their contact info and I can talk them out of it. Or I can take out a small loan and buy it back from them. Why was I ever dumb enough to let Lorraine hang it for sale in the gallery?

No, it's gone. And I can't get it back. My heart feels torn in two, and I know it's only a painting, but it's one of the most beautiful memories I have. From slow dancing with Cole in the kitchen, to the kiss we shared when it was done, to the gorgeous finished product—it's all changed my life.

I want to call Cole immediately, but he doesn't have cell reception. Of course. This is Murphy's Law, right? When I need his comfort the most, he's gone. I sob into my sleeves.

Eventually, the tide comes up and licks at my feet, like a nudge from the ocean telling me it'll be okay. I know it will, worse things have happened. My painting sold and that's a major accomplishment, one worth celebrating.

I wipe my face, go grab a burrito from Mexican Take Out and a Squirt from the liquor store, and take a seat on the dune where Cole and I talked about true love. My painting may be gone, but the small seed of hope I've been nurturing is not. There is always tomorrow, another day, another painting, another promise of love and beauty.

CHAPTER 25

COLE

Just got back, I'm dying to see you. Can I come to dinner tomorrow? Kinda early, like 5 or so?

TIA

YES! Definitely! I'm so happy you're back.

COLE

A week away from you is ridiculous. Okay, cool, see you tomorrow.

———

I'VE SPENT most of the afternoon observing Aunt Mari in the kitchen as she prepares the food for dinner tonight. She's been teaching me as we go through the steps to make chile rellenos and enchiladas, but also relegating me to chopping onions and jalapeños for salsa fresca.

After a long shower and a few spritzes of floral perfume, I'm tying the belt of my sleeveless denim jumpsuit and making sure my gold earrings are secure when I hear Cole's Camaro outside. My nervous anticipation rockets sky-high. I quickly run to the front porch as he parks along the curb to make sure we get a moment before Aunt Mari arrives on the scene.

As he gets out of the Camaro and strides up the sidewalk, my heart squeezes, taking in the sight of him—flip flops, khaki shorts, a powder-blue polo shirt that perfectly displays his tan muscles, a fresh haircut, and a massive black eye.

"Cole!" I exclaim, running to meet him halfway up the sidewalk, my fingers flying up to hover over his left eye. His eyelid and the skin around it is various shades of purple, with a handful of stitches running under his eyebrow. "What happened?"

"Oh, yeah," he says, pointing to his eye and blushing. "It's kind of stupid. Promise you won't judge me?"

"Of course not," I say, putting a hand on his shoulder while my eyes roam over his injury. The stitches are prominent, and the skin there is angry and red.

"I was playing NVG soccer, using the monocle we look through for night vision. I was thinking about you and got distracted. The depth perception is really bad on night vision goggles and next thing I know, someone ran into me and hit the monocle." He winces as he gingerly taps around the wound with one finger. "Popped my eyebrow open and doc stitched me up right there in the field. I may get a bad scar, our docs aren't known for being great plastic surgeons."

"*Osito*," I say, trying to scold him while smiling.

"Do you hate it? My eyebrow scar-to-be?"

"No, not even a little bit," I admit.

He grins, all cute and devilish and kissable, and wraps his hands around my waist, pulling me closer. My arms instinctively go around his neck as he gives me a long, tight squeeze, the kind of hug you give when you don't ever want it to end. Butterflies fill my body as I lean into him. He feels incredible, all strength and firm muscle against my curves.

"Hi, Queenie. I missed you," he whispers, sending shivers across my skin.

"Missed you too."

He lets me go in stages, first loosening his upper arms, then dropping his hands to drape around my waist, then taking my hand in his. I think about tilting my chin towards him to ask for a kiss, but Aunt Mari is going to realize he's here any moment now.

"You ready for this?" I ask.

"Yeah, I'm actually pretty excited."

"Do you speak any Spanish?" I think to ask before we walk in.

"Yeah, I'm super fluent," he says, running his hand over his hair.

"You are?!" Is there anything this guy can't do? Is he real? Is he a simulation?

"No, I was being sarcastic," he says nervously.

"I was about to say—"

The door flies open, and Aunt Mari is standing there in all her cooking glory: colorful apron, dish towel tucked in the waist, and a wooden spoon in hand—red with what I guess is enchilada sauce.

"*Hola, ¿cómo estás?*" she says, half greeting, half challenge. She looks Cole over with an appraising, then appreciative eye.

"Aunt Mari, this is Cole. Cole, this is my great aunt Marisol or Aunt Mari."

"*Mucho gusto*," says Cole.

Aunt Mari beams and I look at him in awe.

"Okay, I started learning some Spanish recently," he says with a blush.

"Come in, come in," says Aunt Mari

"Overachiever," I whisper as we squeeze through the door frame together, his low laugh rumbling through me.

The house smells of onions and spice, and a mariachi band plays through the speaker in the corner of the kitchen. Cole and I sit on the bar stools at the island, surveying the spread of dishes.

Aunt Mari has made chiles rellenos, enchiladas, rice, and home-made salsa—all my favorites.

"Cole, how did you meet Christiana?" asks Aunt Mari as she takes out some wine glasses.

"Well, we met playing soccer," Cole answers. "Then Tia was helping me study. And now we like to...go for walks on the beach sometimes?" He looks at me with a grimace of panic and I shrug and nod reassuringly. That is what we do, it's not like we're hiding anything.

Aunt Mari chuckles and says to me in blatant English, "You have this man and you go for a walk?"

I shoot her a wide-eyed look that begs her to stop any and all suggestive comments. I glance over at Cole and catch him hiding a grin behind his hand.

My dad embarrassed me plenty of times when I was growing up—in front of friends, in front of boys I liked. But I always wondered what my mom would have done in the same circumstances, if she would have been cool, or if she would have been as embarrassing as my dad—or even worse.

Aunt Mari is now seemingly bent on giving me the full experience, so if I ever felt like I was missing out, she's making up for it. I've tuned out of the conversation for a moment, and when I tune back in, Aunt Mari is asking Cole if he makes good money, and he's explaining the Navy pay system based on rank and how much he makes each paycheck. Like, actual numbers. Great—just when I thought this couldn't get more embarrassing.

"You want wine?" she asks.

"No thank you," Cole says politely. I shake my head. The last thing I need right now is alcohol.

Aunt Mari shrugs. "I'm going to have some wine."

She goes around the corner to her wine rack in the front entrance, and I take the chance to put my hand on Cole's knee.

"I'm so sorry if she's getting too personal."

He smiles at me and puts his hand over mine. "It's fine. Actually, I love it. You know me—I'll talk about anything, anywhere, anytime. I chat up this beautiful midfielder on my soccer team about random stuff all the time."

"Oh, you think I'm beautiful?" I tease back.

"Mmhmm," he says, and his eyes drop down to my smile, his wide pink lips reflexively mirroring mine.

"Okay, I'll open this wine and then we'll eat," Aunt Mari announces, and we back away from each other. "Cole...Cole, you have another name, a middle name? Something more Spanish?"

"My middle name is Stephen," Cole offers.

"*Perfecto, Esteban* then. Can you take this to the table?" She hands him the dish of enchiladas, which he obligingly takes to the dining room.

"Aunt Mari, his name is Cole," I say to her in a stage whisper.

"Oh, let me have this, Christiana," she whispers back with a twinkle in her eyes. "He's a good boy. He's not offended."

"Can you not call him *Esteban* the whole night?" I plead.

"I make no promises," she says, grabbing her wine glass and leading the way to the dining room.

I take the seat next to Cole on the left-hand side of the table, and Aunt Mari sits at the head. He reaches under the table and rests his hand on my leg for a moment. The warmth of his palm is comforting, along with the reassuring weight of his hand.

This is all okay. He's okay. I can relax.

Aunt Mari tones down her eccentric great aunt performance a bit as we fill our plates, and I find myself enjoying her interactions with Cole. He's so warm and friendly, I can tell Aunt Mari is quickly joining Team Cole, despite all her warnings about the Navy men around Crown Island.

Cole has the gift of conversation, and he asks Aunt Mari about her life, learning for himself about her and Uncle Gustavo, how they came to live on Crown Island, and a bit about our expansive family tree.

Aunt Mari reciprocates and asks about Cole's job and why he

chose it. I'm proud of the way his character and altruism gently shine through as he tells his story.

All through our dinner conversation, he includes me by asking questions and looking me in the eye. I smile and nod and contribute, all the while content to have him physically near, to hear his laugh in person, to watch the sides of his eyes crinkle when he smiles.

"Your family is in California?" Aunt Mari asks Cole, when we've all pushed our plates away.

"My mom and my two brothers live near Bearstone Lake. My dad passed away very suddenly a few years ago." I reach for his hand where it rests on his leg and squeeze it. He squeezes back.

"I'm sorry to hear that," Aunt Mari says, and her voice conveys how much she means it. "It's been hard for you?"

Cole nods, not able to say anything for a moment.

"Are you the oldest boy?"

"No, I'm a middle child."

"Ah, you're a good son."

Cole shrugs, and I squeeze his hand again to let him know I agree.

"What makes you interested in my Christiana?" she asks, switching the conversation with no warning. I nearly spit out my water.

Cole laughs, with a hint of nervousness. "Um, well, she's obviously beautiful. She's a strong woman, but she can also be kind and gentle. She's smart. Life hasn't always been kind to her, but she keeps going, and she's not one to complain. I mean, there's tons of things I could say, I could keep going all night. And I feel like the more I get to know her, the more I learn about how special she is."

I'm panicking, shooting pleading looks to Aunt Mari to shut this down. Hearing praise about myself has always made me uncomfortable, but this is over-the-top. It's too much. But of course, instead of bailing me out, Aunt Mari throws me into the ring.

"And what do *you* see in *him*?" she says. I have to take another sip of water before I can continue. What do I like about Cole? An infinite number of little things, but how can I match what he said?

"He's nice, polite, kind," I say slowly. I'm butchering this. "I appreciate his honesty and openness. He genuinely cares about people. He's not...dumb."

"Thank you," Cole chimes in laughing.

"I'm so sorry," I say, laughing along with him. What is wrong with me? "Let me try again. Um, he's strong, determined, caring, smart, thoughtful. He doesn't take everything too seriously, just the right things."

Aunt Mari laughs at my feeble attempts to explain the draw Cole has for me.

"*Corazón*, the boy is handsome, I mean *qué guapo*, and he has a beautiful heart, and he loves his family and he works hard and he takes care of people who are hurt."

"Well, yeah, I was going to say all those things too," I add. "Oh, and I like that he's protective and willing to take a stand about things he believes in. Like not harassing people while ordering coffee."

"I do believe in that," Cole says with a chuckle.

Saying all of this out loud in front of someone, a witness, makes it more real. I like him, who he is, what he stands for, his character and values. I admire him and I'm attracted to him.

Something is shifting between us. I find myself focusing on Cole's brown eyes. There's a rope being looped around our hearts, pulling them together, like pulling a boat back into its slip in the harbor.

Aunt Mari chuckles to herself and pours another glass of wine. "Okay, now we see how good you are at washing dishes. I'll let you two be alone, stay as long as you'd like, *Esteban*. Christiana, rest well." Cole stands and thanks her for dinner, and she gives him *besos.* Then she leans over my chair and whispers in my ear, "I like him for you," before kissing my cheek goodnight and sauntering down the hall.

And then it's Cole and me, alone. He leans his elbow on the table and rests his head in his hand, staring at me with a cute, dopey smile. I copy it and stare him down. Then his smile shifts and unmistakable desire fills his eyes.

I haven't kissed him in weeks and I never thought I would be so desperate for a kiss. I want him to make his move just as much as he does. I drop my eyes to his lips, watching them curve into a hint of a rakish grin. I could lean closer, make it a bit easier.

Cole slaps a hand on the table and stands. "Right, kitchen isn't going to clean itself, and I feel like Aunt Mari won't give me her stamp of approval until I conquer it."

He grabs the plates and silverware off the table and carries them off to the kitchen while I nearly tip out of my seat as he leaves me hanging. What a freakin' tease.

"Sit back, I'll take care of these," Cole says from the kitchen.

Well, I'm not going to sit here by myself. I make my way to the kitchen, bringing the other dishes and our two glasses to the sink for Cole to wash.

I take a seat on a barstool, a perfect vantage point to oversee Cole's dishwashing skills. He's obviously not new to kitchen duty and will make short work of everything. Maybe even shorter, if properly motivated. I watch him scrub the rice pot, and his upper arms look like they're putting in a lot of effort.

"Are you flexing?" I ask.

"No," he says emphatically, his neck and face turning bright red.

"You are!" I say in triumph, then wave him off. "You're already hot. You don't need to overdo it."

His hands pause in the soapy water. "You think I'm hot?"

I roll my eyes, but my cheeks are flaming, giving me away.

"Why are the dishes multiplying?" he grumbles in frustration, scrubbing vigorously.

"What do you think of my great aunt?" I ask.

He smiles, his face softening. "I think she's great. She's funny and confident. I never know what she's going to say next."

"You don't mind her calling you *Esteban*?"

Cole laughs. "No, that was hilarious. Don't tell Denny, though, he loves to latch on to nicknames."

"What about Luko?"

"You know Luko isn't his real name, right?"

"Really?"

Cole shakes his head as he rinses off the plates and loads them in the dishwasher.

"It's just a nickname."

"What's his real name?"

"It's Russian, it's spelled v-a-d-i-m, pronounced vah-DEEM."

"Vadim? Wait, Denny called him the Russian bear. Is he really Russian?"

Cole nods. "He's first generation American, I think. His parents were political refugees."

"Wow, interesting."

Not even half as interesting as the prospect of kissing Cole. Luko's immigration history has nothing on the anticipation building in my body with each dish Cole cleans and sets in the drying rack or dishwasher.

I can see he's going to run out of space in the drying rack, so I come around the island and take the towel off the oven door. Cole passes a serving bowl to me and I start drying. It's still warm from the hot water he used to rinse it off. I'm about to put it back in the cabinet when a warm hand gently encircles my elbow, takes the bowl, and sets it on the counter.

Cole looms over me, guiding me backwards until I'm pressed against the counter. His broad chest takes up my whole field of vision, and when I remember to inhale, his cologne makes my senses go taut with anticipation.

He raises his hands to cup my face and tilt my chin up, then looks into my eyes for seconds that seem like hours. I don't care if I drown in the depths of his brown eyes. There are thoughts swirling in my head about *us*. I want that feeling again, the sense of lostness and oneness that I can only get from kissing him. It's been too long.

His gaze drops from my eyes, he steps closer, and finally he kisses me, gentle, sweet and precious. His lips are impossibly soft and smooth. My hands drift to his waist, then up and over his muscular shoulders to the back of his neck, and I pull him towards me. He is very kind, very respectful, but I need more.

"Kiss me," I murmur, "the way you've dreamed of."

He breaks.

Cole wraps me up in his arms, pressing a deep, furious kiss to my mouth. My entire being melts into him, welcoming the smoldering desire behind each sweep of his lips over mine. His hands move up the back of my head, his fingers pushing into my hair as he pulls me to him, closer, closer, ever closer. He tastes my mouth, and my head swims, my knees wobble.

His hands drop to tighten on my waist, and in one quick motion I'm on the counter, wrapping my legs around him. I kiss him back with breathless wonder. When his lips dip behind my ear and press under my jaw, I run my palms over his velveteen hair, dizzy with the newness, the force, the heat, the want. I think I may lose all sense of time and space.

I thought I understood the definition of an amazing kiss, but Cole is showing me I've only begun to explore what it means to be thoroughly kissed. He will wreck me forever. How can anything else compare to being held, cherished, and so thoroughly kissed I can feel it in my soul? Kissing Cole, being kissed by him, is ruination.

He lifts his head for a moment, just enough to look into my

eyes. His pupils are massive black circles, and his chest is rising and falling like he's run a marathon. My heart is racing, my skin is flushed, my lips are tingling.

Us. The euphoria I'll crave forever.

He takes a small step back and I slide off the counter to follow him, his gaze heavy on me. This thing between us—the chemistry, the desire, the passion, whatever was the connection between us up to this point—it's all becoming uncontrollable. It has a momentum of its own.

Cole hooks his fingers in the front pockets of my jumpsuit, pulling me flush against him. He presses his lips to my temple.

"You're it for me," he whispers in a deep, rough voice, trailing heated kisses down to my neck. "Be with me. Be mine."

His words snap me out of the moment and make the lights feel too bright. I pull away from him. The kitchen that was a raging inferno a moment ago is now too cold.

"What do you mean?" My voice is hoarse and hushed.

A tremor runs through him, his arms still locked around my waist.

"Tia, I..."

The instant his expression floods with fear, I put my hands on either side of his face.

"What is it? Why do you look scared?"

"We need to talk," he says with a heavy exhale, pressing his forehead to mine. He laces his fingers through mine and walks us to the front door, a resigned determination in his steps.

"Where are we going?"

"To the beach," he says over his shoulder. "I have some news."

My stomach drops.

CHAPTER 26

W E G O O U T onto the front porch and I close the door behind us.

"What's your news?"

Cole clears his throat, shoves his hands in his pockets, then looks me in the eye. "I just got TDY orders I was not expecting."

"What's T-D-Y?" I ask.

"Temporary Duty. I'm going to do trauma training for seven weeks at a hospital in Raleigh, North Carolina. I leave at the end of the month."

I cross my arms and nod, studying a particularly red geranium bloom as I process his announcement. So this is it, the Navy's curveball, the variable we couldn't account for, the thing outside of our control. In some ways it's a relief to hear it's not worse. He's not deploying, he's not going to a combat zone, he's not leaving forever. But in other ways, it feels like it could be the beginning of the end for us, the point where we start to drift apart. Maybe that's why he said what he did.

Be with me. Be mine.

I shake my head and exhale. "Okay, that's not the worst news in the world. What's trauma training?"

"I'll be at a Level One trauma center, learning how to deal with critical injuries. It's part school, part hands-on learning." I watch him run his hands over his hair and his next breath has notes of frustration in it.

"That sounds right for you," I say, cautiously. "Why do I feel like you're angry about it?"

"Because I have to be away from you for seven weeks. After... that," he says, pointing back to the house, his face flushed.

I nod. "It's only seven weeks, Cole. What's seven weeks between friends?"

I'm the worst liar in the world and seven weeks is a terribly long time.

"Can we just stop trying to pretend about the whole friend thing?" Cole says with a groan. "We are more than friends. We can be boyfriend and girlfriend or dating or anything other than this stupid, odd limbo, and we don't have to promise each other marriage and a baby carriage."

I bite my lip, unable to form any sort of rebuttal.

"Let's talk, let's get it all out in the open, let's go to the beach—"

"Cole, I—"

"Come on, Tia. Let's figure this out. I don't care if we need to argue or fight about it, I just want to have an honest conversation. You can be angry, you can be truthful, whatever, but I'm tired of this in-between. I know what I want and you need to tell me what you want."

I would never say this to him or anyone else, but he's hotter when he's a little grumpy and passionate about something.

"Okay," I say with a nod. My walls are firmly in place, and there is nothing Cole can do to topple my resolve. It can't hurt to talk about it.

"Good," says Cole. "Let's go." He takes my hand and confidently leads me down the sidewalk.

"Wait, I don't have shoes on," I protest. Before I know what's happening, Cole has scooped me up in his arms. "What are you doing?" I squeal. He does the same move he did when I had the stingray injury, maneuvering me onto his back, my legs around his waist, my arms around his neck. He carries me down the sidewalk, past all the white mansions, the field, across the street, past the dunes and boulders of the seawall, until he can set my feet down in the sand.

The sun is dipping lower, and the golden hour is beginning. There's a subtle chill in the air, a promise that the heat of the day is going to cool off soon. Cole instinctively starts moving towards the water.

"It's a beautiful night," he says, breaking the ice.

"It really is."

If I sound anything less than calm, cool, and collected, it's because I've been content to drown in the depths of *us*, and Cole, thanks to the Navy's newest TDY assignment, is now dragging *us* to the surface, forcing *us* to take a breath of reality.

"When we talked about the future, a few months ago," he says, "you said you don't want to date around, you only want to date the guy that will eventually be your husband." I nod as he continues, "And when I said I liked you a few weeks later, you said the Navy thing was holding you back. But then we kissed. Not just once, we've...really kissed. So, I guess I'm wondering, have you changed your mind at all?"

I study our feet pressing into the sand as we walk side by side. "I love that you love your job. I love what you do. I literally could not be more proud of you. But I've talked to Anisha and Lorraine, and it...everything I would go through, in support of you, sounds so hard."

"I'm not going to be in the Navy forever. It's a short season in the grand scheme of things. Sure, there'll be a few moves, some time apart, stressful assignments, but it's all stuff I know you're strong enough to get through."

My self-deprecating laugh comes out like a scoff. "We like to think we're strong enough, but what happens when we're not?

Where does it leave me if I can't handle it?" Crushed—that's where it would leave me. I shrug my shoulders in frustration. "It's not fair. Like, no part of this is fair. I can't stop thinking about you, can't stop thinking about how you kiss me. I want it to happen again every second of every day. I genuinely think you are the best guy I have ever met. I like you so, so much. I truly...I would say more if I thought it would help."

Cole has hope in his eyes, a smile about to erupt.

"But it's so not cool that if I want a future with you, I have to give up"—I hold up my fingers and tick off all the reasons that come to mind—"my job, my family, my community, the places that are familiar to me, my support system, my sense of security. I have to give up all of that and blindly follow wherever the Navy sends you into a wildly unknown future. I hate unfairness, I hate imbalances, and every time I turn it over in my head, I come up with the same answer—it's totally unfair to ask a woman or a man to commit to the lifestyle of a military significant other."

"Okay, but you could say the same thing for baseball wives or oil rig wives or any number of careers where one person has to follow the other. It's not unique to the military."

"And all those jobs would be deal-breakers for me too."

He shakes his head, and keeps trying to frown, then wincing as it pulls at his eyebrow injury. "Cole, everything I've heard and seen makes it seem like I would have to make myself and my needs smaller to accommodate your job and the needs of the Navy. How is that any different from what I just went through with my crappy ex?"

Cole goes wide-eyed. "It's not like that. If you'd have to be anything less than your fullest self, I would say goodbye right now. But I know there's give and take and negotiations and compromise, where each person gives up something not out of compulsion, but out of love."

"I don't know what that's like. I've never had that, Cole. Forgive me for assuming the worst in an effort to protect myself from getting hurt again. All I've known is guys who take sacrifice for granted."

"That's not me!"

There—his spark is turning into a flame, and when he speaks it's not because of anger directed at me, it's because he's fighting for something he believes in. The frustration between us is palpable, but it doesn't scare me. I know we're arguing, but the way Cole argues is almost respectful. He's not making it personal or attacking me, he's attacking the obstacles between us. I can't remember the last time I've felt so safe in an argument.

"I agree," he says, "it is unfair if someone asks you to commit to that and takes your sacrifices for granted. But that's not love. If you are with someone in the military, they should be looking out for you, making sure they're there for you as much as they can be, whether you're together or apart. They should make it clear that they love you and are grateful for you and they see what you're going through."

"I get that, but there's no guarantees."

"Okay, let's stop talking in abstracts. Talk about us, okay? I would guarantee it, Tia. Tell me honestly, what do you think it would look like for you and me?"

"I told you, I'd be jerked around the country, following you and being lonely in new places."

He shakes his head and nearly growls. "You're talking like I wouldn't even be there. You wouldn't have to give up art to date me or even marry me, Tia. Or life in California, for that matter. There's so much that would stay the same. And sure, if we end up together, the honest expectation is that we would have to move from time to time and deal with some crappy situations when we're apart, but just because my career has to be prioritized does not mean it's more important. It's because of the whole idea of 'service to country over self,' not because I personally want to drag you around and make your life miserable. I would want for us to have a happy life together."

I roll my eyes. "A happy life? Okay, go ahead and tell me about your pie-in-the-sky, sunshine-and-rainbows version."

"You want to know what I want? I want you. I want us. I want you to never stop painting. I want you by my side when the going gets tough. I want to support you and encourage you when you doubt yourself. I want to hear you saying you're proud of me and I want to tell you every day that you're my favorite artist. And we can do that no matter where we are in the world, in Fort Huachuca, Arizona or Norfolk, Virginia or Sasebo, Japan."

"Those are three wildly different locations," I mutter, swallowing against the lump in my throat.

"There's two approaches to Navy life," he says, toning down the conversation. "There's the adventure path or the stability path. And we could make a choice together about how we want to do it. If we choose stability, I could request San Diego duty stations as many times in a row as I can. We could try our hardest to be here for 8 years or so."

"But I wouldn't want to hold you back from having an adventure. Isn't that the old phrase? 'Join the Navy, See the World'?"

"Again, we would talk about it. We would figure out the best path forward for us. I would never expect you to be with me under the assumption that I'd be the sole decision-maker."

"You can't guarantee anything, Cole. Eventually something would happen that you'd have no control over, and we'd have to suck it up and deal with it."

"And we would deal with it, together!" He runs a hand over his hair in frustration and stares out at the ocean. "You cannot control life and not everything has to be all bad or all good, Tia. Navy life is not all bad or all good. It's normal for things to be mostly good and a little hard. Or to find a moment of something good in the midst of something difficult."

He's not wrong, and I know it. I exhale and uncross my arms. My mindset is a "hope for the best, prepare for the worst" way of thinking. It's anticipating getting the rug pulled out from under me, so I'm not surprised when it finally happens.

"It's all so...scary. What happens when it all goes to crap?"

"We don't run away. We fight like hell together until it gets better. We buckle down and figure out where things went wrong —and then make it right."

I couldn't have asked for a more reassuring answer. It's all the right words. There's a part of me that's ready to throw away all my concerns and dive into life with Cole. But there's another part of me that says I need to hold out, to be careful. It's okay to take it slow.

"Ugh, that all sounds so...healthy," I say, toeing at the sand, my emotions threatening to get the better of me and spill over into tears.

Cole huffs a laugh. "It's love, Tia. Real love." He puts an arm around me, gathering me to him in the crook of his elbow. "We made a pact to never settle for less and I'm going to hold you to it. You deserve every good and healthy thing." He presses a kiss to my hair. "Okay? You hear me?"

I nod, leaning into him, my mind still a raging inferno of counterpoints and further arguments about why this is a bad idea and how the life of being with Cole is not what I want for my life.

But my heart, my soul, wants to let him win. Forever.

We stay like that for a while, me tucked against Cole, his arms around me. I watch the waves and the gulls and the clouds rolling in as the sun still peeks over the horizon on its way down. I can hear Cole's heartbeat, and in everything he's said I can hear the heartbeat of his character behind his words. He doesn't ask for anything other than me believing I deserve every good and healthy thing.

He raises his phone and gives me enough time to softly smile before he takes a selfie. My heart squeezes when I see the photo.

"I can see it. It could be so easy," I whisper. "I want to believe that it would be happy and lovely."

Cole stops breathing for a moment. Eventually, he gradually exhales and tries to recover his voice, but there's a tiny shake in it. "We don't have to have some big, grand master plan. We don't have to know the end from the beginning. We can just try."

He's right. My soul aches with how right he is.

"I still don't know..." I say, biting back tears. I'm tormenting the both of us the longer this goes on. I'm the one holding us back. "I'm sorry," I whisper to him, shame welling up in my chest. "I'm sorry, it's my fault—"

"Hey, hey, no. Stop." He tilts my chin up to look into my eyes, passion flaring in his gaze. "What I said in the kitchen was on me, I got ahead of us. But we're not going to start regretting anything."

I nod, and his hand curls under my jaw. "I'm leaving in less than a month, let's just give this a shot until then, take it one day at a time. Okay?"

A little less than a month, one day at a time.

A girl in a blue dress and braided pigtails runs by, dragging a kite behind her. She yells for her mom to hurry up because the sun is going down, completely oblivious to the fact that a desperately serious conversation is taking place between the two adults standing a few yards down the beach.

I smile to myself. Maybe I'm taking this all too seriously. What if I gave it a shot, started experiencing some of the ups and downs of Navy life for myself and, shocker, it isn't all that bad?

"Okay," I whisper in agreement. "One day at a time."

CHAPTER 27

I'M in the middle of another long, slow shift at Cafe 22, at the end of a slump of a week. As different school districts start the school year and summer is about to make way for fall, the busy lines are dying down.

It's giving me too much time to think.

Since Cole came to dinner and we talked on the beach, I haven't been able to sleep well. I lie in bed staring up at the ceiling and trying to figure out how I could have all the love in the world for him and none of the bravery to back it up. I stay awake all night wondering how I can grow in courage, if I even can get to a point where I would willingly say yes to being with him. Is it possible?

I shake my head and pull out my phone to banish my incessant thoughts about Cole. I need to think about the next steps for my portfolio and I'm curious to see what other portrait artist's collections look like. I head to Instagram, where the algorithm has been feeding me some gorgeous art.

I head to my explore page where I'm accosted by an unexpected, familiar pair of faces. Sutton posted a picture of her and Bryce at a fundraising event for Congressman X. Bryce is standing tall in a dark suit and a red polka dot tie with a smirk on his face. Sutton has her arms around his waist, her lips on his cheek, and one heeled foot in the air. The caption says "Glow-up."

I snort-laugh.

I could be jealous. I could let my insecurities get the better of me. I could leave a scathing comment like, "Enjoy dating the devil."

But I just feel sorry for them. My hypothetical comment turns into something more like, "I hope you know how to sign up for therapy." Or even, "I hope you find your version of happiness." Maybe Sutton will fix Bryce, or she'll be happy to constantly fold herself into a pretzel to fit his ever-shifting idea of who she should be. Whatever happens, I have no part in it.

I have to admit it stings the longer I think about it, my ex-roommate getting together with my ex-boyfriend, but not as much as I thought it would. I'm so far removed from that life, so much happier, so much more fulfilled, it feels like another century, another timeline.

A text from Cole flashes at the top of my screen and I tap on it.

COLE

> Super last minute, but I want to go home for
> the weekend to see my family before I head to
> HMTT, and I'd love for you to meet them.
> Would you want to come along? What do you
> think? It's not anything serious, just a chance
> for you to meet them. You've already met
> Carson and he's the most serious.

A rush of emotions overwhelms me, right as I have to take an order for a couple and their toddler. I can barely see through my teary eyes to tap all the right buttons on the iPad. Cole would *love* for me to meet his family. He wants me to come with him. As soon as I'm done, I text him back.

TIA

This weekend, like tomorrow?

I don't have work for the next three days, it's the perfect window of time to go somewhere with him. But to meet his family?

COLE

Yeah, tomorrow. Does that work?

He's leaving in less than three weeks, I want to soak up as much time with him as I can, he's met Aunt Mari, I've met Carson, he says it's not serious...and a road trip in the Camaro? I answer before I overthink it.

TIA

Yeah, I'm definitely in.

COLE

Oh, cool. I'd really love that. You want me to come down there tonight and we can talk about the plan?

TIA

I mean, if you're not too tired, I'd love to see you.

COLE

Me too. I need a hug.

TIA

Same. See you tonight.

———

AUNT MARI GOES to bed early, way before Cole finally gets off work, showers, and ends up on the front porch in work-out shorts and a long-sleeved t-shirt. His tired smile lights up when I open the door, wearing linen lounge pants and a tank top.

"Hey," he says, coming in and toeing off his shoes. He gives me a very endearing side hug, pressing a kiss to my head, then a quick series of kisses to my lips. He's quiet, and his arm drapes heavy across my shoulders as we stand in the entryway.

"Hi," I say, leaning into him, supporting him as he leans on me. "Missed you."

"Missed you too."

I squeeze my arms around his waist. "You okay?"

His eyes are bloodshot and he shakes his head. Oh, poor guy.

"Are you hungry?"

"No, I stopped and got a burger on the drive down."

"You want anything from the kitchen? I can make you tea or hot chocolate."

"Tea sounds good."

He follows me into the kitchen and sits at the counter as I fill the electric kettle and turn it on. "What's on your mind, *osito*?" I ask him gently.

He sighs and drags his hands down his face. "There's a lot of drama at work. To be honest, I don't really want to be going to HMTT, and I said something about it and now my senior doc is chewing me out for it any chance he gets. It's not that I don't want to do the training, it's just...I want to be here right now." He shakes his head. "I'm so tired, haven't been sleeping much."

"Me neither," I admit as I pick two white mugs out of the cabinet.

"You okay, Queenie?"

"Yeah, just, you know...everything."

He huffs a laugh and nods. "Yeah, everything."

I drop herbal winter spice tea bags into the mugs and pour hot water over them as Cole yawns.

"Is it okay if I stay the night here? Is there an extra guest room, or can I sleep on the couch?"

"Mine is the only other bed in the house," I say. "I don't mind sharing. You're a gentleman." He matches my glance with a small smile.

"Any other time, I might be tempted to not be so gentlemanly, but tonight I'm beat. Will Aunt Mari be okay with it though? I don't want to cross any boundaries. But it's either that or go to Luko and Denny's. I'm not driving all the way back to the barracks tonight."

"It's fine." Sharing a bed with him is definitely not as chill as I make it sound, but we're both visibly exhausted, not staring each other down with lustful gazes. Maybe we'll finally sleep well, if we're together.

"It's almost a four-hour drive to get to my hometown," he says. "I have to be back at work early Monday morning. I was thinking, if you're cool with it, we can leave first thing tomorrow morning and then head back Sunday afternoon?"

I slide his mug across the counter to him and stay on the opposite side of the island.

"Yeah, that'll work."

Depending on how early we leave, I might miss Aunt Mari entirely. However, I have a feeling if I leave a note explaining that the handsome Esteban and I are taking a quick trip together, she'll be more than understanding.

I study his face as he takes a tentative sip of his tea. "Your eyebrow is looking better."

"Yeah," he says, gingerly tapping around it. "Isn't it weird how my painting won't have this scar? I can't wait for my mom to see the painting in person. She said she might be able to take some time off work and come see it when I get back from trauma training."

My heart drops and my body goes cold. Oh crap. Shoot, I didn't tell him? How did I forget to tell him? Of course, I have to say something, but I know I'm going to cry. I really didn't tell him?

"Cole," I say, my voice dry. "I...there..." I should have made sure his family came and saw it before I listed it or allowed it to be sold. I should have been more thoughtful. "Um...I forgot to tell you something."

"Tell me what?"

"I'm so sorry, the painting sold," I say, my chin trembling as I lean against the counter and study my hands. "It sold to an anonymous buyer. Lorraine packed and shipped it a few days ago."

She had asked if I wanted to be the one to send it off, but I couldn't bring myself to look at it again or else I'd turn into an art thief, stealing my own painting back. I still haven't been back to the gallery, mostly because I know the blank space in the front window is going to rip my heart out all over again.

"What?" Cole whispers. His incredulous tone completely breaks me.

"It was when you were away." I look up at him with tears coming down my cheeks. "I'm so sorry."

"Oh, Tia, don't be sorry." He gets up and comes around, gathering me in his arms, holding me against his chest. "That's good news, you sold your first painting."

Apparently, I'm not done grieving. Cole rubs my back as I sob again over the loss of my painting, an inanimate object with no soul or beating heart, like it's a dying friend. But he doesn't try to placate me, and I know I don't have to hold back my sadness with him. He can handle it just as well as my happiness.

"I understand. That was a special memory."

I nod, venting my combined exhaustion and sadness into his chest.

"I think bed is the best place for both of us," he says. He kisses my head and keeps one arm around my shoulders as we walk through the darkened house to the guest room. I crawl into my side of the bed, weary and weak, while Cole goes around to the other side.

"I'm going to set an alarm for six tomorrow," he says, tapping on his phone, then setting it on the floor. He slides in under the covers next to me as I sniffle one last time.

"Come here," he says, pulling my back against his chest and draping one heavy arm over me. Within a minute, my whole body relaxes, my muscles feeling a slumbering relief they haven't felt in days.

"Sleep well, Queenie," he whispers. "Goodnight."

"Goodnight."

He goes so still and quiet, I can hear his heart beating. When the rise and fall of his chest drops into slow, deep breaths, I find myself trying to match it. He's a hot sleeper, making me feel like I'm wrapped up in a human heating blanket, but I stay under his arm and curl even closer to him. I know I'm safe, protected, and cared for, and that makes me peacefully sleepy.

My favorite thing in bed used to be the coldest side of the pillow. Now I think it's the warmth of Cole Slaeden.

CHAPTER 28

WHEN I WAKE up from the best sleep of my life, my hands are resting on hot skin, my head is on Cole's bare chest, and his wide arms are holding me there. From my vantage point, all I see is sun-kissed skin and muscles. He went to bed in a t-shirt, what happened between now and then?

"You're hot in bed," he whispers, his eyes still closed.

"You're hot in bed," I murmur back, my head rising and falling with his breath.

"Guess I'll sleep shirtless from now on." His finger traces a lazy "S" across my shoulder blade, making me shiver against him. "Or we could get those cooling sheets for our bed."

His chest suddenly stops moving. I roll onto my stomach to face him. His eyes fly open and widen as they meet mine, like he's finally realizing what he just said out loud.

What is happening?

The alarm goes off and now I'm wide awake, shooting out of bed.

I run around the room making the excuse of packing a few things for the weekend, and dash to the bathroom to change into joggers and a t-shirt. But really, I'm avoiding Cole, avoiding the thought of *our bed*. There will be no *our bed*.

Last night, it was supremely comforting to fall into bed together, but when we're awake and looking into each other's eyes over the plane of Cole's muscular chest, it's like setting a stick of dynamite near an open furnace—one step away from completely incendiary.

Cole comes into the hallway fully clothed and I give him a tight smile as I leave a note for Aunt Mari. We get on the road with no further mention of how we woke up, making a quick pit stop for muffins, tea, and coffee. Thankfully, Cole seems to get the memo we will not be discussing our bed. The bed. Bed things.

Once I know we're not going there, I do my best to settle in and appreciate the road trip. Riding shotgun in the Camaro is a mini dream come true, and I pick a variety of songs to play through the Bluetooth. Cole spends most of the drive smiling and laughing, especially when I randomly blast "Cotton Eye Joe" and a few sea shanties. Seeing him laugh with that megawatt grin of his is delightful. Going home is something he's obviously excited about and I love that he has a strong value of home and family.

If I were to say yes to him, if we were to date and completely fall madly in love with each other and get married and have babies, would we bring our kids down this same freeway for Thanksgiving, Christmas, birthdays? Would we listen to kids' songs and play "I Spy" and Cole and I would smile at each other across the middle console and wonder how we got so lucky?

Or would it be me driving solo because Cole is deployed, desperate to take the kids to see their grandma so I can have an iota of quiet, alone time? Would I be frazzled by life and angry at Cole, wondering why I ever got myself involved with someone in the Navy?

The other day, Cole said it's normal for things to not be all good or all bad. Is the answer to my picture of the future C) All of the above?

Cole picks up my hand and squeezes, as if he knows why I've gone quiet. All I've promised him is one day at a time. I have to remember to take this one day at a time.

———

THE LAST HOUR of the drive, we turn onto a winding road that takes us from the flat valley up to the mountains. The brown ugliness of Southern California in the dry season gives way to green pine trees, and when I press my cheek to the window, the glass is freezing cold. The only downside to approaching the cooler mountain highs is the constant curving of the road, reminding me of something I haven't had to deal with in years—I get carsick. I am struggling to keep my nausea at bay.

"Let me know if you need me to pull over," says Cole.

I shake my head. There is no way I'm going to let myself throw up during any part of this trip in Cole's beautiful car. Although it's mildly tempting, just to see him become Hot Corpsman again.

"Tell me your family's names again?" I press my forehead against the cold passenger window.

"My mom is Cathy, my older brother is Carson, my younger brother is Cillian. My dad was Clint. All hard 'C' names."

I gasp as it dawns on me. "That's why you said 'holy crap' when I told you my full name was Christiana. I would fit right in with the Slaeden line-up."

Cole's neck turns tell-tale red. "I've thought about it more than a few times," he admits.

"Mmm." I am fighting so hard to keep my meager breakfast in my stomach and off the floor mats. "Is your mom excited to see you?"

"She's going to be so stoked. Last turn, then it gets a bit bumpy. Roll down your window if that helps."

I immediately hold the window button down, and sharp mountain air hits my nose, giving me some relief. Finally, we pull up a long gravel driveway and park in front of a red two-story square farmhouse with white trim and a generous front porch. I made it without embarrassing myself. Hallelujah.

Cole lays on the horn, and I jump. Carson is the first to come striding through the front door and down the porch stairs in straight jeans, boots, and a Carhartt jacket. The squint on his face quickly turns into a grin when he sees Cole's car. Cillian leans out the door, wearing a thick fleece headband over his ears and a fluorescent running jacket. Cathy shoves her way between them and comes barreling down the front steps in a turtleneck with a flannel shirt over top, jeans and boots, and a long, gray braid draped over one shoulder.

"Cole!" she exclaims.

A whole pandemonium of dogs trail after her, rushing out to greet us: a Jack Russell terrier, German shepherds, golden retrievers, and white long-haired dogs that look like little walking rugs.

"Hello," I say, crouching down to greet the adorable, tail-wagging welcoming committee.

"What a surprise!" says Cathy, throwing her arms around Cole's neck and giving him a tight squeeze, her boots barely staying on the ground. We're surprising them? Everyone is smiling, like this is typical of Cole.

"And who might you be?" Cathy asks, turning to me in a delighted tone. I quickly stand as she comes over to give me a hug.

"Mom, this is Tia Lopez. We played soccer together and—"

Cathy gasps. "You're the artist! Carson showed me the picture. Oh, you have a real gift. That portrait of Cole was just—" She gasps, pressing one hand over her heart. "I wish I could have bought it, but you know, we'll have to have you paint another one. It is so gorgeous. Cole favors Clint's side of the family and I could really see it coming through, and it was just—" She gasps again.

"I'm so glad you liked it," I say as my heart squeezes. I feel awful she didn't get to see it in person.

Carson sidles over and gives me a side hug, which I reciprocate. "Hey, glad you're here. Good to see you again."

"You too," I reply with a smile.

"Killer, get down here," Cole shouts. Cillian jogs out, putting in some earbuds, and gives Cole a quick back-slapping hug. "This is my friend Tia," says Cole. Good, he didn't say anything like "girlfriend" or "my girl" or whatever. Friend is fine.

"Hi, I'm Cillian. Nice to meet you," he says, shaking my hand. "Sorry, I didn't know you guys were coming, Cole. I'm on my way out." Cillian turns to me "I run cross-country and Coach is making us do weekend practices, so I have to run down to the track right now. Look forward to hanging out when I get back." He gives us a quick salute and heads down the driveway.

"If he'd known you were coming, he would have gotten out of practice," says Cathy.

"Oh, no worries," Cole replies. He grabs our hastily packed weekend bags out of the trunk, and Cathy tells him to put them in his room. She links arms with me as we go into the house, followed by Carson and all the dogs.

"Tia, I've waited a long time for Cole to bring someone home."

I hope my smile hides my shock. Cole has never brought someone home before? No, that can't be right. Although I cannot imagine him bringing Ripley here. But "Operation Don't Fall Hard and Fast for Cole" is going to be seriously compromised if I find out I'm the first girl he's ever brought home.

Cathy leads the way across worn hardwood floors to a small kitchen with '90s linoleum that looks like white tiles with little pink roses at the corners. Tucked into one side of the kitchen is a square table covered by a plastic red and white checked tablecloth with four benches around it, enough seating for eight. Cathy pats the tablecloth as she moves past the table to the fridge.

"I hope you don't mind if I ask you to plop down right there in the corner and chat with me while I rummage through the fridge and pull together an early lunch. I think I'll have a delivery today, but I don't want to miss the chance to share a meal with you and Cole. Are you hungry? Tell me about you."

My head is spinning from the carsickness and taking in the details of Cole's childhood home. "Well, I..." I trail off, trying to think of where to start, but I'm drawing a blank.

She jumps right in for me as she fills a mason jar with water from the tap and sets it in front of me. "I'm sorry, it's always difficult to begin a conversation with a vague prompt. How about, where did you grow up?"

"Oh, Los Angeles. Not in a terrible part, but not in a great part either." I take a sip of the water and it's delicious and cool, helping my car sickness to die down.

"And you're an artist? And where do you live now?" Cathy asks with her head inside the double doors of the fridge. "Sorry, Carson recently got us this new fridge, and I can't find anything right now. I liked the old one, but Carson insisted."

One of the smaller terrier dogs burrows under the table, nuzzling at my legs. I scoop it up as Cathy comes out of the fridge with an armful of lunch meat, cheese, condiments, and bread.

"Oh, that's Beau, he's Carson's baby. Isn't he a dear?"

Beau settles down in my lap, resting his chin on my arm. My heart melts. The kitchen and this corner table are so cozy and comfortable and having a dog to snuggle is the cherry on top.

"I live in San Diego," I say, running my hand over Beau's head as his eyes gently fall closed.

"Of course, how else would you have met Cole? Well, I mean there are lots of ways to meet people long-distance these days. No judgment for those apps or websites. People may not know their one true love isn't in their neighborhood, they're on the other side of the country. And you're an artist?"

"Trying to be," I say with a smile. "I just sold my first painting —the one of Cole. I'm hoping this is the start of a new career.

How is your work going? Cole told me you're a midwife and a big inspiration for his choice to become a corpsman."

Cathy laughs and shakes her head. "I hesitate to call myself inspirational." She sets out plates and knives and opens a bag of chips.

"Well, you're definitely a part of Cole's motivation. When I asked him why he became a corpsman, he said he wanted to help people because of you and he wanted to join the military because of his dad."

"Really? He told you that?" Cathy says. I nod, and she looks at me curiously, then shakes her head. "Well, we've always done our best to give each of our boys a sense of service and participation in something greater than themselves. Clint had such a servant's heart, and I'm grateful he lives on in each of our sons."

The last thing she puts out is a massive bag of peanut butter M&Ms. She shoots me an embarrassed smile. "They're a family favorite, and we have them at every lunch and dinner. Lunch, baby boys!" Cathy calls out.

Carson and Cole's heavy footsteps rumble through the house as they make their way into the kitchen, carrying on a hushed conversation that continues as they survey the spread to make sandwiches. I'm tickled over the fact that she calls her grown sons "baby boys" and they respond immediately.

"Hey, you feeling better after the car ride?" Cole asks, turning to me. "You want me to make you a sandwich?"

"Yeah, much better, thankfully. I can get it, *osito*," I say, although I would hate to wake Beau from his snooze in my arms. Carson notices I'm cradling a snoring, snuffling Beau and grins with a nod of approval.

Cole waves for me to stay seated. "No, seriously, I'll make your lunch. What do you like?"

"Okay, um, turkey, swiss cheese, a little mayo, a little mustard, and lettuce."

Cole winks at me and goes back to talking with Carson. It's a small thing, but I've never had a guy make me food before, not even a sandwich. When Cole delivers my lunch, complete with a generous handful of M&Ms, he serves it to me with a grin, like he knows he's slowly and persistently becoming an irreplaceable fixture in my life.

CHAPTER 29

WHEN CILLIAN GETS home from practice and joins us in the kitchen, we're still chatting around the table. But once he's there, the three boys go from casual conversation to thunderous laughter in the time it takes him to make a sandwich. It's all inside jokes, movie quotes, and childhood memories melded together in conversations that move at break-neck speeds. After a particularly loud round of laughter, Beau gives up and hops off my lap to escape to a quieter nap spot.

I love how the brothers fill the room with warmth and smiles and I love seeing Cole so carefree with Carson and Cillian. They all have a wide, easy grin they must have inherited from their dad and their laughter is so infectious, I can't help but smile along, even when I'm not in on the joke.

It makes me miss Julio immensely. Once Dad and I dropped him off at college, we struggled to stay in touch. He craves adventure, so his spring breaks and Christmas holidays were often spent wherever he could score a cheap flight to. Now, he's equally likely to FaceTime from a sandy beach in Jamaica or a mountaintop bar in Canada during ski season. We catch up briefly and we always end by saying "Love you," but we're not regularly in each other's lives anymore. We have a whole lifetime of memories between us and he used to be such an anchor point for me, but we've lost that over the past decade.

Cathy checks her watch, then announces she needs to excuse herself to go check in on some expectant mothers. "Boys, be good hosts, especially you, Cole. And clean the kitchen when you're done." She leaves with a look that I can tell has inspired godly fear in her sons for decades.

We all linger around the table for another half-hour or so, Carson and Cillian both making a concerted effort to include me and ask me questions. I learn that Cillian was quite the cross-country runner in high school, and chose to accept a full-ride scholarship to the local community college a few miles away, where he's studying to get his paramedic certification.

"Did your big brother being a corpsman have anything to do with picking that field of study?" I ask with a smile.

"I'll tell you when he's not listening," Cillian says with a wink.

"Clean-up time," Cole announces, whisking away our plates. The three guys clean the entire kitchen in an orderly, practiced routine. Carson even sweeps and mops the floors.

We retreat to the living room, where I tuck myself into the corner of the worn leather couch. Cole claims the seat next to me, close enough to casually grab my hand, lacing our fingers together with a smile.

"Happy?" I whisper to him.

"Very," he whispers back.

We're all slouching into couches and chairs when Cathy returns with the announcement that no one is in labor, but she needs to put her feet up. She sinks into a recliner next to the dormant wood-burning stove and pops up the footrest.

For a second, the only sound is the faint ticking from the clock over the kitchen doorway, but then the faint crunch of tires on gravel catches the attention of the dogs, who run to the door barking.

"What now?" Cathy says, with a chuckle.

"Okay, okay," says Carson, pulling them back to clear the doorway. "Looks like a delivery." He goes out to talk with the driver while Cathy pulls out a bag of crocheting.

I glance over at Cole and his eyelids are starting to droop, his blinks becoming slower and slower. I run my thumb across the back of his hand, and he smiles reflexively. He's adorable like this, all content and sleepy.

Carson comes back in with a narrow box about four feet high and three feet wide and sets it on end on one of the side tables. He pulls a knife out of his pocket to gently slit the packing tape.

"What you got there, Carse?" Cathy asks, craning to see from her spot on the recliner.

"A surprise for you," he says. Carson opens the flaps of the box, reaches in, and pulls out a black box that looks familiar, but I can't place why.

He sets it on its back on the table and lifts open the cover as Cathy comes to stand next to him. She gasps, and my heart stops, my breath catching in my chest. It feels like time has slipped into slow motion as Carson smiles and Cathy's mouth forms a small "O."

I know where I've seen a box like that—at the gallery.

"Wait," I say, jumping to my feet, suddenly very awake as adrenaline courses through me. "Wait, wait, wait. No, no way."

Carson lifts the box up so we can all see, and safely nestled in place is my painting, the portrait of Cole. I shriek, then suddenly burst into happy tears, pressing one hand over my mouth in disbelief.

"No freakin' way," says Cole, grinning incredulously. "Tia, it's your painting!"

I'm in shock. Is this real life? It's here. Our painting is here. How? How is this happening? My beautiful painting is here.

"No way," I whisper.

"Carson, honey," Cathy says reverently. I watch Cathy, and the emotions crossing her face as she studies Cole's portrait send another round of tears down my cheeks.

"Is she okay?" Cillian asks in a stage whisper.

Cole comes to my side and wraps one arm around my shoulders. He kisses the top of my hair as if to say, *See? You did that.* I would have expected more words from him. But then I look up and see his eyes are tear-filled, and he can't stop smiling.

"This is insane, I am so shocked," I say, a sob catching in my throat. "Carson, you're the anonymous buyer?"

Carson rubs the back of his reddening neck, shifting uncomfortably at all the emotion swirling around the room. "I wanted you to have it, Mom. I knew it should stay in the family, that it shouldn't sell to just anyone."

"Honey, seeing it in person...this is art with a capital 'A'," says Cathy. "Oh, I love it so much."

"We *would* have a fancy painting of you hanging in the living room, you golden boy," Cillian says with a chuckle, ruffling Cole's hair.

This is our painting, mine and Cole's, but now I'm realizing it also belongs to his family, and it belongs here, where his mom and dad shaped his legacy, and raised him to be the exceptional man he is today.

I'm wiping away tears with the backs of my hands like a baby. "I'm so glad you like it. I'm so glad you have it," I say to Cathy, exhaling in emotional, shaky breaths.

"Thank you," says Cathy. "Thank you, Carson, Tia, and Cole. I can't thank you enough." She sniffles and blinks rapidly, then clears her throat. "Cillian, go get a hammer and a tape measure and one of those picture-hanging hooks."

Everyone starts to move around the living room, eyeing the current art on the wall, deciding what should be moved, where to avoid the heat of the wood-burning stove. They're talking as if my painting is the Mona Lisa, and every time they hold it up to test a certain spot, another wave of relief washes over me. It's here, with the people who will appreciate it most. At one point, Cole and Cathy turn to me and ask me a question that I don't hear.

"I'm sorry," I say, laughing through fresh tears. "I'm just so happy."

———

CATHY LEAVES SOON after to help a mother that's gone into active labor, so Carson and Cillian take over dinner prep. Cole and I head up the hardwood stairs for him to show me where I'm staying—his childhood bedroom. The hardwood gives way to hunter-green carpeting that's probably as old as he is, but clean and perfectly suited to the aesthetic of the Slaeden home.

The door on the left is already open and Cole leans against the door frame with a smile, letting me go in and look around his old room for myself. I grin at the row of sports trophies on a long shelf over the window, the big bookshelf in the corner full of old textbooks, comic books, and a modest collection of science fiction novels. A full bed with a solid oak frame and a blue quilt on top sits to one side of the window with a desk and a closet on the other.

"Is this how you imagined it?" Cole asks.

"No, not really. I think...I don't know, I guess this all feels more rugged and mountain cabin-like. I've only ever known you in San Diego, by the beach, so it seems a little off."

"Yeah," he says with a nod.

I take his hand and pull him further into the room with me to ask the question that's been on my mind since we got here.

"Am I really the first girl you've brought home?"

He holds my gaze, never backing down. "Yes. You're the only one I've brought home."

"Why?"

"I know you're afraid of a future of unknowns, and I thought I would take one thing off the list. And you should meet my family, they're important to me and you're important to me, it made sense."

I smile, squeezing his hand in acknowledgement. "That's not exactly what I asked though."

Cole nods and holds my hand against his chest. "Because unlike many of the girls in my past, I'm proud to know you." He presses my hand flat over his heart. "I will never regret knowing you."

My breath catches as I accept with sudden clarity that I feel the exact same way. I stand on my toes and press a quick kiss to his lips. "Thank you for bringing me to meet your family. I love being here."

"You do? You sure?"

"I really do. It's warm and comforting and I feel at ease here. Feels like you."

"Picture this," Cole says, taking my hands in his and wrapping them behind my back. "You and I are together. At some point, I leave for deployment. You move up here to live in my old room, and you paint a grand masterpiece collection of gorgeous woodland, mountainous landscapes that puts your name on the map in the artist world. When you miss me, you dive into the closet and find all my old high school sweatshirts to wear to bed. When you come downstairs for your morning tea, you see my portrait hanging in the living room. And you miss me, but it's like I'm all around you."

"I don't paint mountain landscapes," I say lamely, tilting my chin up at him as he looms over me. "That's not how this works."

Cole smiles, leans down and kisses my cheek, then whispers in my ear, making the hairs on the back of my neck rise. "You would be loved, utterly and completely loved."

"Didn't see anything," Cillian shouts as he passes the doorway on the way to his room. Cole chuckles and follows him out into the hallway, leaving me stunned and speechless.

———

THE HOUSE IS ASLEEP. The brothers—well, three grown men —are having a sleepover in Cillian's room while I get Cole's old bedroom all to myself. For a while after Cole and I said a very chaste goodnight in the hallway and parted ways, there was enough manly laughter going on to make me jealous, but now it's snoring echoing in the hallway.

I love this house. It is the opposite of self-important. It's modest and comfortable, and the Slaeden family has filled it with love. The more I see of the boys' relationship, and of Cathy at the helm of the family, the more I appreciate and enjoy them. Carson is a stalwart oldest brother, and Cillian doesn't let anyone take themselves too seriously.

It's comforting to see that Cole is not an anomaly. His character is genuine and who he is with me is who I see here: an honest, caring man who isn't afraid to show his emotions and feelings, he thinks of others first, has a sweet humility, and he loves with his whole heart.

Why am I still fighting against my growing feelings for him? How easy would it be to say yes to him? I said one more guy in my life, the one I would want to marry. How simple and peaceful would it be if that was Cole?

CHAPTER 30

"Hey, Tia."

A deep voice cuts through my sleep. My body freezes in fight-or-flight mode as I slowly open my eyes. Cole is sitting on the edge of the bed in jeans and a flannel with a Carhartt jacket over it. A black beanie covers his hair. He looks like a mountain man, but my tired brain is struggling to make sense of why he's here, looking like that.

"The house had better be on fire," I say with an exhausted groan.

"The house is fine," he says with a reassuring kiss to my forehead.

"What time is it?" I ask, craning my neck to glance at the window. It's still dark outside.

"Before dawn. I was gonna go on a hike to my special spot to watch the sunrise, but I thought you might want to come with me."

I groan and rub my face. "Waking up before the sun? To hike? How can I say no?"

"It'll be worth it, I promise. It's one of my favorite things in the whole world. And I want you to see it."

"This is not your best surprise." I sigh. "Is it cold outside?"

"Yeah, dress warm. I'll make you some tea and meet you outside in the truck."

I give in and nod, and even in the dark I can tell he's smiling as he leaves. I pull on my jeans and layer a sweatshirt under a denim jacket, but it still doesn't feel like enough layers. Outside of the warmth of Cole's bed, the room is cold, and I imagine it's even worse outside. I take the liberty of rooting through Cole's closet and find a maroon snowboarding coat. I ditch the denim jacket and slide into the coat. It's big on me, but very cozy, and it even smells like him.

When I come down the stairs, the dogs are all lined up against the wall, scarfing down their breakfast from multiple bowls and Cole is waiting for me by the front door.

"Look at you," he says with a grin, his voice a silky whisper. "Here, my mom had an extra pair of boots lying around. You should be the same size." He hands me a pair of Blundstones which fit well after I wrestle them on.

Cole holds the door for me, and we make our way across the crunchy gravel to a big pickup truck that looks a couple decades old, already rumbling. He glances over at me, a sheepish look on his face. "Are you mad I woke you up?"

"Pretend I am so you never do this again."

His relieved smile is endearing. "Fair enough. Hop in," he says, opening the passenger door for me. "There's a blanket there, and your tea is in the cupholder." He points out a black travel mug with a Bearstone Lake Towing logo and I get a whiff of earl gray.

The cab of the truck is warm and cozy, Celine Dion is playing through the speakers, and it smells like a running heater and pine air freshener. I get settled on the worn gray upholstered bench seat with a smile. Everything is clean and tidy, a few pens gathered in the cup holder and a CD holder attached to the visor, CDs filling every slot.

Cole gets in on the driver's side and takes a moment to run his hands over the bumpy grip of the steering wheel. His eyes drift towards a red and white outbuilding across from the house. We sit in the early morning stillness for a while, just the sound of the running truck and Celine singing a love ballad.

"This was Dad's truck," Cole says gently. He tilts his head towards the building. "Sometimes I wonder if he's going to come out of his workshop and tell me to drive safe, the way he did when I was in high school."

"It's a really cool truck," I reply. "What did he do again?"

"A lot of everything. Ran his own handyman and towing company, did some wood-working, installed cabinets, that sort of thing. He was always trying something new, adding new skills to his vast bank of knowledge."

"Did he teach you those things too?"

"Yeah, some stuff. I'm fairly handy with my car and basic fixes around the house. Carson knows way more than me, but he had a head start."

"It's cool that you guys still use his truck. I love it."

He nods with a reflective smile, then lays one arm behind my shoulders as he backs the truck out of the driveway.

We drive on mountain roads for about fifteen minutes until Cole turns the truck into a dirt turnout and parks. He comes around and gets my door for me, and I spy a narrow sliver of trail worn in the dirt behind him as I hop down.

"I'll bring the blanket—it can get extra cold up top," he says, throwing it over his shoulder, then taking my hand.

"How far do we have to go?"

"Not far—and not too steep either."

Sure enough, right as I'm thinking about asking how much longer, Cole pulls me up on top of a giant expanse of rock. We walk towards the edge and a wide view of the valley and the mountains opens up in front of us. The moon is moving off to one side, and the sky is lightening in shadowy, pastel gradients. There's a gentleness to the darkness giving way to day, something more serene than the brilliant fire of sunset.

Cole wraps the blanket around himself, then wraps his arms and the blanket around my shoulders, including me in the warmth.

"I've never really seen the sky like this," I say. "It's beautiful."

He hums in agreement, his chest vibrating against my back. "You're not a morning person?"

"Not generally."

We're both fixated on the light coming from the horizon, growing gradually at first, then picking up momentum, the birds joining in with fast twitters of song.

Cole breathes steadily, and I stay warm in the cocoon of jackets and blankets and his thick arms. My hands come up to rest over his and seem small in comparison. A hopeful peace settles around us, taking a weight off my chest.

If this was all there was in the world, I would be happy. If all we had to do was watch the sun rise and set from a rocky outcropping, embracing each other through the whole of the day, I would be more than content.

Thoughts of reality and responsibilities creep in, and I do my best to shut them out. We're away from life, suspended in space and time in this moment when no one else exists but us. I close my eyes and lean my head back against Cole's shoulder, intent on memorizing every detail.

This is only special because of him, no one else could make this feel so idyllic. He's not perfect, but he's perfect to me. Everything about this is all I've ever wanted—to be at peace, to feel cared for, protected, safe, comfortable, loved. Because of Cole Slaeden.

Cole takes a deep breath, and his arms tighten around me.

"What are you thinking about?" I ask.

"Fear," he whispers hoarsely.

It's so radically different from what's been going through my mind that I instinctively turn around in his arms and hug him tight, my arms dipping underneath his jacket to flatten my hands against his back.

"What are you afraid of?"

"Losing you. That this is an emotional high. That everything is going to crash down on us when we get back. The logistics are going to get to you, my job is going to get to you, it's all going to be a lot. And you'll drift away from me."

I lean back to look into his eyes. "Cole, I will always be here for you. Nothing will ever affect our friendship."

He shakes his head, then looks down at me with a passionate, soul-melting glare. "I don't want just your friendship, I want all of you. Tia, I love you, you take up my whole heart and soul. I want you as mine, and I want to be yours."

I'm speechless, breathless. *Want, want, want.*

Cole looks away, his forehead pinched in frustration. "We can't keep doing this...*I* can't keep doing this. I know I said one day at a time, but we can't do that forever. If we're not meant to be together, then we should be going out and finding who we are meant to be with. You deserve to find true love, even if it's not with me."

"Cole—" I wish I wasn't so scared. I wish I could be brave. I thought courage mattered most in making big life decisions or in stressful situations, but in this moment, I realize it matters most in love. I love him too much to let him go, but not enough to commit to him yet.

"You're right," I say, tears of frustration rising. "I hear what you're saying." I look up at him, my eyes pleading for him to somehow magically make this less difficult. "Doesn't mean it's easy."

"No, not at all," he whispers, giving me a soft, gentle kiss. "How about this? We'll leave it until after I get back. I understand your reservations, really, I do, and I will always respect what you want. We'll get through the next two months and see how things go?"

I nod to him. I hate that we're going to put this pressure on ourselves. I hate that we have started a ticking clock. But it's only fair, it's only right.

———

LUNCH IS the last meal we have together, the Slaeden family and me, tucked into the corner of the kitchen. It feels like we just got here and now all too soon, we have to say our goodbyes. Of course I give hugs to all the pups as we gather on the front porch. Then Cathy steps forward and hugs me tight. "I am so, so glad I got to meet you, Tia. You're a gem. Thank you for painting my boy. I hope I get to see lots more of you."

"You're an amazing woman, an amazing mom," I tell her, hugging her back.

"No pressure," she whispers, "but I see the way Cole looks at you and I want you to know I would love to have you as my first daughter."

I immediately tear up, making it hard to let go of her. She is the sweetest.

"When are we going to see you next?" she asks, as she turns to give Cole a hug.

"We'll be in touch," is the line Cole settles on as he embraces her.

Cillian and Carson give me brotherly hugs, then backslapping hugs to Cole, then Cole and I are in the car backing down the driveway. Everyone waves until we're out of sight.

"Why am I crying?" I protest through my tears. "They're not even my family, and I only met them like twenty-four hours ago."

Cole pats my leg and smiles. "I'm glad you like my family." He turns the radio to a country station and I roll down the window to prep for the winding roads.

The whirlwind of a weekend sinks into my brain. Sweet Cathy, the brothers together, driving in Cole's dad's truck, the mountaintop moment Cole and I shared. Most of all, the overwhelming love of family. I really need to be better about my relationship with Dad and Julio, not take them for granted. I'm so grateful I have them. If the Slaedens were to become my family too, I'd be doubly lucky.

As the emotions settle once we descend the mountain, some stark facts rise to the surface, like islands emerging from an ocean fog. The biggest being the fact that Carson bought my painting. Not exactly the major art win I was hoping for. It's nice to have a sale under my belt, and I am forever grateful the painting is staying in the family, but...that's it. There's no next steps, no new thresholds to cross, no collector interested in further work from me. I'm right back where I started in my attempt to launch my career.

Crap. I don't want to think about that now. I glance over at Cole. He's running his hand over his hair and studying the road with a pensive, furrowed brow.

"*¿Qué estás pensando?* What are you thinking about?" I ask.

"Things are going to pick up the pace when I get back." Cole starts walking me through his schedule, detailing the variables of his travel plans, including leaving his car at Luko and Denny's.

"You can use it while I'm gone if you need to," he offers.

"Really? You'd let me drive the Camaro?"

"Of course," he says and moves on to talking about getting his plane ticket.

I don't want to talk about his plane ticket. I'd rather talk about anything else, but I listen gamely and nod along, making notes of the dates and times in my phone calendar.

The closer we get to San Diego, traffic builds up, and Cole's getting more and more clipped with his words. We end up respectfully arguing about whether we should get dinner, whether Cole should come in, whether he needs to immediately get on the road back to base or stay until traffic dies down. Basically, everything. I'm getting more and more worried about whether he's mad at me or I'm actually mad at him, but not expressing it well. No, I'm not mad at him, I'm just...ugh, everything is off.

I don't understand it. We just had an amazing, wild, emotional twenty-four hours, but now we're both acting like it was all too stressful.

"Cole, it's going to be okay," I say as he parks in front of Aunt Mari's house.

He rubs his face. "I need to shave," he says, looking in the rearview mirror. "Dang it, I forgot to get a haircut. Guess I'll have to do a barracks cut."

I reach over, grab the front of his flannel, and kiss his cheek, rough with blond stubble after two days of not shaving.

"What's worrying you?" I ask, running my thumb along his jaw.

"There's just a lot going on."

"You worried about work? About leaving?"

He nods, leaning into my hand. "All of it." His eyes close, and he exhales heavily.

"It'll be okay," I say softly.

"Yeah. Okay." He gets out of the car, comes around, opens the door for me, and brings my bag up to the front door. We share a quick kiss and a whispered goodbye. I'll see him again before he leaves, but the way my stomach still flips in fear does not bode well.

I wave to him with a smile as he drives off, but once the rumble of his car fades away, the reality hits. I have things to figure out, decisions that need to be made. He has work, and his own mental and emotional journey to navigate. And we'll have to do it on our own. It's hard not to feel an impending sense of dread looming over us like a black thundercloud threatening rain. I can see it coming, and there's nothing I can do to stop it.

CHAPTER 31

COLE

Finally got my flights from SATO, the people that organize our travel. I leave in a week. I need to be at the airport no later than eight in the morning next Saturday.

TIA

What time is your flight?

COLE

It leaves at 8:50 am.

TIA

Your confidence in your airport abilities is astounding.

COLE

Can we plan to meet at the beach at 7:30 am that day to say goodbye? Please?

TIA

Aren't you leaving your car at Luko and Denny's? We should meet there.

COLE

Very practical, very unromantic.

TIA

Touché. I will meet you at the beach at 6:30 and you will leave for the airport no later than 7:00. Final offer, deal or no deal?

COLE

Haha, fine.

———

I DRESS in jeans and a tan hoodie with shaking hands and a pit in my stomach. I take the Mustang to Ocean Beach, where Cole and I decided to meet to say goodbye. I park and stare out at the sand and the gray ocean and the gray sky.

I feel sick.

I hear the rumble of the Camaro and I go stand on the sidewalk, my arms wrapped around me. Cole gets out of his car in a black hoodie, tan pants, Vans, and a black hat from a local brewery. His travel outfit is cool, but his face is stressed, his eyebrows knitted together, his fresh scar making him look extra upset. The chilly gray morning is matching his expression. A salty breeze catches my hair, forcing me to keep dragging it back from my face.

"Hey," I say in a light voice, a seagull echoing my greeting.

"Hi," he says flatly.

"C'mon, what is it?"

"I don't want to go."

He steps in front of me on the sidewalk and I go to him, wrapping my arms around his waist. In an attempt at comic relief, I try to pick him up, unsuccessfully, until he finally wheezes out a laugh.

"Okay, okay, put me down," he says. I memorize every millimeter of his smile.

"*Osito*," I say in a whisper. His eyes snap down to mine, and he takes my face in his hands.

"Let me kiss you goodbye."

"It's not goodbye yet. We have a whole twenty-seven minutes left. Let's go walk on the beach. It's our thing."

Cole drops his hands from my face and wraps his arms around me in a giant bear hug. He walks us backwards until I'm leaning against him and he's leaning against the car, and he doesn't give a hint of letting go. I'm nestled against his chest and the warmth of his hoodie, and I soak it up because I won't have this for a whole seven weeks.

It all comes rolling over my heart like a sleeper wave. I won't have this for seven weeks. I grab his sweatshirt in my fists and press my forehead to his chest and fight against the sadness that's now drowning me. Dang it, I was doing so good.

"I'm going to miss you so much," I admit, unable to fight it anymore.

"Really?" he asks, leaning his head down to press his cheek against the top of my head.

"I knew I would, but it didn't really hit me until this moment."

"I'll be home soon. It's just a month and a half."

"That's so long."

"You'll have time for yourself. Think of all the paintings you could do, and I'll be a better corpsman for it."

I can't imagine saying goodbye like this over and over and over for longer and longer periods of time. I know Anisha does it, but how? My respect for her shoots up times one million.

"The homecoming will make it all worth it, okay?" Cole murmurs to me, running his hand over my hair. "That, I can promise."

"Are you going to be too busy to call?"

"I don't know, I hope not. But if I'm clingy and calling you every night, you'll get annoyed with me."

"Please be clingy. Please be needy and desperate and call me every spare moment you have."

Cole laughs, and the deep vibration of his chest shakes me along with him.

I squeeze him tight until he huffs a laugh and eases my arms away from him. I sniffle. "I swear, I was not even sad, I was ready for you to go, and then you hugged me, and I realized I have to live without your hugs for seven weeks, and I don't know. It just got to me all of a sudden."

"You want a kiss to make it better?" he asks, looking down at me with the sweetest, saddest brown eyes.

"Yes, please," I murmur.

He reaches up to turn his hat backwards, then wraps his hands around my face, and gives me the most comforting kiss of my life. It's beautiful and unassuming, powerful and commanding at the same time. His affection for me is not at the mercy of our circumstances. He tells me things with his kiss, things that sink deep into my soul, wrapping me up in love.

Slowly, in subtle movements, Cole turns us around, until I'm the one leaning back against the car. He cages me in with his arms, his mouth never leaving mine. My hands hold his face, and I pour my whole heart into kissing him back. We keep up this public display of deep affection, a feeble attempt to make up for all the days we won't get to kiss each other.

Cole presses his forehead to mine, and when he tries to say something, he's breathless. "It...it'll be okay, right? You'll be okay?"

"Yes," I say, my breath ragged.

"Can I be honest?" I nod. "I'm freaking out. How are we supposed to do this?"

I run my hands up the back of his head and pull him back down to meet my lips. Kissing him has slipped into something that offers both solace and the promise of addiction. And I'm supposed to let him go, just get back in his car, drive away, and leave for seven weeks. But whether we want it or not, it's happening, so the only thing I can do is try to make it easier. I ease his face back to look in his eyes.

"We're going to be more than okay. I swear, we're going to be great, Cole."

I can feel the effect of my words as his shoulders relax under my hands and his pinched expression disappears. He straightens up, stands tall, there's even a hint of a smile as he looks down at me.

"Oh, I almost forgot—I got you something." He opens the back passenger door and pulls out a small brown gift bag with white tissue paper sticking out. "I'll never leave you empty-handed," he says before he passes it to me.

"Should I open it now?" I ask.

"Yeah, go for it."

I walk around to the back so I can set the bag on the trunk. Cole leans against the side of the car, his hat still backwards, his face a handsome portrait of tension.

After taking a layer of tissue paper out of the bag, I pull out something carefully covered in more tissue paper and unwrap it to find a delicate gold desktop frame with a picture of us in it.

It's the selfie Cole took of us on the beach. Our faces are pressed close together and I'm softly smiling, my hair whipping around in all directions. I love it so much. I don't think I've ever bothered to frame a photo, so knowing Cole took the time to buy a frame and get this printed in the midst of his demanding life makes it that much more valuable. I hold it up and grin, misty-eyed.

"Cole, this is so special."

"I know it may be kind of cheesy, but I made myself one too, to have with me in North Carolina."

"Not cheesy. Not cheesy at all," I reply, giving him a quick— then lingering—kiss. "Thank you."

"And this," he reaches for something from his back pocket and slides it into my hands, "is to keep you busy."

I turn over the little envelope and see it's a gift card to my favorite art store. For a significant amount. I look up at him wide-eyed, my mouth hanging open.

"Don't argue. It's yours," he says. "You'll make me happy if you spend it all before I get back."

My heart overflows at his thoughtfulness and generosity. He knows exactly how to make me feel seen and loved, and he does it willingly.

"Now I kind of want you to leave so we can start the countdown to you coming back. I hate this," I say with a laugh, brushing away tears.

"When I come back though..." says Cole, trailing off.

"I'll be here," I promise. I look into his eyes, then memorize his face all over again. He is so beautifully handsome. My possessive need for him grows the longer I look at him. I don't ever want to let him go. "Please, just rip the band-aid off."

He nods and wraps his arms low around my waist.

"Bye, Cole," I say, as I hug him, memorizing every curve of his body against mine.

"Bye, I love you." He gives me a long, passionate kiss that ends in a dip, then sets me upright and jumps in the Camaro. I stay on the sidewalk and wave to him until he's out of sight, my heart dropping the whole time.

There's a ringing silence when I get in the Mustang and close the door. My chest hurts, and each time I try to take a deep breath, it's accompanied by squeezes of panic. It all feels so wrong. A part of me is missing, traveling farther and farther away with each passing minute.

My love...

I'm so in love with him.

Not just, "Oh I love him, what a great guy."

I *love* him, I need him, I want him. Forever. The feeling scares me with its forcefulness, the desperation and raw need.

I'm in love. I love Cole.

I'M RUNNING for my life on my third loop around the island. The palm trees are loudly rustling and the wind pushes against me, offering more resistance as my feet pound the pavement.

I'm running scared.

So what if I love him? So what?

It doesn't mean I have to marry him. I can love him and keep it to myself and never make any sort of commitment to him. We could date until it fizzles, or the Navy could ask him to move to the other side of the country, and I could just say goodbye. I do not have to rearrange my life or my plans because I happened to fall in love with him. Plenty of people love people that they can never be with. Call it a curse, call it your soulmate, call it true love, but it doesn't mean that's who you get to spend the rest of your life with.

Doesn't matter that he kisses me so well.

Doesn't matter how hot he is.

Doesn't matter how well he cares for me.

Doesn't matter that he is the most trustworthy person I've ever known.

Doesn't matter that I love his whole heart and soul, his mind and his body, his triumph and his tragedy, his strength and his gentleness.

I love him.

I love him with my whole heart and soul, in a way that I have never loved anyone before.

I LOVE HIM, but I'm going to stay sane and rational and figure things out in a logical way first. That's what I tell myself over and over as I shower and change and wearily flop onto my bed. Saying the word "love" in my mind is changing everything. And he's gone now. I groan into the mattress in frustration.

Burrowing under the covers gives me little relief from the pressing sense of longing and absence. The pillow next to me still smells a little like Cole, and I hug it to my chest, burying my nose in it as I cry. It seems pathetic to be crying when he's a phone call and only three time zones away, but I don't care. If I pretend I'm not sad, I'll hold it in until something reminds me of Cole. The Gulf War veteran will come to the coffee shop, and then I'll break down in ugly sobs, and no one wants that. Better to let it all out now in the comfort and privacy of my room, snuggled in bed.

My phone vibrates with a text from Lorraine asking me to come by the gallery as soon as I can. I'm tempted to give her some excuse. I want to wallow.

But I can't afford to fall into a pit of despair. These seven weeks of Cole being gone are supposed to be all about next steps for me, moving forward in my career in any way I can, so I shouldn't ignore anything from Lorraine.

I give myself five more minutes of sadness. Then, after washing my tears away, I take a slow walk over to the gallery. The warm, emerging sun comforts my face and the bougainvillea bushes trailing over fences offer some cheer with their pops of magenta.

But he's still gone.

———

I STEP INTO THE GALLERY, composed and calm. Lorraine takes one look at me and says, "Oh, what's happened?"

"Nothing," I say, double-checking behind me to make sure I haven't grown a tail.

"No, you look so sad," she says, coming out from behind the register and meeting me in the middle of the gallery floor. "Has something happened to Cole?"

"Oh, he left for some training today, a seven-week course in North Carolina. I'm kind of missing him already." Really missing him. Really wanting him back. Because I'm in love with him.

"Well, I'm happy this news has come today," Lorraine says, giving me a big hug. I welcome it, hugging her back.

"Listen," she says, pulling back to look me in the eye, then leading me to the computer. "An acquaintance of mine is a renowned portrait artist turned art instructor. Her name's Giada Burke. She was in my MFA cohort, and she was always head and shoulders above the rest of us, but very kind and helpful. Anyways, I asked her if she has any spots available on her next art intensive, and at first she said no, but I sent her the pictures of the paintings you've done, including Cole's portrait, and she said she could add a spot and make an exception for you in her next class. It's in four weeks."

"What?" I say, a smile growing on my face. "Are you serious?"

"Here, come to the computer and look. See if you're interested."

A website is already up on the screen, and I start scrolling, my mouth dropping open in amazement. The photos show a small circle of six students painting a live model, while a tall woman clothed in boxy black linen offers instruction. They're in an airy room with tons of natural light and pale hardwood floors, their easels evenly spaced apart. All their faces look positively delighted.

"I don't know what to say," I tell Lorraine. "I'm speechless. This looks like a very elite course."

"She's an excellent instructor and I highly recommend you take the spot she's offering you."

"It's in Marina Del Rey," I say as I scroll more. I'd have to commute, it's nearly three hours one way.

"There's a residency option, for which Giada offers a scholarship."

"It's a one-week course. I'd have to take off work."

"I'm sure you have some vacation time."

"I guess I'd take the train up there? Actually, I could drive the Camaro—"

"Tia, are you trying to find reasons not to do this?" Lorraine asks, putting one hand on her hip and furrowing her eyebrows at me.

"No, I'm just..." Worried I won't be good enough, scared of being the worst painter there, intimidated by the aesthetic of the class already. And I'm tired and sad and want to curl up in a ball.

"Listen, Cole is gone. Now is the time to invest in yourself and do something that will further your career. I'm not saying he has to be gone for you to do those things, but as a former Navy wife, I'm telling you it's good to keep yourself busy."

I bite my lip and scroll some more. "Thank you for putting in a word for me," I murmur. I know I need this. I know I need a shot in the arm to keep me going with my art. The time is now. I have to take the plunge. "I won't let you down."

"Don't worry about me," Lorraine says, waving away my statement. "Do it for you. Prove to yourself how talented and brave you are."

CHAPTER 32

I HAVEN'T HEARD Cole's voice for ten days now. I should just ask him when we can talk, but I've been chicken, not wanting to impose on his time. We've texted back and forth at the end of his day, but I miss his voice. And I know if I hear his voice, I'm going to miss his physical presence even more than I already do. I ache without him around. My brain says I don't have to put up with something in my life that hurts like this, but my heart is saying this is proof that I love Cole.

I've googled quotes about absence and longing and found a particularly poignant one by Comte de Bussy-Rabutin,

"Absence is to love what wind is to fire; it extinguishes the small, it kindles the great."

I think what Cole and I have is "the great." It's big and wild and scary and incredible.

"Okay, so, why are you staring at your lock screen?" asks Jules, a mug in one hand and a silver milk pitcher in the other.

I turn it towards Jules so she can see the picture from Cole's FMF pinning ceremony. "I'm having a hard time."

"Yeah, we noticed, friend. Did you and Cole break up?"

"No," I shake my head. "He's on the east coast for training. For seven weeks."

"Aww, so you're missing him bad, huh? I can imagine missing my boyfriend something fierce for seven weeks."

"He's not my boyfriend."

Jules slams the pitcher on the counter in shock. "HE'S NOT YOUR BOYFRIEND?"

"No."

"Why not, Tia? Why the heck not? Girl, don't fumble that!"

"Well, he's in the Navy—"

"Tia, wait. Stop for a second. What is happening? I love my boyfriend, I am practically engaged, but I'm not blind. Cole is handsome as hell and worth his weight in gold. Has he ever dropped the ball on you? Like, messed up, cheated, left you hanging or anything? Is there some secret gross fetish I don't know about? Is he actually a shady con man or something?"

"No," I say with a defensive laugh.

"And your main complaint is he's in the Navy?"

"Yeah."

"Because that life is too hard or something?"

"Well, it's...demanding. And it requires sacrifice. I wanted to have independence and build my own life, make my own choices, not twist myself into some version of me that operates around him."

"Tia, who exactly is asking you to do that?"

No one. Cole made it clear when we talked on the beach that he would never ask that of me.

"Well...there's a lot of unknowns." My only rebuttal sounds weak, said out loud.

"Instead of being worried about those unknowns, maybe think of it as the one, big, great unknown, full of exciting things. You two are the cutest little teammates I've ever seen. Think of the adventures you could have, the things you could see. Think of how stable your life would be if you and Cole got together and lived out your passions side by side. It could be the best thing you ever do."

A life with Cole *could* be the best thing I ever do. Emphasis on the conditional, hypothetical quality of that statement.

———

ANYTIME MY PHONE DINGS, vibrates, or lights up with a notification, I jump to see if it's Cole. It rarely is, but I'm still in a constant state of checking to see if he's texted or called. I've started to resent anyone sending me a funny reel or the DoorDash app letting me know my order was confirmed. I need a project.

I decide to put Cole's gift card to good use and stock up on supplies for my upcoming art intensive. I take an Uber to Luko and Denny's house and pick up the Camaro for a test run before driving it up to Marina Del Ray.

Once I get over the initial anxiety of driving someone else's car, much less Cole's dreamy ride, I grin. I allow for a moment of self-satisfied happiness as the car roars onto the freeway. Bryce who?

After finding all the items on my moderate list, I'm ready to head home and get things organized, get back into a routine of painting for practice. The Camaro makes a worrying squeal when it starts. Oh, no, please not this. Not Murphy's Law. I just want to get home.

The temperamental sky decides to open up and pour down torrential rain as I put the car in drive, the kind of downpour that has the windshield wipers going back and forth at full speed and I still can barely see. Really? This is supposed to be California in September when a late summer hits, not D.C. with its East Coast summer thunderstorms.

My phone is hooked up to the Bluetooth, and the navigation voice keeps shouting directions at me as it takes me on surface streets to avoid traffic. The constant updates keep cutting into what was supposed to be calming classical songs.

Suddenly, the songs stop altogether, and the FaceTime ring tone blares through the car. I check who's calling and my heart leaps. It's Cole, now known as "Osito" in my contacts. I hurry to try to answer it, but I can't really focus on looking at the phone in the middle of the rain.

"Hey, hi!" I say loudly, doing my best to sound positive and happy.

"Hello?" says a voice that's definitely Cole's, but garbled and chopped up. I glance down at the screen and see a pixelated mess of camouflage. "Hello? Tia?"

"Hi, can you hear me?" I yell, looking around for a place to pull over.

"Tia? You there?"

"Cole, your connection isn't great," I shout, every nerve pinging with overload.

"I can't hear you at all."

I swear under my breath, remembering the Bluetooth can be finicky. "Hang on, I'm going to pull over and fix it," I say loudly.

"I don't ha...ton...time, just want...ay hi...quick."

"Hang on!"

I finally spy a strip mall to my right and cut through a lane of traffic to pull over. I try to hit the Bluetooth button and swipe and turn it off, and when I go back to the screen with the call on it, Cole's face comes through clearly for half a second. I nearly cry with happiness and relief to see his handsome smile and his tired eyes. My love, my heart. He waves, and the call drops.

In a daze, I put the car in park and unbuckle my seat belt. No, that did not just happen. I grab my phone and try to call him back over and over, each time getting an error message about no connection. Hot tears fall down my face. I want to talk to him—I *need* to talk to him. I miss him so much. Stupid cell reception. Just one minute—that's all I ask. Is that too much?

When I finally walk into the house audibly crying, Aunt Mari rushes to my side in alarm.

"*¿Qué pasó, Christiana?*"

"I miss Cole. And it's really hard. And I don't want to feel this awful. I want him home."

"Okay, we'll fix this," she says, with a sense of urgency. "I'll make empanadas and we'll watch a movie. Here, have some wine." She pushes her glass into my hand. "I think you're having a hard time being in love."

"I am," I say through my sobs.

"Oh, *niña preciosa, mi corazón.*"

———

TIA

Can we FaceTime tonight?

I FINALLY TEXT Cole my request the next day, once I figure he's out of class. I don't know if he's super overwhelmed with his training, or if he's trying to give me space, but either way, I'm over it.

OSITO

Yeah. Can you send me a picture of whatever you're up to right now?

I'm in a paint-splattered black t-shirt, my hair piled on top of my head in a messy bun, no makeup, my gold hoop earrings the only redeeming accessory. But I pull out my phone and snap a selfie with me in the foreground smiling, my easel behind me holding a portrait of Aunt Mari halfway done. I send it.

OSITO

swearing emoji I miss you.

TIA

I need one of you.

It takes a minute, but he sends a picture of him staring down into the camera, in uniform, with a cheeky little grin, looking ridiculously sexy and adorable at the same time. He kills me.

TIA

Miss you so bad. Call me tonight?

OSITO

You got it, Queenie.

———

I SIT CROSS-LEGGED on the bed as my stomach flutters full of butterflies and my heart pounds. He said he'd call at five my time, and right on the dot the phone lights up with an incoming FaceTime.

"Hi!" I say suddenly and loudly as Cole's video comes online. Holy crap, there he is, standing in his uniform pants and black belt, olive green T-shirt, and his usual short pale hair. Does absence make the heart grow fonder, and your love interest sexier? I wouldn't be surprised if there were cartoon hearts pouring out of my eyes right now.

He adjusts the camera on his end. "Hey, Tia. Is the video all right, is it working?"

"Yeah, it's just small."

"Oh, are you on your phone? I'm on my laptop. Wanted to see your face as big as I could."

Stop it. He is too cute. I turn my phone sideways, and he takes up more of the screen now. He looks good—healthy but tired, handsome but drained. He pulls up a chair and sits down, leaning forward towards the camera.

"How are you?" I ask.

"Um..." he says, rubbing his eyes, "I have seen more blood this past week than I have in my entire life. A lot of bones and stitches too. It's the real deal. We're assisting in the trauma bays to help prepare us for battlefield-type injuries and it is...gnarly. Definitely not just temp checks and handing out Motrin. I am learning a ton, though." A yawn cuts him off. "Sorry, it's a lot of high-adrenaline and learning, and then I crash at the end of the day. Sorry I haven't called more."

I do my best to be understanding, given what he's just told me. I imagine the way he responded to my stingray incident but ramped up to one hundred times the intensity. "Don't worry," I say, "I've been busy in my own way too. Guess what?"

"What?"

"Lorraine has this friend who's this renowned portrait artist and teacher, and she does these special workshops out of her studio, and long story short, I'm going to an exclusive artist intensive in Marina Del Rey, for a week."

"What?!" Cole shouts with a massive smile taking over his face. "That's awesome! That's amazing. And you're just going to, like, learn and paint for a week?"

"Yeah, I got the time off work, and I got a scholarship to pay for the residency portion, and I get to focus on getting better at portraits and exploring new ways to express my style."

"Tia, that is awesome!" Cole says, the smile never leaving his lips. "I'm so excited for you."

"I'm nervous. I think it's going to be great, but it's also going to be really intense. I leave in two weeks."

"You're going to do great. Listen to the kindest voice in your head—you're going to do so well."

I can't stop looking at him, a grin permanently etched on my face.

"What else are you up to?" he asks.

"Anisha is thrilled I'm a TDY widow right now—her words, not mine. She and Sarah are going to come over next week and we're going to have a wine and paint night and some girl chat."

"That sounds really fun. I bet they'll love it."

My cheeks hurt from smiling. I thought FaceTime would be a

poor substitute for real-life conversation with Cole, but it's surprising how refreshing it is to see him and hear him at the same time.

"Do you have studying you have to do? Anything I can help you with?"

"Oh, yeah, we do have some stuff we'll be tested on but it's nothing like studying for the FMF pin. I'll be fine. Um, but I did want to talk about something I've been thinking about in random little moments of time."

He sits up straighter, squaring his shoulders, and his tone becomes more serious as he talks. "I think I need to take some time to myself. Not in a selfish way, more like, I need to stop avoiding the things I need to deal with on my own. Like, I need to be okay being by myself and being just me. I was reading about contentment as the antidote to relationship insecurities and I realized I need to learn to be content on my own, with my own life, whether or not you decide you want to be a part of it."

I don't know how to respond to that. It makes sense, he's not wrong, but it feels like he's taking a step back. Fear wraps around my throat and chokes me. What if I'm not the one that ends us? What if I run out of time with him?

He continues, "When I first got here, I was having really bad anxiety, like not sleeping and my heart would start pounding and my breath would get short whenever I thought about you potentially walking away. It was out of control. I don't want to be like this obsessed, possessive person that haunts you until you say yes. I'm starting to feel better about being okay with whichever way things fall now, but I think the best thing I can do is focus on myself for a bit. So, what if we decided to do that for the rest of HMTT, take time for ourselves and not talk until I get back?"

Wait, what? That was not what I was expecting. How is that his conclusion?

"Not talk for five weeks?" I ask, my voice cracking as I rub one hand over my eyes.

"Oh, I didn't mean to upset you," he says, his voice softening. "I thought you might be on board."

"I'm not crying," I say with a rueful laugh. "I'm just shocked. Five weeks, no contact?"

"Yeah?"

"That's ridiculous."

He blinks. "Why?"

I splutter, waving my hand in the air as I try to piece my words together. "Do you know how much I live for a notification from you? For a text, a GIF, an emoji, anything. I freakin' miss you so bad, I am holding on by a thread, the only thing that keeps me going is hearing from you. I hate being apart."

He hesitates, biting his lip.

"Cole, I think it's a bad idea."

"But what if it was real life? What if I was deployed to a place with no reception, no internet, and the only way I could communicate with you was through letters?"

"You're going to put me through some little deployment simulation? Is this a test?"

"No, no, it's nothing like that. I'm saying I need this, I need to grow, I need to be okay just being me."

It's as if my worst nightmare has come to life. The man I love, taken away from me by the Navy, and all channels of communication cut off.

"For the record, I do not support this plan. You told me you wouldn't do this. We've barely hit a comfort zone of making this work."

"But isn't that how we grow, by making ourselves uncomfortable and then adapting and overcoming?"

I roll my eyes in disbelief. "Please. You have one thoughtful internal monologue and now you're all hot and insightful."

He laughs, a sexy, deep chuckle that makes my heart squeeze with longing. His absence really is making my heart want him more and more. There's no way I'm letting him make a unilateral decision for us.

"You understand you're gambling here? You're betting on me being willing to put up with five weeks of not talking to you?"

"I'm betting on you being stronger than you give yourself credit for."

"Cole...how long have you been thinking about this?" I ask.

"Like, a week."

"Have you run it by any of your friends?"

He shakes his head no.

"I don't think it's a good idea and I am positive Luko and Denny would say the same thing."

He runs his hand over his hair, waiting for my verdict. "Please? I may be making a mistake, but can we try?"

I bite my lip and study his expression. "Starting now?"

"No, starting tomorrow."

I groan. "I hate that I like you enough to say yes to this." I love him, but now is not the time and over FaceTime is not the place to say it. "I hope you get what you're looking for."

He nods. "Thank you. I know this isn't what you were expecting."

Understatement. I'm biting back some choice words and I'm sure he can tell by my silence.

"I'm sorry for being a wet blanket."

Again, understatement.

"Can we talk about something else now? It's a Friday night, I'm free for the rest of the night. My favorite comfort movie is *Pacific Rim*."

He offers up that piece of information and I know I have a choice to either smack it down in anger or keep up a little volley until we reach a point of easing back into conversation.

"Mine is *Mulan*."

Cole grins. "Do you think that played into you honoring your father's wishes to not study art?"

"Cole Stephen Slaeden," I say, my eyes nearly rolling out of their sockets as he chuckles. "Don't get me started on why you probably like Pacific Rim."

"You'd probably be right," he says. "What else is your comfort go-to?"

We talk for hours, keeping Cole up way too late. We talk about anything and everything, from childhood memories to stories from the coffee shop or from when Cole was in boot camp. We laugh and stare at each other longingly and I wish there was a way to send a kiss through a computer screen. When we finally start to say our goodbyes, I'm snuggled in bed, Cole propped up against the pillow next to me.

"I should let you go to bed," I say.

Just like when he left, the goodbye is hitting me way harder than I thought it would. Five weeks of not talking is stupid and unnecessary and I don't know if I'll survive. Tears fill my eyes and drop down my cheeks as I stare at the screen, memorizing for the millionth time every curve and corner of his face. I'll have to go paint it from memory tomorrow. He is my eternal fixation.

"You're really going to leave me by myself and not talk to me for five weeks?"

He sighs, then nods. "Next time we talk, it's going to be in the airport, face to face, after I've kissed you senseless."

———

WHEN I WAKE UP, I find one more notification from Cole—a text message with a link and a heart emoji. I snuggle into my covers and tap the link. The webpage opens to reveal "Endymion," a poem by Henry Wadsworth Longfellow. I gasp—he sent me a poem as a final sign-off. The moving stanzas and the thought of Cole picking this out make me feel like I'm both anchored and flying.

...like Dian's kiss, unasked, unsought
Love gives itself, but is not bought;
Her voice, nor sound betrays
its deep, impassioned gaze.

It comes, —the beautiful, the free,
the crown of all humanity,—
in silence and alone
to seek the elected one...

CHAPTER 33

WITHOUT THE NEED to constantly check my phone to see if Cole has called or texted, my days seem freer, but in a hollow, empty way. I miss Cole's voice, his tone, even the way he expresses himself in a text.

I get back to running regularly and going for long walks with a soccer ball on the beach. And I have more time to focus on my friendships. It just feels like everything is happening under a foggy sky when it could be in the warm sunshine.

Anisha comes into girls' night at Aunt Mari's brandishing a blank eight-by-ten-inch canvas and a bottle of Merlot. "Wine, painting, snacks, girl chat—so therapeutic," she says as she sets everything on the dining room table.

"Very true," I murmur in agreement as I pick at the seal on a bottle of paint. I've set up three stations for each of us girls with disposable palettes and two paint brushes, one thin and one wide.

"*Hola,*" Aunt Mari says in greeting as she glides into the kitchen in a burnt-orange silk skirt, a white sleeveless blouse with an exaggerated collar, and loads of her signature silver jewelry. "*Bienvenida,* I'm Tia's great aunt, Marisol."

"Aunt Mari!" Anisha exclaims. "So nice to meet you, you have an amazing house. Wow, you look fantastic."

"*Gracias*, I have a date."

I gasp, then smile in surprise. "Aunt Mari! *¿En serio?*"

She nods as she tucks a few things in a cobalt-blue clutch. "He's very handsome, very rich, and very good at picking out the best restaurants. We're going to STEAK tonight, that fancy place at the end of the main avenue." She's cool, calm, and collected on the outside, but I can tell her subtle smile is one of excitement.

"I hope you have a fantastic time," I say as the doorbell rings.

"I'll get it," says Aunt Mari. "*Adiós, chicas.*"

I hear her briefly exchange greetings with Sarah and the front door closes as Sarah comes in with her own canvas and a tote bag with a pack of Oreos peeking out of the top.

"Was that your great aunt?" Sarah asks. "I thought it was Rita Moreno for a second."

"She's going on a date," says Anisha.

"Nice! Good for her!" Sarah lays out pretzels, gummy bears, and Oreos on the table. "Okay, I brought the snacks and my canvas, what are we painting?"

"It depends on what you two want to do," I say, as we sit down. "We could either all paint the same thing or we could turn it into a bit of a therapeutic session of just painting for the calming effect of painting."

The girls choose the latter and Anisha fills our wine glasses as I give a few tips and tricks. I chose to get acrylic paints, since they're easier to work with, to keep things simple. I show them how they can blend colors both on and off the canvas and the room falls quiet as they quickly become engrossed in painting.

"This is seriously calming," Anisha whispers. "You should host these as a side gig—wine, art, and silence nights. Military spouses would go feral for it." Not a bad idea. I file it away. Eventually, I'd like to do something to give back through art.

My phone vibrates on the table. Denny's calling me. Why is he calling? My stomach suddenly drops in fear. It couldn't be about Cole, could it? That's not how it works if they need to notify someone that something bad happened, right? Or what if he's changed his mind and he called Denny to break up with me because he said he wouldn't talk to me until he got back? No, that's insane. This no-talking thing is driving me crazy.

"I'll be right back," I say as I take my phone and rush to my room, adrenaline jumping through me as I answer. "Hey, is he okay?"

"What? He? Oh, Cole?" Denny says. "Oh, sorry, you're worried I'm calling because something bad happened? No, no, he's fine, I'm calling about me, actually."

I take a deep breath and let it out through my lips.

"Sorry, Tia, I didn't think I would scare you."

"No, it's okay, no worries," I say with a relieved laugh. "What's up?"

Denny sighs. "Um...I was hoping you could give me some girl advice."

"Oh, okay," I say, sitting down on my bed and crossing my legs.

"Remember Ellis? Get this, I just ran into her at a restaurant. And she seemed pretty happy to see me. And then I was saying goodbye and we were in this little hallway and it was like a habit...I kissed her. On the forehead!"

I gasp. "Denny! Oh my gosh!" It sounds like something straight out of a romance movie, the long-lost lovers reunited.

"She seemed like she was happy about it, she didn't go weird on me or anything." He exhales and mutters, "She smelled like coconuts and sunscreen. Do you think I should ask her out? Is that a good move or do you think it'll scare her off?"

I bite the inside of my bottom lip, weighing what he's told me. "What do you hope will happen, if you call her?"

"Obviously she'll admit that she's still hopelessly in love with me and all she wants in life is to marry me and raise a bunch of blond babies and ride off into the sunset together."

He groans as he finishes his sentence, like he knows how far gone he is. Poor guy. I can't imagine being in his shoes.

"Well, the worst that can happen is she says no. Just go into it assuming she'll say no and if you're already hurting for her, can it hurt worse?"

"Tia, if there's one thing I learned from letting go of the love of my life, it's that it can always get worse."

His words hit my heart like the thunk of an ax against a log, threatening to break apart my stubbornness about Cole and Navy life. I look over to my nightstand, to the framed picture Cole gave me. If I let him go, would I be in pain forever? And what's worse, the pain of a challenging life with him or the pain of trying to pretend I'm okay without him?

"Then text her," I tell Denny. "Keep it casual, no expectations, something chill like getting coffee or ice cream or something."

"You think I should go for it?"

"Be brave and dare greatly. Be the man in the arena, nothing is won by standing on the sidelines. Babe Ruth said, 'Never let the fear of striking out get in your way.' Sorry, I've been reading a lot of quotes about courage."

Denny chuckles. "Okay, I'm going to do it."

"I hope she says yes."

"Thanks, Tia. How's Cole doing?"

Someone asking me for updates about Cole is sweet and thrilling. As in, I'm the person who would know the most about him and what he's doing right now. I wish I knew how he was. I wish I could tell Denny about every wild and wonderful thing he's learning. But I won't know any of that for weeks still.

"Uh, I think he's fine. He said he's not going to talk to me until he's back."

"He what?" Denny screeches incredulously.

"He said he needs to take some time for himself. He wanted us to like, take a break from communicating. I'm not entirely mad about it, for the record."

"Huh...that sounds really dumb." I feel validated that I'm not the only one who thinks so. "Okay, well thanks for the advice."

"Anytime, Denny. Good luck."

I've never considered myself a romantic, but the way I'm rooting for Denny and Ellis to work things out and get back together makes me wonder if Cole is well and truly converting me to believing in true love.

"Was it Cole?" asks Anisha, as I make my way back to the table.

"No, it was Denny, actually," I say. "Hey, what's the name of the girl he's obsessed with? Ellis—"

"Ellis Montclair, her dad recently became the admiral of Third Fleet."

My mouth drops into a big O-shape. I met her mom. And her dad is admiral of the fleet? I know more about Marine Corps structure than Navy structure, but that sounds incredibly important. I hope it goes well for Denny, despite it seeming like the odds are stacked against him.

"How's Cole doing by the way?" Sarah asks.

"Where are you guys at with things?" Anisha asks. "Are you even dating?"

I shake my head. "We're...kind of past that. We both know we want all or nothing."

Sarah goes wide-eyed as she takes a sip of wine, swallowing hard. "Hang on, you guys have only known each other for like three months. Frank and I have been together for five years and we're not even engaged."

"The timing is the least of my objections," I reply. "It's just whether I'm able to accept that life with him will look...different from what I imagined as a secure and stable life."

"Their timeline is not uncommon," Anisha chimes in, "especially for military couples. I've known people who eloped within twenty-four hours of meeting."

"Watch that be Luko," I joke.

"For real," Anisha replies with a laugh.

"Remember how you said it takes love and bravery?" I say to her. "I keep feeling stuck when it comes to the second part. How does someone get more bravery?"

Sarah shakes her head. "You can't force yourself to be okay with a situation you're not okay with. I think you either have the courage to do it and the love helps you overcome your hurdles...or it doesn't."

"You probably have a lot of latent courage," says Anisha. "Like those people who don't think they're strong and then they can suddenly lift a car off a person. Once you start pushing your limits, you'll see how much you're actually capable of."

"Maybe..." I reply. "I think if it was anything less than what Cole and I are talking about, which I'm pretty sure is committing for life, then it would be something that I would suck it up and do. Like painting, I just need to put my brush in paint and start. But I take commitment and marriage seriously, so I...I don't know if it's like a 'try and see how it goes' kind of thing."

I finally pick up a paintbrush and start swiping some cobalt-blue paint across my canvas in broad swoops. I let it sit for a minute or two, then come back in with some titanium white, blending and mixing and making more dimensional waves.

"How's Mick?" I ask as I think about him on the aircraft carrier, bobbing up and down in the middle of the sea.

"He is so done with deployment," says Anisha. "The last month is always the hardest, it seems like it never ends. People are stressed on the ship, he's getting more and more impatient, and it's hard to maintain a good attitude. Thank the Lord he's not getting extended."

Sarah puts a lot of focus on giving some shadows to her clouds, then sets her paintbrush down. "If you could go back to the night you met Mick, and you could decide whether to go talk to him or not, knowing everything you know now, what would you do?"

"Easy," says Anisha, dropping her chin in her hand, with a smile. "I'd walk right up to him and say, 'Hi, handsome. Life is going to suck really bad sometimes, but would you like to go through it together?'" She taps her phone to wistfully look at the lock screen photo of her and Mick. "He's my person, he's totally worth it."

————

LATER THAT NIGHT, I lie in bed piecing together my thoughts of the day, thinking about Denny and Ellis, about Mick and Anisha, about how much I want to call Cole.

Love is so humbling. It's taken over my pride and plans and forced me to reckon with the limits of my selflessness and capacity for sacrifice. If I could go back and decide whether or not to meet Cole, what would I do?

Cole feels like an inevitability, like he was always meant to be a part of my story, from the moment I locked eyes with him in the liquor store. Choosing an alternate reality where I never interact with him would be battling a predestined fate, fighting a battle I could never win. I'm living in a state of war when I could enjoy blissful peace with Cole.

CHAPTER 34

"Drive safe," says Aunt Mari, handing me a travel mug of tea as I do a mental run-down to make sure I remembered everything for the art intensive. "*Disfruta tu semana*. I'm sure you'll learn a lot."

"*Gracias*," I say, giving her *besos* before getting behind the wheel with excitement and anticipation. The Camaro starts up well, thanks to Luko and Denny, who took a look and figured out it was a squeaky belt they could easily replace. I wave as I leave the driveway, then take the main road off the island, over the bridge, and onto the freeway. The sky is deeply blue, the ocean is sparkling on my left, and my Karol G playlist is matching my mood.

But as I get onto the 405 freeway, with forty-five minutes left to drive to Marina Del Rey, a pit forms in my stomach. I turn off my music. I have no idea what the other workshop participants will be like, what Giada will be like, what the atmosphere will be. What if they're all stuffy art elitists and I'm the one who barely got in thanks to a favor from a friend? What if I'm not as good as I think I am? What if Giada is demanding and brusque and we don't get along?

You're going to do great. It's going to be awesome.

Cole's kind voice comes into my head as clearly as if he was in the car with me. It sucks that I can't talk to him, can't hear his voice in real time. There's so much I want to tell him, and I want to know how he's doing and what he's learning. It's ridiculous to have a favorite person in the world and not be able to communicate with them.

I run my hands over the steering wheel, the one his hands are usually wrapped around. He believes in me. I can believe in myself too. There's no reason I have to be self-deprecating and allow negative thoughts to take over.

I whisper a new-to-me Winston Churchill quote out loud: "Fear is a reaction. Courage is a decision." I switch the song to Karol G's "*Mi Ex Tenía Razón*" as I slip on my sunglasses, and let the Camaro roar a little as I head north.

I PARK in the driveway of a narrow, but tall modern concrete building in a residential neighborhood. According to the website, there's an apartment set-up on the ground floor and the open space where our classes will take place is above it, on the second floor.

A tall, willowy woman in a black linen caftan, her gray hair elegantly done up in a French twist, comes out of the apartment to greet me.

"Hello, hello, hello, I'm Giada. You must be Tia Lopez."

"I am, thank you for having me," I say, as she gives me a quick handshake with a pat to the back of my hand.

"I'm very glad Lorraine reached out to me, I'm always looking to have newer artists in my workshops. I am selective, you know, but I think you're going to have an amazing experience. I'll show you your room, then we can get your things set up in the studio."

I grab my bags out of the trunk and follow her into the apartment, a sparsely furnished space reminiscent of a dorm room, with one couch in front of a small TV. There's a tiny kitchen in the corner with a stove, sink, microwave, and refrigerator, then a hallway with two bedrooms across from each other and one bathroom at the end of the hall. It's all white walls with natural lighting, macrame wall hangings, and light oak floors, reminiscent of the pictures I've seen of the studio upstairs.

"It's small, but perfect. You won't be spending much time down here anyways," Giada says.

The itinerary was emailed out a few weeks ago and my mouth went dry when I saw that we would be painting under instruction from eight a.m. to noon, then listening to presentations from guest artists during lunch from one to two in the afternoon. After a break from two to four p.m., we would gather for art critiques over dinner from four to six, then one more round of painting from six to eight p.m. Intensive was the right word for this week of instruction.

"Make yourself at home, then once you're ready, bring your supplies upstairs and we'll get you set up at an easel. Also, all the food will be in the dining room off the studio. We only have the one intro session today, from one to four, so no rush, but it'd be best if you were ready to go by quarter to one." She smiles as she glides out of the room.

I set my bags in the corner and take in the petite bedroom with a twin bed covered in white linens, a small leather chair in one corner, and a wardrobe across from it with a fake green plant draping down the side. It's austere, but comfortable and perfectly suited for a one-week stay. The first thing I do is pull out the framed photo of Cole and me, and prop it on the nightstand.

I take a picture and send it to Aunt Mari to let her know I've arrived safely. She responds with a GIF of a baby saying "¡Qué linda!" which makes me laugh. She has date number two with her rich love interest tonight and I ask her to tell me how it goes.

My next instinct is to text Cole, but I exercise the utmost self-control and hold back. I wonder what he's doing right now, what he looks like. I picture him in uniform or scrubs, sterile blue gloves on his hands, maybe some blood, like he alluded to. But his face would be intent under a surgical mask, his eyes focused. He'd be in control of the situation, making calculated decisions and—

No, I'm not going to spend mental energy daydreaming about him. This is my time, my week, my realm.

———

I AM DEFINITELY in over my head. At one o'clock on the dot, Giada had us pick up our paintbrushes and start in on a portrait of a live model. The woman sits across from me in a wingback chair, in front of the semi-circle of six artists and their easels. She looks like something from a Gothic novel, in a white high-neck dress, her black hair streaming down past her shoulders.

Giada's instruction was to paint the woman's portrait in our usual style, using our usual methods. She offers advice and direction as we work, pointing out different things about the lighting, background and shapes we could use to refine our portraits. She stops by each of our easels as we work, noticing the distinctions between each of us artists.

I'm hesitant about my brushstrokes, trying to think ahead and plot the whole painting in my mind so I can control every detail and dimension.

Giada breaks through my thoughts as she speaks from across the room. "If you have the larger value shapes right, that's eighty percent of the portrait done. The other twenty percent, the smaller details aren't nearly as important. Your outline sketch is the surest foundation. Again, if you have the larger value shapes right, that's eighty percent of the portrait done."

Her words fly into my brain, coming to rest in my heart, resonating with meaning. I can easily outline a sketch with confidence. My brush starts to fly between my palette and canvas and in no time, Giada is looking over my shoulder, nodding at my canvas in approval.

———

THE NEXT MORNING, I start in on another portrait challenge—high-contrast colors. As I paint the background with cadmium red, bright as a bell pepper, I keep turning over the eighty-twenty analogy that Giada told us yesterday.

When I left D.C. to come to San Diego, I only had eighty percent of the picture. I knew I could stay with Aunt Mari, that I could get a job to earn my own money, that I could be happy. I didn't know the other details, which was fine, but those "details" became the best surprises of all. I didn't know I would make such great friends, that I would grow in my artistic abilities, that I would meet the incredible Cole Slaeden.

It dawns on me that if I say yes to Cole, I'm not looking into a future of one hundred percent unknowns. I just have to trust the eighty percent that I do know—the larger value shapes of the love Cole and I have for each other, our character, our personal values. And the other twenty percent...well, I can choose to not let it worry me. I can choose to move forward. I can choose to stop holding back. I can let my love run free and not be fettered down by unknowns.

That night, I read through my collection of courage quotes again and find what I'm looking for from Lao Tzu: "Being deeply loved by someone gives you strength, while loving someone deeply gives you courage."

I love Cole Slaeden deeply. My love for him ignites my courage, which fuels my willingness to do whatever it takes to be with him.

Once I stop trying to temper my love, desire, and want for Cole and finally admit it, it shocks me as it courses through me, powerful and ecstatic. It's a relief to stop arguing with myself and surrender to my indomitable love for Cole. My heart is pounding in my chest and adrenaline shoots through my body traveling outwards to my fingers and toes. I feel alive and awake and *ready*. Finally, finally.

Courage.

———

THE NEXT MORNING, I struggle through our prompt from Giada to use contrasting colors to create depth. I achieved the desired effect to a degree with Cole's portrait, but I'm trying to incorporate stronger colors this time around. However, every time I add a paint color to my palette that feels like the logical choice, it mixes together wrong. I want to smear my canvas with alizarin crimson, then layer it with French ultramarine, to see what will happen with the violet hue, but that seems like a crazy leap. I stand in front of my easel, paralyzed with indecision.

My phone vibrates in my pocket, in a rhythm that tells me I have an incoming call. It's not Cole, I know it's not him, I know for a fact it's not. I don't even need to check.

I still want to double-check.

I pull out my phone and nearly drop it. Cole is calling. Actually, he's FaceTiming. Is this a test? Am I not supposed to answer it? Oh, screw that, even if it's a pocket dial, I'm answering. I set my brush down and take my phone across the hall before answering.

"Hey, Cole."

As soon as his face fills the screen, he starts talking, his voice slightly echoing like he's sitting in a stairwell. "Hi. I am so sorry. I don't know what I was thinking about not talking to you." He clears his throat. "I feel so terrible. I left and then I left you alone and that was the wrong thing to do. I'm so sorry, I should never have done that."

A weight rolls off me and I take a deep breath full of relief. "I'm not mad," I say, with a soft smile.

"Just disappointed. That's the worst. I totally deserve it too."

"What's prompting all of this?" I ask. I hope Denny didn't go chew him out after our phone call last week.

"There's a guy here on the course who's married and he calls his wife every night and every morning. It started to eat at me that he probably had it figured out, that he was doing the right thing, and I was the one who was doing it all wrong."

"Oh, okay," I reply, relieved to hear his reasoning.

He sighs and adjusts his angle. I can see he's in uniform, with a surgical mask in one hand and he is sitting in a stairwell. "I totally understand being mad, I really do. You don't deserve that."

"Well, did the past week or two give you time to yourself at least?" I ask.

"No," he says with a deep, rueful laugh. "All I did was think about you. Turns out, everything isn't black and white, yes and no, talking or not talking. You're part of everything I do now."

I understand that feeling all too well. I bite my lip and look down at my shoes for a moment. The minority voice in my brain thinks he really needs to grovel his way back into my good graces, while the overwhelming majority says, *Isn't it incredible, to hear that he couldn't stop thinking about you?*

Cole sniffles, drawing my attention back to him and his penitent face. I think love is going to win this round.

"After all my promises and reassurances about being there for you, no matter where I was in the world...I'm so sorry, can you ever forgive me?"

In his humility, willingness to admit wrong, and ability to genuinely apologize, Cole illustrates exactly why I trust him, why I can forgive him quickly and easily.

"Yes, I can. And I do."

He sighs and I watch his shoulders sag in relief. "It won't happen again. All I want to do is talk, I'm dying to know how you are. I miss you so bad."

I hear Giada giving instruction, then she pops her head out of the classroom to scan the hall for me. I give her a sheepish grin as she waves me back to the class.

"I miss you too. I'm on my art intensive right now and it really is really intensive," I tell Cole in a hurried whisper. "I think I won't finish class until you're asleep. We can at least send messages throughout the day and I'll check them when I can. I'd love to hear how you're doing too. My instructor is waving me back, I have to go now."

"Okay, sounds good, love you, bye."

I press a kiss to the screen and hang up.

Giada glides over to me as I hurry back to my place. She takes a glance at my palette, then my blank canvas.

"Let your heart and your mind go where they want to go, don't cage yourself in with ration," she murmurs to me. "Just like love, art has its own logic."

She moves on to the woman painting next to me and I blink hard. Okay...okay.

I close my eyes and refocus my mind from the excitement of my conversation with Cole back to painting. After a moment, I decide I'm not going to mess around with a background of melded colors, I'm going to use them as shadows and highlights. I'm going to paint a portrait in red and blue on a yellow background. I allow myself some titanium white to create different tints of the alizarin crimson and French ultramarine, add cadmium yellow to my palette, and dive right in.

As I add the colors in the hollows of the cheeks and the bridge of the nose, my mind rearranges the sagacious phrase Giada said earlier, repositioning the words. Just like painting, love has its own logic, and I cannot cage it in with ration.

That's exactly what I've been trying to do. I've been trying to take the love I have for Cole and shove it into a cage and it's not working because it was never meant to. I can't reconcile my own box-shaped plan with a love that will not be contained, because they are incompatible. I have to decide whether to stick to the cage of what I think I want from life, or go with the wild, ecstatic life of love with Cole that scares me with all its unknowns.

How does everything in this art class also apply to Cole and me?

Over dinner, we all take turns critiquing each other's work. Giada has set the tone for our feedback to be encouraging and positive, and I've learned so much by listening to how everyone processes and receives each other's art.

When it comes to my yellow, red and blue portrait, the table oohs and ahhs.

"This, this is what happens when you don't overthink," says Giada. The other participants chime in with phrases like, "Interesting and eye-catching," and "I wish I had thought to try that," and even "I'm obsessed with this idea."

My cheeks heat at everyone's praise. As I've learned more about each of my fellow participants and watched them work, I know I'm in the company of greatness. To have their admiration is incredible, and I leave the table for the evening round of painting floating on cloud nine. I think tonight will go down in my personal history as the night I feel I've arrived as an artist.

———

BY FRIDAY, I'm a new woman with half a dozen portraits I've produced in a frenzy of painting and the new-found freedom of working with the strange logic of art, instead of against it. I've experimented all week, under Giada's helpful eye, and we're both a little in awe of what I've done. She gives me a big hug as I get ready to leave. "All you have to do is let yourself be inimitably you. See what you're capable of? You don't even realize how strong you are and how well you can rise to the occasion until you try. Please stay in touch, I know you're going to do great things."

I am capable of great things. I am capable of loving fully. I am brave enough. I am courageous.

CHAPTER 35

ELISE COMES by the register with an armful of new Cafe 22 t-shirts that I helped her design, stacking them by size into piles of navy blue, tan, and gray in the baskets underneath the counter. I already know I'm going to snag a navy-blue one for Cole.

He and I have kept up good boundaries with talking: not staying up too late, not taking away from the time he needs to study and the time I need to keep up my painting momentum. Sometimes our communication is a short and sweet good-night text, sometimes it's hours on FaceTime.

Cole reserves the last hour of his day for journaling, a new habit he's adopted in an effort to spend time with his own thoughts. After about a week, he told me he actually looks forward to it and he wishes he would have known to do it before. We're growing individually and together while we're apart, and it's reassuring that we're not letting go of our own identities or ignoring the things we need to work on.

Cole is also letting his hopeless-romantic flag fly proudly.

The afternoon I got home from the art intensive, a big bouquet of fluffy pink and purple dahlias was delivered with the note, "I hope I get to talk to you every day for the rest of our lives.

Yours, Cole." This week it was a dozen red roses with an excerpt from "The Building of the Ship" and a note:

> *It is the heart, and not the brain,*
> *That to the highest doth attain,*
> *And he who followeth Love's behest.*
> *Far excelleth all the rest!*

"From your favorite poet, HWL. Love you, Cole."

"Tia," says Elise, interrupting my thoughts. "I was looking at the schedule for next week and you're off for four days in a row. Any fun plans?"

I tilt my head sideways. "I thought coming back from the art intensive, I'd be catching up on some shifts, but I guess not."

"Nope, you're free as a bird for those four days."

What could I do with four free days? My natural instinct would be to stay home and paint, but why do that when I could—

I have an idea.

I call Dad on my way home and make sure it sounds like a good plan. My passport is still valid from when I went to Mexico to see my grandparents a few years ago. The weather looks decent, no tropical storms on the horizon. The tickets are not terribly priced and I can use some points to book them. I'm all-in and my reservations are set before I even walk through the door to Aunt Mari's house.

I text Cole about my exciting new plans.

OSITO

That's an amazing idea, that's perfect! You're going to have the best time.

I still have some hesitations about seeing Dad and telling him I'm a full-time artist now, given that I don't have much to show for it. But this is climbing another rung on the ladder towards courage. I can't chicken out on going to see them because I'd rather avoid the topic. I'm going and we're going to talk about it and it's going to be great.

———

AS SOON AS I roll my carry-on into the baggage claim area of Aeropuerto Internacional de Cozumel, Dad and Julio raise their arms and yell, "*Gooooooooooolllllll!*"

Everyone turns to look at them and they grin at their successful attempt to embarrass me. I roll my eyes, smiling the whole time. Dad's wearing a sun-bleached Panama hat and a white guayabera that contrasts with his deeply tanned skin, browned by days under the sun on his fishing boat.

Julio is standing tall in a black t-shirt and gray shorts. He has new tattoos covering his left arm and I am shocked he told me nothing about them. Combined with his sharp black eyebrows against his lighter skin, he looks striking.

"Nina," says Dad, folding me into a hug. He takes a gasping breath as he holds me. "Oh, I have missed you so much and I didn't even know it."

A faint scent of corn tortillas and Old Spice is woven through the fabric of his shirt, and it makes my heart happy. "Me too, Dad."

I turn to Julio and wrap my arms around his lean frame. "*Hermana,*" he says as he gives me a hug. "*Ha pasado mucho tiempo.*"

"Oh, like you know Spanish now?" I say, poking him in the side.

"Since he's noticed the cute girl who works at the marina," says Dad. I shoot a smug smile at Julio as we walk outside the airport and cross the street to the parking lot. I'll ask him about it later.

"You have a good flight?" Dad asks.

"Yeah, it was great," I say as I get into the back seat of Dad's little white hatchback. Julio slides into the passenger seat and adjusts the seat, sending it flying back into my knees. I reach around the headrest to give him a throat-crushing hug.

"I'm so happy to see you," I squeal.

"*Vamos a celebrar,*" says Dad, turning on the local radio station that's currently playing a merengue classic.

It's a twenty-minute drive to Marina Caleta, where Dad's mini fleet of three boats are docked. We pass dozens of cinderblock and concrete buildings painted every color of the rainbow. Little red motor scooters carrying couples dart around, and every so often a bright mural outside a school or park catches my eye.

Giada encouraged me to try new mediums for painting, so I brought a travel watercolor set and a small sketchpad on this trip. I want to go back to landscapes and scenery for a bit and see how my skills have grown in that area from all my practice of portraits. If all goes well, I'll head back to San Diego with a small postcard collection of watercolors.

The city gives way to dense forests of tropical trees as we get closer to the marina. The whole drive Julio and Dad and I chat about how the fishing is going, funny stories from Dad's latest charters, and what kind of fish is popular to catch this time of year.

"Wait, so you're helping Dad with charters now?" I ask Julio. "Like, long term?"

"I'm still not sure. I'm going to delay my application to business school for a while, we'll see," he says. "But in the meantime, it's been awesome being down here. And yes, my Spanish has gotten better, solely because of living here and being immersed in the culture."

Dad and I exchange a glance in the rear-view mirror that says we both know better. We park at the marina and Dad walks us down the pier. Julio keeps looking around, like he's looking for someone specific, but he relaxes once we get to the boats.

Dad gives me a short tour of each of them, then we settle down for a drink on the middle one, *La Sirena*. Dad pops open the lid of a cooler and hands bottles of Modelo beer to Julio and me. "I can't remember the last time we sat down together like this," he says. "Having you two here...it's the best."

"It's been way too long," Julio replies.

"You're always the one jetting off to new and exciting places," I say.

He pauses with his beer midway to his mouth. "Because I never heard you guys say otherwise."

I look at Dad to back me up, but he's looking at Julio with his head tilted to one side. Julio looks at Dad, who finally looks at me.

"Did we just never...communicate?" says Dad. I shrug.

Julio leans forward, his elbows resting on his knees. "I always wanted to come home from college and have a quiet Christmas with you guys, but freshman year, my roommates talked me into a ski trip, and I was desperate for friends, so I went."

"What about the next Christmas?" I ask.

"You took a winter session community college course for extra credit. So I planned another trip."

"What about the one after that?" A strange sense of dismay rises in me. A sense of missing out on something that could have been. "Was that the one I went to Mexico to see Abuelo and Abuela?"

We look at Dad, who holds up his hands in surrender. "You both had made other plans for two years in a row, so I assumed you were done with coming home for Christmas. I took my first trip here to check things out."

"What about summer and Thanksgiving and all those holidays?"

"Once you two had jobs and lives and you weren't in college anymore, I thought you wouldn't want to hang out with your old dad. I moved here and you never mentioned wanting to visit."

I look around in disbelief. "All this time we could have seen each other way more?"

"Dang," whispers Julio. He laughs to himself and sips his beer.

I can't believe it. There's no way this is a simple miscommunication issue. No way. And yet...the way Julio recounts it does add up. We're each as much to blame as the next person. Schedules got full, jobs got hectic, we just drifted out of orbit with each other.

"Well, let's never do that again," I say.

"Yeah, for sure," Julio chimes in.

Dad laughs. "You guys still want to hang out with me?"

"Obviously," says Julio. "You were the first destination on my list when I got laid off at the bank."

"You got laid off?!" I shriek. A twinge of regret follows my shriek. When I got laid off, Julio was nothing but kind and comforting. I set my beer in a cup holder and go give my brother a tight squeeze around his shoulders. "I'm sorry."

He pats my arm. "Right back at you."

"Would it make you feel better if I told you what I'm doing now?"

"Sure," he says with a laugh.

"I'm an artist." I go back to my seat without looking at either of them, giving them a moment to process. "I know you never were a big fan of me having an art career, but it's what I want and I'm really enjoying it."

"*Mija*," says Dad when I finally look at him. "You're an adult, your own woman now. I've grown, you've grown. I'm sorry for what I said when you were younger. I wasn't trying to be mean, I only wanted to protect you from disappointment."

"The arts are hard," Julio chimes in. "It's risky. So many people try and fail, barely scraping by and taking hit after hit when they can't get their career off the ground."

Dad shoots Julio a glance that tells him to stop talking. "Nina, I'm proud of you for trying," he says. "I'm sure you'll be amazing at it."

"Thanks, Dad," I say with a grateful smile. I can tell his words have genuine feeling behind them. "Oh, and I'm kind of seeing someone now actually. His name is Cole, he's a corpsman in the Navy."

"*Es un nombre gringo, ¿no?*" Julio says.

"*Cállate,*" I hiss, trying to find a way to kick him. "This girl must be really cute if you're learning Spanish for her. You hate Spanish."

"*Es el lenguaje del amor.*"

"You in love is new. And gross," I say, like we're back in high school.

"So, Cole. He's a nice guy?" asks Dad.

"Really nice."

"How serious are you?" asks Julio.

"Really serious," I say, taking another sip of my beer.

"Like commitment-serious?" asks Dad. I nod and watch him and Julio exchange a glance. Dad looks skeptical; Julio's going to be a hard sell.

"*Mija,*" Dad says, stretching back in his seat. "Are you sure it's not just because he's the first nice guy you've been with?"

"He's..." I trail off, thinking of how different it is to describe him to say, Jules, versus to Dad and Julio. They don't care how strong he is, how pretty his eyes are, how sweet he is when he's tired. They care about things like is he going to break my heart, how is he going to protect me and provide for me. "He's very caring, very kind, he's thoughtful and encouraging. He's dedicated to his job. He loves his family. Aunt Mari loves him too. He's... amazing."

"I am worried for you," Julio mumbles, finally looking up. "Navy guys are not all good. What if he turns mean and cheats on you? What if he drags you around the country and he doesn't take care of you?"

Dad leans forward. "I worry you may not understand what it means to marry someone, Nina."

"Dad!" I exclaim. "I'm not a child, I know what marriage is."

"Does he, this Cole?"

"Yes, he had a very good picture of marriage. His dad was a wonderful husband to his mom. He died a few years ago." A lump wells up in my throat and I look out across the marina, blinking back my emotions. "Where was all this concern when I was dating an absolute loser?"

I pick at the gold label on the stubby brown beer bottle. Where was all this questioning when Bryce was making me feel small and less significant than him? How come no one asked me the hard questions before it was too late?

"I think when you're gone," Dad says, slowly, cautiously, "I have an image of you as a grown-up woman, confident and self-assured. But when you're sitting right in front of me, I see my little Nina, the one who grew up begging her brother to play futbol and would ask me to read princess stories before bed."

"I feel the same," Julio says. "I think about you working in D.C. and being some powerful woman who wears heels to work every day. It wasn't until you called us from Aunt Mari's that I realized you're not that. Not in a bad way, just...you're still you, still young and vulnerable."

"I'm sorry I didn't protect you better," says Dad. "No matter where you are, you're still my girl."

Julio nods. "We need each other. I mean, look at how Dad's been here for me, Aunt Mari's been there for you. *Familia*, you know?"

It's Julio saying "familia" that makes my heart crack wide open.

"That's it," I say, with a laugh as I tilt my head back to keep my tears in my eyes. "We're having a family reunion, every summer and every Christmas. I don't care where we are in the world, we're going to make it happen. And you're going to meet Cole and I know you're going to love him. Now stop making me cry."

Dad and Julio both come over and squeeze me tight as the boat gently sways under us.

———

PAINTING IN COZUMEL IS A REVELATION. I thought I might feel irked by not having my regular studio set-up and controlled atmosphere, but it's actually freeing and energizing to be painting wherever Dad takes us. My sketches are quick, my color studies of the ocean are vibrant turquoise and aquamarine, and I love having the island as its own subject.

We all go snorkeling one morning and I spend the afternoon painting as many fish as I can from memory. If I had more time, I'd settle in and do actual oil paintings and pull together a theme. As it is, I fill my sketchbook easily by the end of my visit.

It illustrates what Cole said on the beach when we were talking about the future, about me painting anywhere. If Cole and I were together, and we would have to move to wherever the Navy sends us, there would always be something new and interesting for my creative brain. I can take my supplies all over the world, I can find inspiration anywhere, and being an artist is actually one of the most liberating professions I could choose for myself right now. I don't have to give up any part of myself to follow him, I simply have to find my anchor points, find my routine, and get to painting.

I can go anywhere with him.

By the time I hug Dad and Julio at the airport, I'm sad to say goodbye to them, but so ready to be one day closer to Cole being home.

"Okay, so Christmas, yes?" I say, looking each of them in the eye.

"Christmas here?" asks Dad.

"Christmas at Aunt Mari's?" I counter.

"Talk to her first before you invite us all there," says Julio.

"Okay, Christmas at Aunt Mari's, pending an invitation."

Dad chuckles. "Even in your late twenties, you're still my *niños*." He suddenly calls out to a passerby who must be a friend of his, asking him to take our photo. He puts one arm around each of us and beams. When he texts it to us, all I see is pride emanating from his whole demeanor. He may be Julio's dad, and my uncle, but he's our rock.

"Love you, Nina," he says, giving me a hug and multiple *besos* to my cheeks.

"Love you, Dad. Thank you for everything. Thank you for still being here for us, even though we're adults."

"We'll never be too old to need a hug from you," Julio chimes in as I turn to hug him.

"I hope it works out with the girl you have a crush on," I whisper to him.

"Aww, thanks, Nina. I hope it works out for you and *el gringo*." I poke him hard in the ribs, then give him one more hug.

"*¡Hasta Navidad!*" I say as I walk away, waving to both of them.

"*¡Hasta Navidad!*" They shout back.

CHAPTER 36

SEVEN WEEKS AGO, I said goodbye to Cole with the heaviest weight of dread on my chest. So much has changed since then, it feels like a lifetime has passed. But it also feels like I snapped my fingers and now I'm getting ready to pick him up from the airport.

If I thought I had butterflies around Cole before, nothing compares to the way my entire body is taken over by flutters and nerves knowing he is on a flight back to me. This homecoming thing is unreal. I never knew I could be so excited and totally terrified at the same time. Not that I'm terrified to see him, but I'm just so nervous.

I put on a blue-and-white polka dot off-the-shoulder cotton dress with a ruffle around the bottom, some neutral sandals, and decide at the last minute to leave my hair down. I swipe on some makeup, spritz on some perfume, and check my phone. I still have fifteen minutes to kill.

Well, I'm going to spontaneously combust if I stay here a moment longer. I'll have to find parking at the airport anyway, so may as well head out. I connect my phone to Bluetooth and dial Anisha as I drive over the bridge.

"Tia! What's up, girl?"

"Um, I'm heading to the airport to pick up Cole and I am...is it normal to feel numb one second and overly hot the next second and then like I'm going to throw up?"

Anisha screams into the phone, then laughs. "That's going to be me in five days! Isn't it the best worst feeling? Oh, my gosh, homecomings are insane! When Mick came home from his first deployment, I thought I was gonna cry buckets of tears, but instead I laughed like a crazy person. Literally, I could not stop laughing, and it was not cute. It was half-cackling, half-braying. Tia! You're doing it!"

Now I'm the one screaming to let out the nervous energy and massive swell of emotions rising in me. Anisha screams with me, and then I'm laughing, my eyes welling with tears. "I have never felt anything like this!"

Anisha sighs. "Right before he walks into the baggage claim, you're going to get this kick to the heart. You'll know he's right there, and then he'll see you and run to you, and it will be the best moment of your life."

———

I'M CLUTCHING my purse in a death grip, standing on my tiptoes as if I'll see him sooner if I'm just a bit taller. People are calmly walking into the baggage claim juggling their water bottles and neck pillows and backpacks, completely unaware my life is about to feel whole again the minute I'm in Cole's arms.

I have to remember to breathe. I keep scanning the crowd, hoping I won't miss him, that I'll see him the instant he comes through the security doors. Every time I see a blond male or a guy wearing a hat, my pulse doubles. I can't wait to kiss him, to hug him, to smell him.

Suddenly my heartbeat trips and my whole body starts shaking. He's here, he's steps away, I can feel it. I'm smiling, but a giant sob is welling in my throat. We made it.

Cole Slaeden bursts through the crowd, running towards me with his unmistakable, megawatt smile. I run to meet him, and he drops his backpack to scoop me up in his arms. I wrap my arms around his neck, clinging to him so tightly, only loosening a fraction to kiss him. He kisses me back with short kisses over and over, then one long kiss that he holds forever, like he's been waiting his whole life for this moment.

I eagerly press my lips to his. My choice is him. I gladly, willingly relinquish all of my stable, safe plans for myself and I choose Cole. I choose the most incredible man, I choose true love, I choose the Navy life. I want it all.

I can feel Cole's whole body shaking when he pulls back to look me in the eye.

"Hi," I whisper, relishing the feel of his short hair under my hand, the smell of him, the ripple of his muscles as he adjusts his hold on me.

"Hi, Tia," he whispers back. He slowly sets me on my feet. "Oh, it's so good to see you," he says, taking my face in his hands to kiss my forehead. "You're so beautiful."

I can't say anything or I'll cry, so I wrap my arms around him in a tight hug, pressing my forehead to his.

"Hi," he says again, letting go of my waist and possessively taking my hand in his.

"Hi." I give him the biggest grin as we make our way to the baggage claim to grab his sea bag. "How was the flight?" I ask, awkwardly breaking into normal conversation as bags drop onto the carousel.

"Fine. You look so cute in this dress," he says, hugging me from behind, pressing a kiss to my neck. "I want to have you all to myself for the rest of the day."

I turn and trace his jaw with my finger, making his arms break out in goosebumps. I nearly say, "How about for the rest of your life, my love?" but I press a kiss to his cheek instead.

He grabs his sea bag, hoists it over his shoulder, and takes my hand, picking up his backpack in the other. "Lead the way."

I slowly navigate us back to where the Camaro is parked. We stop no less than six times to kiss and look into each other's eyes.

"I can't believe you're here," I whisper, pressing my hand to his cheek. We haven't stopped smiling yet and I don't know if we ever will.

"I love you," Cole says, his hand against the small of my back, pulling me flush against him for another kiss.

I had a whole thing planned, a special location, a mini speech, a declaration, and finally, the three words I've been holding out on saying. But in the mix of excitement and euphoria, they come tumbling out halfway down Section S of the parking garage as I wrap my arms around his neck.

"I love you so much, Cole."

He freezes, looking at me with wide eyes. He turns around to glance around the parking garage, spies the Camaro, and says, "Hold that thought."

———

COLE PARKS alongside the dunes of Crown Island, opens my door for me, and practically drags me out onto the beach. We dash across the warm sand, and I giggle at Cole's sense of urgency. The blue skies, the way Cole keeps looking over his shoulder at me with a wide smile, the way my hair and my skirt dance in the wind; it all feels like the happiest version of sunshine and sea breezes.

When we reach the cooler, packed wet sand, I run ahead of Cole, and grab his hands in mine.

"I love you so much," I say, threading my fingers through his.

"How much?" he asks, looking down at me with hope and expectation.

"Enough to fill a lifetime."

He blinks a few times, letting my words sink in. "A lifetime?"

"Yes," I say with a nod. "I want to go where you go, I want to be by your side for all of the wild, beautiful, chaotic life we could live together. I want to be yours, for every goodbye and every homecoming, every tough night, and every accomplishment. I want to be the woman who's there for you through it all."

He looks down at me for a long minute, and I give him time to process what I'm saying.

"Are you serious?" Cole asks, smiling as tears start trickling down his cheeks.

"Completely serious, I mean every word."

Cole takes a few steps back from me, running his hand over his hair, then wiping his eyes.

"I'm really overwhelmed," he says with a laugh. "I'm so happy, but I can't believe it. But I'm so relieved too. And I'm wondering if this is a dream, but it's too good even for a dream. I feel like I need to yell or something."

He takes a deep breath, filling his cheeks, and blows it out in a whoosh. "I've wanted this for so long now." He pauses as his voice shakes with emotion. "Since that day we talked about love. I wanted to kiss you for what felt like forever, and I thought I could live with just that, if it was all you'd give me. But I've been living like a man half-starved until this moment, until you said you love me. Now I am just...overwhelmed and happy and—"

His eyes darken, focus on me, and before I know what's happening, Cole comes charging towards me, scoops his arms around my legs, and spins us around, up the beach and back towards the dunes, yelling in delight. I squeal and laugh, bracing my hands on his shoulders as he runs in circles. Suddenly, his footing in the sand shifts, and I'm falling backwards with a yelp.

But Cole cradles my fall and ends up on top of me, lying in the sand. He lowers himself until our foreheads are touching. Then, finally, finally, he presses one, long promise of a kiss to my lips. It's a simple kiss that carries the weight of countless meanings and hopes and dreams and plans.

"I love you," he whispers to me.

"I love you," I whisper back.

My hands frame his face, and I meet him in every press of his mouth, matching every fragment of his desire and adoration and hope and love with my own, kissing him until there's a sense of wholeness. Cole's frenzied, passionate kisses relax as he takes his time, settling in like he could keep me here like this for hours. I would not complain.

———

WE EVENTUALLY END up back at Aunt Mari's house, after Cole did his best to brush all the sand off my back and tidy my hair. I can't wait to show him the collection I did during the art intensive, but as soon as we walk into my mini studio, I'm overwhelmed with gratitude for him. If he wouldn't have let me paint his portrait, I don't know what random side paths my artistic journey would have taken me on. I take his chin in my hand and press a kiss to his mouth. "You mean the world to me."

"We're here to talk about your art," he murmurs against my lips.

"Well, then, check it out," I say with a smile, turning him to look at the wall where my newest collection hangs, filling the space nearly from floor to ceiling.

They're all loosely sketched portraits in vibrant, high contrast colors of random models from the workshop, full of life with expressions of joy and hilarity. They turned out exceptionally well, proving to myself that Cole's portrait wasn't a fluke, I actually had upped my skills with all my practice. My vision came to life as soon as I stopped trying to control everything and granted myself freedom and latitude. I am so proud of what I've accomplished.

"What the...Tia, this is awesome," Cole says, his eyes lingering on each painting with appreciation. I love that he takes his time looking at them, not rushing through his observations. "How do you feel the class went overall?"

"It was definitely an elite level of instruction. We jumped in immediately on day one. Giada does not waste time—she is efficiency personified. There was no time to be nervous, I just had to pick up my brush and start. It forced me to move along at warp speed instead of agonizing over each step."

"These colors are super cool—very eye-catching. They'd make a great gallery collection," Cole says.

I can't stop grinning. How did I ever think I would be okay with letting him go?

"Anyway, just wanted to show you that," I say, hot and blushing.

I turn to leave, and Cole grabs my hand, reeling me into his arms. "I love you. Your mind fascinates me. I tried to draw something for you once and it was a total bust. But you, you create art over and over and over, like it's second-nature and it's incredible."

"I love you," I say, accepting his effuse praise, and ready to dish it back to him. "You're so brilliant and you have a brain like a steel trap. I couldn't memorize half the stuff you know and then you're out there handling physical wounds and real-life people. I would be paralyzed the second someone came to me with a cut and you'd just make comfortable small talk and take care of it like it's no big deal."

"I guess all our kids are going to come to me for band-aids and they'll come to you for artistic help with their science fair displays."

"Oh, we're talking about kids now?" I say with a nervous laugh as Cole swoops one arm around my waist, takes my hand, and starts slow-dancing with me.

"I'm talking about everything with you, Tia. The longest, fullest, most beautiful life."

"Buy a girl dinner first," I whisper, grinning.

"I'm gonna kiss you so you stop talking," Cole says, a deep rumble shaking us as he laughs, then kisses me.

CHAPTER 37

A FEW WEEKS LATER, it's my favorite holiday of the year—Halloween—and we're all gathering at Luko and Denny's for a team party. The doorbell goes off repeatedly as I'm putting the finishing touches on my up-do in the mirror of the master bathroom. Cole got off work late, rushed down here, quickly showered, then started putting on his costume with minutes to spare before the party starts.

"Zip me up?" I call out.

He comes sweeping into the bathroom in shiny black shoes from his dress uniform, a rented black tuxedo, and a massive, flowing black cape. What is it about a man in a cape? I go wide-eyed, my mouth making an O-shape.

"Oh my gosh," I say in an incredulous whisper. "You are so freakin' hot right now."

"Says the woman with a dress barely clinging to her shoulders," Cole says, his gaze raking up and down my body, his eyes going dark.

"Zip me," I say, before I let myself fall for that look in his eyes. My wide skirt swishes around my feet as I turn my back to him. The second I feel his hand against my dress, I press my hand to my stomach, my skin breaking out in goosebumps as the back of Cole's fingers trail against my spine, pulling the zipper up. When I turn around, my cheeks are hot pink and Cole's eyes meet mine in the mirror, dark and wanting.

"We should go down," I whisper. I never would have guessed dressing up as Christine and the Phantom of the Opera for Halloween would have been this sexy. Cole would have made a natural Raoul, but the Phantom is so much more iconic. Cole finally nods and picks up the white mask from the counter. When he slips it on, I press my lips together.

"Don't even think about serenading me with a seductive ballad in front of our teammates."

Instead of smiling, Cole's face goes serious and he pulls the mask off.

"What is it?"

"I feel like they're going to give us some...looks."

I give him a questioning look. "They're our teammates. They love us already."

"I know, I'm just...it's going to look like I jumped into another relationship, like I'm a true serial dater."

"They're not going to judge you."

"Mm, kinda feel like they are."

"Neither of us picked this timing, it just happened. That's love, it has its own logic."

Cole nods, running his hand over his hair.

"This isn't all one-sided, you know," I remind him, putting one hand to his cheek. "I'm here with you. I chose to be by your side. And I trust our friends will be happy for us."

"Okay," he says with a deep breath and a brave smile. He puts the mask back on and tucks my hand in the crook of his elbow. "Okay, let's go."

We head down the stairs in a sweeping grand entrance. Anisha, dressed as Rey from Star Wars, and Mick, dressed as Obi-Wan

Kenobi, are the first to see us. Anisha's jaw drops. "You win Halloween, forever."

"Hi, friend," I say with a laugh, giving her a big hug. She hugs me back so tight, I can't breathe, but I can feel her elation.

"Tia, this is Mick! I actually have a husband."

"Mick!" shouts Cole behind me. "Dude, good to see you."

"It's good to be back," says Mick, before turning to shake my hand. He's a lot taller in person, but he has a warm friendliness about him that matches Anisha's energy. "Hi, Anisha's told me all about you. Thanks for winning that championship by the way."

"Oh, gosh," I say with a laugh. "I've loved getting to know Anisha. She's awesome."

Denny comes around the corner, dressed as Robin Hood, complete with an endearing pair of wire frame glasses. He takes one look at us and whistles.

"Damn, you all are way too good at Halloween."

He never told me how things went with Ellis, and in the whirl of my trip to Mexico and Cole coming back, I've forgotten to ask. We all migrate to the kitchen where Luko is pulling brownies out of the oven. At first glance, he looks like he's dressed up as Maverick from Top Gun, but unfortunately, he's actually getting ready to head into the squadron for a night flight.

"Denny," I whisper, coming alongside him with the excuse of grabbing a cookie. "What's the latest with you-know-who?"

He glances over his shoulder, to where Luko is setting the brownies on the counter.

"That's another story for another time," he whispers back with a wink. He seems fine, but sometimes Denny is a hard one to read, always putting on a cheerful, upbeat attitude when he could be dying inside.

Sarah and Frank roll in to round out the group, dressed as Thor and a Valkyrie, of course. Sarah shoots me a wink and a smile when she sees Cole and I hand in hand.

"Okay, so last season's team was victorious in more ways than one," says Frank. "I was rooting for you guys."

"Seriously?" asks Cole.

"Well, hello, in case you haven't noticed, it's Tia we're talking about," says Sarah. "She's gold."

"So is he," I say, squeezing Cole's arm with a grin.

Frank, ever the team parent, gathers us all in a big circle in the middle of the kitchen. It's like we're back in the pre-game huddle.

"Hey, let's crush it tonight. Give out more candy than anyone on the block, down some drinks, and have a good time. Luko, what you got for us?"

"Do not add to the population." He shoots a pointed glance at Anisha and Mick, making Mick blush hard. I press my lips together to keep from laughing "Do not subtract from the population. Stay out of the hospital, newspaper, and jail—"

"If you do find yourself in jail, establish dominance quickly," Denny rattles off. "Hands in, Goal Diggers on three!"

"One, two, three, GOAL DIGGERS!"

⸻

AFTER THE DOORBELL stops ringing and most of our friends have gone home, I trade my big pink dress for a matching black sweatshirt and sweatpants and shake my hair out and Cole trades his sexy cape and tuxedo for charcoal joggers and an olive-green USMC sweatshirt. He needs to get back to base tonight and I know I'm going to crash as soon as I get back to Aunt Mari's. We walk out to our cars together, Cole's arm hooked around my neck in a sweetly possessive gesture.

"You're the best. Thanks for being game to dress up with me," I say.

"Of course." He drops a kiss to my hair.

Once he puts his stuff in the trunk, and gets ready to say good-night, I hug him, pressing him backwards until we're both leaning against the Camaro. His arms come around me, his hands tracing lines up and down my back. My head rests over his heart, and I can hear his pulse thumping away.

"I love you, Cole Slaeden," I murmur. "I love who you are. I love that I get to say my boyfriend's a corpsman in the Navy. I'm so happy I get to be by your side."

"I love you, Tia Lopez," he whispers, suddenly choked with emotion.

I melt. All of my future now centers around him. I want to take care of his heart and love him well, to gently tend to his kind soul.

"We're going to take care of each other," he promises, echoing my thoughts. "I'm going to love you so well, forever and ever. You will always be the first thought in my mind, and I will do everything I can to give you a beautiful life. I am yours, you are mine."

I stare up at him with nothing but adoration in my eyes. One of his hands leaves my back, drops into his pocket, then holds up a gold ring between us.

"Marry me?" Cole asks.

My stomach flips, my heart pounds, tears form instantly. This moment is beautifully real. My legs feel weak as I'm floored with gratitude and love.

"You want to marry me?" I ask, a mini sob interrupting me mid-sentence.

"I want to marry you, build a life with you, live every moment I can with you. Will you marry me?"

"Yes. Yes, of course," I say, crying as I press one hand to my mouth.

He slips the ring on my finger and I hold my hand up to the light. There's a rectangular diamond, emerald cut I think, set horizontal with diamonds wrapping all the way around the band. The minimal amount of setting I can see is gold. It's exquisite.

"Do you like it? I spent hours looking at rings online after class and this one felt like you."

"You got it during HMTT? Have you been carrying it around in your pocket this whole time?" I ask, with a laugh as I wipe my tears.

He laughs. "Yeah, anytime we're together. I wanted to be able to propose whenever the right moment came along."

"You're so sweet," I say, sobbing again. "I love you. This could not be any more perfect."

A wave of emotion comes over me as Cole holds me and kisses me thoroughly. So much has happened in our lives to lead us to this moment, it's awe-inspiring. I'm engaged to the most incredible man and we get to love each other for a lifetime. Cole was right, he did tell me so—to love and be loved truly is magic.

I pull back a bit to wipe the tears off my cheeks. "We're going to get married?"

Cole nods. "This is it, Queenie. You and me, forever."

"I'm so happy."

CHAPTER 38
EPILOGUE

"*Osito, ¿dónde está tu hijo?*" I yell out from the bedroom.

"*Carlitos está en la sala,*" Cole shouts as he comes down the hall from the bathroom. "*Está jugando futbol con Titi.*"

"*¿Está listo su biberón?*"

"*Sí, está en el refrigerador. Vamos, mi amor.*"

I put in my signature gold hoop earrings as I swish across Aunt Mari's guest room in a long pink floral dress with a deep V-neck and sheer long sleeves.

"You look gorgeous," says Cole, putting his left hand on my waist to still me long enough to steal a kiss. I glance down to make sure he has his wedding ring on today, which he does. He has a tattoo on his ring finger, since he doesn't wear a ring to work, but for special occasions, I like to see the flash of gold on his hand.

"You don't look so bad yourself," I say, patting the navy tie resting on his white dress shirt as I pass him. It's an understatement. He looks ridiculously handsome, and the way his khaki pants hug his butt is the icing on the cake. I take his chin in my hand and pull his mouth down to mine for a quick kiss.

"*¿Listos?*" asks Aunt Mari as we come into the living room. She's seated on the rug, tossing a mini soccer ball to Carlos. I'm very grateful she is still willing and able to host us and babysit an almost two-year-old. Her handsome husband, my new great-uncle, is unfortunately away on a golf trip at the moment. Carlos loves him only a tiny bit less than he loves his Titi.

"*Sí, gracias por ayudarnos con Carlos,*" says Cole, in perfect Spanish. I bite my lip. The man is too attractive for his own good sometimes.

"*No hay de qué,*" says Aunt Mari, as Carlos drops the ball in her lap. "*Disfruten la fiesta.*"

"*Gracias,* Aunt Mari," I say, leaning down to give her a quick kiss and squeeze the chunky cheeks of my little brown-haired, brown-eyed baby.

"I'm going to go to a little party now, okay, baby? You're going to play with Titi Mari and I'll be home soon. And tomorrow Tio Julio and Abuelo will be here."

"Titi!" exclaims Carlos, rushing Aunt Mari with a big hug around her neck that nearly knocks her over. Our squishy, hefty chunk of a baby has my looks and Cole's enthusiastic personality. He's just the best.

"*Adiós, Carlitos,*" says Cole as he opens the front door for me.

"*Adiós, Papi,*" Carlos calls back in his adorable little voice. I press a hand to my heart and exchange an emotional glance with Cole. We both melt whenever Carlos speaks Spanish.

"How is he so cute?" I ask as we start down the sidewalk.

Cole grabs my hand and kisses the back of it with a grin. "Because he's our baby. I always knew we would have the cutest kids."

The breeze picks up, rustling the palm trees under the gray June sky. I close my eyes and take a deep breath, relishing the fresh smell of the ocean wafting by. We live relatively near the ocean at our current duty station, Camp Lejeune, North Carolina, but the air isn't fresh and crisp enough for my picky beach tastes. There's something magical about being back on Crown Island, being in the place where my life really began.

"Can you believe we're walking down this sidewalk talking about our son?" Cole says. "And almost six years ago, you and I walked this same path not knowing if we would even be together?"

"Wild, isn't it?" I say, squeezing Cole's hand.

"Wildly awesome," he says with a big smile. "You're incredible."

"Only because you're amazing." I feel like I won the universe's grand prize, the greatest lottery in the world.

We pop into Cafe 22 to say a quick hello to Elise. Jules married her boyfriend and they moved up to Seattle a few years ago. We still exchange Christmas cards and Jules always signs hers with cute little digs like, "Told you you'd end up with the hot corpsman!"

And then it's time for the main event at Lorraine's gallery. It all feels extremely surreal as I turn the corner, hand in hand with Cole. Lorraine is standing outside wearing a fuchsia linen maxi dress, her hair cut into a chic silver bob. "Sweetheart!" she exclaims as soon as she sees me. She holds her arms out wide, her bangles clacking on her wrists, and folds me into a big hug. "Oh, I'm so happy to see you in person instead of over FaceTime."

"Me too," I say with a wide grin.

"Hi, Cole," she says, giving my husband a big hug and a pat on the shoulder. "Thank you for getting her here."

"Of course. Without you, there'd be no us. It's almost the six-year anniversary of the famous portrait." He drops a sweet little kiss to her cheek.

"Aww, what a time, what a memory. Well now that you're here, I think we're about ready to begin. Come on, let's say hi to Giada."

Giada spies me coming into the gallery and says, "Is that the great Tia Slaeden? Hi, you!" She squeezes me in a tight side hug. "I am so excited for this new collection. When you told me the concept, I thought it was so brilliant. What are you working on after this?"

There's a flicker of nervousness as I brace myself to tell Giada my plan. "I'm actually taking a break from painting for a bit. I'm going to partner with a military spouse nonprofit for a year to expand their offerings for art therapy classes."

Giada's eyes go wide. "Oh, that's so perfect for you. Tia, that sounds incredible."

I smile with relief. "Thank you. I've been anxious about taking time off, so I really appreciate your encouragement."

"Well, you've been churning out collections left and right, I think a break is well-deserved."

Cole wraps his hand around mine and squeezes. The many collections I've released over the last two years were a byproduct of him being deployed and me struggling to cope with being a new mom and solo parenting and us being stationed on the East Coast. It's been a rough season, demanding a lot from both of us and our marriage. Art was always there for me and my collections have done well, but to be honest, I'm a little burnt out.

Now that Cole's back for a while, the chance to paint alongside other military spouses and equip them for processing their stories through art is a perfect fit for the year ahead.

"Okay, are you ready?" asks Lorraine, handing Cole and I a flute of champagne. I press my hand to my stomach to still the butterflies. Cole glances over, then puts his arm around my shoulders and gently turns us so our backs are to the modest crowd. He tickles my sleeve with his fingers so I look away from the drop cloth draped over my largest painting in the collection and into his warm brown eyes.

"You are my favorite artist," he whispers. "You have created a stunning collection of paintings, and I am so proud of you. I love you. You got this."

I nod and he presses his lips to mine with love and confidence as Lorraine calls for everyone's attention.

"I love you," I whisper to him before turning back to the small crowd gathered.

Lorraine raises her voice to be heard to the back of the gallery. "Thank you all for being here today to celebrate the unveiling of the latest collection from Tia Slaeden. I'm going to turn the floor over to her for a few brief remarks."

I step forward and Cole takes a step back. I pull my phone out of my pocket and open up my short speech in my Notes app.

"I want to start off by thanking Lorraine. If you weren't already aware, Lorraine has been there for me from the moment I decided I wanted to have a career in art. I walked into this gallery as a heartbroken woman who had just quit my job in D.C., and decided I would paint something worthy of being displayed here. Coincidentally, that's how I fell in love with my husband." I turn to Cole with a wink, and he blushes under his collar as he raises his glass in acknowledgement.

"This collection is called 'Art is Long and Time is Fleeting.' It was inspired by the idea of mentorship, the kind shown to me by Lorraine and Giada Burke. It's also about following in the footsteps of those who have lived bravely before us, in big and small ways, people like my great aunt and my grandmother. Looking to those ahead of me in life has given me so much encouragement and I hope I can inspire others to study our own personal heroes. I'd like to read an excerpt from Henry Wadsworth Longfellow's poem, A Psalm of Life, which is also where I got the title for this collection."

Lives of great men all remind us
We can make our lives sublime,
And, departing, leave behind us
Footprints in the sands of time;

Footprints that perhaps another,
Sailing o'er life's solemn main,
A forlorn and shipwrecked brother,
Seeing, shall take heart again.

My dear friend, Mr. Longfellow, stays with me to this day, a kind and thoughtful muse.

"In this collection, you'll see everything from the mentorship of father to son, to the corpsmen who inspire my husband in his work, to the women who have poured into my life and made me who I am today. I hope you enjoy it."

I reach behind me and give a gentle tug to the drop cloth. It falls away to reveal my largest painting in the collection, a thirty-six-inch by thirty-six-inch portrait of three women painting, their backs to the audience. The woman in the middle is smaller and shorter, with a braid down the center of her back. She stands in front of a canvas with only a few brushstrokes on it. The other two flanking her have nearly complete paintings on their easels, and they are pointing at the middle woman's canvas, offering advice and encouragement. The woman on the left has a silver bob, and the woman on the right has her hair done up in a French twist.

Lorraine and Giada gasp and within a few moments of recognition, there's not a dry eye in the house. I am grateful my vision has translated to the audience, even though it means Cole has to go find a box of tissues for all of us.

The rest of the event passes by in a blur of congratulations, well-wishes, and a lot of sales. The special paintings, the ones most meaningful to Cole and me, will never be sold. I learned my lesson on that point. Cathy graciously keeps my paintings at her house since I don't trust them to survive military moves. Carson and Cillian will drive down with her later this week to hang out with us and pick up a couple from this collection that I'll be keeping.

After everything is concluded at the gallery, I say a quick goodbye to Lorraine and Giada. We'll meet for brunch later this week, then again to package my sold paintings.

"I can't believe they all sold," I say, bubbly on champagne as Cole and I walk to Mexican Take Out for burritos. I giggle when he swings our joined hands back and forth.

"Never doubted you for a second," he says. I pull him in for a kiss.

While we wait to order, my phone dings with a notification, a new message in the group chat we still call "Military Goal Diggers." It's Cole and me, Anisha and Mick, Denny and his wife, and Luko and his wife in the group, and it is constantly pinging with a message or GIF. I gasp when I read the text.

MICK

Just dropped my paperwork to go SELRES.

Anisha immediately replies with a string of GIFs of dancing, applause, and partying.

Cole's also looking at the message on his phone, smiling as Anisha keeps sending the GIFs and the guys give a simple thumbs-up to Mick's text.

"It feels like just as quickly as it started, it's all going to be ending," I say. "Mick's going reserves and he's only a few years from retirement now."

"Crazy," Cole says, sliding his phone back in his pocket.

"Crazy," I say, shaking my head. "It's the one-word tagline for military life."

———

LATE THAT NIGHT, Cole and I snuggle up in the guest room bed while Carlos sleeps across the hall in his pack-n-play in what used to be my mini art studio. Even though he's only a few steps away, we miss him so much, we're both scrolling through our phones and looking at pictures of him, melting over his big brown eyes and chubby baby face. Now feels like the right time to bring up the thing that's been on my mind for a while.

"Should we have another baby?" I whisper.

Cole shakes his head with a rueful laugh. "Queenie, I barely survived you giving birth to Carlos."

I smile at the truth of it. I decided I wanted to try to have Carlos at home and Cathy was my midwife. Cole hated seeing me in pain and he was stressed the entire labor and delivery. All his corpsman instincts went right out the window and his protective, caring instincts towards me took over. At one point Cathy asked him to help by refilling my water bottle and he yelled, "I'm not letting go of her hand, Mom!"

I bait the hook a bit. "Yeah, but what if it's a girl? Can you imagine Carson and Cillian and Julio being uncles to a little girl? And your mom and my dad would be over the moon."

Cole sighs and I think I'm gaining ground.

"What if she's a cute little blondie with curly hair and she takes after your dad's side of the family?"

"Oh my gosh," he groans, rubbing his hand across his eyes. "But what if it's a boy?"

"Then Carlos would have a brother, like you and I have brothers. They'd be adorable little troublemakers."

Cole wraps his arms around me and pulls me against his bare chest, snuggling his face into the curve of my neck with a kiss that makes me melt. "You really want another one?"

"I really think I do," I say, running my fingers across his scalp. "Would you be okay with another one?"

"If it can be delivered by a stork onto our front porch."

I giggle. "I think that's how they come nowadays."

"Okay, perfect."

———

ONE YEAR LATER, baby Carina is born with a full head of blonde hair and our family is complete. Cole weathers her birth bravely and tears of joy run down his cheeks as he kisses us both.

"My girls," he says with a grin.

As I sit on our bed with Carlos tucked next to me, and Cole

holding Carina, I see our wedding photo over our bed in the reflection of the mirror across the room.

It's a photo of Cole dipping me with a kiss, in front of the arch of swords at the end of our ceremony. Denny was the one who tapped my butt with his sword and said, "Welcome to the Navy, Mrs. Slaeden." For a brief moment, as everyone cheered, I wondered how I would feel about being a Navy wife, five, ten, twenty years down the road.

Now, I can confidently say I couldn't be happier. It's not easy to live at the whims of the Navy, to move and leave friends and have Cole be deployed and work demanding jobs. But with Cole, I am home. Wherever we go, whatever we do, we do our best to care for this love between us, this incredible gift we've been given.

THE END

———

The My Navy Romance series continues with
Denny and Ellis's story, coming in 2025!

For updates, subscribe to Hope's newsletter,
Hope's Happenings, via her website,
hopesnyderwriter.com

ACKNOWLEDGMENTS

I've been dreaming of writing this story for years, and I could not have done it alone. There are so many wonderful people who contributed to Tia and Cole's story becoming the book you hold in your hands.

Thank you to Pondlife, my amazing alpha readers. Anna, Charlotte, Erin, and Kate, I could not do this without you. Each of you are such a blessing.

Thank you, thank you, thank you to my beta readers, Keira, Ella, and Marie, for your fantastic feedback and encouragement.

Thank you to Priscila Perales at Loving the Book Life for strengthening my weak Spanish and doing a sensitivity read for me.

Thank you to MaryAnn at Ascension Edits for proofreading my manuscript.

Thank you to the Marines who answered all my questions and gave me some insight into the culture of corpsmen. I'm so proud to know all of you.

Thank you to all the military wives who have cheered for me to write this book. I wish I could hug you all, and I hope you know how incredible you are. Our job is never easy, never boring, and rarely celebrated, but we're a tough bunch, full of love and courage.

Thank you to my amazing husband and sweet kids. I published this book during a demanding sea tour (the definition of insanity) and that meant a lot of grace and understanding from all of you. I am so thankful for all the ways you showed your love and support. You are the best dream come true.

From my grandmothers, to my great aunts, to my aunts, and

most of all, my mom, I owe so much to the women in my family. Writing this story was so humbling as I was continually reminded of the lasting, positive impact they, and other older women, have had on my life. Thank you for everything.

Thank you, God, for giving me these words, for shaping me as a writer, and giving me the strength to keep going. This book is an answer to years of prayer. All glory to you.

ABOUT THE AUTHOR

Hope Snyder writes love stories full of courage and kissing. She's a Navy wife, a mother of three, an avid reader, and a proud California girl. She has a Certificate in Creative Writing from the University of Cambridge Institute for Continuing Education and has lived in South Korea, England, California, Virginia, and the Pacific Northwest, thanks to the Navy. Her favorite Jane Austen book is (of course) *Persuasion*, the one with the most naval references.

Hope is also the author of *Trust Me: A Black Swan Protection Novella*.

 instagram.com/hopesnyder_writer

Made in the USA
Las Vegas, NV
08 October 2024

96521519R00204